Praise for *Love and Famine*

"One should add 'Politics' to the two abstractions of the title, for Chin's fictional world is infused with the cultural and personal consequences of Mao's Great Leap Forward.... Because the author is an engineer who's lived in the U.S. since 1978, the novel has a particularly autobiographical feel. Both epic and personal, this novel chronicles two decades of love, loss, history, and culture—and the complex tensions that arise from these forces—during the turbulent Mao era."

—*Kirkus*

"Set during the turbulent years of Mao Zedong's rise and into the Great Leap Forward, Love and Famine is a rich and detailed look at the lives of both Chinese intellectuals and peasants alike. Han-Ping Chin's autobiographical novel offers a glimpse into the way the Chinese lived during the formative years of China's communist regime.... Dapeng's struggles and slow rise to triumph pull the reader along hoping for a semblance of a happy ending in the face of the near-insurmountable hardships surrounding him. A fascinating look at life during the Great Leap Forward, and a fine addition to the study and literature of the period."

—*Historical Novel Society*

Love and Famine

A Novel

To Sylvie Carberry,
my teacher & friend,
with best wishes.
Han-ping Chin

Han-ping Chin

Harvard Square Editions
New York
2017

ISBN 978-1-941861-45-5
Printed in the United States of America
Published in the United States by
Harvard Square Editions
www.harvardsquareeditions

PART ONE

Foot travelers returning from our neighboring province, Hunan, shouted for several days, "Japanese troops are coming!" Without radio, newspaper, or telephone, nob~' knew exactly where the invaders were. Early on t' June 19, 1944, I ran four miles to t' County, where a large crowd was an announcement. Through the open doo. ...e town hall we heard the clicks of a one-key transmitter connected to a battery, *di, di, di-di, di-di-di-di* ... The usually noisy marketplace was quiet except for that mysterious sound. I watched the grownups' faces for a clue to its meaning, but they only gazed at each other in dismay.

Over my head, men argued about how far we were from the battle lines; some said 50 kilometers, others 35. But they all agreed that, without tenacious resistance, the Japanese would swoop down on us the next day.

At noon, the county's Emergency Order of Evacuation, a handwritten poster with the red seal of the county government, was pasted on the front wall of its office building. It called for immediate evacuation, leaving nothing usable by the enemy; helping government armies to fortify our defense.

Though only ten years old, I felt my hair bristling at the patriotic slogans at the end of the order: "Let's unite with one heart and one mind, we share a deep hatred of the enemy. The final victory belongs to us!"

Pingxiang, a county of west Jiangxi, bordering Hunan Province, had been a safe corner during the war due to its distance from the Japanese occupation on the coastline and in North China. Now, six years after my family had fled Wuhan, enemies were approaching our second hometown.

Mother shook me awake at daybreak, "Get up, Dapeng! You're the man of the house now." Half-awake, I saw her faint shadow, cast from our oil lamp, moving along the ceiling, but I fell asleep again.

She'd been up all night, trying to pack everything we owned into our few boxes. Every now and then, when Youzhi, my 15-month-old brother, cried himself awake, she stopped to rock his cradle.

"Where are Father and Haitao?" I rubbed my eyes, "People say the Japanese troops have already encircled Hengyang."

"I hope they aren't trapped there. Father's a nice man, Heaven knows. The problem is, they face at least four days' hike and will have to row a boat to get home. And bandits are everywhere on all the roads now."

She started sobbing. I suddenly felt our family's lack of men: just me, helpless with a woman and a baby.

This year, she had decided to cancel our Chinese New Year's celebration, using the money she'd saved for the annual festival to buy me new clothes, and to treat 20 guests to my tenth birthday party. She'd clearly told me then her expectations of me, "When a real boy reaches ten, he should be as ambitious as his father and dare to act like the head of the household."

I made a vow to myself: "I'll be a real boy."

I got out of bed and found, among a mass of scattered clothes, shoes, and kitchen utensils, a long, narrow towel to tie at my waist the way I'd seen ancient heroes do in picture books. Into my pocket I put my cloven deer hoof, a weapon street fighters carried secretly, which my friend Little Tiger had given to me for self-defense. He'd preserved it with herbs and hard liquor, and had dried it so the ankle stiffened at a right angle. He also taught me how to grip the shin, putting the two sharp, horny parts of the hoof between my index and middle fingers. "It's as hard as iron," Little Tiger said, "and will arm you, and boost your guts." Now his family was evacuating to a place far away from where my family was headed.

Still holding my little brother, Mother dozed off in bed. I tinkered with pots, rice, and mustard greens, trying to make a meal for us as I'd seen Mother do every day for years. Watching my first attempt, she tickled Youzhi's neck with her nose. My little brother giggled.

After breakfast, she asked me to go with a porter to help carry our two suitcases into the private coal mine that Auntie Wu's brother owned. There we'd hide our best clothes and small items, anything of possible resale value, for after the war. The mine's small entrance led to an extensive maze for excavation. A miner pushed a cart with our possessions along wooden tracks while holding an oil lamp by its string with his teeth. I crawled after him into the deep, dark labyrinth, memorizing the route. After our boxes were safely stored with some other families' things, I followed him back out of the mine.

On my way home, I found no armed sentry at the town hall for the first time. Only a few people were on the street. I hurried home and saw two single-wheeled carts waiting outside. Our sleeping rolls and several small bags had already been loaded. I helped Mother to stuff clothes, pots, pans, and our remaining rice and cooking oil into a big bamboo basket. Except for a three-drawer desk and a lightweight bed, we left the furniture we'd accumulated over the past six years.

We fled with five other families from Hubei Province. The only highway in our area had been destroyed by wide, deep pits, dug to impede Japanese cavalry or motorized troops, leaving only a zigzag of narrow embankments for us to pass over. Soon after we reached the edge of the basin, many local families scattered to nearby mountains, where they had relatives.

We continued hiking farther south, following the path the coal miners and peasants had taken during the 1927 uprising as they retreated to the red guerrilla base. We were headed for a place where a Hubei refugee's son-in-law, Zhong, had arranged for us to take shelter in his family's ancestral temple. I used a short shoulder pole to carry two baskets with cooked food and kitchen pottery jars, trudging amidst a fleet of wheelbarrows.

With her bound feet, a tradition imposed on women since the Song Dynasty, Mother had difficulty walking on the ragged road. Most of the time she held Youzhi and sat on one of the two sideboards of the single-wheeled cart, a position sometimes used to transport pigs, which squealed at every sharp bump. I knew how hard her ride was. As we gained elevation, the mountain trail wound along the edges of ravines flanked by steep rock slopes. I constantly worried about the carts turning over in an accident.

In the morning, I was energetic, enjoying the babbling creeks and the jade-like peaks under the azure sky. Whenever our carts got stuck in ruts, I'd rush to help the porter by pulling the rope. In several places, I set down my load to catch grasshoppers or drink the spring water seeping out from rock fissures. Every hour or two, Mother asked me to check on Mrs. Wu's family, who trekked ahead of us separated by some local travelers, to see if they needed help. Her husband was on the opposite side of the battle line, and she had three daughters, aged twelve, seven, and five. Following the custom, we, all children of Hubei-refugee families, addressed her as Auntie Wu.

At a tiny roadside temple, our two families had lunch together, sharing the cold food we had brought with us. Auntie Wu complained of a stomach problem and wouldn't drink the spring water I fetched in an enamel cup, so I offered her a hot drink from our thermos. She was touched. "In troubled times, it's nice to have sons, especially one like Dapeng."

Auntie Wu's words echoed in my head, reminding me I was the only man in the two families. At dusk we arrived at a primitive village and took refuge at Zhong's ancestral temple.

Although Mother wept every day over Father and Haitao,

here she braced up, swaddling Youzhi on her back and leading me to build our temporary nest, a room in the west wing of the temple. In the kitchen we shared with two other families, we made a stove with stones and earth. She asked me to haul water from a well and to gather firewood from the mountainside. Thorny twigs and bushes scratched me, scarring my arms and legs. I cried but didn't let her see.

Ten days later, Father and Haitao fled the war zone and found their way to us. The children in the temple's big yard cheered, "Uncle Liu and Haitao have come home!"

I rushed to take Father's bag, while the other kids thronged around them, and the adults asked, "Is Hengyang still in our hands?"

I led Father by the hand to our home, where he sat on the stone threshold, and faced the crowd. Standing outside the circle, Mother held Youzhi, wiping away tears with the back of her hand. When our neighbors offered hot water, and packed tobacco in a water pipe for Father, he answered, "In the early morning of June 26, while our enemies were occupying the airfield, a local worker ushered us to a trail that led out of Hengyang. Two days later, the city was besieged."

Haitao added, "The casualties were horrible, and the Japanese fired poison-gas shells to kill our soldiers."

Haitao was 16, short but sturdy. He naturally took over the duties of replenishing our water and fuel. At first I relaxed. Then Mother asked me to take water and firewood to Auntie Wu in the east temple wing. She had no sons to help with chores, a problem especially now that we were in a wild area, where stragglers and disbanded soldiers looked for chances to rob and rape. Her three daughters greeted me as if I were an old family friend and a man.

For three days and nights in the middle of July, rifle shots mixed with rattling machine guns echoed back and forth from the surrounding mountains. Nobody knew where the Japanese were. Parents nervously kept survival bags handy and forbade their children to go outdoors. Everyone was ready at all times to climb the hill behind the temple.

I found a popular novel left on our neighbor's bamboo bench, a story of a legendary general of the Tang Dynasty and his conquest of Korea. Though I didn't know some of the words, the story lured me to guess them and read the book through.

On the third evening, the gunfire let up. A detachment of our government soldiers retreated to the temple to rest, and their team of porters followed with ammunition. I read by the setting sunlight, but no sooner had they started filling their bandoliers with bullets than a mortar shell screamed overhead, lacerating the air above us. It exploded in a rice field just outside our window. I dropped the novel and dashed into our room. Children cried, and dogs barked. Father and Haitao hurried to gather our belongings while Mother, trembling, with Youzhi in her arms, muttered, "Buddha, bless us," over and over.

In the front courtyard, a commander whistled his soldiers into marching formation and shouted. "Folks, keep calm! We're resisting the enemy." Then they ran off in a flash.

Father carried our food, clothes, and blankets on a shoulder pole. My older brother Haitao had Youzhi swaddled on his back. Mother held a walking stick to steady her balance. Even with bound feet, she carried two bags tied together over one shoulder.

My parents believed no enemies or local bad guys would search a ten-year-old boy, so they sealed their two gold rings and a few silver coins into a small shoe, then tied it under my waist belt. "That's the last bit of our family reserves," Father said.

"Don't worry," I said. "I know how to protect it."

My other task was to safeguard our salt, which was as scarce as gold during the six-year Japanese blockade of China's coast. Father had painstakingly procured it and saved all we had in a tin can. I stuffed it into a sack that held a winter jacket that doubled as a cushion.

The back door of the temple was already jammed by the fleeing, shouting crowd. "If Japanese soldiers see so many bullets here, they'll think we collaborated with government troops and burn the whole temple for revenge." In the tumult, Father asked Mother and Haitao to go ahead while he and I picked up bullets strewn around our living room and the multi-family, shared temporary kitchen. "Hurry!" Father said.

Until then, I'd never known how heavy bullets are. We gathered hundreds. Gritting my teeth, I carried my fully loaded basket while Father ran back and forth twice. We dumped the bullets into a rice paddy outside the brick wall.

As we dashed to catch up with Mother and Haitao, a woman in a roadside shop called desperately, "Help! Help!"

People around us sighed. "She's being raped," someone said. "Either a Japanese or government soldier cornered her." Her hopeless shrieks only intensified our horror and fright as we, the escaping herd, ran up a narrow, sloping path. The human wave separated Father and me. We called to each other but were soon drowned out by the babble of others.

In the midst of strangers, I recognized a grocery clerk from our town. By intuition, I thought him a nice man and addressed him as Uncle. That night, I stuck with him, and we slept with a crowd of fleeing villagers in the woods. He put his two large baskets between us, and I served as his human shield, guarding his property on the other side. It was the first time I'd spent a night away from my parents. I believed they were nearby. I prayed I'd find them the next day.

In the ominous darkness, sick adults used towels or clothes to muffle their coughing, while young mothers stifled crying babies with their breasts. To keep my family treasures hidden, I tied the small shoe against my belly and lay on my stomach, using the sack, with the tin can inside, as my pillow.

The next morning, I woke to find the store clerk sitting on his shoulder pole, supported by the two sturdy round baskets, and sucking a pipe. I felt hungry and worried. When the explosions and volleys were receding, he descended to a lower elevation to spot anything suspicious in the valley. I shifted to the outskirt of the pine woods and looked for anything edible. The sweet potatoes were not ripe, but as big as carrots. I dug one out and rubbed away the dirt from it on my pants. I hastily chewed, but had difficulty swallowing it, remembering Mother's teaching not to take anything from another family. Instead, I picked wild gooseberries. They soothed my parched throat but made my stomach rumble louder. All night, I was too faint to react to the attack of mosquitoes. They bit; I jerked.

The third morning, as the sun rose, I heard someone faintly calling, "Dapeng!" Gradually, I recognized Father's trembling voice. Escorting him was a bunch of children with Hubei accents, also shouting my name, their voices rising one after the other. Chuju, Auntie Wu's youngest daughter, only five years old, was also trudging along with them. Her sharp, high-pitched voice was set off from all the others and sadder than I could bear. I huddled myself up, slid down the steep slope, and staggered to greet them. My young friends swarmed to hug me before Father could ask me how I'd fared the night before.

Mother smiled through tears to see me, after two nights of fear and worry. She went to each family scattered among the pine trees to offer gratitude for their children's help, and she repeatedly told me to find ways to repay their kindness.

Another day passed. Sporadic gunfire sounded beyond the mountains then dwindled to quiet. Young peasant men snuck back to their villages and found no enemies. Following them, we returned to the ancestral temple, where the hard boards used for beds, and the freshly cooked rice with a few vegetables, seemed luxurious treats after our nights in the woods.

While our parents worried about our safety and their

livelihoods, we children had great fun, despite itching all over from mosquito bites. On sunny days, we boys played soldiers, carrying sticks on our shoulders, imitating government troops in goosestep, singing, "Compatriots, take arms! Brandish your broadswords and cut off the enemies' heads!"

The girls skipped rope for hours. While one or two jumped, the others sang folksongs and kept rhythm. With her hair fluttering, Chuju swung her arms wide and kicked her legs high, punctuating the group movement. She had the clearest, most melodious voice:

> How many stars dot the sky?
> How many people dwell on Earth?
> Too many stars dim the moon.
> Too many people disrupt peace.

One evening, while the sun was still bright, a group of us, boys and girls alike, wandered a half-mile away and ran into a gang of wild boys from another refugee center. Forming a half-circle, they marched menacingly toward us, yelling, "Defeat them! Catch them alive!"

Outnumbered and scared, we retreated. With my hand in my pocket on the cloven deer hoof, I walked backward, facing our enemy. Then, before we could engage in hand-to-hand combat, one of the boys sneaked behind us and pushed Chuju into a rice paddy.

I shouted, "Stop running away! Don't let them think we're cowards!"

Chuju couldn't survive long in such deep water. Her head was submerged, hands thrashing and legs kicking. Our leader, a chubby sixth-grade boy, stopped and brandished a stick. "Brothers, throw rocks! Shield Dapeng so he can rescue Chuju."

We cheered his resolve and felt braver ourselves. "Beat them! Kill them!" We rushed them and pushed them back.

Bubbles sent up from her mouth scared me enough to make me sprint. With cold hands and trembling knees, braving the raining stones, I tried to reach Chuju. A spring scene flashed in my mind, a water buffalo pulling a plow through the paddy, the water high enough to reach its belly. In desperation, I held her ankles and leaned back, trying to add my body weight to my arms' strength. The reaction of her jerking body was so strong that my feet went out from under me. While slipping into the deep, muddy water, I kept my back hard against the dry slope and quickly wrapped my arms around her knees. Then, I struggled to turn and lift her out of the water.

Slumped on the bank, she shivered and coughed convulsively, then burst into tears. I bent over and patted her back. "Don't be afraid. You're fine now. I'll take you home." She held my waist, and her sobbing ceased.

Our leader stood defiantly in front, as in the ancient battles we saw in the theater, challenging the rival commander to a one-on-one wrestling contest. "If anyone has the guts, step up!" Nobody on the other side took him up on it. During the confrontation, two screeching girls from our side had led a bleeding boy back to his parents. Soon the fathers and older brothers rushed to the scene and stopped the fight.

Worried women relayed the frantic report: "Chuju was almost drowned!" Auntie Wu wailed the loudest. When she reached us, I was using bean-vine leaves to get mud off Chuju's face.

My parents scolded me. "Why did you wander out into that field?" my father said. "If you get hurt, we have no doctor or medicine. We already have too much to worry about. How can you be so thoughtless?"

Before Father could heap more blame on me, Chuju's mother hurried into our room. "Your son is a brave man. He saved Chuju!"

Father smiled through a stern face. "You flatter him. He's still wet behind the ears."

Chuju had tagged along, hiding behind her mother, holding a

corner of her blouse. Her eyes glittered. Fresh from a bath, her dark, slick hair contrasted vividly with her pink face.

Our neighbors clucked. "How dangerous it all was. If she'd been in the mud much longer, she would've been finished."

As she was about to leave, Auntie Wu put a hand on my shoulder and whispered, "Good boy! Study seriously and become a big shot. I'll give you Chuju as your wife." My face and ears went red.

2

In September, soon after the Japanese troops left our town to go farther into Southwest China, we returned home. Our school reopened for the 1944 fall semester, but two thirds of the students had dropped out due to their parents' lost livelihoods. We fifth graders shared a classroom with the second grade, and the aisle served as the demarcation line. When the one teacher talked to one class, students on the other side were supposed to be quiet. One day, two second-grade boys were caught playing with silkworms, their heads sticking out of the eggs that the boys kept inside their underwear and hatched with their body temperature. As a punishment, our language teacher ordered them to stand for the rest of the lecture.

Zhong, the assistant principal, taught us mathematics. He was famous in the community for the quality of his teaching and for sticking to the doctrine, "Whipping is indispensable to the training of first-rate scholars." We seldom saw him smile. Once, he praised me for completing the optional parts of an assignment. That misled me to think he would tolerate my occasionally careless work. Later, he held up my messy homework in one hand and a neat copy chosen from the second graders in the other. "Which one looks nicer?"

The students answered in unison, pointing to the second grader's exercise book, "That one!" Facing two classes, my humiliation seemed doubled.

He didn't stop there. Pacing up and down in the aisle, he said, "A gentleman must exert himself and strive hard ceaselessly." Then he stood by my desk. "Your pleasant facial features and scholarly manner tell me you must have a decent upbringing." Waving my homework book, he continued, "But this ugly sheet doesn't match your handsome appearance. You're able to write neatly, but you don't. Shame! Shame!"

I slouched home and ate little for dinner. Mother put her palm on my forehead. "You might have a fever. Are you sick?" After repeated questioning, I told her what had happened at school. She fully agreed with Zhong's criticism of me, adding to her rebuke my reluctance to babysit my toddler brother or assist her with housework. To wrap up her lecture, she said, "You're lucky to have such a strict teacher, don't let him down. Stay away from the wild boys and behave like a grownup. Share the hardship with Father, and be an excellent student. Otherwise, you won't be able to stand on your own two feet and be someone in the future."

I didn't know what to say. Then, she decided to let me take responsibility for family worship. "Be sincere! There are deities three feet above our heads."

After that day, every morning and evening, I planted burning joss sticks in the ash bowl without missing a single day. Any bad day, when I got a low grade or harsh comments at school, I would worship longer than usual. The big characters, 'Heaven, Earth, Emperors, Ancestors, and Teachers', looked grim from their commanding position, as if the invisible beings were reminding me of my insufficiencies. They certainly knew how pious and sincere I'd been.

Teacher Zhong's sting and Mother's inspiration conspired together to push me to work like a man. Soon, I reached the top of my class and was treated as an honor student. Both my math and language teachers considered me a promising seedling. With fatherly concern, they wanted me to decide on my future goal or choose a profession: science or letters? Meanwhile, Zhong appointed me student head of our school, which mainly required me to give a weekly speech at the Saturday afternoon rally. It was a ceremonial role, and I was supposed to say something along the lines of our principal's aphorisms. Several times, I was embarrassed by not knowing what to say, but everyone said it was good training.

After school, I fetched water from the well, bought coal that I carried with a shoulder pole, and ran errands for Mother. Sometimes, I picked edible herbs, such as purslane, from the grasses on a stream bank, to substitute vegetables. Father left home, trying to find his former employers in Hunan and Hubei Provinces. Youzhi was a two-year-old toddler. I had to take him with me if I went out to play. Whenever we passed food stands, although I didn't have a penny, he'd yank on my sleeve and beg for a snack. I would open the split in his pants and slap his bare skin. He cried even harder then, and I'd drag him away from the laughing crowd. Once, in a quiet corner, I squatted to hold him, saying 'sorry' to him. My strange sobbing voice stopped his tears. He pushed my forehead away from his chest and embraced my neck tightly. Gradually, he grew closer and closer to me, following my requests more willingly than our mother's.

In the autumn of 1946, when Father was still looking for a job away from home, I passed the tough entrance exams and became one of the hundred new students to get into the only public middle school in our county. Among all our elementary-school graduates, I was the only one accepted. Except for two students from rich families who went to private school, my other friends became child workers, peddlers, or peasants. I knew I owed my good fortune to the sacrifices made by my parents. With my admission notice to the school on his knees, Father enjoyed the bubbling of his water pipe and the smoke slowly rising from his mouth. "Not easy. A thousand took the entrance exams, only one hundred were enrolled. I've always believed, 'Heaven will never let a sincere person down.' I knew you'd make it."

Mother paused while mending my pants. "Auntie Xu next door is jealous. She didn't talk to me for ten days because her first son failed the exams."

Father sighed. "Women have long hair but short vision, Dapeng still has a long way to go, he has to finish university to become an engineer. I hope he'll be the first of our relatives and friends to annoy Auntie Xu to death."

That was when I heard what Father expected of me for the first time. My grandparents died early, and, at the age of 11, he'd became a child worker at an oil-pressing factory, then at a grocery store. During three years of study with a private village teacher, he learned how to use a brush pen and memorized a few easy-to-read books on Confucius's ideas. As an apprentice at the grocery store, he had learned to calculate with an abacus.

Mother looked at him coldly. "A university education means we have to make do without his help for another ten years. A machine-shop job lets Dapeng earn money much earlier. It is more secure, pays more than being a coolie, and only requires a three-year apprenticeship. Little Tiger, Dapeng's best friend, is going that way. In three years he'll be earning a wage, and his parents are thinking about marrying him to his cousin."

Father sneered at her, "Little Tiger hasn't got the makings of a student. His parents see only what's under their noses. In this world, only skills difficult to attain are worthy of esteem. Extra years in education deserve big rewards."

After a long silence, she sighed, "It would be nice if, in ten years, Dapeng became an engineer."

3

As the first one from the refugee sub-community entering the public middle school, the parents of other families suddenly regarded me as a role model for their sons. Two cousins from Xu's family, Zhongyuan and Jiujiu, both born in Jiangxi and five years younger than me, began to follow me like my disciples. If it wasn't raining, Zhongyuan would go hiking with me and recite prose on a hilltop in the early morning, hoping to improve both his asthma and his poor scores. Jiujiu was more rebellious, and was often involved in scuffles with the local kids. His father was paralyzed in bed. When his mother got odd jobs, she would bring him to my home, asking me to supervise his studies and keep him out of trouble.

In the middle of my eighth grade, a rich local family invited me to be best man at their son's wedding. They dressed me up, took me to a barber shop for a haircut with pomade polishing, and hired a sedan chair to carry me to a hotel in the county center, where the ceremony was conducted. Many guests complimented me when they spoke to my father, "Your son will become a handsome statesman." He smiled and replied, "I hope your propitious predictions can come true." Privately, he told me, "Politics is dirty. It's noble to make a living by crafts and skills."

With engineering as my long-range goal, I made a special effort with math. During that winter vacation between 1946 and 1947, among the 50 students in the class, I was the only one who tried to solve the one hundred problems listed at the end of the textbook. Though I'd only solved 70 or so and left the rest blank, Teacher Tang praised me at the beginning of the next semester. I didn't quite catch his words in the noisy room but I never forgot the image of his lanky body, and his voice constantly hoarse from energetic lecturing, and what he wore that day, a loose overcoat with the hem dropping to his ankles.

Our PE class was in the late afternoon, arranged as a spare-time recreation. We had only a basketball and a volleyball for the 50 players, and sometimes I failed to touch either one within the hour. Frustration drove me to visit the library, reading newspapers and magazines. As a result, my writing scores rose and I had an audience eager to hear about the Civil War and international news.

In spring 1947, during my second semester of seventh grade, Teacher Meng began our instruction in classical Chinese literature. He wore a long robe, its hem just above the cuffs of his Western slacks, quite stylish at the time. Physically taller than the average South China man, with a high, slender nose and high cheekbones, he gave people the impression of peace and wisdom. His crew-cut hair made him appear humble and he was close to the students.

I'd first heard Teacher Meng's name in 1943 when Chiang Kai-shek established the Nationalist Youth Army, educated young men preparing for a coordinated counterattack against Japan with the Allied Forces in the South Pacific. Still only nine, I was thrilled by the stirring couplet printed in the margins of wall calendars: 'Every inch of lost territory will be recovered with an inch of blood; one hundred thousand young men equals one hundred thousand trained soldiers.'

Answering the call, Teacher Meng took the lead by registering. Inspired by him, several high school students hurried to enlist in the Youth Army. People of the town praised him for *renouncing his pen for a sword*, as a Han Dynasty hero had done.

To prepare for a ground war in the north to expel the Japanese, Meng endured heat, mosquitoes, and strenuous drills along with the younger soldiers. He fought in the jungles of Burma for two years, until the Japanese surrendered in 1945. Then, when the Youth Army was dispatched to fight communist forces in Northeast China, he returned to teaching instead.

In the middle of the semester, he assigned us the subject, 'If I Were Somebody', to write as a composition. I finished an essay with the title 'If I Were Monkey King'. As I used recent phrases from newspapers to criticize the ill phenomena of our society, and imagined myself a hero like the Monkey King in Chinese mythology, using my supernatural power to change the world, Teacher Meng was excited. He couldn't resist copying my essay in fist-sized characters on red poster paper and pasting it on the wall. The success of my essay made me feel close to my teacher.

February 1949: the government had lost three decisive battles in the north, and its armed forces beat a hasty retreat that overwhelmed the railroad. Frequent train rumblings and shrill whistles sounded plaintive cries for the defeated. Our campus stood on a hill, facing the Pingshi River. The railroad, skirting the ancient city walls, crossed the river at a right angle, and trains slowed there to pass north into a station. Through the large classroom windows, I could see stalled trains lined up for miles, and demoralized soldiers roaming around.

In the odd, confusing atmosphere, we still celebrated completing ninth grade and graduating from middle school. I bought a silk-covered autograph album and reserved the first page for Teacher Meng to write some commemoration. He surprised me by inscribing my album right away.

> Young men should be ocean waves
> unfolding magnificently,
> Not dead water in a marshy pond.

His elegant calligraphy impressed me, and the inscription signaled the end of an era. I sensed from the overtones of the inscription that he had made specific observations about me.

All three years, he had approved of my coursework and my goal to become an engineer. Now, when our principal and discipline supervisor had stopped showing up and schooling became semi-autonomous, pro-government students looked listless, while leftist activists strode around energetically. My quiet manner must have disappointed him.

In April, the railway was back to normal, the government army had fled without a trace, but the communist forces hadn't yet arrived. Outside the window of Teacher Meng's office, bright sunshine reflected off oily green fields. The charming scenery, during the political vacuum, made me feel ill at ease. Suddenly I felt Meng belonged to a secret group, and was treating me as a friendly outsider.

I blew on the page he had written on. The ink dried. I closed my album and was ready to go. Meng said, "The school will be closed two months earlier than in normal years. We'll gather at an elementary school in a hidden valley of Grapes Hill, around four kilometers from the West Gate. You can find me through the old keeper of the Wu Family Memorial Hall. He's our sentry."

"What are you doing there?"

"Singing songs and practicing a popular rural folk dance. We'll have a lot of fun to prepare ourselves for greeting the dawn. Please come, it's the best chance for you to catch up with the times."

I made a deep bow to him. It was the last time I practiced this old-society ritual.

That summer, when all kinds of rumors flew around, I wondered what Teacher Meng and the left-wing group were doing at an elementary school deep in a mountain recess. But Mother wouldn't allow me to endure the four-hour round-trip under the scorching sun.

4

At a midnight in late September 1949, three consecutive explosions shook our neighborhood. The retreating nationalist (KMT) government had destroyed the three railway bridges near our town. The deafening blasts sounded like the funeral fireworks of the old regime, whose members were now called KMT reactionaries by the victors.

During the following two days of nervous serenity, my older brother, Haitao, returned with his bride. He had been a small-time news reporter for a local newspaper in Wuhan for a few years before 1949; after his boss, the newspaper's owner and a local KMT Party branch head, was executed by the People's Liberation Army (PLA), he'd fled to Jiangxi. I surrendered my room to the newlyweds, sleeping on a bamboo bench wedged into my parents' room. Still, I kept doing my worship as usual: making a deep bow with burning incense, taking three strides forward, and then kneeling under the altar.

The PLA passed through our small town, chasing the routed KMT troops toward Taiwan. Along with their marching song, they repeatedly sang, "But for the Communist Party, there's no China." I recalled that my schoolteachers had taught us that China has a five-thousand-year history of civilization. I kept asking myself the question until the following year, when the song was revised to, "But for the Communist Party, there's no *new* China."

When some of the troops stationed themselves in our small town to rest for a few weeks, we residents were obliged to make room for them, our liberators. My family of six rented a two-bedroom, barrack-style bungalow originally built for coal miners; the only space we could surrender was the sitting/dining room. Now the infantry soldiers were everywhere. With grass-green uniforms and puttees, they distinguished themselves by fixing red stars on their hats.

Sitting or lying on the floor, they took my space for the three strides and blocked my way to our family altar, a narrow bench leaning against the wall facing the street door, on which an incense ash bowl and a pair of candlesticks stood. Above the bench, the big characters on red paper, 'The Sanctuary of Heaven, Earth, Emperors, Ancestors, and Teachers', remained, spiritually dominating our home, but my daily duty of burning joss sticks in the ash bowl was interrupted.

As the rifles rested against the altar, with their muzzles aimed at the big characters, I sensed the blasphemy against my ancestors and the threat to my living teachers. Mother asked me to stop worship for the time being; it wasn't our fault. Still, I lit joss sticks and edged my way toward the bowl, squeezing amongst their bodies and weapons. When I moved a metal pipe laid along the bench, one of them yelled, "Don't touch it! That hand torpedo can blow up the whole row of houses."

Another said, "You little diehard, go shove your superstition."

Their buddies roared with laughter. I found myself surrounded by tall northeastern men as if in a forest. In fear and disgrace, I remembered the order issued by the PLA headquarters, the Three Main Rules of Discipline and the Eight Points for Attention, which was posted on the streets and sung by the soldiers. I said, "Don't forget *speak politely*, that's one of your Eight Points for Attention."

They stopped hooting. And we stopped worship for the rest of their two-week stay. Mother knew the communist regime denied the existence of deities, she nevertheless resumed her worship until the supply of joss sticks and other 'superstitious material' petered out.

The victors immediately took retaliatory strikes for communist martyrs and living class brothers who'd been persecuted by the old regime. They killed Mr Xiao, the last KMT town magistrate, in the second day of their occupation. They recruited Coyote Tian, a bully from my elementary school, as a messenger because of his proletarian family background, as his father was a blacksmith. Xiao's horse, the only one in town, was confiscated and assigned to Coyote Tian for shuttling emergency documents between our town and the county center. Coyote Tian let the horse trot along a stone median strip through the dirty street, imitating the manner of a war hero. After finishing sixth grade, he sold water chestnuts, assisted a Taoist monk catching ghosts, and served the gangsters at various gambling dens. He earned his nickname by his strong muscles and sneaky attacks.

My father's employer, Bin Shu, was a mining foreman and got rich quick by trading coal after the war. The new powers held him accountable for the death of a communist in the failed uprising of miners in 1927, and immediately arrested him. During the three-day custody, his son, around 11, carried food to him once a day in two bowls wrapped in a towel, one covering the other. I saw the boy walk timidly along the fence of our school to the two-floored house, originally owned by a landlord and now the headquarters of a local militia, where his father was jailed. Listening to the whizzing bullets of revolutionary vengeance and the cheering crowds at the rally ground, Father looked pale. Fear or sadness? I couldn't tell.

A year before, in my early insomnia, I listened to my parents talk in the dark. Father worried how long he could delay the answer to Bin Shu's request to let his daughter be my future wife. That showed how much his boss trusted him. Now, I was no longer afraid of the planned arranged marriage. But I wanted to know what exactly Bin Shu had done 22 years before, and if he deserved capital punishment. Perhaps lest his words would contradict the Party's propaganda, Father spoke evasively. To stop my mumbling, he finally said, "Revolution is a class action. It's not like a bank, setting up an accurate account for its every enemy. For victory, it must kill by category."

People I knew in our neighborhood all respected Principal

Zhang of my elementary school due to his knowledge, righteousness, and majestic looks. Unfortunately, he served one term as town magistrate and carried out the KMT government's conscription. The only victim, whom he found hiding in a water vat and sent to the anti-Japanese front line, had come home safely and was now leading the peasants shouting, "Down with the despot landlord Zhang!" With arms and hands tied, Zhang knelt on the stage facing the agitated crowds. I couldn't stand the sound of his grunting under torture. The sight of a large lump suddenly appearing on his forehead and the sound of human bones hit by a wooden stick sickened me, forcing me leave the scene. While his son was looking for special medicine to cure his wounds, the military sent Zhang to a remote place, and he never came back.

I started my school with hard physical and ideological training. The mess hall was run by students in turns, and only one cook was hired. Housing was free, though I lived, with other boys of our class, like a pigeon in a basement with 20 double-decker bunks. Such a thrifty life made me feel better for the way in which it made the financial burden on my parents bearable.

On top of all the other courses, we had to intensively study the History of the Development of Society with a textbook abbreviated from one of the series, *Cadres' Essential Readings*. It divided human history into five stages and five corresponding societies. As the final touch, it concluded that socialist society will inevitably replace capitalist society. It was an inexorable law, independent of man's will. Therefore, capitalism was doomed to extinction, and socialism would prevail all over the world.

Our lecturer, the first curly-haired man I met in China, repeatedly explained why Karl Marx said, "Revolution is the locomotive of history," and Frederick Engels said, "Violence is the midwife to the Revolution." I tried to use the two catch phrases to justify the beating of the principal of my elementary school. I found the better way was to forget him.

5

My tenth-grade school year started in October amidst the revolutionary frenzy. An underground Party member, Li, surfaced and took control. As a decision maker and an embodiment of truth, though he remained a student in my class, he dethroned the schoolmaster as the figurehead. Li used to be a truck mechanic in a large city, he then hid among us middle-school students although was ten years older than us. Physically big and tall, resolute in speech, and endowed with a mysterious history, he drew immediate support. Under his leadership, the Youth League (YL) set up its headquarters to supervise the administration, and branched out into every grade to discipline and guide students along communist principles.

We no longer bowed to our teachers when meeting them on the street nor stood up when they walked into the classroom. The county government shot the two military drill trainers, posted by the nationalist regime during World War II. A teacher who once worked as discipline supervisor, and another who was in charge of the boy scouts before 1949, lost their jobs. One chilly November day, along the riverside by our school, I saw a peasant lead along my ninth-grade chemistry teacher, Song, with a rope. Wearing only an unlined shirt and straw sandals, he was hurried away because he had owned a piece of farmland. He never came back.

Our former English teacher, Hu, hadn't shown up since the regime change. He's unforgettable, especially because of his dark whiskers, thick glasses, Jiangxi accent and amusing stubbornness. That winter, we saw him standing in front of a winnowing blower wearing only underpants. After splashing him with cold water, the peasants cranked the handle of the blower. It was a common way to pry hidden gold or silver out of landlords. After that incident of *beating out floating assets*, Hu died of pneumonia.

The remaining teachers resembled birds startled by the mere twang of a bowstring. No matter how reverently they followed the guidelines issued by the new government, they'd get in trouble for their personal history or a slip of the tongue in the classroom.

The army made off with half of the healthy boys in our school as the first wave of students joined in order to carry guns. Then it took most of the lively, pretty girls to enlarge the military propaganda troupes. The students remaining on campus became restless when the local government demanded pure and reliable young trainees to replace the workers left over from the old regime. In a few months, our grade had shrunk from 110 students to 23, and merged into one class. The public mood shifted. For many, going to university rather than into the army was not honorable. Though the pressure was increasingly strong, I decided to stick it out with my studies, no matter how rudely I was jeered, with phrases such as, "Fear of military hardship," or, "Sticking to bourgeois dreams is despicable."

It was not easy for my parents to keep me at school for the last five years. Now the new government would train engineers and medical doctors as a part of its proletariat ranks, following its requirement would make our family life less difficult than before. University education was free, and the government would assign every graduate a job. For the final four years, I wouldn't be a burden on my parents. This simple calculation told me that my parents would only have to go through difficult times for the coming three years of my high-school studies.

One evening, two teenage boys came to our home, jubilantly talking about their plan to join the army, and urging me to take the same action. Soon after they left, Father said,

"The nationalist government has been overthrown. It makes no sense to expand the army."

I said, "The PLA needs students to replace the illiterate peasant soldiers, because the Party wants to liberate all mankind."

"High-school students are rare. It's a big waste of future talent, like killing the hens to get the eggs."

His remark helped me survive the peer pressure, even after all my close friends left school.

However, it was hard to part from Hao Ding, a native-born boy who'd grown up with me. He'd defended me against bullies at school, and we'd played together almost every day during the summer vacation of 1949, the transitional time of our history. We seemed to have an informal treaty between us. Sometime during eighth grade, when Teacher Meng taught us a story about two ancient heroes from a poem, we felt inspired to vow that we'd serve in the army and become generals.

While he still remembered that solemn pledge, by then I had begun to doubt my ability to become a general and regarded our impulsive words as childish bragging. I'd studied seriously, working toward the goal of going to university, and my parents had suffered for that purpose during the previous five years, especially 1945–46, when they often went to bed before dark to skip dinner. They suffered many hardships to keep me in school. If I gave up my goal, they'd be heartbroken.

The day Hao Ding went to register at the PLA recruiting station, he and his mother detoured to come see me. He wanted to try to persuade me one more time, while Auntie Ding wept and asked me to help her keep her son. In ten years, I'd seen his father only once. He joined the KMT army to fight the Japanese, and nobody knew where he was now. Finally, I told Hao my true thoughts. "I'm not a fighter. It's easier for me to be a student. I hope you can stay with your mom. Her life is tough."

Auntie Ding sobbed more uncontrollably, but he was

determined to go. We waited an hour at the recruiting station to see him off. Standing in formation, he was harnessed with a knapsack, four grenades, two belts stuffed with two hundred bullets, and a sack of rice. The gun slung over his shoulder almost touched the ground.

The first letter I received after he marched toward the coast proudly reported his journey.

> We hiked from morning to evening, about 50 kilometers a day. At night, our meetings focus on the Three Checkups: class origin, performance of duty, and will to fight. In these short four weeks, my political consciousness has been greatly heightened. My feet are blistered all over and it's painful to walk, but my spirits are high. Soon, we'll liberate Taiwan.

The second letter was filled with despair about me.

> Every dawn, when the bugle blares, urging me get up, I'm excited for another day chasing the routed KMT troops. At that moment, I imagine that you're ready for another day in the classroom. I know you still want to attend university and pursue a cozy bourgeois life. My friend, I'm worried about you. Without a lofty idea of communism, you might be cast out by the Revolution.

I privately asked my geography teacher what he thought. He said, "Joining the army is glorious, but going to university is also patriotic. The experience of the Soviet Union tells us nationwide industrialization will follow military victory. I predict China will soon feel a lack of scientists and engineers. They will come from university graduates."

His advice gave me the strength to face down the pressure

to join the army. Yet I couldn't get over my sadness about Hao Ding's leaving and his disapproval of my choice.

It was the end of November. Along with his letter, an unbroken spell of wet weather seemed to press the sky low, further dampening my spirits. Mud and puddles covered all the open areas. YL members and supporters occupied our classrooms every afternoon. With no place to be alone for fresh air and a quiet moment, I found a small basement where the janitor's tools were stored and a door opened to a steep slope. Standing there for hours, I watched the rain falling like a curtain. The mist above the ravine blocked my vision, just as my dear friends had all disappeared from my horizon. I was sure I'd never see Hao Ding again.

The rain kept me melancholy, and I felt anxious about what was going on in the noisy classroom. The YL branch meeting might be celebrating the acceptance of a new member, and non-members were invited so that they would be inspired. Or perhaps a veteran cadre was telling the story of his struggles so young students could cherish a hard-won victory of the Revolution. Officially, participation in spare-time political activity was voluntary. Actually, absence from it was a sign of petty-bourgeois liberalism, harmful to the Revolution. Now, all students were divided into 'progressive', 'backward', and 'middle'. Though there wasn't a list publicizing the statuses, everybody knew where he or she stood. I was keenly aware that a man watching the rain alone outside the collective was an image of a political laggard. I felt that they must be collecting my faults as raw material for Marxist analysis.

The athletic boys, who behaved like gangsters during the KMT rule before the summer, had become zealous YL members. I was grudgingly in awe of the Party's magic power to convert troublemakers into ethical guards. In fear and confusion, I picked up their cold air toward me, an indicator of their class scorn toward backward elements. One of them, a member of our school basketball team, had been warm to me two months before. We'd spent a Sunday afternoon with another guy at a former Confucian temple, chatting happily and eating pop-rice without water to drink. He began snubbing us as soon as he joined the YL. My isolation kept me ill-informed; I worried something hideous might be brewing against me. The secret diagnosis of me would soon become open fire.

The hubbub in the classroom was leaking from the windows and trickling down the stairwell. In my solitude, the collective power and strength seemed irresistible and alluring. I held the wooden rail, stepped up, and stopped, trying to distinguish some meaningful words from the noises. Gradually, I reached our classroom. When I turned the doorknob and popped my head in, Comrade Li shouted, "Come on in, you're welcome!"

The erupting applause sounded like cheering for a lost child returning home.

6

Months later, when the land-reform campaign engulfed all the 'newly liberated' areas, our school prepared an opera to incite the peasants' class hatred of landlords. The drama team offered me a supporting role. I found it a warm and lively social environment. Unlike the tough, rigid boys in my class, the open and joyful performers from various grades gave me much-needed shelter.

Our regular rehearsal fostered a warm bond among the teachers directing the show and the students performing it. After school and on Sundays, we boy performers would often get together to swim in the river by the foothills or hike on the mountain trails behind our campus. While feeling at home with the others, I often forgot the stern faces in my classroom. The next morning, sitting at my assigned desk, I became keenly aware that I belonged to this regimented unit and was under collective monitoring.

Since the new educational system emphasized physical labor as a way to reform the world and remold educated people, we spent a lot of time opening up wasteland around our campus and doing volunteer work for the county. I dreaded it because I couldn't compete against the athletic students. They were all YL members. Whether plowing earth with a hoe or transporting coal from a pit with a wheelbarrow, I tried hard every time, and still I accomplished less than they could. The accusation that I held an incorrect attitude toward labor became lodged in their minds. To avoid giving them a chance to attack me, I'd grind my teeth and struggle not to lag.

In the meantime, I wanted to keep up my coursework, and not let it be interrupted unnecessarily. When eight of 'the dregs of the KMT reactionaries' were killed near downtown during a lecture, the curious boys cut class and walked half an hour to get there. One day while we were shoveling dirt to level a building lot, a volley of bullets erupted from nearby bushes. We stopped working, looking around and at each other's faces. When the firing squad left the execution field with their guns on their shoulders, the boys laid down their hoes and rushed over to find 12 headless bodies left behind by the execution squad. They came back describing the scene graphically to scare our female schoolmates. I didn't join the crowd to look at the nauseating scene.

Sometime between these two mass executions, a former KMT soldier was singled out from a mob of peasants attempting to rob a state-owned granary. He was shot in a roadside paddy that had dried in the winter, 50 yards from our campus. A mischievous guy in my class watched at close range and counted the shots: 37 rounds. Then, after the corpse had been removed, he found the wooden spike which had been tied to the dead man's back. While the criminal's name and a red cross remained on it, local people believed the spirit of the dead would haunt anyone hit by the inauspicious spike. One night, when we were walking back to campus after a rally at the county hall, the mischievous boy picked up the spike and hid behind a wall, no doubt planning to scare the girls coming along behind us. I yelled at him, "Don't play mean tricks!"

He said, "Shut up, sissy."

Now, the 12 abandoned bodies lay next to our workplace. When most male students from the seventh to twelfth grades thronged to watch, "The disgraceful end of the counterrevolutionaries," I, 17 already, felt on edge for staying among the girls. On my way back to school, I followed the last few timid young men to have a glance at the corpses. The surrounding shrubs were smeared with their brains and blood, and the strong stench lingered terribly. I quickened my steps to leave.

Nai, the KMT Party chief of the county, was one of the dead. He left a son, Peinan Nai, one of my classmates, and a daughter, who was two years older and then attending the Revolution University at Changsha, a city around a hundred kilometers from our town.

Peinan lived in the same large room with me and the other boys of our class. Li and other YL members had worked on him to accept his father's death sentence as required by the Revolution. He looked prepared for the result, but didn't eat dinner that day, curling up instead on his rolled-up comforter. Unable to repel the bloody scene or disperse the pungent odor from the morning, I had no appetite either. Speechlessly I stood by his bunk for a long while. He was short, thin, and a little hunchbacked. His overgrown hair and pale face dotted with acne made him look even more miserable. When I finally asked him if he needed something to eat, he shook his head and kept staring at the wall.

Over the next few days, Big Brother Li and his close followers lectured Peinan to convince him that his father, an enemy of the people, deserved the death penalty. Peinan made a public confession about the reactionary influence he had received from his father, but didn't satisfy the audience judging his examination because he simply parroted the words the YL members used to criticize him. Worse, he looked sad, rather than hateful toward his father.

News came about his sister, who in peaceful times always looked neat and pleasant but was now undergoing an ordeal. She had enrolled at the Revolution University to demonstrate her repudiation of her reactionary family, but the six-month cadre-training program was tough. She had to be cleared before being entrusted with a political mission. Her self-criticism, round after round, failed to reach the standard for, "Correctly recognizing her father's crimes and clearly drawing the distinctions between her father and herself." In desperation to confirm her sincerity, she rushed into a kitchen and chopped off three of her fingers.

Such cruel self-injury, including suicide, was normally explained as a show of resistance against the masses' scrutiny. Still, I expected the sad news would evoke sympathy for her younger brother, and my classmates would let him go. Instead, Peinan was criticized again and again until he sobbed uncontrollably. He barely passed his trial for his father's anti-communist crime by pledging to dig out the dead man's political and emotional influence on him.

The fate of Peinan and his sister baffled me. Should everybody be hammered on an anvil like an iron machine part to be prepared for the Revolution before joining it, or should they willingly be trained and hardened during the process of revolution? Before I could find an answer, I was criticized for my sympathy with Peinan and for my silence at the recent struggle against our history teacher, Chen, for distorting

Marxism. Big Brother Li orchestrated the criticism and self-criticism meeting on a Saturday afternoon. After my confession of my deficiency, about ten or so YL members pointed out my malady and how to cure it.

Li spoke last to summarize their opinions, "In the life-and-death battles to defend our newborn red power, Dapeng has lost his bearings. Why? Because he doesn't understand class exploitation and class struggle. His petty-bourgeois sentiment makes him tender toward class enemies like Teacher Chen. His pity for Peinan has reduced our effort to help an enemy's child find the right point of view. We should give him a loud shout, 'Comrade Dapeng, your bad attitude is leading you unconsciously to slip into the enemy camp!' Do you guys agree?"

They cheered.

I jotted down every criticizer's words and mumbled that I'd correct myself with collective aid. Li nodded with menace, "We'll check what you say against what you do. Show your political consciousness!"

7

Our history teacher, Chen, was fired after being publicly denounced. For a whole month, no faculty members wanted to fill the vacant position. At that time, not even university experts dared write texts on world history, for insufficient mastery of Marxism would draw severe attacks. Without an alternative, Teacher Zhou, the first post-Liberation principal, took the extra job of teaching us. He was the schoolmaster left over from the KMT era. As a transitional figure to keep the campus in order during the revolutionary takeover, he nominally kept the title but got little respect from YL members. Nevertheless, some senior students praised his lectures, so I felt lucky to have such a teacher. Like those fans, I believed his prestigious position in the old society had reflected the Confucian principle, "Excellence in scholarship leads to officialdom."

He started the class with a narrative of the 1789 French Revolution. Without a textbook authorized by the government, Zhou had to trim his knowledge to fit an official guideline and gingerly read it to us. Sometimes, forgetting censorship, he'd put aside his printed outline, take off his glasses, clean them, and exultantly tell us what happened in France in the late eighteenth century. Sitting in the second row, I was fascinated by the stories he brought forth and deeply moved by his energetic manner, and passion for history.

In his early forties, he was full of confidence and enthusiasm. Fellow teachers and parents of students respected him because he was both moral and learned. I liked him and hoped he would have a long life. His sturdy body, swarthy skin, and vigorous stride all looked blessed. However, the YL members appeared reserved and cold toward him.

One day, talking about how the Industrial Revolution of England had inspired Japan, Zhou made a comment. "The Japanese were good at copying what the West had invented, but lacked creativity."

I raised my hand to stop him. All my classmates waited for my words, and my face and ears became hot before I could say anything. Having no way to retreat, I blurted, "You're wrong to say that. We should distinguish between the laborers in Japan and the exploiting classes."

It was a cliché used in newspapers and by political cadres, but this was the first time it had come from my mouth. Teacher Zhou modestly accepted my critique. "Yes, you're right. I retract my wrong comment. It was unfair to the Japanese working classes."

During lunchtime that day, as I walked down the slope toward the mess hall, a large hand landed on my shoulder from behind. It was Big Brother Li. "You've made big progress.

Keep going."

The next week, I passed Zhou's younger daughter, a ninth grader, on the library staircase. Worried that her father might have complained at home about my behavior in class, I pretended not to notice her.

Did I, indeed, care for the dignity of the Japanese proletariat? Or had peer pressure prompted me to take Zhou's off-guard words as elitism against the oppressed classes? I tended to believe that my real motive was to make a gesture to please Big Brother Li and his protégés. I apologized in my heart for the cowardice that weakened me enough to hurt a senior teacher, the most vulnerable man on campus after 1949.

On the other hand, I wanted to forgive myself. I had given up my worship for my ancestors and teachers under the circumstances, was that enough to comply with the Revolution? Didn't I have to further fulfill the calling of the Party and its YL?

At the end of the winter of 1950, when the Chinese People's Volunteer Army marched into North Korea, newspapers reported that many evicted landlords were spreading rumors of an imminent KMT counterattack. The threat justified cleansing the teachers' ranks of potential enemies.

Before our final exams, I heard from a senior student that during his youth, Teacher Zhou had joined the Rejuvenation Association, a short-lived, somewhat secret society affiliated with the KMT.

Soon after the Chinese New Year of 1951, when we students were still enjoying the holidays, all teachers and staff from all schools were called to return and undergo political screenings. At my school, Teacher Zhou bore the initial, hard brunt of the campaign. His misstep many years before was quoted as sensational news copy for mobilizing the masses.

Unexpectedly, Zhou resisted the interrogation conducted by his fellow teachers and supervised by cadres from the county. At the beginning of the 1951 spring semester, a whole school rally was held in the sports field to increase the pressure on him. Like a bear standing in the center, Zhou had to turn to face a criticizer from any quadrant of the large circle. Soon after Comrade Li's opening address, the younger students came to dominate the scene. I repeatedly raised my hand to join the shouts.

"We won't withdraw our force till victory is complete!"

"If the enemy refuses to surrender, smash him!"

A seventh-grade boy stood out from the crowd. "I've eye-witnessed his ugly reactionary features. The day after three US fighter planes were shot down by our air force, he was reading a newspaper in the teachers' sitting room, and I happened to pass by. He slapped his thigh and moaned, 'What a pity,' as sad as if hearing of the death of his parents."

The crowd was in a tumult. Above the hushing and booing came the scream of a young female teacher. "Mourning the downed US airplanes, Zhou's exposed himself as an active counterrevolutionary, not only an historical one."

Zhou lost his composure and yelled to the boy accuser. "You liar, making up a story. I hailed it as a 'Great victory!'"

The evening after the rally, we classmates had to talk about our ideological gain from the rally. Everybody made similar points during the rotating speeches. A few students raised their doubts about the seventh grader's statement, but they were in the minority. Comrade Li challenged me for my opinion. I said, "Teacher Zhou slapped his thigh, about that there's no argument. But what did he say? I believe each side might have a 50 percent probability of being true or false."

A radical said, "How can you take a neutral stand between revolution and counterrevolution?"

Another said, "Don't play the lute to a cow. He's less

intelligent than the seventh-grade accuser."

I said, "You both violate Chairman Mao's teaching, *seek truth from facts.*"

Li stepped in. "First of all, we should praise the vigilance of the seventh grader against class enemies. Later we'll verify the facts about what he revealed."

The continuous yelling and pounding of tables pushed Zhou to his limits. When the senior student guarding the improvised staircase detention room fell asleep before dawn, Zhou snuck past him and groped his way up the stairs. He jumped from a third-floor dormer window headfirst onto a rocky slope below. At the ground floor three more guards stood talking and smoking on the sidewalk. They were supposed to prevent class enemies outside campus from collaborating with Zhou. The object flying over their heads frightened them and put them under criticism. The next morning, I delayed a few minutes before entering our classroom, lingering around the outcrop of sandstone near the building foundation, it was yellowish brown and stained with Zhou's blood. I mourned him in silence.

Nothing changed on campus. Another teacher was assigned to lecture us on the modern history of China instead of world history. I couldn't forget Zhou, and his death pricked my conscience. I didn't know how much my criticism in class had hurt him. He might have ignored it as the parroting voice of an immature student, but he might have taken it as the last straw. The inconstancy of human relationships carried by it must have chilled his heart, making him less fond of the world. I would detour to avoid meeting his younger daughter, who was two years younger than me, in order to keep my peace.

Mourning him in my heart, I collected views of him from old-timers on campus, including trustworthy teachers, senior students, and an elderly librarian. They all said Teacher Zhou was an upright man, attentive to his own morals, but too rigid to be bent.

During the 1951 spring semester, while the Chinese People's Volunteer Army fought desperately along the 38th parallel across Korea, hatred of the US and our 'domestic class enemies' prevailed everywhere in China. Rising to the new demand for patriotic propaganda, our drama team undertook a fairytale opera, *The Happy Mountain*. The mountain symbolized China, and its now-removed wolves and tigers, hunted to extinction, implied Western imperialists. Foxes remained, representing wily reactionaries, foreign and domestic alike. Two hunting brothers, led by Old Hunter, valiantly continued to rid the mountain of predators.

Since our more accomplished singers had by now graduated and gone to university, I got the lead, playing the younger brother, along with a cast of inexperienced student actors. We rehearsed tirelessly, and our prodigious effort paid off. By opening day we could sing and dance the 90-minute opera without conspicuous flaws.

During rehearsals, our music teacher was too busy to spend enough time helping every performer. Whenever I had difficulty singing correctly, our assistant director, Teacher Meng, who taught me reading and composition before 1949, would come to sing along with me and encourage me. Having the common mission of putting on a great show revived many pleasant feelings between Meng and me.

I was one of his favorite students, but I sensed a chasm between us because I hadn't joined the activities to greet the Liberation, which he organized in the summer of 1949. At the end of September that year, PLA troops marched into our county center. To the rhythm of drums and cymbals, the students trained at Grapes Hill now swelled the streets ahead of the PLA troops. I saw Teacher Meng striding along in the student column, leading the chorus in singing.

When I started tenth grade, Meng continued to teach ninth. The Liberation of China from the reactionary regime suddenly made me a stranger to him. Every time we met on the road, his doubting and searching air repelled me. Besides our no longer being in the same classroom, I must have seemed aloof about the summer camp he'd been dedicated to. In his mind, no doubt, I remained a droplet of 'dead water in a marshy pond.'

No sooner had *The Happy Mountain* brought me back to Teacher Meng, than he was thrown into the fire, accused of being a live agent of the US imperialists and their lackeys in Taiwan. An interrogation was arranged in the afternoon. Besides faculty and staff members, militant students were picked to strengthen the force.

Suddenly, the lull after Teacher Zhou's death was broken, and the Campaign of Suppressing Counterrevolutionaries turned its spearhead toward Teacher Meng. On the eve of attacking him, Comrade Li quizzed me, "How do you see his service in the KMT Youth Army from 1943 to 1945?"

I answered, "As preparing for the counterattack to recover our land occupied by the Japanese."

"No, you've been deceived by the KMT's propaganda. They flew under an anti-Japanese flag, while their real purpose was planning the anti-communist Civil War. You must enhance your political consciousness."

This new definition of the Youth Army gave the campaign leaders an excellent opportunity to stir up the slackening masses. His interrogation was conducted on the third floor. The clamor seeped down to our classroom on the ground level. Haunted by Zhou's sad ending, I wished that Teacher Meng would be mentally strong. I also wished that his sister, Qiaohon, who'd joined the PLA and married a general, knew he was under fire.

8

The closed windows and doors couldn't fully muffle the furious shouting and thunderous table-pounding. The intimidating voices didn't make me believe him guilty but they made my heart sink. One evening I murmured to Mother, "If Teacher Meng's brother-in-law, General Sheng, were here, the mobs would treat him less brutally. I wish I could fly to Wuhan and find his younger sister, Qiaohon. But we don't have the money to buy train tickets."

Mother seemed to have a solution. "You should go. Your grandpa told me that if someone has taught you, even if only for one day, you ought to respect him as you do your father for the rest of your life."

She took off her apron and led me to a narrow alley to see an old woman who was also a war refugee from Hubei. Her son, Winter Born, was an engine driver and famous for his filial piety. Mother made it clear what we had come for.

He readily promised to take me on the train. "Dapeng can stay in my driver's compartment all the way to Wuhan. Around 12 hours. Then come back the next evening. You'll have the greater part of a day to do things in Wuhan."

I chose a Friday night to start my trip and asked a schoolmate on our block to present a written request for a one-day sick leave for me for Saturday. Teacher Meng's father was touched by my move. He had formerly been our school's principal for many years, and local government preserved him as a reusable man left by the old regime. With a trembling hand, he wrote a short letter to his daughter. He repeatedly tapped the address on the envelope before his words came out. "Anything you can do to save my son would be a great blessing."

I started off with a lunch box and two yuan in my pocket. The driver's assistant kept adding coal to the burner. During the first hour, his extra steps and exaggerated shoveling forced me to huddle on the slope of the coal mound. Later, he looked tired and sat on a bench, smoking. I took the shovel to feed the coal, working slowly but giving him enough time to let his cigarette burn at a leisurely pace. As the tension between us relaxed, I had a catnap and ate my food in the early morning.

At Wuhan's eastern railway station, Winter Born let me take a shower in the drivers' dorm. After putting on clean clothes, I took a bus and ferry to look for the hotel where a suite was assigned to General Sheng as his family's residence. It was my first time coming back to the city since I'd left it at the age of four with my parents, and Mother worried I might get lost. Its vastness and busy traffic made me anxious about how long it would take me to reach Qiaohon's place and whether she and her husband were at home. I ran all the way to transfer from the bus to the ferry, then from the west side of the river to another bus. The Revolution had indeed changed the residents. Unknown crowds would blame anyone cutting in line, or yell at others, "You're lacking in political study."

The hotel was one of the most luxurious in Wuhan, taken over by the state to house its high-ranking cadres and generals. I waited at the reception counter, appreciating the red lacquered wood floor and the well-carved banisters along the staircase. Soon, Qiaohon appeared with an armed guard. She was 19, but no longer the elegant girl of the old days. Her quick and militant gestures looked like stage moves, much affected. Perhaps she'd acquired them from the army performance troupe. She stretched out her hand. "You look very familiar. Are you from my hometown?"

"Yes, I'm two years your junior and now continuing my study."

Her guard was watching the surroundings. I lowered my voice. "Your father gave me this address because Teacher Meng is in trouble."

Her face turned pale, but she kept calm. "Thank you for

coming all the long way. I want to catch up on events in west Jiangxi. My husband is busy now. I'll tell the guard to ask him to join us for lunch."

I followed her to the second floor, where her family's suite was situated. The hardwood floor, leather sofas, dining table, and large writing desk were all red. She asked me to sit down and let the orderly serve me tea while she read the letter from her father.

While I was absorbed by reading the certificates of merit given to her husband, she punched the cushion of her sofa. "As soon as the Japanese surrendered, my brother went back to school. He didn't fight in the Civil War. How can he be treated as an anti-communist?"

"That's what I was wondering."

She tried to hold back her tears. "He also helped the Party underground take over, especially to protect the coal mines from KMT sabotage."

"I heard that Teacher Meng and your father raised thousands of silver dollars to pay off the KMT commander who'd threatened to blow up the county's only power plant."

"My father used his influence as high school principal and city council chairman. My brother risked his life as a go-between. The local cadres are ungrateful idiots!"

Around lunchtime, General Sheng came home. I stood up to let Qiaohon introduce us. In his early forties, his gentle appearance didn't match his valorous image as the famous commander of an elite division during the Civil War. Now he headed a whole army. Behind his stately manner and stoic air, I sensed a sharp edge.

The couple excused themselves and went into their study and shut the door. As the orderly set up the round table with chopsticks, bowls, and spoons, the general's voice was a muffled buzz while his wife's curses were clear and crisp. "You're playing it safe…. A tiger on the battlefield but a mouse inside the Party. If you don't do anything, I'll do something."

Soon, they came out and asked me to sit down. The soup of pork ribs and seaweed, diced ham with sweet rice, and bass steamed with ginger were all delicious. At the table, Qiaohon didn't eat but looked aside with lips pouted. The general urged me to eat more, then put a hand on her wrist and cajoled in a fatherly voice. "You've been in the army almost two years, and now you're a military staff member, but your petty-bourgeois sentiment remains. Revolution is not fair play. It's bloody." He ladled more soup into my bowl. "Have the masses at your school beaten Teacher Meng with sticks?"

"Not yet. The table-pounding, yelling, and intimidating are enough to crush him."

He nodded at me, then at his wife. "The campaign at your school is a gentle breeze with a mild rain. During the 1942 Rectification at Yan'an, a normal school near our headquarters had half its students confess they were KMT spies, and some cadres died in the torture caves at the hands of their own comrades."

I felt my hair stand on end.

He sucked in some soup. "Our high combat strength comes from our tough cleansing of the ranks. That tells you why the KMT spies had difficulty penetrating our ranks, while our underground Party members felt at home playing mahjong with their generals' wives and dating the daughters of Chiang Kai-shek's top aides. So, don't make a fuss about the campaign at your school. It's normal routine to me."

"General," I said, "the PLA's Eight Points for Attention say, 'Do not ill-treat captives.' If Teacher Meng is a prisoner of war, shouldn't that be applied to him?"

He smiled. "We treated prisoners of war nicely to demoralize the KMT army and encourage surrender. Teacher Meng isn't a prisoner of war. He has to pass through fire to prove his loyalty to the Party."

Qiaohon jerked her hand from his grasp. "My ears can't bear your rubbish. No matter what you say, I'll write a letter to remind local cadres not to torture a confession out of him."

Struck dumb for a second, her husband showed a calm face. "Don't be silly. The only thing you can say is to ask them to help your brother cooperate with the mass movement."

And I'd thought it might be enough to let the county leaders consider Teacher Meng's status as a dependent of a high-ranking cadre. What could my desperate trip achieve?

After lunch, Qiaohon drafted a letter, rewrote it after her husband's corrections, and tied it up with a box of tonic herbs. "Give it to my father. He'll forward it to the mayor, who used to be a staff officer under my husband."

I put the package into my shoulder bag and was ready to go. "Thank you for the lunch. I'm excited to have met General Sheng. Since the freight train needs time to refill with water and coal before leaving, I have to wait for the engine driver at the eastern station."

Her husband rushed out from another room to shake my hand. "We should buy you a ticket for the express train." He turned to Qiaohon. "Please arrange a jeep to take him there and inform the engine driver about his express train ride."

9

I returned home on Sunday morning. Though terribly drowsy, I ran to deliver the letter to Teacher Meng's father. The gentleman, highly respected in the old society, now looked like a frightened deer. Shrunken and hunchbacked, he gripped my hand, his bony fingers like a chicken claw. "I don't know if the mayor can receive me or read the letter personally."

The next day, I went to school as usual. In the nice April afternoon, when most students were playing in the sports field between the library and the lecture building, I stayed on the balcony of the library, reading a newspaper and enjoying the sunset. A howl arose from the midst of the moving crowd in the field, and all heads turned to watch a human figure climb out of a dormer window and jump off the roof of the three-story lecture building.

I ran downstairs and out the door. Above the shouts and my own footsteps, I heard a sharp metallic creaking and squealing. Running the 60 yards up the slope, I hoped it wasn't Teacher Meng. I jostled through the circle of onlookers and saw him wriggling on the ground. After jumping, he must have instinctively grabbed the rain gutter, but its lightweight tin didn't stop his fall.

Blood and teeth swished about in his mouth. He moaned three words, which nobody understood, over and over. The campus doctor arrived and said Meng was saying the name of a painkiller injection.

Several muscular students found a door and a wheelbarrow to carry him to the county hospital. When they laid him out, his disfigured face and much shortened body frightened me. As the team and the doctor moved down the hill, Big Brother Li spoke to the newcomers. "His fear of death overrode his reactionary will, the coward. Both his knees are broken, and the shin bones have been pushed up into his thighs."

I believed that when he grabbed the gutter, Teacher Meng's desire to live had overcome his intellectual's pride. Li's dancing eyebrows and joyful gestures sickened me. I walked away to keep my tears from revealing me as an ideological captive of the class enemy.

After Meng's disappearance from campus, the Campaign of Suppressing Counterrevolutionaries ceased all mass activities, though nobody had declared its ending. We had half a year of peace, and I hoped no other teachers would be in danger.

Then, a new storm came in the winter of 1951 and lasted to

the spring of 1952 when our last semester began. The Campaign against the Three Devils—Corruption, Waste and Bureaucracy—found Teacher Tang as its first and primary target.

Tang taught me math in the 1946–47 academic year when I was a seventh grader. After 1949, his good reputation and diligence had persuaded the new authorities to select him as the school financial officer, an honor without extra pay. He didn't realize the danger of being the only one on campus with money flowing through his hands. In February 1952, when the hunting of embezzlers became frenzied, activists interrogated him around the clock. One morning, as the struggle extended from the previous night, I saw him in the center of an empty classroom, sitting in a student chair, surrounded by seventh-grade girls. They held placards: 'Leniency toward those who confess their crimes; Severity toward those who refuse to.' Pointing at him, they chanted, "Embezzler, open your eyes! There are only two roads for you to choose. One way lets you out, the other leads to ruin. One is bright, the other's dark."

I peeped through the door until the bell rang marking the start of lectures. After the cursing girls had left Tang for their class, I rushed to the teachers' sitting room to fetch a mug of warm water. The gurgling sound Tang made swallowing the water, and my heart's pounding, almost panicked me. I was ready to parrot the girls' chant if someone approached in the corridor, but feared that my trembling voice would betray me. Fortunately, nobody showed up. I ran to the other building and apologized to the geometry teacher for being ten minutes late.

With the specters of Teacher Zhou and Teacher Meng hovering above my head, I worried about Tang in the following days and months. Miraculously, he endured the ordeal, swallowed his pride, and lived. Despite not yet having official rehabilitation, most people believed him innocent.

May 1, 1952, International Labor Day, was the last time I joined a rally in my hometown. After the ceremony was over, Hot Chili, the eleventh grader who'd played the part of a village girl in our performance of *The Happy Mountain*, asked me to accompany her to see Teacher Meng. She was a tomboy, and her nickname paid tribute to her sharp tongue and petite physique. Though we both still held the now outdated sentiment of cherishing good teachers, I said, "Aren't you afraid of the backlash?"

"Why do you worry so much? My father worked for the old regime as a personnel manager at a state-owned coal mine, so I carry a class curse you don't have, but I dare to visit him."

"Fine, please show me the road."

Through the ragged, slab-paved streets and alleys, she led me to the city gods' temple. Before 1949, the city gods were considered the local administrators of the netherworld, but now, atheists had turned the temple into a warehouse for a state-owned paper-pulp company. Through the grid of the temple's front gate, I peered at stone arms, legs, and the heads of granite statues scattered around its yard. Books confiscated from landlords were piled in huge heaps, soon to be added to the recycling pool. Some of them were printed on glossy paper and brought there from Shanghai, they were not affordable for ordinary people.

We found Meng's family in a row of low-roofed shanties against the west side of the high fences. The bare walls told of the utter destitution of the family, which had obviously been swept out of its former residence. A layer of rice straw formed their beds. Pots and pans lay all around on the ground.

Our former teacher lay motionless on the straw. He couldn't stand. His wife was decocting medicinal herbs on a coal stove. A boy of three or four stood by, watching his mom expressionlessly. Stretching her sleeve to dry her tears, she sobbed. "He can only crawl with his hands and pull his body forward. His salary and free medication are all cut off. I don't know how long we can live."

Hot Chili whispered, "His brother is a music professor, and his younger sister married a PLA general. They should give you some money."

"Forget about that. They won't give us a penny. But they shouldn't have written all the crap to blame him."

I was shocked. Had Qiaohon's letter made things worse for Meng? Or maybe the letter hadn't reached the city leader before Meng attempted suicide? I punched my chest and cursed myself, "How dumb I was. Things would've been different if I'd gotten her letter two days earlier!"

"They only care about protecting themselves," Meng's wife said.

Neither Hot Chili nor I knew how to console the miserable couple. We just awkwardly sat on tiny bamboo stools for ten minutes.

Teacher Meng said not a single word. I could only bear to glance at him once. Without teeth, his mouth and chin had flattened. With cheekbones squashed, his former oval face had been slanted sideways. We stood next to him awhile. I hoped our grieving silence conveyed our condolences. When we said goodbye, I mentally bowed to him as I had when we met on the street before the Liberation.

After we left, Hot Chili said that Teacher Meng had nodded to us, but I hadn't seen it. Perhaps it was indistinct or I was less sensitive than she was. On the street, we promised to keep our visit secret. Then, I recited the words Meng had inscribed in my album two years before, on the eve of the Liberation. I sighed. "He greeted the Revolution with rapture. Now this."

"You used to be his favorite disciple. You need to see him as a mirror and get rid of what's between you and the Revolution."

"How about you?" I said. "You think the Revolution favors a hot temper?"

"Don't worry about me, I'm going to be a doctor. And marry a worldly-wise man."

"A henpecked husband."

"Not like that. And not like you, either."

I was stunned for a second. "Touché."

During a discussion on how to correctly view Meng's attempted suicide, I held back until Big Brother Li challenged me. "You must have a lot of thoughts and feelings about this event."

"No, I don't have much to say."

Li smiled. "We're students receiving the Party's education. Revealing any doubts or wrong ideas is fine. We can help each other to get the right answer. That's the only way to make progress."

The few active YL members had pens and papers ready, waiting for my speech. I had no difficulty figuring out what the correct speech should be. Like shifting rosary beads, I said word by word, with pauses between them, "By the regulations published by the Ministry of Public Security, any officers of the KMT military are counterrevolutionary elements if they ranked higher than, or equal to, the company commander. Meng held the title of Major Instructor, equivalent to a battalion commander. Regardless of when or how he joined the Youth Army, he is a counterrevolutionary."

Li and his close followers looked at one another in blank dismay. I took in a long breath and continued. "The Party and revolutionary masses have shown enough patience toward him, but he chose to commit suicide, the worst way to resist the Revolution. He has only himself to blame."

Li said, "So far, you've respected Meng as a good teacher, failing to know his harm to our newborn red power. I'm glad you've made a clean psychological break with Meng. I hope you can cut any sentimental ties to him. To defend the victory of our Revolution, we have to suppress counterrevolutionaries thoroughly and completely. Any sympathy with them will give imperialists and the KMT a chance to restore their rule over China, and millions of innocent people will be decapitated."

10

Toward graduation from high school, we had to pass a political evaluation, which included self-examination, group criticism, and a personal rectifying statement. The system looked unclear, even mysterious, and the school administration seemed to be excluded from the political operation. The frequent appearance on campus of a female cadre, a member of the county Party committee and the wife of its secretary, hinted to us that there might be a single line, connecting through her, to Big Brother Li. The final conclusive appraisals of us would be written by the YL branch, sealed in the individual's dossier, and sent to the university to which he or she would go. Our class was divided into four groups, and each one was headed by a reputable YL member. Big Brother Li personally presided over the group I belonged to. We six classmates sat in a small room for a whole week, enduring the July heat, to conduct our mutual ideological dissection.

Father hadn't owned any properties before 1949 nor served the old regime. His lowly status benefited my smooth progress through the general check of family class origin and social ties, the first phase of the evaluation. While some students were grilled for having an immediate relative who was executed, jailed, or put under surveillance after the Liberation, nobody asked me any questions in that category. Nevertheless, to prevent any later accusations of dishonesty with the Party, I searched through my memory to look for dubious people among our relatives and anyone my parents knew. As a result, I wrote down the name of Mother's niece, who'd married an engineer serving the KMT Air Force and escaped to Taiwan. I emphasized that I'd never met her because her family escaped in a different direction from ours during the Japanese invasion.

The second phase, self-examination and mutual exposure, turned tough for me. The radicals took the chance to vent their accumulated rancor against me, presenting all the evidence of my disdain for political activities and especially my sympathy for Teacher Meng. I tried to explain away the facts they quoted, but in vain, because some senior teachers facing the same accusation had admitted their true thoughts and repented. The Campaign of Ideological Remolding was surging forward on all university campuses, and every day *The People's Daily* would print model confessional speeches given by famous scholars and scientists in Beijing and Shanghai. Their surrender to the Party of their past political impurity and their association with the old regime seemed morally wholehearted, and it inspired me to make my penitence at a group meeting.

"From a Marxist point of view, a man's economic status determines his political attitude. My father isn't a capitalist, but he held the dream of becoming one. His illusion about the old society must make him dual-minded toward the Revolution. My excessive tenderness toward Meng, a historic counterrevolutionary, might have reflected a petty-bourgeois wavering, the shadow of my father. Also, my mother taught me to be compassionate with wretched or miserable people. Her belief in Buddhism has hindered my plunge into class struggle. I've failed to treat Teacher Meng and Teacher Zhou as unarmed enemies, as Chairman Mao dictates."

Li's nodding approval let me feel relief, but one tough kid didn't let me pass any farther. "Did you help someone hide property during the Land Reform?"

"No!" I was stunned, unable to make heads or tails of the question.

"Don't pretend to be stupid. During the Land Reform, our classmate Zhang and his two brothers were ordered by the poor peasant association at their home village to appear for the final search of their premises. You can't forget that day."

A year and a half earlier, when my friend Zhang was about to leave the classroom, I said to him, "It's cold. May I borrow your scarf?" I kept it until the day he left for Shanghai to join his parents, when I put it back around his neck. The same day I'd borrowed the scarf, the poor peasant association had taken the three brothers' woolen sweaters, and they'd come back to school with ragged clothes.

To buy time to regain my composure, I spoke slowly. "Zhang's family passed the Land Reform Campaign with the title of 'enlightened landlord' because they surrendered everything voluntarily. Though his father used to be a judge for the Hubei Provincial Superior Court before 1949, he managed to set certain Chinese Communist Party (CCP) leaders free from KMT prison. That's why he was kept on as a court worker in Shanghai after the Liberation."

"No matter what the situation is with Zhang's father, you helped him to hide a piece of property. Am I correct?"

"I had no idea about that. Who could expect the clothes on their backs would be counted as property?"

A female student said, "I don't believe you had such motives, but objectively, your actions helped him keep the scarf."

I took her compromise as an opportunity to back down, but not too far down. "You're right. I didn't have bad motives, but I should've foreseen such an effect."

"You shouldn't have borrowed anything from the son of a landlord," Li said. "If you don't enhance your awareness of class struggle, you'll soon get into big trouble."

I nodded humbly.

Round after round, the rotating self-criticism and collective help went on. One morning, my hearing lasted two hours, and I felt nitpicked by ravenous peers, as if each of them were holding a magnifying glass. I didn't go home that Sunday. Worried, Mother hiked to our hilltop campus with her bound feet and brought some salt pork for me. When I told her what was going on, she smiled, as peaceful as ever. "Take it easy. Under a low eave, no-one can walk upright. Just bow your head and go through." Her words soothed me, and I showed more patience.

The third phase of the evaluation was designed to display the ideological harvest of the mini-rectification, as shown by everyone's summary statement. The big shots in Beijing and Shanghai had offered us samples of a self-flagellating writing style. No matter how stiffly I mimicked them, my writing seemed to glorify the Party and socialism. Some newspapers also quoted university students unloading their dirty minds. One of them said he'd been poisoned by the novel *Gone with the Wind*, which stimulated the growth of bourgeois individualism in his heart. Since my classmates had blamed me for preferring Chinese classics and Western novels to proletarian ones extolling Soviet heroes, I figured out where to attribute the origin of my petty-bourgeois sentiment.

Besides blaming my parents' negative influence, I sweepingly accused the books I'd read of dragging me away from the Revolution. The Chinese classics carry feudal ideas, and Western literature spreads the decaying capitalist spirit. Still, I felt my statement was weak and devoid of persuasive content.

That evening, I asked my older brother, Haitao, for help. Though currently weighing coal, which was transported by wheelbarrows, at a station, he knew more history than I did. He helped me find Karl Marx's criticism of some Western novels, such as Defoe's *Robinson Crusoe* and Goethe's *The Sorrow of Young Werther.*

During my final confession, I read the quotation from Marx. "Young Werther's sorrow is actually the sorrow of the urban petty bourgeois. Robinson's image is nothing else but that of a colonist." I passed the evaluation, taking a pledge to seriously study Marxism to rid myself of poisonous influences from ancient and Western cultures.

11

The day a photographer took our collective picture as a memento of our high-school graduation, most of us looked happy, cherishing the last chance to be together. I almost forgot the friction and conflicts caused by the political evaluation, though quite a few others remained hostile and ignored one another.

Soon after we were dismissed, I walked down the hill and found Teacher Tang in a shabby riverside house. He and his wife rented a room there, living like peasants.

Though it was the first time we sat face-to-face and had a private chat, he acted as warmly and intimately as if he were my uncle. In addition to the coarse tea he made, he fetched a bottle of hard liquor from under the bed. Since I'd never had a drink, he drank alone. He smacked his lips and sighed. "I've watched you grow up. I hope I'll hear you named as a big shot. But be cautious, there are so many pitfalls on the road ahead. As a university student, the Party will no longer treat you as a juvenile."

"I know. Teachers Zhou and Meng joined the wrong party or the wrong army when they were young. They didn't have a chance to correct their mistakes."

"No." He leaned forward. "Their real mistake was sticking

to an obsolete idea: righteous intellectuals should die rather than accept insults. I used to be like them. Seeing their death, I've changed my mind. They should've put survival first. Personal dignity and self-esteem mean nothing to the Revolution. Only mutual suspicion and insults are effective in leaving enemies no way to hide."

"Ironically," I said, "in his article attacking Leighton Stuart, the US Ambassador, Chairman Mao declared, 'We Chinese have backbone.'"

He waggled a finger. "We can show our backbone only to the US and the KMT. Within the Revolution's ranks, we should bow our heads and accept torture or humiliation. A veteran cadre in the county's Party committee privately warned me that my rehabilitation would take time but not to hold a grudge. During the internal purges at the guerrilla bases around the Jinggang Mountains in the early thirties, many Red Army soldiers were executed, as KMT spies, with knives or spears to save revolutionary bullets."

"I heard stories like that from the 1942 Rectification at Yan'an," I said. "It seems to happen every ten years. We should be prepared for the next cycle."

"I hope it won't go on too long. Once the Party consolidates its power, it'll ease off."

The kettle whistled. He added boiling water to dilute the homemade tea, which still gave off a strong smell of smoke.

"In 1949," I said, "when some teachers were fired, Teachers Zhou and Meng were kept on. They must have been considered useful. They should've held out in the storm, which was much less brutal, and lasted for a shorter amount of time, than the one in 1942."

He nodded. "Heaven hadn't cut off all escape. Even if they'd been sentenced to prison, they would've been pardoned before their sentences were over, as soon as the Party badly needed senior teachers."

I finished a third cup of tea. It was time to leave. "I'm glad you've survived the disaster. As the proverb says, 'Those who don't die in a calamity must have a huge fortune ahead.'"

"Forget fortune. What I need is peace."

Walking me outside to the riverside, he held my hand tightly. "Friendship between gentlemen appears indifferent but is pure like water. Thank you for the mug of water that morning after I'd been interrogated around the clock and harassed by those seventh-grade girls. You did that, risking your neck."

"That's not big enough to be worth talking about."

"It was a big thing that not many people would dare to do."

I took a few more steps. "My parents worry about me in the future."

His overgrown eyebrows, like that of Taoist immortals, seemed to accent his wisdom. "They can't help you at all. You have to learn to swim upstream by yourself. Life would be easier if we forgot the old Confucian ethical codes."

The last day of our scattering and going home, Big Brother Li called on us to do our alma mater some good turns. Some cleaned the roads on campus, and others mended broken books in the library. I walked around and found, almost hidden under a coat of whitewash, four characters on the wall facing the entrance gate, and eight on the opposite wall, representing the four ethical principles and eight cardinal virtues. Each had been painted red with a white background, as big as a truck wheel. They were hastily covered up in 1949, but were still faintly visible, and a source of nostalgia for old-timers, especially obsessive people like Teachers Zhou and Meng.

I invited a classmate to help me, and we got enough white lime. He kept mixing the material to make the slurry, while I used a long-handled brush to smear a white layer onto the walls and totally conceal the 12 characters. In the late afternoon, when we were using up the leftover lime to trim the

edges and corners, Big Brother Li came by. He laughed loudly.
"Great job. You've made a true contribution. Down with
Confucius!"

I laughed too, but for the reason Teacher Tang had given
me. Obliterating the old tradition would help individuals to
throw aside personal dignity and suffer insults in order to
survive.

12

I graduated from high school in the summer of 1952 when the
news media was exalting the country's First Five-Year Plan for
economic development, a strategic step toward realizing
Stalin's idea for socialist industrialization in China. Being an
engineer was suddenly the most fashionable, glorious
profession. Even a fine arts' lover, a genius among my
classmates, switched course to enroll in a military engineering
school.

About that time, a popular alumnus arrived home for a
visit. Two years older than me, he was studying electrical
engineering in Beijing. In 1950, he had emerged as the best
singer in our high school and had played the lead role in a
revolutionary opera.

I visited him at his parents' home and asked, "Do you
regret your career choice?"

"Not at all. But if I'd known the tremendous potential of
China's water resources, I'd have chosen water-resource
technology rather than electrical engineering. I feel it more
strongly every time I cross the Yangtze and Yellow Rivers."

He recommended Wuhan University. "It's famous for
water-resource and waterpower engineering. The campus on
East Lake is the most beautiful in China. I especially love the
swimming pool, fitted in a bay of the lake. In the early autumn

of 1950, I watched young couples swimming the backstroke side-by-side, gazing up at the blue sky."

His enthusiasm was contagious. I made my decision.

The campus of Wuhan University was as beautiful as I'd imagined. Built on twin hills, with sports fields set in a flat valley, its modern Western architecture was artistically harmonized with the ancient Chinese roof styles. The two hills ran from west to east and extended to the beach, and the exquisite villas on the ridges and slopes were reflected in the clear lake.

As I soon learned, its enchanting setting contrasted sharply with our regimented life and strict ideological surveillance. From 6:30 am, when loudspeakers blared the PLA's 'Military Anthem' to wake us, until 10:30 pm, when electric bells commanded us to turn off our lights and get into bed, our schedule was filled with collective activities. We ate together, attended lectures together, and did homework together. Our hour-long daily physical exercise was conducted under a system called Physical Readiness for Labor and National Defense. We climbed ropes, threw dummy grenades, vaulted boxes, and ran together. On Saturday nights, in the school auditorium or on the sports field, we sat in an area assigned to us and watched revolutionary movies, most dubbed in Mandarin from Russian.

My small dorm had five double-decker bunks and two desks, leaving just enough space for us to move sideways. Every night, ten roommates crammed in there to review texts and solve problems together. Anyone walking in or out would disturb everyone else.

Our ideological space was also confined. One third of the new students had transferred from army and government organizations. Officially called cadre-students, they'd been trained to conform to a military lifestyle and commissioned to remold the university and guide us, the regular high-school graduates. Every Tuesday evening, during our two-hour group criticism and self-criticism, they sounded like clergymen and court judges. They also always complained that the coursework was too heavy, and even hazardous to their health. The Party leaders accepted their demands as public opinion, pushing teachers to shrink our curriculum and slow the pace. We regular students had more spare time and finished the reduced workload with much less effort than before.

The YL branch secretary for our class was Jianlin Mo. This woman, born in Henan, had served in the army for three years and seemed to be on a mission to convert me. I loathed her slovenly dress, carelessly cut hair, yellow teeth, and the food scum on the front of her jacket. If she'd taken better care of her appearance, no doubt a military commander would have kept her in the army or married her. Still shy, she talked to me from her perceived higher moral ground. One cold December evening, after I spent half an hour helping her with math problems, she asked me to take a walk with her. I was nervous but prepared for another inquisition, as, in the previous months, two other YL members had quizzed my political stance.

She smiled. "What are your true feelings toward the Party and the YL?"

I replied slowly. "I've studied the book *How to Be a Communist Party Member*. It lists eight standards for judging if an applicant qualifies to join the Party, or if a Party member is worthy of being called a communist. YL members are loyal assistants and a reserve force for the Party." I recited the eight standards. "Ideal Party members should be fearless in war and selfless in peace. They are respected by the masses as role models and vanguards, and function as a bridge between the masses and the Party."

She frowned. My tone must have been too flippant. "Have

you applied the Eight Points to check your own thoughts and deeds?"

At my wit's end, I remembered an article in a magazine criticizing a common misconception that existed among established scientists. I thought, as a student, committing a popular mistake like the big shots would be funny, that it would be blamed as ignorance at most. "They're too high and remote for me. I want to be a Bolshevik outside the Party."

She gaped with astonishment. "I've never heard that strange phrase. How can you become a Bolshevik outside the Party? My theoretical level is low. Let me ask Yonghon Huo to talk to you."

"No, please, don't talk to him, I was just joking."

"It's no joke." She left in a fury.

Yonghon was the toughest Party member in our department and one of my roommates. Though physically short, he often awed others with his high principles and his loud voice. One afternoon at the end of 1952, when only he and I were in the dorm, he suddenly asked me, "Did you say you want to be a Bolshevik *outside* the Party?"

I kept reading the local newspaper. "It was a casual joke."

"It can't be a joke. It must be deeply rooted in your mind, but you're not the only one with this delusion. You must've learned it somewhere, some bourgeois scholar who uses stupid phrases to cover up defiance toward the Party."

I glared at him. "Don't throw me into that weird category. I have faith in the Party, I'm enthusiastic about the socialist cause, I want to remold myself. But I don't make a big show of it."

He sneered. "Pure fallacy. There can't be Bolsheviks outside the Party free from iron discipline and the collective fight. Anyone who wants to stay away from the Party is alienating himself from the Party, and most likely slipping into anti-Party crime."

"What about the author Lu Xun? He didn't join the Party, but Chairman Mao praises him as a great proletarian fighter."

"So you throw yourself into the category of brilliant exceptions? Don't make me laugh. Lu Xun and other literary masters supported the Party in its most difficult time but stayed outside the Party to conceal their true identities. The Party strategically planned their roles to achieve the best effects. They weren't acting on personal preference."

I couldn't win this argument. I took a breath and nodded thoughtfully. "They were bona fide Bolsheviks projecting the image of liberal intellectuals. That was the best way they could help the Revolution. I'm one of the ordinary masses. My blind imitation of Lu Xun is laughable."

"And dangerous. We have only one road open to us: to remold ourselves, and to catch up with the Revolution's developments."

"Thank you for your insight."

13

One Saturday evening in October, Huihe Lin and I were assigned to guard our dorm building against burglars, class enemies, or US and Chiang Kai-shek spies, while the other students went to the auditorium to watch a Soviet movie. I had a book to kill the boredom.

I quietly assessed Huihe under the light bulb hanging from the concrete awning. His head was oddly large for his lean body, and the rear of his skull stretched backward like a hanging crag. His accent, from a mountain area of Hunan, made him hard to understand, and his peasant attire and never-washed bedding repelled his urban classmates. Nevertheless, I recognized his intelligence and felt he was being honest with me. My sympathy for him at the time of his father's suicide had brought us closer than before.

We sat on tiny stools at the front door. While Huihe vigilantly watched every moving shadow and analyzed any audible sound, I thumbed through *Selected Poems of the Song Dynasty*. My silence seemed to make him uneasy. He glanced at me every other minute, and a half hour later, couldn't help asking, "Why don't you talk?"

I looked up from my book. "Do you remember seven months ago when you got the letter from home about your father's suicide? You sobbed inside your mosquito net. I brought you dinner from the mess hall and fetched hot water from the boiler room so you could wash."

"I'm very grateful. How could I forget that?"

I raised my voice to a loud whisper. "At the first group criticism, most classmates cursed your father, a pre-1949 landlord, as a class enemy, and said your grief proved you had a wrong political stance. You just cried."

"Please don't rub it in."

"Unlike the others, I stood up and said that mourning your father is a natural human reaction, and the difficulties he left for your mother and sister were enormous. I suggested you not let your sadness stop you from studying. I wanted to cut the smell of gunpowder from the air."

"I know and appreciate that."

I slid my stool closer to him. "At the end of the second round of criticism, you denounced your father as an exploiter and his suicide as a way to resist the Revolution. Your sudden elevation of class relations above blood relations made me blush. When the others cheered your phenomenal change, I wanted to fall through the floor."

He bowed his head. "Did you know, immediately after that first meeting, my student aid, mainly free meals, was suspended? I did what I had to."

"The problem for me is your sudden image change. Your

confession at the second criticism meeting plus good exam scores and lots of volunteer work have remade you as a newborn baby of the Revolution. You're quite glorious now."

He turned his long face toward me but said nothing.

"I guess you'll be a YL member soon. Am I right?"

He stammered a little. "A month ago I turned in my autobiographical report about family background, social ties, and how I've changed my world outlook and political stand. If it's considered okay by the YL branch, I'll fill out an application form. Please don't report my progress to anybody, it might get turned down."

"I believe you'll soon jump out of our circle of political misfits. I hope you can help us and care for us."

"Don't say that! The YL committee tries to convert all eligible students, except those whose parents were executed, jailed, or put under surveillance after 1949. It wouldn't be hard for you to join the YL if you're enthusiastic with the collective and if you're critical of the backward masses. Also, don't read ancient stories or foreign novels. Oh, and respect the cadre-students, you'll get instant results."

I was astonished by his well-thought-out plan. "I can accept some of your suggestions. But your attitude toward politically idle people annoys me. We both know most of them are humane and honest. Why loathe or betray them for our own progress?"

He scratched the patch of scalp behind his right ear. "I don't ask you to loathe or betray them. But the line between the Party's interest and your friendship should be clear. Criticize them if they spout anti-Party or anti-socialist opinions to your face, and don't spare anyone's feelings."

"And our friends will shun us."

"Yes, if you get close to the YL, they will shun you. Isn't that better than your current situation? It's a revolution, you have to take sides. The humanity and honesty you see in the backward masses are actually their fatal weaknesses, it blurs their consciousness of class struggle. There're so many newspaper stories about class enemies using the backward masses as their shelter. You feel comfortable with political laggards, so you don't see the danger. If you don't change your attitude toward them, you'll soon find it's too late to regret it."

I said, "Some of our classmates are shy, unsociable, or difficult to communicate with. They're loyal to the Revolution, but they don't speak aloud or express their love and loyalty to the Party in public. It's unfair and wrong to treat them as backward elements."

Huihe shook his head. "Those are character defects. To defend the Party line, a revolutionary should shout at the top of his voice. You're not one of those shy, tongue-tied clods, so don't pretend to be. Stand up to the challenge, my friend."

14

No matter how depressed I was by the boredom and pressure on campus, I tried to persuade myself the revolutionary lifestyle was designed to temper and purify us into new-style professionals worthy of the Party's trust. The future would be nice.

As I sat in class every morning, the sun cast its rays through our huge theater hall and brightened the red characters written on the wall, 'Communism is Soviet Political Power plus Nationwide Electrification.' Lenin's simple formula had profound meaning for us and directly charged my profession with the mission to build a dreamlike paradise, our communist society.

The goal of our department, Hydraulic Structural Engineering, as printed in the documents issued by the Ministry of Education, was 'to provide the nation with qualified engineers for the design and construction of key water-control projects.' China, we were often told, had the richest waterpower resources in the world.

During my first year, a popular Soviet movie about building a dam gave me a picture of my future life. Red flags fluttered atop towering cranes, monstrous concrete blocks rose from the river, and the shafts of hydraulic turbines, ready for installation, gleamed in the huge plant.

The protagonist, a handsome young graduate from a Moscow university, quickly matured into an honored engineer, replete with Bolshevik values and aspirations. Sporting a distinctive black leather jacket, he moved easily, talking with the crews and arguing with inarticulate bureaucrats. He lived in a neat brick bungalow set apart from the shabby laborers' sheds. His wife, a graceful art student, had left college and urban life. She hummed Russian folksongs while cooking dinner, ran to greet her husband when he came home, embraced him warmly, and danced with him at a workplace club. Clearly, their honeymoon would go on forever.

That dynamic Russian engineer in his black leather jacket, with the beautiful wife, framed my university daydreams and often distracted me with thoughts of my own future marriage. Between the two of them, I imagined, they spoke their minds freely, without secrets or censorship. When cuddling together and watching trout swimming in the water, their sweet prattle was carried on the breeze like the soft chirping of swallows. In freezing winter, burning a chunk of firewood, they would drink vodka and recite Pushkin's poems instead of talking political crap, like the couples in some Chinese novels and movies did.

When my mind returned to the blackboard, I would scan the backs of female classmates' heads, each had long, dark hair. They sat together in the front rows, mostly to avoid the male students. A chasm separated me from them. The female cadre-students, like their male counterparts, were older than me.

They were poor at coursework but sharp about picking out other students' ideological faults. Their high-sounding phrases matched their standard, gray Lenin-style blouses. I kept a respectful, cautious distance.

In the winter of 1953, when Huihe Lin's father had committed suicide and Huihe Lin was found weeping inside his mosquito net, a female cadre-student pointed a finger at him during a meeting. "The day Stalin passed away, you didn't cry, but now your heart's broken by the death of a reactionary. Why? What's your political stance? Answer me now!" After that, even the most cynical boys, many of whom gave stellar performances in sports and academic subjects, were wary around such women.

With these Big Sisters as role models, younger girls who enrolled directly after high school quickly learned the Party line. They competed with each other to show their toughness, not only during formal meetings but also in casual conversations.

15

Earlier in my freshman year, to celebrate the 1953 Chinese New Year, the student union organized a show. Through my high-school friends studying at the same campus, the drama group found me and asked me to take the main role in the play, *Spring in Mining Mountain*. A Cantonese girl with a Westerner's look from the Russian Language Department came to help us as the prompter during our dress rehearsal and performance. Still in her first year of study, she'd already become a public darling on campus. Until then, I didn't know her name, but often heard male students around me affectionately call her 'Foreign Doll' because of her oval face, deep-set eyes, and aquiline nose.

Her presence made me look forward to our performances. Even her Mandarin, carrying a strong Cantonese accent, sounded melodic to my ears. Unfortunately, her brief appearances only let me know her name, Ziwei Cao, but didn't offer me a chance to chat with her. Unlike our high-school drama group, where innocent affection promoted harmonious relationships, intensified orthodoxy on the university campus brought a dreadful solemnity to our rehearsals, curbing any natural interaction between men and women. In such a monastic atmosphere, Ziwei had assumed a reserved manner that precluded any possible social contact with her. She was unattainable.

During our dress rehearsal, the propaganda chief of our university's Party committee, a stocky man with surly manner, came to inspect the play's content and our performance. He'd also invited the art director of a military cultural troupe, a skinny expert with dark-rimmed glasses, to give us professional instructions. At the end of our show, the director held my hand, and talked to our team members, "Look at Dapeng. He's built like a well-proportioned statue. His light-complexioned face, white touched with red, indicates good health. These are excellent natural conditions for an actor to represent socialist heroes on stage."

The propaganda chief echoed, "Yes, I agree. His high nose ridge, dignified carriage, and intelligent eyes lead me believe he has innate gifts to play the part of a wise, great Party leader."

The director turned to me with a solemn tone. "However, you act more like an intellectual rather than a miner. Why? Lacking stage experience is one thing. The more important aspect is your lack of proletarian feelings. So, I suggest you learn as much as you can from workers, peasants, and soldiers, while sharpening your performing skills."

The propaganda chief said, "We'll follow your advice and help Dapeng and the other performers improve their skills and enrich their proletarian sentiments."

The director promised, "I'll come to see your next program. Our professionals like to cooperate with you amateurs in order to discover rare talent."

A year later, in 1954, a Soviet singing-and-dancing troupe was to perform in downtown Wuhan for a few days. It was my sophomore year. Tickets were allotted to our school only for those who had participated in the amateur performances. Sitting in the audience, I felt intoxicated by the Soviet artists' brilliance and, of course, thoroughly enjoyed being absent from the weekly group criticism.

Returning to school, we took a ferry across the Yangtze to the bus terminal. It looked dreadful, full of passengers strung out in a hundred-yard-long line. At that hour, buses ran infrequently. Many of us decided to walk the four miles back to campus rather than wait. Going east, we soon passed a commercial riverside district. The streetlights were dimmer, and vehicle traffic nil on the newly poured concrete road. Near the rear of the horde of hikers, I spotted the charming Cantonese lady, who had once been our prompter.

It was mid-March, and most people were wearing sweaters or jackets, but she had on summer clothes. Taller than the average Cantonese woman, she had especially delicate features and an attractive figure. Her smooth beige skin and pretty face added to her allure as one of the hard-to-meet South China cuties. Unlike the baggy blouses and shapeless pants of most female students, her plain, light-green cotton clothes fit closely. Her shortened slacks revealed curvaceous calves, and her trimmed hair swung like that of foreign women I'd seen in government documentaries.

From her frequent glances toward me, I knew she sensed my gaze. Gradually, we both walked behind our fellow travelers. Without the others around, I felt at ease approaching her. Falling back to walk alongside her, I awkwardly twisted my tongue to speak in Russian. "Hello, Comrade Ziwei Cao."

A winsome smile flitted across her face. Immediately, she dropped her reserve. "I remember you. You played the lead role in *Spring in Mining Mountain.*"

"Please don't mention that lousy performance. I made a fool of myself."

"Don't be so humble. You did well. Ji, who played your wife, is my classmate, but she's too delicate to play a peasant woman well. My female classmates suggested that Ji and you would do marvelously in a play about an ancient romance between a gifted scholar and a beautiful lady. If only such work hadn't been banned."

"Don't you remember what the campus propaganda chief asked us to do, cultivating our proletarian sentiments? How can you encourage me to play the role of an ancient scholar?"

She chuckled, and her teasing shrunk the distance between us. We were no longer worlds apart. I tried a joke. "You made a poor decision today."

"How?"

"You're too ladylike for this hard walk."

She smiled. "I can be tougher and more athletic than you. Test me on the sports field."

"Okay, okay. I just meant that you seem different from most other female students."

"Really?"

"You probably graduated from a missionary girls' school."

"How did you know?"

"You're feminine and poised, which is rare on our campus. All missionary schools were taken over by the government and went coed by the time you graduated, but the old tradition has shaped your manner and style."

"Are you flattering or criticizing me?"

"Praising you, of course."

"Don't you believe my heart and soul were poisoned by the

church?"

"Don't be so touchy. Ideological remodeling requires we all find something wrong with everyone else. Your classmates must've beaten to death your missionary contamination. So take it easy. We should get used to harsh criticism."

"You don't know how hard it is for me to satisfy my picky classmates. They always make me feel wrong and inferior to them. Oddly enough, women are more critical than men."

"Women are jealous of you because you're so beautiful."

"Don't say that." Her hands crossed to hold her upper arms and her body swung a little away from me, as if flinching from a sting.

Still, I noticed something sweet in her protest. "Okay, let me put it another way. When people exalt militancy, rudeness, and boorishness as the spirit of our times, they consider pretty, graceful women inherently incompatible with the Revolution. That's why some radicals are harsher toward you."

She fell into silence, perhaps chewing on my words.

To avoid the awkwardness of talking too personally, I switched to the Soviet movies and novels about the Great Patriotic War. I mentioned the color film *Capture of Berlin* and its magnificent scale and panorama. "But I prefer the classics, such as *Resurrection*, adapted from Tolstoy's novel, and *Crime and Punishment*, from Dostoevsky. They're marvelous, with a long aftertaste. Films cheering the October Revolution and the following Civil War give you little aftertaste."

Returning my trust, she said, "I prefer Pushkin to Mayakovsky."

I leaned toward her, as if evading eavesdropping. "You never get tired of reading Pushkin's poems. Mayakovsky's verses sound like political slogans to me, no matter how highly Lenin praised his work."

We'd gotten separated from our fellow hikers, and only the rustling leaves and our own steps accompanied us. "Hurry," she said, "let's catch up." But she didn't quicken her pace.

We strolled side-by-side. Soft spring breezes brushed our faces, and Wuchang willows, made famous by ancient poets, welcomed us from both sides of the road. A chorus of frogs and the night's fragrance drifting from nearby orchards seemed to unite our tastes and temperaments. I couldn't keep from singing a folksong I had learned in the summer of 1949.

> Breezes from the south ripple a pond in
>   spring.
> Around rice paddies, grasses turned oily
>   green.
> She walks ahead; on her heel I follow.
> Fretting, she stamps her foot, pleading,
> "Ah my man, don't tail me!
> If others see, how embarrassing!
> Don't think me fickle
> But idlers' gossip is torturing.

The music and my feelings seemed to travel afar and linger in the dark field, intensifying my feelings of restlessness and uncertainty. I caught Ziwei looking at the ground—perhaps I'd been too bold.

After a few minutes, she raised her head. "You have a good voice."

"Just average. But I'm brave enough to show off my mediocrity."

On the final stretch, the lights glittering from our hilltop alerted me that I'd soon have to part from her. I slowed, rallying my courage. She abruptly asked, "Are you a comrade?" It was a pet phrase, in the early fifties, meaning a Party, or YL, member.

It was an eligibility inquiry and gave me no room to be elusive. "No ... Not yet."

Off the highway, the country road leading to the campus

was paved with sand and gravel. The gritty sound of our steps punctuated my regret and frustration. We finished the journey without talking. Eventually, we reached the marble archway, our campus gate. Under a French parasol tree, we said goodbye. I hadn't worked up my courage until the moment I shook her hand.

"May I have a chance to meet you again?"

"It's easy to find the coed dorm." Her voice was jittery. "I think we can meet at the group activities in the student union."

The next morning in the classroom I tried to shake off Ziwei's question, *Are you a comrade?* Lost in reflection, staring out the large window of our classroom, I absently watched sailboats glide across the lake, oblivious to my instructors' words and the chalk lines that were drawn on the blackboard. My thoughts slipped away, through the screen of tender willow branches, to the lakeside lined with Japanese cherry and French plane trees. From the glittering fishing harbor, to the far horizon where East Lake touched a blue sky, what a fantastic scene the sunlit day held for Ziwei and me.

Now I was faced with a political condition stemming from the popular mood and peer pressure. Whenever a top scientist or artist joined the Party, people liked to say, "Whoever understands the times is a great man." Ziwei's challenge represented a conventional requirement of our times.

To be a comrade, I would have to speak like a priest or judge, even in private, and replace my independent thinking with Party doctrine. To win a lady's heart by gaining Party affiliation, I might be able to try. The most difficult part for me was to attack and estrange the 'backward elements', for I saw them as more truthful and compassionate than the political vanguards. Huihe Lin's worldly wisdom came back to me and compounded my confusion.

Over the next several days, I found myself making a detour

past Ziwei's dorm in the hope of seeing her dear face. But whenever I did, she was rushing about, and I lacked the courage to approach her. Instead, I slipped into the crowd and berated myself. This was not a dignified way to win her heart. Either forget her or approach her in triumph.

16

I had difficulty accepting political prerequisites for love. Loathing the public mood on campus, I scrawled nonsensical words in the margins of my textbook. Among them was a children's folk rhyme written one thousand five hundred years earlier by Emperor Wu of Liang, a master of both pen and sword. The emperor-author, wearied by wars and court conspiracy, yearned for a simple life like that of Mochou, an uneducated, rustic woman. Driven by the legend of Mochou— Carefree—he named a large lake near his capital after her.

> Flowing east, the river passes Luoyang,
> Where a carefree girl is called Mochou;
> At the age of 15 she's married off to the Lou
>   family
> At 16 she gives birth to a son named O'Hou.

My childhood friend Chuju, Debuting Daisy, was 15 now. As her image floated across my mind, I missed my youth, a time when I was held in esteem by my childhood friends and their parents. Especially Auntie Wu, Chuju's mother; she had praised me and called me 'a dutiful son and good student'. Now, with the campus a temple of the Party, my early merits counted for nothing.

At the end of the spring semester of 1954, I wanted to visit my parents, with the ulterior motive of seeing Chuju, the youngest daughter of Wu's family. Four months of rain had caused the biggest floods on the Yangtze in a century. I overheard Party members talking about organizing volunteers to support the anti-flood troops to defend Wuhan. But the railway south to my hometown was still open, and I decided to go and spend two weeks with my parents in west Jiangxi, and try to win the affection of Chuju, now a slim, supple girl. I could join the volunteer flood battle when I returned to school.

One afternoon, I entered Chuju's home when her mother was next door. She greeted me like a neighbor that she saw every day. From the desk, I picked up the copy of her recent black-and-white photo, taken at the shop, and asked her, "May I have this?" She snatched it away and went to their kitchen. When she came back with her hands empty, I was turning the pages of one of her exercise books. She hurried to grasp the book and shut it with both hands, standing on her tiptoes to add pressure. She was only five years younger than me, how could she be childish like that?

Seeing the scene, her mother laughed, "Stupid girl, Dapeng is our distinguished guest. His knowledge is more than enough to teach you. Why don't show him the places marked by your teachers with red crosses? Don't be shy. Let him help you."

I spent two hours helping with her geometry and algebra worksheets. She became more amiable and friendly with me than when I had just arrived. Then, I asked her, "Where have you hidden the picture?"

She tilted her head and teased me. "You can search. If you find, you'll have it."

Auntie Wu invited me to dinner. Chuju sat as far from me as she could. Glancing at her, I wistfully thought of how, as children, we'd been carefree together, catching fireflies in the threshing fields, picking camellias on the hills, always at ease. Now she was shy and reserved with me, neither asking a single word about my political status nor showing any sigh of awakening to love. I swallowed her mother's special meal, barely tasting it.

That dinner would be our only encounter that summer. Her mother sat at the table with us, a gracious, generous hostess. After dinner, Chuju brought me a basin of warm water with a new cotton towel submerged in it. Ordinary families rarely used a new towel except for a distinguished guest. I gently wrung the towel and lightly skimmed my face with it, careful not to get it stained.

A few days after I arrived home, the railway back to Wuhan was flooded. Every morning, I was on edge while reading the newspapers posted at a street corner. Streets in Wuhan were now lower than the water level of the rivers, and the three towns of the big city, naturally divided by the Yangtze and its tributary, were walled by high levees. While photos and articles publicized anti-flood heroes, I knew the danger areas were expanding and casualties were rising. Staying at home, I couldn't do much to help my poor parents or make them happy, and Chuju's cold reception made me think I should've stayed at school. Though bored by the regimented life on campus, being detached from the collective now made me feel lonely and insecure. A strong sense came to me that my future would be tied to the fate of our country.

I went to Chuju's home to say goodbye, but she wasn't there. Her mother smiled at me. "Chuju isn't as gentle or refined as her two older sisters. She's a little mischievous now. After you left the other night, she joked the towel you used still had the scent of a man." The small joke intrigued me but gave no meaningful clue.

In late July, I somberly left home. Since numerous stretches of railway were under water, from Changsha I would spend 17 hours making a detour by steamboat along the Xiang River, across Dongting Lake, and back to the Yangtze. From the mouth of the lake to Wuhan, the Yangtze had become a sea, its boundary the horizon. The wooden basins, doors, and cottage roofs floating on the river told me what devastation the flood had done to our people. Guilt seized me, and I felt like a deserter finding his way back to his ranks.

Passengers huddled on the bare metal deck while the waves tossed the boat about. As the churning of the propellers made me sleepy, I recognized that my home visit was a wrong move during such a natural calamity. Chuju was not yet awaking to love, and my nostalgic feelings for our childhood affection caused no resonance with her. Living in the backwater of our hometown, what kind of woman would she develop into? Most likely, not as I wished.

Women at the engineering departments were rare, and almost all the suitable ones had paired off, making the single men panicky. Only one remained available in our large classroom, where 150 students took the same lectures. She once admired a boy, who was the cream of our class and a member of our university basketball team. As soon as she approached him, still in correspondence with her high-school sweetheart a thousand miles away, our YL branch criticized her 'bourgeois casual attitude toward love' and foreclosed her right to date anyone else on campus.

As the boat cleaved the waves speeding to Wuhan, the image of the campus beauty, Ziwei, with her foreign, compassionate air, was hovering above the bow. My activity at the drama group had allowed me to meet ladies outside the engineering disciplines, and she was the best one in public view. Why should I be annoyed by her prerequisite for accepting me? Perhaps I was being too idealistic, considering that true love should be unconditional. Reviewing the oft-quoted love stories in our history, how many didn't carry the ethical stigma of the times? I should admit her requirement of Party loyalty as a reflection of the entire society. She wanted to save me from being a political outcast and let me fit into the mainstream in order to realize my aspirations. If I kept resisting self-remodeling, I'd have no chance to win her and never be a part of the new order.

Though we'd just gotten to know each other, and the distance between us was big, I believed that her early Christian education and my upbringing under my mother's Buddhist influence would be compatible, bringing harmony to our conjugal life. And our common love for classical literature, both Chinese and Russian, would be the catalyst to make us a congenial couple. Judging from her breadth of spirit and imposing manner, she would persist in professional pursuits, and I could count on her willingness to struggle along with me as a fighting couple. Compared with the fantastic scenario, her prerequisite seemed reasonable to me, or not too harsh, as I then understood it.

While the whole population of Wuhan was desperately fighting the flood, with students and soldiers at the core, my joining the university's volunteer team would strike a pose on the battlefield to show my patriotic spirit. It would be a quick way to fit into the mainstream, then I would join the YL as a step toward becoming a Party member. Above all, it would remove a hurdle in my road to approaching Ziwei.

Campus now looked like a logistics' zone near a front line. Due to its higher elevation, the regional garrison parked their vehicles in every space between the buildings.

Before going to my dorm, I went to meet Jianlin Mo, the YL secretary of our class, and registered to join the volunteer team. After lunch, I carried my sleeping roll to report for duty at a university branch office of the Wuhan Anti-Flood Command Headquarters. When I walked by Ziwei's dorm, I pulled down the brim of my straw hat to shade my face, and speeded up my pace.

I was assigned to join a group conveying greetings and

appreciation to the huge contingent along the riverside, singing revolutionary songs and helping the cooking crews. I worked diligently for a few days but missed the glorious battle. I asked to become a member of the taskforce, but the section commander said my job was equally honorable.

One day, I delivered a basket of buns and a metal bucket of stewed cabbage with pork as lunch to the squad reinforcing a levee. On my way back to the kitchen shed, a column of water suddenly sprouted from the lower part of the slope. It signaled an immediate danger, a *piping failure*, when seeping water would form a torrent to erode the soil around the hole. I threw aside my shoulder pole and baskets, desperately hitting the bucket with the ladle and yelling for help. People began to run toward me, converging from all directions. I tossed away the bucket and ladle, and darted to lie down, covering the hole with my back.

My weight made the water spill sideways, and the ground began to yield. The piping leak turned out to be a surging fountain. Soldiers and students swarmed up to form a human wall, weighing like a mountain on my body. Muddy water splashed across my head and choked me. I stuck it out, waiting for the emergency repair to be finished. Soon my hands and legs turned numb. Suffocated, I could hear the noises from the crest of the dyke, where the shock forces were piling up caged stones and bagged clay to stop the seepage on the water side of the levee. Suddenly, a landslide removed the human wall and buried me in the mudflow.

I struggled to raise my head for air, but my arms and legs were numb. The ten-foot-long cylindrical cages, filled with rocks, were rolling down to block the channel cut into the slope by the fountain. The large troops carried bags of clay, and were going to fill out the gaps between the cages. I knew this would be my natural grave, and my parents wouldn't be able to survive with my misfit older brother and unfledged younger one. Then, the cages and bags fell away with the enlarged landslide, and the turbulence washed me down the slope, joining the confluence with the ditch flow along the toe of the slope. I was drowning, my consciousness fading. Multiple spots of pain still emitted flashes to my brain, and I felt I was flying in a dark sky for a moment, and falling in an ocean of mud.

A rescue team found me in front of a trash filter-rack, where surface water was flowing back into the sewerage system. While my consciousness was slowly coming back, I was lying across the back of a water buffalo, facing the road pavement. The pressure on my chest and stomach helped to drain the muddy water out of me, and my coughing and choking hurt my throat and nose badly.

In addition to my dozens of cuts and the symptoms of a drowned patient, the sewerage sludge gave me severe diarrhea. In a field-clinic tent, I was treated with an intravenous drip, an enema, and penicillin shots. Large cuts were dressed with gauze and ointment, and minor ones were brushed with red mercurochrome and purple gentian violet. Therefore, my face was painted with both red and purple strokes. A nurse told me that the doctors that worshiped Germany preferred gentian violet, but those who admired the US liked mercurochrome more. For neutrality, she used both, whichever was available.

Ten days later, still weak, I resumed service in the kitchen. Stopping leaks with a human body was honorable, but it happened frequently at the frontline. I was especially praised for my timely hitting of the metal bucket. A frontline commander said at a rally, "Only bravery is not enough for revolution, you must be also good at revolution."

Both Huihe Lin, the guy who wept after his father committed suicide, and I were awarded a third-rate citation by the waterfront command post.

17

At the end of October, when the Yangtze River's water at last had fallen below alert level, our university's brigade came back from the flood-fighting front. We had a homecoming rally in the auditorium. The student union chairman, Xiaohou Ban, read the Wuhan Municipal Government's citation for the meritorious service of our model laborers and gave a triumphant speech.

For days, loudspeakers were blaring. "Wuhan is as important to China as Chicago is to the US! Chicago is flooded now! Wuhan will not be!"

"We've won the equivalent of a battle in the Korean War!"

"Comrades, our victory has proved the socialism is superior to capitalism!"

I quietly checked the news with the professor, who got his PhD from the University of Illinois and taught me hydrology. He said, "I have neither foreign newspapers nor radio. From the fragments from our media, I understand that the Chicago area is flooded now. Chicago is second largest city in the US, densely populated and highly industrialized. Since that area is flat and has several rivers around it, and it is near Lake Michigan, along with the recent heavy rains, the flood might cause severe damage. But I guess their disaster area is smaller than ours, and the duration of flooding from their rivers is relatively shorter than that of the Yangtze. Anyway, we've kept the flood from entering downtown Wuhan."

Before he shut the office door, he admonished me, "We should trust in *The People's Daily*, the Party's tongue and throat, which is responsible for educating us."

Having missed six weeks of the fall semester, I had to struggle to catch up with my coursework. In the meantime, I signed up for volunteer work taking care of casualties from the anti-flood battle, especially those who'd fought in fields infested with blood-flukes and then had been diagnosed with snail fever. Injections to kill the parasitic worms often led to comas and a high fever. If people recovered at all, they missed at least a semester of school. Normally we had a midday rest including lunchtime, two and a half hours for summer or one and a half hours for winter. To help a sick classmate with his hydraulics studies, I gave up my noontime snooze and all other fragments of free time to create a weekly folder of tutorial materials. In neat writing, I put together my classroom notes, detailed equations and solutions, and answers to common questions.

Each student unit, or 'class', had a three-person leadership in a troika system copied from the USSR and officially called the Class Triangle. It consisted of the YL branch secretary, a class leader, and a course representative. Our current course representative was weary of the tedious work and wanted to quit, so the other two members of our troika suggested I take the position. I threw myself into the volunteer job, shuttling between instructors and students to collect homework, hand out supplementary notes, and arrange makeup exams. When an athletic roommate returned from a swim meet in South China, I couldn't shirk from helping him pass his midterm.

A public view of me as a progressive element soon emerged, allowing YL members to see the maturity of my conversion. Meanwhile, my friends who remained politically idle and aloof began to grow distant. Approval from the vanguard made me feel I was fitting better into the new order and gave me the courage to approach Ziwei.

For several evenings in a row, I went to the Arts and Literature library, which was filled mainly by students from those departments. One night, when I was browsing new arrivals on a shelf, she came in and sat just a few chairs from where I had all my things. Flustered, I tried to slip out. But it was too late. She spotted me and nodded. On my way back to my seat, I picked up a Russian grammar book and drifted toward her. Bending over the table, I whispered, "Would you help me with some sentences? I'm confused."

I trembled as she turned the pages of my book carelessly. Suddenly, she smiled. "Congratulations! I saw your name on the honor roll posted in the main library."

Her easy manner, as if chatting with a classmate, calmed me down. "Not worth mentioning. I just followed the crowd."

"You acted like a man. Let's go outside."

I threw my things in my bag and rushed out with her. We ambled along the veranda, where magnolia trees rustled in the autumn breeze, turning the regimented grid of light from the street lamps into swaying sparkles on the ground. The curtain of night and the foliage offered perfect privacy, and I tried to release the words I'd composed for her. They were all choked up.

Instead, I started to gossip about some cadre-students. "They're dumb and lazy. No matter how loudly they sing 'Study Hard for the Revolution', their scores are much lower than ours. We even defeated them on the History of the Chinese Revolution and the Fundamentals of Marxism."

She stopped walking and shook her head. "You can't talk like that. You can't even think like that. They'll smash you politically, like killing an ant."

"I know, I know. I've tried to stay at a respectful distance, but they don't leave me alone, always prying, trying to read my mind."

She nodded. "That's a good sign. They want to convert you into a comrade. Don't wreck your chances."

"You're right."

"What I'm scared of," she said, "is the midterm in political economics. It's boring, but we have to pass it to graduate. If I get a low grade, everyone'll say I lack reverence for Karl Marx."

"The material and teaching method for that course are

copied from the Soviet Union. It's the same for all third-year university students. The instructor reads the pages word-for-word, like a bee buzzing in a summer garden."

She laughed.

"He puts me to sleep," I said. "But don't worry. I have a way to guarantee you a good score."

"Are you kidding?"

"The instructors just want us to memorize and believe what they've planted into our brains like seeds in soil. So, if you remember all the lecture notes, you'll get high scores. Otherwise you'll flunk."

She stomped a foot, "I don't have that kind of diabolic memory."

"I have an idea. We mark the text with a series of Qs and As to make it like a script, and take turns playing the A-and-Q parts. After practice, you'll answer the questions fast and fluently, like pushing the buttons on a machine. For instance, if I ask, 'Why is the proletarian revolution inevitable?' you should immediately say, 'Because the contradiction between socialized production and private ownership cannot be overcome by the capitalist system itself.' Or, if you ask me, 'What is the law of a socialist economy?' I'll answer, quick as lightning, 'Rapidly developing production, in a proportional way, under a centralized national plan, to satisfy people's needs to the maximum extent.' Unless we get that fluent in our responses, we'll never get over this hurdle."

She smiled. "Unlike the guys in my class, you can almost make it sound like fun."

Electric bells went off, both near and far, marking 10:00 pm, the end of evening study. A half hour later, when the lights went off, all the students had to be in their dorms. Ziwei said, "Sorry, I almost forgot your question about Russian grammar. Let me see your book."

"It's too late, I need ten minutes to walk back to my dorm.

Can I see you Sunday? Besides tutoring me in Russian grammar, we can start our politico-economics review."

She put a hand to her forehead. "How about ten am?"

"Perfect. I'll meet you at the newspaper-and-magazine room of the faculty club."

"But we're students."

I grinned. "No problem. I often read there at naptime, and the lady in charge knows me. It's a quiet place, especially on weekends, when most teachers are doing household chores."

She said goodbye, then slipped away like a swallow into the shadows.

18

The faculty club, a two-story building set back in a cluster of bamboo along a quiet path, had a large reading room upstairs. Besides newspapers and magazines from socialist countries, there were bulletins from the embassies of friendly capitalist countries, such as India and Switzerland, and publications from Western communist and labor parties, which carried tidbits of information about the West not available in domestic newspapers.

I arrived first. The scarlet-painted hardwood floor, the purplish velvet window curtains, the sets of tea tables and sofas, and the floor lamps all looked more enchanting today. A large oval mirror stood in one corner, in a frame of fragrant red sandalwood carved into flying dragons and dancing phoenixes. The wood's smooth sheen suggested the antique dated from the early Qing Dynasty. I imagined an ancient beauty preening her head ornaments in front of the mirror, her long gown spread out on the floor behind her.

On a campus strictly organized like a military base, what a nice place I'd chosen for our first date. Listening to chirping birds, I nervously waited for Ziwei to show up, worrying that she might not come.

As soon as I sat down at the tea table, I glanced down at my black Mao jacket, a sort of uniform for school and university, checking the four pockets and the central column of five buttons to make sure they weren't wrinkled. My shabby attire imbued me with a sense of inferiority that whipped up my dignity.

After lengthy minutes, I heard her steps on the staircase. At the door, she popped her head in and gingerly looked around.

It was a mild October day. Her jacket with a long zipper and waist belt was beyond the craftsmanship of inland tailors. Both the blue shell and pale pink lining were made from fine fabrics. With her white, close-fit khaki pants and dark, low-cut casual leather shoes, she was decked out like a sporty overseas Chinese person of the sort never seen among the people I knew.

She took books and notes from her bag. "Have you been waiting long?" I smiled and shook my head. She began to adjust a hairpin, arching her right arm overhead like a swan's neck, her movements revealing a natural grace. The antique mirror afforded me an unblinking look at her, a Westernized fairy in the oval mirror guarded by dragons and phoenixes. Her oval face and broad forehead were seldom seen among my compatriots. Along with her widely-set eyes, they sent forth an air of a sanguine disposition, bringing peace and cheer to her surroundings. Gazing on her profile, her up-turned, high nose and cherry-like lips mesmerized me, and I began to search my memory: which photo of the sculptures collected in the European picture album resembled her the most? Her long eyelashes looked like twigs of weeping willow forming a screen for a spring field, and then, through the screen of her eyelashes, I saw a crystal mental world.

Now she was assessing my stupid stare at her reflection. Before I could avert my eyes, she coolly asked, "Why don't you make the best use of the time to sort out your problems with

Russian grammar?"

"Something funny happened in our department. One Saturday night, a man recited the Chinese version of a Pushkin poem in a vacant classroom. He had two listeners, a man and a woman. Later, the woman reported it to the YL branch secretary as evidence of his bourgeois taste and indecent flirtation with her."

"Which poem?"

"The famous one, the first few lines of which many students can remember: 'At the fascinating transience, you emerged before my eyes, like a mirage lasting as shortly as epiphyllum blooming at night, like a fairy of purified beauty.'"

She giggled. "That's a shoddy Chinese translation."

I stuck out my tongue. "I see. If I recite it to you, will you report me?"

She blinked quizzically. "I should, but I won't." She tapped the books on the table. "Let's get back to our subject."

Quite relaxed, she started tutoring me in my recent Russian lessons. Without many problems, I enjoyed her feminine handwriting scratching on the paper, soft and neat, and her mellow Russian, spoken with confidence and a Cantonese accent. Once in a while, I peeped at the mirror, infatuated with our images bending over the table. Often I warned myself not to be skittish.

An hour later, I presented my folder of Qs and As summarized from our textbook and lecture notes. I let her ask the first question.

"How does a capitalist exploit his workers?"

I pressed my forehead like a button and made a popping noise with my lips. "By seizing the surplus value of products which has been created by workers' surplus labor. Now, why is monopoly capitalism the last, declining, and rotten stage of capitalism?"

She hesitated. I said, "Push your button. Where is it?"

She touched her nose with a forefinger, like a little girl, very cute. She couldn't stop giggling.

After the first round of practice on the 22 items, we switched roles and asked and answered the same questions.

When we finished, Ziwei said, "I'm sure I'll pass the midterm with a good score."

"We can do this again before the next midterm or final. And I wish you could tutor me more in Russian."

"No problem. Your Russian is better than most students not specializing in linguistics. Under the university curriculum, you'll have two more semesters of grammar and then be able to read some Russian novels."

"It won't be easy."

"But you can give it a shot. I have a bilingual copy of Turgenev's *Fathers and Sons*, which you should try to read next summer vacation with the help of a dictionary. Then, I'll find out how smart or stupid you really are."

Her joking bathed me in renewed hope. Still, she was so beautiful, my chances had to be slim, so I told myself not to get too cocky.

As we got ready to leave, I plucked up my courage, "There's a daisy exhibit at the East Lake Resort where artists display watercolors among the flowers. The weather's great. I'd love to go to the exhibition with you."

"I've never gone out with a man. The gossip would drive me crazy. Once anyone saw us stroll together by the lake, rumors would fly like a swarm of locusts all over campus. We're just beginning to get to know each other, so how could you parade around with me on the lakeshore? I don't want my back shot full of arrows."

"Sorry. I didn't think of all that." I took the latest *Pictorial of Poland* from the magazine stand and sat on the sofa. While pretending to pore over photos of Poland, relatively liberal among the socialist countries, I tried to rationalize her apprehension and compose myself.

She sat next to me. As we both gazed at pictures of Polish fashion models, I felt her cheek touch my shoulder. Like a spring breeze brushing my face, she said, "I can go out with you when you've joined the YL."

19

In March 1955, all third-year students in our department were scheduled to go to the Huai River for three months of field practice. A week before leaving, the YL branch held a special meeting to discuss my application, and they unanimously raised their hands to accept me. Although the result had to be endorsed by the university YL committee, I'd never heard of anyone being denied during this final phase.

I celebrated silently for having achieved a milestone on the road to becoming a red engineer and a worthy candidate to be Ziwei's lover.

The next Sunday morning, I walked to the coed dorm and boldly knocked at Ziwei's door. Getting no response, I stood listening, but heard only my own heartbeat.

To my relief, she opened the door a crack, popped her head out, looked up and down the corridor, and then cast an assessing gaze on me. The glint in her eyes showed surprise but not irritation. She opened the door all the way and walked out. She hadn't expected me but looked proud of how she was decked out for the day. Her sapphire-blue sweater, hand-knitted and a close fit, set off her shiny dark hair and brilliant dark eyes. With a hint of a blush, she averted her eyes and gave me a delicate smile.

"You devil, how can you come without an invitation? Lucky for you, my roommates are out."

"I'm leaving on Tuesday for three months of field practice.

I'll have no chance to see you, not even your shadow. You know how much I want to talk to you."

"You must have good news to be so bold."

"You're sharp. I came to say thanks for pushing me so hard."

"Weirdo. Has the YL branch accepted you?"

I smiled.

"Congratulations! I knew you'd make it."

With a trembling voice, I asked, "Could we go to see the daisy exhibition at the East Lake Resort today?"

"How about in the afternoon, after I finish my laundry?" She paused. "Let's take the ferry separately and meet at the exhibition around three."

To add to the excitement, a high-school classmate, by then an army corps sergeant working to repair North Korea's bombed railway, sent me 15 yuan, friendly support for my final stage of university study. This was a large portion of his meager salary, and it not only warmed my heart, it filled my empty pocket for an entire month.

Inside the bright gallery, mixing with locals and tourists passing through Wuhan, we leisurely browsed the many species of daisies on display. Above the pots, framed paintings of flowers, birds, and landscapes created a fitting background.

At closing, we followed the crowd to a noodle house, where we had a simple dinner, standing with our bowls in our hands. Outside the restaurant homeward-bound tourists chased the setting sun as they scattered to the west. Ziwei stopped to buy a tin of crunchy Xiaogan sesame candy. She popped one in her mouth, offered me one, and laughed. "I can't get enough of these, I eat them all the time."

We soon found ourselves alone in a vast plaza while the bosom of the lake turned dark purple in the twilight, and a remote chain of hills undulated at the foot of the evening firmament. We stopped at a waterfront deck that extended from a teahouse and was covered by a huge awning. Quite popular in the daytime, it was closed now, its chairs upside down on the tables. We sat on a bench above the water, facing each other and leaning against two columns. She started the conversation. "Do you know I got five for my midterm politico-economics." That meant Excellent under the Soviet grade system.

"You're smart."

"No. Thanks for your help."

After I briefed her on the Meishan Reservoir and its multi-arch dam, the place I was going the next Tuesday, we talked about each other's families. I was astonished that her father had been a Hong Kong businessman. In the period of 1946 to 1949, he spent most of his time in Canton. After that, he left her mother and younger brother in Canton, rarely coming home for a brief visit.

The dusk seemed to bring out a tender femininity, quite different from her feigned toughness in the daylight. I could tell how happy she was about my advancement, though she didn't explicitly say so. For a long while, she kept silent. The swishing waves rhythmically slapped the retaining wall beneath our feet, while *Swan Lake* wafted toward us from a nearby resort for high-ranking Party cadres.

She asked, "Have you read *And Quiet Flows the Don?*"

"Yes, but it's too long. I skipped some pages and sections."

"It's a masterpiece. Sholokhov got a Stalin Prize. I plan to read the Russian version this summer. I'm studying some tutoring articles about this epic to better understand it."

"From the Soviet photo exhibitions we can see on what a magnificent scale the deserts and barren land in their mid-Asia area are being transformed. Only the canal connecting the Don and the Volga is unthinkable. Someday we'll travel there, listen to a Volga boatman's song, and watch trout swimming in the Don. We could carry the book in the Russian original and sit under the sunflowers on the river, reliving the epic. And—"

She shrugged. "A fantastic pipe dream."

The last ferry was almost empty. An old lady and a girl around ten, apparently her granddaughter, sat on a crossbeam opposite us. Their outfits—blouses with buttons on the right side, baggy pants, cloth shoes—were all homemade. The bed sheet knotted to hold their baggage especially marked them as countryside travelers. The girl fixed her innocent gaze on Ziwei, no doubt admiring her lovely figure, stylish jacket, and leather shoes.

The old lady was warm and talkative. After a brief greeting, she complimented us with a wide grin. "You two make a handsome couple, a match made in Heaven."

Ziwei wriggled uncomfortably and turned her head toward the stern. I smiled. "Grandma, you flatter us."

Ziwei pinched my wrist. I couldn't decipher a definite meaning, but the sharp pain gratified me and left a sweet memory.

We left the boat and walked behind other passengers. After they scattered to both directions of the western lakeshore, I ran across the road and stood by a cherry tree. Seeing her peer around and follow me, I took the trail through the botanical garden, the shortest way to reach her dorm, on the south side of the main library. She kept a distance from me, and the thick foliage shaded our path from the starlight. Soon, we strolled side-by-side. The chorus of frogs accompanying us seemed to be the same as what we heard the year before when we hiked from the riverside to our school, and that night they sounded intimate, as if they even carried a welcoming touch.

Hand-in-hand, we passed a gallery formed by two rows of gingkoes and the arched roof made by their interwoven branches. I couldn't help pulling her toward me. With cold hands and my heart irregularly pulsating, I hugged her. She ducked her head to hide her mouth, and wriggled when I kissed her neck and cheek. The next moment, she held my face with both hands and pressed her lips on mine in a flash. She turned to run. I caught up with her at the end of the gallery and pulled her back in the shade, where we kissed, without knowing for how long, until a large soaring bird startled us awake.

"Have a safe trip. Please write to me from Anhui." She hurried to climb the rocky slope to the back of the main library. I escorted her from far behind. As soon as she reached the granite sidewalk of the west wing of the building, I descended the slope. Feeling weightless, I sang a female Beijing opera song in falsetto, 'The Drunken Imperial Concubine', all the way toward my dorm, speeding past the plantation.

20

Our three-month engineering practice was a non-paying summer job, but it was crucial for preparing us to conduct our final project for graduation. The construction site at Meishan, Anhui, was managed in a paramilitary fashion, with a former PLA division at the core of the labor force. The work style and quality control were rigorous, but its construction machines and tools were simple, even primitive. We students were scattered to live with the local workers, mostly demobilized soldiers, as Chairman Mao had called for. Their bamboo huts had a door at each end. Two parallel benches along the longer walls served as beds. I occupied a 30-inch-wide slice.

The tough environment was far different from what Soviet movies depicted. Here, even senior technicians and young engineers who'd done honorable work lived in intolerable quarters, like dump sites, reminding me of World War II refugee camps. I took it as necessary in order to condition myself for the future, but worried that Ziwei would be unwilling to settle down with me in such harsh living conditions.

I imagined that her future job, most likely as an interpreter escorting Soviet experts and big-shot bureaucrats, would display her charm and grace. The powerful satyrs would offer her comfort and luxury. Who could say if she'd be strong enough to resist? With such a grim picture ahead, I had difficulty mustering joyous words to write to her. My letters seemed as dull as the reports we listened to at the construction site.

Contrary to my expectations, however, warmth and fanciful imaginings about our engineering project flowed out of her notes to me.

Normally, I'm not interested in postwar Soviet literature, especially reportage. But recently, Bolievyi's collection of short stories, *People in Stalin's Era*, attracted me just by the description on its jacket. The stories tell how the Soviets work and live on water-conservation construction sites and how they use daily tasks to glorify Joseph Stalin. Apparently, they love their present lives, which are victorious transitions from past struggles to a wonderful future.

Now you're on the Huai River battlefront, witnessing how socialism is changing our land. Do you know a woman in our class suddenly started to pry me for information about you? I guess she probably saw us at the daisy exhibition. Though annoyed by the rising rumors and gossip, I feel a kind of closeness to you. It makes me want to read the whole book.

Since you have left campus, I always feel your

absence. I remember how the stage lights brightened you in the costumes of socialist heroes. Offstage, you impressed me by your hard work. How lucky I am.

Her sentimental linking of the book and my professional training sounded like a harbinger of the message I wanted. I replied:

Dear Ziwei,

This year, May 1 fell on a Sunday, so we celebrated Labor Day along with Youth Day, May 4, in an unconventional way. The local YL committee led us on a hike to a former guerrilla war headquarters, a bunch of thatched houses high on mountain ridges among clumps of trees. A Party veteran, who fought here eight years ago, worked as our guide. Nearby, many dead Red Army soldiers were buried in a roughly kept cemetery. Our guide made use of the scene to bring forth his point. "Comrades, you're a new kind of university student, trained by the proletariat. I hope you can prove by your deeds that our martyrs didn't shed their blood in vain."

The veteran's speech persuaded me to evaluate my current work with an historic view, while your letter lets me integrate our shared personal future with our nation's destiny. In the Party's sunshine, our relationship should develop like a bud unfolding into a full blossom.

Recently I read Pavlenko's *Correspondence from the South*, an epistolary novella of five letters from a Soviet geologist to his wife. His deep love for his Soviet motherland was manifest in his dedicated exploration of Antarctica, where he endured harsh weather and unbearable cravings for his wife. Please read this small, highly refined book, knowing that the five letters perfectly reflect what I want to say to you.

Love,

Dapeng

At the end of June, a week before we left the site, the university authorities sent a letter to the Construction Bureau's political department. It contained a notice officially verifying my YL membership, and the Party secretary at my working unit handed it to me in a ceremonious style. I immediately wrote to tell Ziwei the good news. A dream of a romantic summer vacation with her seized me. She would tutor me on my Russian reading and we would row a sampan across East Lake.

On the way back to school, the bumpy truck ride and muggy boat voyage couldn't interrupt my dream. After the forthcoming year of our sweet dating, we would write each other's names as revolutionary spouses, and the university would assign us to the same city, even the same working unit. I would never speak roughly or loudly to her like Father did to Mother. Our mutual love and respect would set an example for many other couples.

21

Back on campus, a sudden storm broke the peace. A new campaign, Eliminating Counterrevolutionaries, was launched to interrogate five percent of the campus population. All students, faculty, and staff would be confined to campus for the whole summer. Nobody could ask for leave.

On the afternoon after final exams, I went to Ziwei's dorm.

As I arrived, she walked out of the lavatory with an empty washbasin in her hand, wearing a pair of clogs and underclothes. Transfixed at seeing me at the far end of her corridor, she hesitated a second, then rushed up and whispered, "I'm in trouble. Please don't come again."

"Could we talk outside for a few minutes?"

"No, this is a bad time." She quickly looked around. "The inquisition group searched my belongings and took away all the letters my father sent to me. Now go away!"

A cadre-student, identifiable by his faded military uniform, came out of a room and stalked towards us like a thief. He held a notebook with a red cloth cover, specially designed for security workers. It was a political fashion carried by inquisitors, a symbol of the Party's trust. To make it sanctified, the hundred pages of blank paper between the covers were numbered at the corners, and the book had to be returned to the security office at the end of the campaign.

Like a bully peasant cadre, he jerked his head up to question me, and his bristly unshaven chin brushed my shoulder. "What's your name?"

I turned my body and disdainfully brushed off my shoulder. "My name? What's your name?"

"I'm a member of the leading group. It's my duty to ask you."

His covetous air revealed more of his jealousy than his political vigilance. I said, "You have no right to ask me anything unless you find a way to reach me through our department."

Ziwei pushed me to go. "He's a nasty mangy dog who's pestered me for three years. Just ignore him."

I pointed a finger at him. "Don't take advantage of her as a campaign target. Anyone fishing in troubled waters will be exposed to the light of day. In your case, I'll make sure of it."

A political hurricane swept across campus. All day long, orchestrated shouting and table-pounding burst from every dorm building and faculty office. We were forbidden to inquire about suspects in other units so could only guess what was going on outside our enclosure.

Our professor of structural analysis became a key target due to his pre-1949 connections with local KMT officials when he owned a small construction firm. He extricated himself by jumping off the roof of the six-floor building. Cadre-students accused him of, "using death to resist the Revolution."

Huihe Lin, a fan of the respected professor, couldn't hide his sorrow. In the swimming pool, a bay separated from the lake by posts, he tried to say something serious to me, but was afraid of our classmates listening to us. He splashed water at me. "He was a rare one, not trained in the West but able to teach this tough course. He was only in his early forties. He should've had a brilliant future."

I splashed water back at him. "He was too tender for the mass movement."

At the height of a big rally to stir vigilance against latent enemies, local policemen handcuffed and led away our Russian language professor, whom I'd frequently contacted because I was the course representative.

One day, before dawn, roars and rapid steps startled me from sleep. Qing, a male student from Hong Kong, was attempting suicide by electrocution, and the volunteer security guard was shoving him away from the switchbox of our dorm building. Qing was two years younger than me, usually gentle and well groomed. Along with the security guard, one of Qing's roommates was praised. The day before, immediately after Qing left the lavatory, the roommate had rushed in to pick up the smeared, stinky paper from the wastebasket and turned it over to the inquisition group—a letter from his father in Hong Kong. The act was held up as an example of "exceptionally high alertness against an enemy's attempt to destroy evidence of a counterrevolutionary crime."

Our unit of 24 students didn't have anyone from overseas. To fulfill the quota, the campaign leaders dug out two male students, Yang and Hua, as suspected hiding enemies. After 50 days, they found Yang guilty only of a fondness for banned novels and spreading rumors about top Party leaders' young wives. Hua's problem was his visit home in the winter of 1953, when former landlords and their children had met with him. He confessed they yearned for their properties, expropriated during the 1950 Land Reform, and hated being treated as public enemies. The campaign leaders accused him of plotting with the landlords to overthrow the new government.

Besides other common forms of punishment, a few radical classmates moved Hua's bunk into the second-floor corridor, directly facing the staircase, which had a large landing with steps on both sides. They decorated the bed with a proscenium arch, replete with cartoons and posters bearing captions such as, 'This Counterrevolutionary is as Cunning as a Fox', and, 'Smash Enemies Who Refuse to Surrender!' On display like a caged animal, he suffered unrelenting humiliation and sleep deprivation. Some classmates hated him for steadfastly denying the charges against him, but more began to believe his innocence.

Everybody knew the tougher they treated the targets, the more political credits they would get. On the contrary, any sympathizers would have trouble; at the least bad job assignments upon graduation. Most people were kept wavering between their consciences and pragmatic results.

Out of self-preservation, I joined my shouting, table-pounding classmates, against Yang and Hua during every struggle session. Whenever I imagined how Ziwei stood like them, bowing her head to accept the insults and intimidation, my voice was weak and my hands were heavy when I raised my fists.

When more and more suspects were sent to campus detention centers, the campaign leaders assigned some fresh YL members like me to be amateur security guards. Every week I sat for ten hours on a staircase landing with another young man, both of us armed with sticks, guarding an exit from the basement in which the suspects from three water-related engineering departments were imprisoned. After midnight, I often dozed off, propped up with my wooden stick in front of me until the stench of sweat and urine from below would wake me.

Ziwei was now in the same category as the detainees, although she was on our campus, female suspects remained in their dorms. She had urged me to follow the conventional track toward success, and I quickly saw that her wish represented the public mood of the new society. Who could expect that I would so soon hold a stick against a group of people that included her?

When the 1955 fall semester started in early September, the mass movement abruptly ended. Hua, the son of the pre-1949 farm owner, mistreated the whole summer as a class enemy, could move back in with his roommates, and the Russian language professor was released from prison. The wretched campaign targets cautiously dodged crowds, typically eating at mess halls after most diners had gone. Ziwei must have acted the same way. For three consecutive days around noon, hidden behind a hedge of clustered bamboo, I waited by the path connecting her dorm to the mess hall, watching countless students pass by. At one point she walked near me, but others were around, and so I only gazed at her haggard figure disappearing down the road.

The fourth noon I was intercepted by Jianlin Mo, our class's YL branch secretary. Stalking up from behind, she scared me with her freezing words. "Do you want to show your sympathy to Ziwei Cao or do you have secret information for her?"

I avoid looking straight at her uneven haircut and yellow teeth, but retorted, "The campus roads are open to every student. The campaign is over."

Her voice rose in anger. "I want to protect you. You should appreciate the favor. How do you know the campaign is over? Her case is complicated by an overseas relationship."

On Chinese New Year's Day, February 12, 1956, when our university shut down its temporary prisons, and my classmate Hua ended up with only a political verdict, "Severely departing from the correct class stance," rather than a criminal conviction, I waited to see Ziwei. The student union held a large ballroom dance party in the gym, and the YL branch committee encouraged its members to be warm and dance with campaign targets for the unity and harmony of the big revolutionary family.

Outside the circle of onlookers, Ziwei showed up without a trace of her past joy and vitality. I pulled her to the dance floor. "Everybody should look happy."

She quietly followed me. Taking her in my arms, her body felt light, easy to lead. She must have practiced dance. In the midst of the pushing crowd, I whispered, "Do you have a verdict from the inquisition group?"

"Yes, but not what I wanted."

"How was it phrased?"

"It said the investigation has verified that I'm not involved in my father's activities abroad."

"Weird. They should've clearly said you're innocent. Please wait. It isn't a final conclusion. I know how difficult it is to live with a political shadow."

"Ai-yo!" She grimaced in pain from my tight grip. I noticed frostbite on the back of her hand. I didn't blame the cold winter in Wuhan or not having a heat supply. Political isolation had shut her off from physical exercise and caused her to suffer from poor circulation.

We danced for only a few minutes. Then she returned to her place near the door and excused herself.

"What's your hurry? The dance will go on until tomorrow morning, and there's a nice midnight snack at the mess halls."

She bit her upper lip. "I failed my final exams in two courses last semester. I need to prepare for makeup exams."

"I hope you can find some peace of mind and do it well." I walked her to the hillside dorm. "Good luck. Please let me know what happens."

I leaned against the dorm wall and watched the window of her room turn bright. I hated that I couldn't take care of her. In the gym, a Soviet-made record sounded remote and alien to me as it played 'Moscow Nights'.

22

With the spring of 1956 came a soothing political breeze when Premier Zhou called for the March toward Science. I was one of six students nominated by our university to study in the Soviet Union. The opportunity to get a higher degree and to make a pilgrimage to the socialist holy land made me exuberant.

I asked Ziwei to go with me to see the Soviet Industrial Exhibition in the city center. She accepted my invitation with little hesitation.

On the ferry, surrounded by strangers, a sense of closeness descended upon me. Speaking above the engine's noise, I cupped my hand to her ear and told her about my windfall.

She lowered her head and kept rubbing her fingers. The frostbite had left purple patches on the backs of her hands, and tears trickled down her cheeks. She suppressed a sob.

"Everything's going to work out for you."

"For us," I said.

"For us? No."

"I thought you loved me. What about our future together? We'll have good jobs and practice Russian at home. A happy, dramatic life."

She pulled her hand away. "That's your fantasy, but it's a mockery to me."

The newly built Soviet Exhibition Hall was huge and majestic. Besides heavy machinery, it featured consumer goods, but none of them could enchant Ziwei. We passed a group of young students flocking around the glass counters displaying wristwatches and fountain pens. A college boy pointed at the pens and sneered. "They look ugly, nothing comparable to either Gold Stars or US Parkers."

Another student moved his chin to indicate the Moscow wristwatch. "Blunt and unreliable."

The Russian vendor, who understood Chinese, got angry. He smashed one of the Moscow watches on the cement floor, then picked it up and thrust it into the face of the young man. "See? Still running. Can you do that with a Swiss watch?"

A female Chinese guide arrived to disperse the boisterous kids. A faint smile flitted across Ziwei's face.

We found a Cantonese restaurant not far from the Exhibition Hall. While we waited at a corner table, she finally spoke. "Going to the Soviet Union will also make you a Party member even sooner. It's the shortest way to become a red expert. I'm happy for you."

"For us."

"You go your way, I'll go mine."

"Why?"

"My cousin, a med student, and her fiancé, a jet fighter pilot, grew up together and made a commitment at an early age. Last year, when the man asked for a permit to marry her, he was denied by the political commissar of his Air Force base because her father was a landlord."

"Don't worry. The security regulations are really tough for pilots, but I'm going to be an engineer in water resources, and I can't carry a dam to surrender it to an enemy."

Her jaw tightened. "No jokes. Having a father overseas is more dangerous than being the daughter of a landlord under neighborhood surveillance. Can't you see our political polarization? I won't let my background ruin your future."

"I care only about our common fate. We should go through thick and thin together. If, upon graduation, the government should dispatch you to a harsh place due to your political liability, I'll go with you to set up our nest in the vile circumstances."

"Dapeng, be realistic. Our future won't follow your will."

I tried to persuade her to eat. "This is our first chance to eat at the same table. The roast pigeon is tasty. And the rice porridge with filleted fish is famous." But she had no appetite at all.

She stopped eating and wiped away tears. "I failed my makeup exams."

"It's not your fault. People understand. Can you ask your department chairman for another chance?"

"I also failed a recent midterm. I've lost my memory and can't focus. My mind goes blank when I try to study. A doctor told me that healing from a nervous breakdown isn't quick, and his pills make me feel worse. I want to take a leave of absence for a semester or two."

"Where will you go?"

"Home."

"You have a diploma almost in your hand. If you have to repeat a semester or a year, it's no problem, just bite the bullet. You're not alone. I'm in the same boat as you."

"I have to take the exams by myself. You can't help me at all."

"Be practical. Focus on the final four courses, the ones you failed. I can outline your graduation project. We can start it this summer. Afterward, wherever I am, I can use my spare time to help write it."

"How can you do that?"

"Your classmate, Ji, who acted with me in the play, says you can choose a topic from a wide range. You can pick a Soviet author or his work. Since there are tons of Chinese articles about that, I can read them. Believe me, I can compose a passable essay in Chinese. Then you can translate it into Russian."

"It wouldn't be as easy as you're making it sound."

"Or as hopeless as you think. Let's overcome the crisis together. In any case, it's better to stay at school than go home. If you're here, the university leaders will want to rehabilitate you. Otherwise, they'll forget you."

"No matter what you say, I can't study anymore. I just want to go home."

"Quitting school would be the worst move you could make." I looked at her and fought back tears. "Please don't abandon me."

"Enough. My nerves can't take it." She covered her face with both hands. "You'll fly far and high. It would be stupid and selfish of me to grab onto your wings."

In a sullen mood, we kept on eating. I appreciated the tasty, expensive food and cherished our meeting after her ordeal. I believed she had the same feeling.

On the ferry back to campus, she stood by the bow, where the guardrails were welded pipes with large, unsafe openings. I stood next to her. The rumbling engine and splashing waves offered us no peace to resume our conversation. She stared out at the wide river and braved the wind. The free end of her blue kerchief fluttered like a bird's tail, and I sensed that her heart was also poised like a bird's, ready to take off.

Our final bus ride covered the road along which we had walked and chatted the first time. Behind a wall of standing passengers, we sat in a back corner. With her body snuggled against mine, her melancholy silence told me more than words could.

As she was determined to go home, I accepted that leaving her classmates, who had tortured her for a whole summer, might be helpful for her recovery. Later, returning to school, she'd gain friendship from the new faces. I searched for a gift for her, but found only a book, *How to Cure Your Nervous Breakdown*, which was practically helpful to her. The author, an experienced medical doctor, pointed out many misconceptions about nervous breakdowns, explained the cause of such physical and psychological disorders, and suggested their cure using alternative methods rather than medicine. I read it through and thought that it was enlightening and instructive, and would certainly help her.

We parted two weeks later at the Wuchang railway station. Besides my wish for her speedy recovery and our future meeting, I gave her the book, and said, "It's better than any doctor to cure your nervous breakdown."

At the last second, I gripped her hand in an attempt to salvage the tender feelings about to be carried away by the train.

23

As I was waiting for a letter from Ziwei, out of the six candidates for studying abroad, the university authority allowed only the three Party members to take the qualifying exam. We three YL members had been left out. We understood, that as the YL was defined as the assistant, and reserve, force to the Party, we were less qualified. Later, only a small portion of the YL members would pass the rigorous clearance and tough political testing for eligibility to enter the Party.

I wondered if we'd been used as stooges to make the selection process look fair. I kept the feeling to myself until Jianlin Mo came to see me.

Outside the drafting room for our graduation design, standing in the corridor, she said, "I'm sorry you didn't get chosen this time. You're young, there'll be more opportunities. I hope you're not bothered by the higher-ups' decision."

I shrugged casually. "It's logical, I'm not a Party member. If I were a leader, I'd make the same decision."

"Aha! You're peeved. Party membership is crucial, but you have the potential to join the Party soon, and your other qualifications can offset your present shortcoming. The directors of the personnel office and our department's Party secretary have discussed your case carefully. As other universities sent non-Party members abroad, they did root for you. But the overseas relationship you're trying to establish has them spooked."

I lurched backward. "You mean Ziwei Cao?"

"They didn't name names, but I didn't misunderstand their implication. From their tone, I feel there's still some room for you to maneuver. Can you cut your ties with her? If you can, Yonghon Huo and I will lobby on your behalf. If you can't, you'd better accept the current decision without a grudge."

Her offer churned my anguish. If my hopes had been dashed two months earlier, Ziwei wouldn't have felt herself to be a liability and might have stayed on campus. Now, if I gave up the reignited hope for a golden future, there was no guarantee that she'd come back to me.

In the corridor, I walked rapidly, turning sharply. Jianlin walked beside me calmly for a while, and finally said, "Don't let the opportunity of going to the Soviet Union slip; it will never come again."

I stopped to face her. "I want to keep my relationship with Ziwei Cao, the chance of a lifetime."

"Fine, that's your decision. Don't forget to help her take a correct attitude toward the 1955 campaign."

I lost no time writing to tell her about the cancelation of my candidacy for studying in the Soviet Union. "The major barrier is gone, please come back to me."

24

In late July 1956, we got our certificates of graduation, red-covered books that looked like passports, and had a rally as our commencement. The Party committee secretary and administrative head gave speeches like the generals did to the military cadets leaving school for various fighting posts. They sweepingly addressed the places we were designated to go: the Party's Scientific and Technological Front Lines. Representatives for the graduates swore on the stage, "The Party's need is our personal goal. Going to the most difficult spots is the most glorious achievement." We shouted and cheered to support their oaths, pledging to accept any jobs the Party was going to assign us.

Unlike the times of the old society, we had neither private celebrations nor could we invite our parents. Just after our commencement, the university treated us to a sumptuous dinner. Tables were set out on the East Lake waterfront and lights hung from cherry tree branches.

Before we picked up our chopsticks, a clerk from the personnel office walked among our tables to hand everyone a letter. We opened them and found our job-assignment notices. Some looked joyful, and others sullen. Among three hundred graduates in various water-resource disciplines, only eight were assigned to the Chinese Academy of Sciences—the best place, we thought. Seven of the eight were Party members, and the eighth was an academic champion and politically maturing to soon become a Party member.

Those who were upset by their assignment found no room to bargain with the authorities, given their written and oral oaths. They would swallow their frustration to fulfill their obedience to the Party. Against the collective disdain, a few of them requested that the leaders make certain changes, but they couldn't achieve what they wished.

I was among the next five to get desirable assignments; in Beijing at a newly established national lab affiliated with the Ministry of Electric Power. The Party emphasized electric industry as a top economic priority.

I got a two-week vacation to visit my parents, and drained the cash in my pocket for the train tickets.

Three generations of our family were cramped into a single dingy room in a shaky house we shared with four other families. A hanging blanket created the only partition between the sections. My younger brother, Youzhi, slept on a camp cot beside my parents' bed on one side of the curtain. Haitao, his wife, and their three children lived on the other side. An elderly retiree from a railway repair yard lived upstairs, immediately above our family. He was kind enough to clear space in his room and invite me to stay there for two weeks.

Upon my arrival, Mother beckoned me to sit by our coal stove, where a square table was always set, ready for three generations to eat, or for guests to have tea.

Father came in with a parcel and looked at me quizzically. "It's for you, from Guangzhou."

I opened the package. Inside was a Russian–Chinese dictionary, an expensive one that few university students could afford. I felt its weight and the sentiment it carried. Inside its hard cover, I found Ziwei's letter.

July 18, 1956
Dear Dapeng,

Every day for two months I tried to write you, but my mind was blank, so I gave up. I often cried with your photo by my pillow. Mother showed it to a fortune teller who predicted that you have a big fortune and honors ahead. Concerning whether harmony or conflict is predestined between us, the fortune teller's equivocal answer made her worry about our union. Still, she loves your looks.

Father isn't superstitious. He praises various boys we once knew whose attributes he pieces together to create an ideal young man he wants for me. Soon after you and I met, my intuition told me that you might be the right man to be his son-in-law. At least your communication skills and quick learning would delight him. Unfortunately, such a dream is impossible to realize, as you live in a different social system from his.

I miss our campus, especially the library where you used to sit and gaze at me from an inconspicuous corner. At the beginning, your bold, edgy interest annoyed me, but now I yearn for it.

I enjoy your changeable expressions, sometimes playful like a child, sometimes solemn like a mature man. Your quiet efforts to fulfill my wishes show the most valuable qualities a man can have. Reading Pavlenko's epistolary novella, as you recommended, I imagined we would live together poetically like the Soviet couple.

Then, at the advent of our long-awaited happiness, disaster befell me and shattered our dream. Suddenly, my classmates and roommates became a herd of beasts, brandishing claws and roaring at me for months.

I've been bored and irritated in Guangzhou, but I have no way to return to you. Seeing my dark future and the dead end of our relationship, I've decided to go to Hong Kong for a while. Miraculously, the local authorities have already granted my passport, and I'll leave here in about ten days. Since I will go abroad legally and will come back, please don't worry.

Goodbye, Dapeng. A man with great potential, you shouldn't be as maudlin as when I last saw you. I have confidence in you. Don't be frustrated at losing your chance to go to the Soviet Union. Other good luck awaits you.

As a memento, please keep this dictionary, which shall accompany you and help you master Russian.

Love,
Ziwei

I silently cursed. The hen had flown away and the eggs in the coop were broken.

Father fondled the dictionary, appreciating its obvious value. During my childhood, he'd had only one book, *An Extensive Collection of Sample Correspondence*, which he used to rewrite letters for his boss and his illiterate friends. Now, his son was studying a foreign language, something unprecedented in our family.

I stuffed Ziwei's letter into my pocket and rearranged my belongings on the bamboo bench. Mother stood beside me, watching. She gingerly picked up the 3x4-inch photo taken at Iron Bird Photoshop, in Wuhan, the day Ziwei and I visited the Soviet Industrial Exhibition. It was hand-tinted and backed with stiff cardboard.

Mother clicked her tongue. "Wow! She's a gorgeous city girl. Stylish hair, so rare nowadays. Look at her bright, noble eyes."

Father snatched the photo from her, looked at it, and frowned. "Must have been brought up in a rich, modern family. Too delicate for our humble family. Our chicken coop can't keep a phoenix."

25

I heard noise in the parlor. My older brother, Haitao, returning from work on the streets, rested his cart against the wall, handlebars up, and chatted with a neighbor, a cobbler.

Since I left home in 1952, he had worked as a store clerk, then as a substitute teacher in an elementary school. In 1954, a family friend helped him find a teaching job at a coal miners' evening school, which looked relatively stable. But he lost it within a year, and now made a living as a porter.

Father cursed gutturally. "He's home early, with the sun still high. Rotten wood cannot be carved into a statue."

I looked at Mother and waited. She tilted her head toward me and murmured, "Last year, he was fired after two months of public humiliation."

I turned to my father for details. "What were the charges against him?"

"All his troubles came from his filthy mouth. He said things like, 'The US is superior to the Soviet Union in science and technology.' His colleagues tattled. The 1955 campaign was chasing the secret followers of Feng Hu, the writer whose arrest Mao had ordered. Haitao was found guilty of echoing his ideas. For instance, that the boss of film production should be the director instead of the Party secretary. They accused Hu of attempting to abolish the Party's leadership, and Haitao became his follower."

Tears came to her eyes. "That night, sometime in late August, while we were eating dinner, he came back with his sleeping roll, looking like a defeated rooster. Your sister-in-law said nothing but just put down her chopsticks and wept. With two children to feed and one more in her belly, she felt Heaven had collapsed. He should have repented and pleaded for mercy."

Haitao walked in, drying his sweat with a long towel draped across his shoulder. He picked up Ziwei's photo. "Her eyes have an air of confidence and serene dignity. Tell me about her."

"She's a year younger than me and had almost graduated from the Russian Language Department. Then she had to quit school and go home."

"Why?"

I took the photo back from him. "She fell into the same trap you did last year. Her father is in Hong Kong, so the campaign leaders interrogated her as a foreign agent, and she had a nervous breakdown. Now she's going to Hong Kong. She says she'll come back, but who knows when?"

Haitao sighed. "Since 1949, every family who had someone escape to Taiwan or Hong Kong has had no peace. Break it off, and quick."

Father resumed his authoritative manner. "Going to Hong Kong is like jumping into a muddy river, she'll never wash clean. Just think of her as dead." He jerked his head toward the bamboo bench. "And burn that photograph before the wrong person sees it." He went to the front yard to mix coal with clay to make briquettes.

Mother began to sweep the floor of the tiny kitchen, which was also our dining and sitting room. In the middle of her task, she held the broom and straightened her back for a rest.

"Auntie Wu will have you over for dinner. She's proud of you, the first university diploma among our Hubei refugees. She never changed her mind about Chuju marrying you. The girl is even prettier than two years ago."

"Chuju is still a child."

"Don't be silly. You'll have a headache your whole life if you marry an educated woman. Chuju is thrifty. She won't complain no matter how poor you might be. Unlike the women in big cities, we know Chuju's family down to its roots."

"We grew up separately, we don't really know each other."

"The war brought our two families together; you met by fate. Every time her mother asks about you, Chuju hangs around with her ears pricked, as if looking for something."

"Mama, I'm too tired for this."

She dropped the broom and sat down, shrinking back with her hands folded on her belly and her shoulders slouching. At 22, I shouldn't have behaved like a willful child. I sat down next to her on the bamboo bench and held her shoulder.

Haitao stretched his hands to both ends of the narrow bench and tilted his head. "As your older brother, I wish you the best of luck, and that you will rise up to honor our ancestors. But who knows? We have to prepare for bad luck."

Mother sat up straighter. "Look at how your sister-in-law toils along with Haitao. A highly-educated woman in such a situation would've run away from him a long time ago."

I smiled. "Mama, don't push me so hard. Ten years ago, when Haitao was dating at a young age, you said something about how a man should worry about gaining honor and official rank rather than a wife."

In Father's absence, Haitao spoke like a guru. "Chuju is a flower in our town. It's not easy to find a nice girl in a new place. You have advantages because you're childhood friends, and because her mother has settled on you."

"Human affairs are unpredictable. I'm still naïve, and I'm going to live like a soldier for years to come. Everything is uncertain."

"I know what you mean. You should keep in touch. She might be a good choice for you, and there's no harm in keeping your options open."

That evening, Mother found clean sheets for me. I stood and listened to her marital advice once again. I had to stop her interminable chatter. "Mama, you must be exhausted from a long day taking care of your grandchildren. We can talk later."

I had just finished four years as an impoverished student and felt I could finally draw breath after the embarrassment of not having enough money to buy even textbooks and drawing paper. With an entrance job in Beijing, I'd be no better off than the vast majority of poor workers. For my large family, it looked even gloomier. After the war, Father had found a job as an accountant in 1947, but lost it in 1953 when the firm went bankrupt. At 60 he was still pushing wheelbarrows heavily laden with coal, or sieving sand at a quarry. My younger brother was going to be in eighth grade.

Clearly, my rosy dreams had been possible only on campus, an artificial setting, far from home and reality. My hope of a cozy life, as depicted in the Soviet movies, had become weaker since my observations on the Huai River. The poverty and desperation at home wouldn't let me forget that I was the only family member who would have a regular salary. My obligation to my parents was great.

I tossed about in bed that night as Ziwei's letter announced, over and over, 'I'll come back, I'll come back.' Through the thin, shaky floor, I could hear the cries of children, my sister-in-law grumbling, and Father scolding my younger brother for coming home late. The noise depressed me. When an early morning breeze carried the crowing of distant roosters, I put

my hands behind my neck and raised my head. Reality
wouldn't yet allow me to start a family.

26

Over the next three days, Mother kept pushing me to see
Chuju and Auntie Wu. I lacked the enthusiasm, though it
would take only ten minutes to walk to her home. The distance
between Chuju and me now seemed greater than when she'd
been hundreds of miles away.

On the fourth day, I was reading in a library room at the
county's cultural center, which had been a Confucian temple
before 1949. It was the only quiet place where I could escape
the din at home. After skimming the tedious newspapers, I was
totally bored. A clump of bamboo in the side yard shaded me
from the summer's heat, and the rustling leaves made me
drowsy. With drooping eyelids, I looked out the window at
moss-covered stones beside red-washed walls. Just then a
familiar figure flashed through the circular door to the side
yard. Chuju!

I sprang from my chair to greet her on the brick path. As I
stood before her, she barely glanced at me, avoided my gaze,
and with one hand self-consciously fiddled with a bamboo
stalk. I hadn't seen her for two years; she was now 17 and
looked like a fully-grown woman.

As we stood in silence, the bamboo swayed, and scattered
rays of sunshine danced on her light-green, short-sleeved shirt
and casual white slacks.

The blush faded from her face, and she looked at the
ground. "Congratulations on going to the capital. Please don't
forget us small-town bumpkins."

Weighing Mother's persuasive words, I gazed at her.

At last, she looked at me. "Why don't you say anything?"

I fumbled for words. "Maybe you can study in Beijing. On holidays, we could climb Fragrance Hill, the highest peak on the west side of Beijing."

She snapped off a bamboo leaf, held it to her lips, and blew on it to try to make it whistle. No luck. She smiled. "You're a sweet talker, but don't make fun of me. You'll be dazzled by those sleek Beijing girls."

Charmed by her misty eyes, I put my hand on her arm. She looked around and swiftly retreated. She stopped at the circular door. "Mom asked me to invite you to dinner tomorrow, but I didn't want to come to your house to ask, so I'm telling you now. If you don't want to come, please tell Mother yourself." She ran into the street like a gust of wind.

The next afternoon, I went to her home. After exchanging pleasantries with me, her mother returned to making dinner in the common kitchen, a former landlord's sitting room now shared by three families. Three brick-lined stoves and three large, glazed water vats occupied most of the space. All the corners, except where doors were hung, were filled with piles of coal.

Chuju's two sisters were in other provinces. The oldest one married a KMT battalion commander, who'd been jailed by the CCP somewhere, and the second oldest was in a college. Chuju's father worked in an iron mine hundreds of miles away, she lived with her mother in a single large room. With only one full-size bed and one single, the space was big enough to serve as living room, dining room, and bedroom. The small backyard offered a private retreat. It was a secluded area, surrounded by four walls with the eaves slanting toward a shallow pool about the size of a ping-pong table for collecting rainwater. The locals called such an enclosure a sky well. Along the perimeter of the pool, under the eaves, a brick walkway offered a lovely place to spend a summer evening.

I sat at the small dining table in their room while Chuju

pretended to help her mother fix dinner in the kitchen. At intervals, she rushed in with a cup of tea, a plate of peeled pears, and a pomegranate. More than once I overheard her mother say, "Go talk with your guest. You can't help much here." For a time, only the sizzling wok broke the silence, followed by the jingling of a metal hook from a shoulder pole and the sound of pouring water as Chuju came back from the well.

I looked for something to read. Near Chuju's pillow I found a well-known novel, *Days and Nights*, a translation of Konstantin Simonov's story. At the front, defending Moscow from Nazi troops, a Lieutenant Sahalov, the hero, falls in love with a nurse in the trenches. I'd read this book a few years before and liked its liberal, even bold, themes. The lieutenant was a man of great willpower, but he didn't try to conceal his fear of death from the nurse. Such realism was almost unimaginable to readers in China. In our literature, fearless fighters, mad with class hatred, charged our enemies without regard for their own safety.

Two thirds of the pages of the novel were rolled back over the spine; Chuju had almost finished it. As she read, did she have fantasies about men?

I was putting the book back when her mother came in with a large dish. "Chuju is honoring you with a rare treat. This grass carp is hardly ever available, but she got up early, before I woke, to stand in line for it."

Walking in immediately behind her mother and carrying a bowl of fresh eggplant and another brimming with mustard greens, Chuju moaned. "Mom!" She stomped her foot on the floor.

Sampling everything, I especially savored the pork rib soup, boiled with winter melon and seaweed. Eventually, I slowed down. The food was sumptuous, in contrast to the lukewarm demeanor of Chuju, who sat opposite me, just beyond reach. But her mother's warmth offset Chuju's coolness. She used a large spoon to deliver lotus roots, fish, and meat from the dishes to my bowl, even as I shyly tried to stop her. "Auntie, I've already eaten too much."

Chuju tittered, "Mom, please don't push him. A gentleman doesn't eat much in public. Let him keep his scholarly manner." We all laughed politely.

The outdoor heat faded at sunset. Darkness fell. Auntie cleared the table and prepared her bath. When she laid a large wooden basin between the two beds, I stood up to leave. But she told Chuju, "Why don't you take our guest out back? The air is cool there."

Chuju took two stools and I followed her to the sky well. After she closed the door between their room and the yard, we were enveloped in twilight, the sky a deep-blue backdrop illuminated by the moon. Sitting side-by-side under the eaves, we quietly watched stars blink down on us. One after another, patches of clouds floated across the open sky.

Chuju broke the silence, saying she couldn't name any famous constellations. I pointed to the seven stars that form a spoon. "That's the Big Dipper. But I don't know many either."

She straightened, tilting her head to the sky, unbinding and re-braiding part of her long pigtails. She blinked slowly, and I marveled at her contented glow. At last she said, "There's a myth I particularly like. Every July 7, the Goddess of Western Heaven permits Girl Weaver to meet her lover, Cowherd Boy, on the other side of the Silver River." The Silver River is the Chinese name for the Milky Way.

She pointed to a crowded, bright cluster of stars. "When I was little, my oldest sister told me that was the Magpie Bridge. Countless magpies, sympathetic to the lovers, make themselves into a bridge for Girl Weaver and Cowherd Boy to cross. She worried that it would be chilly and lonely in that high place."

Her profile in the bright twilight reminded me how much the women in our town admired her. The teenage girls in her neighborhood would often say she looked like a well-known ingénue, a mountain girl from an ethnic minority appearing in a recent Chinese movie. At the happy ending of the movie, her suitor, the heroic young hunter, steals a kiss from her cheek and runs away.

As time quietly flowed past and the moonlit sky, framed by the rectangular well, isolated us from the outer world, our intricate society faded away. In the shade of the eaves, the cute and innocent Chuju appeared permanently immune from corruption. *I should do that—steal a kiss from her!*

With less courage than the hunter, I inched my hand around her shoulder, but felt her tug instead of melt. I was nervous but not discouraged. Gathering my will to kiss her, my thoughts raced. What if she screamed? At the very least, her mother would think me bad. Still, my instincts told me Chuju wouldn't protest, so I raised myself enough to launch a quick kiss. When my lips touched her cheek, she raised a shoulder and shoved my face away. I sat back down hard on my stool, both hands holding my chin.

Chuju giggled, "Are all men so shameless?"

I kept silent. The light of the kerosene lamp inside leaked through the seams of the door and threshold, and we heard her mother pour her bathwater from the basin into a bucket, then dump it in the front ditch. It was time for me to leave.

Chuju stood on the porch to see me off while her mother raised her voice in farewell, "Say hello to your papa and mom, and come back before you go to Beijing."

The day before I left for Beijing, I went back to Chuju's home and talked briefly with her mother. After I said goodbye to Auntie, Chuju walked me out. At the front brick steps I asked her, "Could you come to meet me around eight o'clock at the east gate of the old city wall? The chance of running into anyone who we know over there is slim."

She smiled but shook her head. "I've never gone out with a man, even in daytime."

"Your mom will let you to go out with me. I'll ask her." I turned back toward her home to go ask.

She stretched her arms out to both sides to block me. "Nobody asked you to do that for me."

I looked into her eyes. "Then you'll come?"

She nodded.

I hurried home and had a bath. After dinner, I lay in a bamboo recliner, mentally preparing for our meeting. From the south end of the bridge, we would walk along the river. Following a trail branching from the bank, we'd pass an orange orchard, then climb the hill where a schoolyard offered breeze and a bird's-eye view of the city at night. Leaning against the guardrail, we'd have much to discuss. But on what topics?

Haitao sat down and warned me that I'd already lost the ideal opportunity with Ziwei; if I let the practical one with Chuju pass by, I'd be falling between two stools. Despite his status as a political outcast, he spoke like a pundit and quoted a verse to describe the hopeless state of a great Tang Dynasty poet, who lived in the ancient capital, Chang'an. "Our capital teems with ranking officials, while you're alone and look haggard." His words reminded me of my immediate future, as shown in documentaries, in which millions of ordinary men in Beijing marched like ants and lived like bees. While bars were forbidden and ballrooms limited to within working units, a technical recruit like me would stand little chance of finding someone like Chuju.

I should persuade her to take the national exam for university entrance and, with her average scores, aim at a suitable school in Beijing. Living in the same city, our mutual support and understanding would lead us to realize our parents' wishes for us. That was my only possibility at this moment. To accomplish the basic training of a profession was one thing, while to refine someone culturally was another.

At a time when many young people took brutality as bravery, rudeness as frankness, and courtesy as bourgeois hypocrisy, Ziwei had preserved her demeanor and humanity under pressure. Why? Her upbringing in an educated family and spending her formative years in a missionary school might have been the answer. Perhaps, tradition and religion had cultivated her noble values and emotional appeal. Imperceptibly, they worked together like filters to prevent the misconceptions of solemn propaganda from settling in her mind. That's why Ziwei was so exceptional, and what I loved most about her. Could Chuju possess the same values and taste that Ziwei did? No, she didn't have the makings of a refined lady.

The Revolution had created many new words. One of them was *pei-yang-gan-qing*—to foster affection. In 1949 and 1950, when the PLA seized Central and South China, its arts troupes and propaganda teams recruited large numbers of high-school and middle-school girls. Over the next couple of years, all the suitable young women were unwillingly swept from their own towns to marry army commanders. To push through their hasty matching, administrative efforts were needed to persuade the women to accept the men. A popular form was to arrange one-to-one meetings for the couples to exchange opinions. That, added to many other forms of pressure, became the procedure to foster affection.

Perhaps I could borrow that term and foster affection with Chuju, but we'd do it naturally, without administrative aid. I'd patiently remold her into a refined lady like Ziwei. Gradually, my vision seemed to clear, and my plan looked feasible.

I arrived at the bridge ten minutes early, knowing Chuju wouldn't be there yet, not while the sky was still light. Vigilantly watching all the shadows approaching from either side, I waited. Time went slowly. Only boys diving from the middle pier and their splashing distracted my fretful attention.

The sky turned dark. Children caught fireflies. Another hour passed. Parents called their children home: "Damn it, you don't know how late it is!" and, "Come home *right now* or I'll skin you alive!" The slamming and latching of home gates followed.

I was a solitary pillar, attached to the granite bridge banister. Electric lamps had been installed at both ends of the bridge sometime during my university days. Their low voltage and small bulbs gave off poor illumination. At the appointed hour, I looked around. Of course, she was a little late. At 15 after, I wondered if I should leave.

I waited until midnight, two hours past Chuju's strict curfew. I knew she would never come now.

"What a stupid joke." A brisk breeze swept across the water.

27

In early September 1956, the best season for sightseeing in Beijing, five of us, all former classmates, reported for work at a research center in an eastern suburb of the vast capital city. The highway passing by our compound was busy with the rusty buses and old trucks of all types running between Tong County and Beijing. Their speeds were influenced and controlled by horse-drawn carts full of goods.

The sky was clear, the air crisp, and the scent of delicately sweet osmanthus wafted about us as we strolled along the red wall of the Forbidden City. Like a lovelorn soldier, I felt myself alien to the charming scenery and the musical dialect of pure Mandarin.

The 1956 salary adjustment had just been concluded.

According to political or technical ranks, the old-timers received raises plus sizable amounts of extra cash because the effective date of their new pay was set several months retroactively. Those senior engineers and cadres joyfully frequented department stores, browsing and buying high-quality clothes, watches, bicycles, leather goods, and even wristwatches imported from Japan and Switzerland. Now senior cadres were dressed up in woolen suits and long, fur-lined coats, a vast improvement compared to the coarse uniforms of the PLA commanders in 1949 during the march into Beijing. They rode sightseeing sedans with their children and beautiful young wives, all smiling as brilliantly as if they were fresh blossoms.

The privileged echelons pushed the whole society into a spending spree. Nearby stores set up installment plans through our accounting office. Anyone could get zero-interest loans, which would be deducted monthly from salaries. I felt sorry for the poor secretaries and lab trainees. Under peer pressure, they ate the cheapest unpalatable food for months to save enough money for a pair of woolen pants or leather shoes.

A wad of cash, 62 yuan, would be delivered to my desk on the fourth day of every month. I spent only about a third, mainly for the mess hall's plain food. Housing was virtually free, at 0.8 yuan a month for a bunk in the bachelor's dorm. Thus, I could send another third to my parents. The remaining third would be my reserve, mainly for emergencies or a home visit.

I understood the nation's low-salary policy arose from the urgent need for funds for military strength and industrialization. Psychologically and practically, I prepared for financial hardship. I was insulated from envy by a passion for study and knowledge stronger than my desire for pricey retail wares. Despising the waves of material longing which slapped me every day, I decided to steer clear of romance until my professional position became more secure.

The Party's March toward Science began in earnest. An air of exaltation for science filled the streets, and even some barbershops hung notices on their windows: "High-ranking intellectuals have priority, no need to wait in line." At our institute, noteworthy professors were invited to teach us graduate math, applied mechanics, and specific topics related to the work of each division. To encourage us to concentrate on professional subjects, political studies were substantially reduced. Still, the daily work and political activities were hectic. Being content with the materially drab life, I craved more free time to study.

My division director, Old Ma, a humble, tolerant man, often appeared to be confused. He was 15 years older than me but had graduated from university only ten years earlier. Many young graduates treated him harshly due to his lack of leadership, skills and achievement, as well as his long-windedness. In his eagerness to join the Party, he'd volunteered to be an ideological watchman, and hence had hurt some senior engineers. They hated him, and one of them called him The Star-studded Sky behind his back, making fun of his pockmarked face.

I respected him as an honest elder, though under pressure he'd insulted others. In return, he trusted me as his main assistant, letting me draft our division's annual plan and other reports. I often represented him at meetings that my low rank didn't qualify me even to attend. I was grateful for his help in advancing my career.

Sometimes I worked as his public relations secretary, which put me in a sorry position. One day, I acted as an escort to pick up Professor Chen from Qinghua University. He'd been hired as the adviser to our division and came once a month to deliver a two-hour lecture, or review our reports or plans. He normally seemed modest. I admired him for his PhD from Harvard in 1948. After the Korean War, he had returned to

China, following the patriotic tide surging among the overseas Chinese scientists. As the road in the residential area of the campus was narrow, the driver who came to pick him up parked the jeep a hundred yards away. No sooner did the professor walk out of his home than he started to complain. "Why park so far away? Can't you see the road?"

I apologized. "I said the same thing to the chauffeur, but he makes the decisions. Have you heard, Professor, that he who holds a steering wheel or a stethoscope can be the most arrogant in a poor country?"

The prewar US jeep was dirty and rickety. To make things worse, it cut out twice in the 40 kilometers before we arrived at the school. The driver asked me to crank the engine by hand, which took strength and endurance. Away from our guest in the car, I did it as a pleasure.

By the time I opened the jeep door for the professor, he was glowering. I apologized, "Sorry, our only sedan was already dispatched for something else before I got my application for transportation endorsed. Next time, I'll do this ahead of time."

On the way back to our institute, the jeep cut out twice again. The first time, I worked the crank well, though it exhausted me. The second time, I strained every muscle in my body. Though the November weather was cold, I streamed with sweat. The driver yelled, "You look like you've been starved for three days."

He was cocky because Chairman Mao stressed that intellectuals have to learn from workers, peasants, and soldiers. As a former PLA soldier and a proletariat worker now, he was doubly qualified to look down on me.

In the rearview mirror, I could see the professor's angry face. Did he deserve such privilege? A half-day consulting per month, and 50 yuan for moonlighting. I didn't have the answer, but decided not to crank a car for him again.

On another occasion, a parallel research center affiliated to the Ministry of Water Resources invited the Russian expert Simenchuk, who was working in our division on a one-year contract, for an academic exchange. Since our organization, the Ministry of Electric Power, was newly established, we lacked high-ranking professionals. As usual, Old Ma asked me to accompany Simenchuk and the interpreter.

As we walked into a spacious room, five Soviet-trained Chinese engineers sitting around the conference table stood up to greet Simenchuk. They were about ten years older than me and, in contrast with my four-pocket blue jacket, they were dressed in the three-piece suits preserved from their days abroad. They introduced themselves, their subjects, and where they'd studied in the Soviet Union, all stuttering terribly. When the formal discussion began, they resigned themselves to letting the interpreter do the job.

I might as well have been invisible. I took a low stool and sat under the window in a corner, four yards away from the table. I waited for somebody to ask me to sit with them, but nobody even looked at me for two hours. Their arrogance and breach of etiquette humiliated me, while their servile manner toward Simenchuk made me laugh. I began to despise them. Nevertheless, I carefully listened to their Chinese conversation with the interpreter and found the technical content all banal and shallow. Compared with what I'd read from the current US journals, I evaluated their knowledge as mediocre.

One of my former classmates, a comedian and sharp observer, worked in the same division as the five snobs. He had made a comment. "By political trickery, they grabbed the chance to study in the Soviet Union. Academically, they're a bunch of straw bags."

I had doubted his remark, which sounded unkind, even venomous. Now, at the end of the meeting, I found my friend in a lab on the same floor as the conference room. He walked me to the parking place of our Warsaw. Before Simenchuk and the interpreter came, I described the scene that afternoon. He consoled me. "Don't let it bother you. When General Xin Han was young, he submitted to the disgrace of crawling under a street guy's legs. Later he became one of the founding fathers of the Han Dynasty. Sooner or later, you'll defeat those straw bags."

"The problem is how to convince people I'm better than these guys."

He smiled, slowly rotating his palms together as in the past. "Learn from ancient heroes. They spent ten years in the high mountains sharpening their swords before the decisive battles."

28

Searching for the secret to success, I wrote a letter to a former teacher who'd taught me hydraulic structures. I asked him why so many researchers who'd struggled their whole lives achieved so little. He replied:

> One of the common reasons is their lack of solid basic training. *Luxuriant leaves come from deep roots* is a good metaphor. The Beijing opera stars are good in four fundamental skills: singing, speaking, acting, and acrobatics. I strongly suggest that you concentrate your early days on math, physics, foreign languages, and some newly emerging technologies.

Now I saw my sword and how I'd have to sharpen it. Every Saturday evening or Sunday morning, I stayed alone in the lab while my coworkers went shopping or to the movies. Whenever I was too sleepy and wanted to quit, I'd remember the ascetic ways of two ancient scholars. To study at midnight, one tied his long hair to a rafter. The other jabbed an awl into his thigh. I simply stuck my head under the tap and let the icy water keep me wide awake.

Sometimes, daydreams distracted me, and loneliness bit like a poisonous snake. How had the two ancient scholars purged their minds of romantic desire?

In 1956, a politically relaxed year, the ban was lifted on some movies and songs from the thirties and forties. Every weekend, a ballroom dance was held in the auditorium of a technical school next to our compound. The breeze kept sneaking love songs and drumbeats into my ascetic tower of learning. I moved my desk to the alcove of the lab, which had only one window, and pasted paper slips around the frame and along the central joint. My coworkers approved of my method of keeping out the winter wind and dust. I didn't tell them I was just trying to make the room soundproof.

Someone got a poster from the Japanese Industrial Exhibition advertising a sewing machine as an exquisite gadget and hung it on the wall facing my desk. I hated that poster. It featured a beautiful reclining lady fondling the machine. Her body was wrapped in thin gauze with its end floating in the air, as if at any moment she would emerge nude. One day when the YL branch secretary came to collect membership dues, I challenged him. "How can you tolerate such capitalist crap?" He immediately tore down the poster.

The purified environment had indeed improved my focus on study. In two months, my reading speed of the English book *Foundation Design* had accelerated from a few lines per hour to a few pages per hour. I started to refresh the math and Russian I'd taken in college. However, to make further progress, I needed stronger mental power. It wasn't enough to just remove a model's photo from the wall, especially when a living model, Anna Lin, was flashing around.

Anna had graduated from a four-year technical school for

those who'd finished only ninth grade. Once, when my friend Aiming and I talked about her, to avoid mentioning her real name, I used the heroine's name from the Russian movie *Anna Karenina*, which had recently been dubbed into Chinese. Through her small talk with our officemates, the real-life Anna I saw every day in no way resembled the famous literary character. But her slim figure, almond-shaped face, and delicate demeanor prompted my whim.

Aiming slapped his thigh. "She looks just like the Russian actress who played the young Anna."

That reminded me of the screen image, right down to the low-cut summer dress and the long braids swaying over her slender arms and full bosom. The only difference was the color of hair. Unlike the blonde Soviet star, our officemate had sandy dark hair.

She was born in Harbin, the city in the far north from which most Chinese ballerinas had emerged. Her pale skin and curvy lines made me curious as to whether she was of mixed blood, Russian and Chinese, but I hadn't had the chance to ask her. She wore attractive dresses, which the thrifty majority considered a negative distinction, was reluctant to speak publicly, and avoided political activities. Party leaders saw such people as typical backward elements.

Every day, along with disapproving looks, she received covetous gazes from male colleagues and strangers alike. Women with little political ambition outspokenly praised both her prettiness and her good luck. Her father, a senior engineer in the railway system, gave her money, while most of her peers had to support their parents.

After the one-month orientation and lab training for new recruits we got to know each other. Every now and then, once we heard the research facilities of certain other industrial ministries had imported a new instrument from Japan or Western Europe, young fellows would pester our leaders to let us go over and have a look. That would be a chance to tour downtown Beijing with free transportation. Strolling through the streets and lanes, I would crack a joke with her whenever she looked in a good mood. My exaggerated 'aarrr' sound to imitate the Beijing dialect, mixed with a southern accent and improvised into tongue twisters, made her laugh. At least she didn't have an aversion to me.

I believed she was a nice person but spoiled by her parents as an only child, too delicate for our militant collective. She also looked too glamorous for my humble position. We belonged to different groups, but often met at division meetings, which were held in the largest room. As others sat around the central U-shaped counter or scattered in the four corners, I often moved my chair next to her. She would sit straight up and hide her legs under her skirt. I tried to focus on the speakers, but felt her charming smile and graceful carriage baking my side like the heat from an oven. If there was an occasion, when the other listeners were distracted by a side issue, I would find a trivial or meaningless question to whisper to her: "Was your middle school owned by the Christian church?"; "Does your mother have natural feet or are they bound?" Then I enjoyed her pure Mandarin and mellow intonation, interrupted by her delicate gasps for breath.

Whenever, sitting far from her, I saw affection in her glance at me, I'd warn myself it was a hallucination. Then I'd deny my previous judgment and assure myself she really was sending me endearing messages with her bewitching eyes. Then I'd negate the negation of the negation, which annoyed me no end.

29

In November 1956, soon after the Soviet Red Army smashed the Hungarian Uprising, we had a week of study and debriefing. Every employee of the institute, lab worker, field engineer, theoretical worker, or translator, made very much the same statement of his or her position, speaking in rotation and repeating the Party's declaration. We all blamed Western imperialists, former fascists of the Austro-Hungarian Empire, domestic reactionaries, and liberal Hungarian intellectuals. We all praised the Soviet Red Army for having carried out its sacred international communist obligation. Due to the CCP's thorough elimination of counterrevolutionaries and persistent remolding of intellectuals' minds, we all believed that a Hungarian-type uprising, started by students and liberal artists asking for freedom, democracy, and human rights, would never happen in China.

In the middle of January 1957, as if making a summary about the Hungarian issue, the authorities arranged for us to watch a Chinese documentary, *The Truth about the Hungarian Incident.*

A truck and a van shuttled four hundred employees in two loads each from our compound to the downtown movie theater. Crowded like bundled sticks, we had a rough ride. I stood on the truck bed by the tailgate near Anna. A piercing wind penetrated the many crevices in the canvas awning and side covers and whirled in from the rear of the cab. Men tightly tied the flaps of their padded caps. Women shrouded their heads with woolen scarves.

The driver handled the truck skillfully, but bumpy suburban roads and merging traffic caused him to swerve and make sudden stops that threw us off balance, banging into each other. Once when the driver swerved sharply, Anna and I instinctively clutched each other's waists. Soon, the downtown asphalt gave us a smoother ride, but our hands remained around each other in that sudden intimacy for the rest of the half-hour trip.

At one point, as she stretched up a hand to hold the metal

frame of the truck awning, the lower hem of her leather jacket rose, letting me grip her warm sweater and feel her supple waist. Whenever one of my hat flaps met her upturned collar, they formed a shield retaining the faint fragrance from her face and hair, as if exclusively for me. I felt overwhelmed by the unexpected favor of being so close to her, a woman coveted by hundreds of men at our institute, and whom none dared touch.

The movie theater was unheated. Sitting in metal chairs, we all stamped our feet and rubbed our hands, filling the hall with background noise. The film was mostly still photographs with voiceover narration. It showed the bloody corpses of the local Hungarian Party cadre chiefs and security police that the rebels had slain, but no injured protestors. I was bored but obliged to watch to the end when Russian tanks rolled through Budapest, the streets lined with young girls waving and tossing flowers.

During the 40-minute film, Anna sat away from me and didn't look in my direction. I wondered, under her calm appearance, whether she feared that the subtle feelings between us might be detected by watchful comrades. I just hoped that she would stand next to me again when we rode back to the institute.

After the movie, we all waited on the sidewalk, letting sick and elderly colleagues board the van first. Then the young men and women swarmed onto the truck bed. In a wordless understanding, Anna and I were last to climb up and squeeze into the crowd near the tailgate. Immediately, we put our hands on each other's waists and enjoyed the bumpy ride back to the institute.

At a division meeting the next day, while our coworkers bragged about their ideological gains from the movie, I mulled over my sweet time with Anna, who sat far away from me like a stranger. Perhaps our embrace in the confining crowd had been only a friendly reaction to the rough ride and had made no impression on her at all. On the other hand, she normally kept her distance from men. Our temporary closeness at least seemed to imply that she could get along with me. To avoid making a fool of myself, I took her warmth as impulsive and lacking deep feeling.

One Saturday night, alone in the lab, I had just begun to study when she approached my corner desk, walking as lightly as a cat. Her smile instantly dispelled the stale lab air and brightened the dull room. I was dazzled by her new tailor-made clothes, rare even in downtown Beijing. Certainly she dared not wear them on workdays or among poor crowds.

I raised my head and smiled. "Why are you still hanging around a boring lab on a Saturday night?"

"For tonight I found a vacant bed in the women's dorm. It's terrible to wait for a bus and then get squeezed by the human stampede. I'd much rather enjoy a leisurely ride early Sunday morning."

She lost no time modeling for me her short-sleeved, close-fitting, blue wool outfit that perfectly set off her dark hair and white skin. It was a preseason fashion show, and I felt privileged to be the only person in her audience. But I didn't know what to say to please her. In the dim light of my desk lamp, as she turned and showed me her front, back, and profiles, her shadow dancing on the wall, I wondered how she really felt about me.

"You're a blue angel, descending on me to prophesize my good luck."

Looking complacent, she said nothing. Overcome with awkwardness, I pulled out from a drawer of my desk a small book, a collection of 50 popular songs, and asked which she liked best. She suggested the Yunnan folksong that I'd learned in 1947 and recently heard sung by a mezzo-soprano on the radio. It assumed the tone of a girl expressing her love to a young man.

You're a dragon in the sky,
I'm a flower on the ground.
It wouldn't rain if the dragon wouldn't leap,
Without rain the flower wouldn't blossom.

We held the page, opened our mouths, and repeated the words until we had synchronized our singing.

She pointed at the last two lines. "What does it mean?"

I smiled. "You know. Please explain it to me."

Her hearty laugh turned into giggles. The lab became silent except for a buzz from the electric wall clock. She sat on the edge of my desk and faced me. Her alluringly posed body glowed with affection. It had happened so quickly, so easily, it all seemed unreal.

Thud! Thud! Thud! It came from outside the window. Someone must have climbed up to the windowsill to peep into the lab. I guessed that it was a certain demobilized soldier, a young man from our machine shop, spying on us. By claiming to struggle against evildoers and evil deeds, he indulged in voyeurism. A few months earlier, he claimed to have witnessed a Party branch leader of our division having sex with a female YL member in this very lab. He had dragged the Party committee into an investigation until a hospital report verified that the woman's hymen, 'virgin membrane' in Chinese, was intact. Now the pervert was on the prowl again.

Anna and I hadn't touched each other, but to avoid a possible bite from his poisonous teeth, I said, "This is trouble. We'd better leave right away."

"Where?"

"On the other side of the highway, north of the No. 42 bus stop, there's a brick kiln near a large locust tree. You can't miss it."

We left separately. She made a detour by her dorm for her leather jacket. At our rendezvous, the land spread to the horizon in all directions. In summer, a green curtain of sorghum and corn offered a perfect trysting place, but now only wheat seedlings lined the gray fields. I draped my arm across her back, and we walked along a trail between patches of wheat. Under the starlight, her eyes shone enigmatically, contradicting her innocent nature. Unlike her timid public character, she now strolled with a straight back that showed pride, and self-confidence.

I didn't know what she had in her mind. Her savviness about women's fashion and her craft in stretching a limited budget were impressive, but I'd never seen her read or carry a book in her purse. She seemed oblivious to what was going on in the larger world, and it was odd that she showed no interest in knowing. Ironically, her political inertia had helped her avoid big storms, though several times she had cried at group meetings when criticized for trifles blown up into the behavior of a bourgeois hedonist.

She was the first to speak. "You looked so nice in Western clothing."

"You mean when I recited that poem at the October Revolution anniversary last November? I borrowed that suit from a guy at the Hydraulics Division. He probably inherited it from his capitalist father. I wish someday I could wear clothes like that every day, like the Soviet experts now waltzing down our streets."

"You'll make it when the time comes. I heard you get up at 4:30 am to study and even read on the train. It's rare nowadays."

I led her westward, toward the lit horizon. Her now shambling steps told of her hesitation. After a few silent minutes, she stopped. "We'd better go back."

I embraced her tightly. She deflected my kiss with closed lips gliding across my face, far from the scene I'd dreamed of.

In dismay, I shuffled back to our compound. Still holding her hand, I tried to gather the courage to challenge her seriousness. I didn't utter a word until we could see the shadow of our office building in the distance. "You must have many suitors orbiting you like satellites. I doubt there's any space in your mind left for me."

She giggled, kissed my cheek like a dragonfly touching water, and ran across the highway toward her dorm.

The following Monday, when we met in the office as usual, she treated me as if I were just another coworker.

30

The Youth Art Theater was showing Shakespeare's *Twelfth Night*, which we took as a proper response to Chairman Mao's announcement the previous May: "To artists and writers, we say, let a hundred flowers bloom."

The translation and performance of the play were excellent. Tickets were expensive, but people interested in Western culture still thought them worthwhile. Aiming arranged for seven colleagues to see the masterpiece, and we all met in front of the theater.

I was shocked to see Anna arrive with another man. She looked uneasy, and when Aiming asked the man's name, she sheepishly introduced him to everybody but me: Professor Yao, a specialist in aerodynamics. His attire and manner identified him as a postwar graduate student trained in the West. He looked about 15 years older than Anna, and had a small physique and boorish Hunan accent; not a nice match for her at all.

I stood outside the circle and read a synopsis of the play, assuming that nobody noticed her omitting me.

During the intermission, Aiming asked me, "Why didn't Anna introduce her boyfriend to you?"

I shrugged. "I was just standing too far from the rest of you."

Aiming said that Professor Yao had finished university in 1943, and had been sent to the US by the KMT educational authority in 1946 to be trained as one of the experts serving postwar reconstruction. After the Korean War, the CCP painstakingly launched a campaign to get the elite group of aeronautic engineering experts back. He was one of them and was now working at a research institute affiliated with the Defense Science Commission, he had the military rank of colonel though he wore plain clothes.

A bell ended the intermission, and we returned to our seats. My mind frequently wandered from the stage, only to be brought back by the audience's laughter.

The next evening, Aiming found me in the corner of our dining hall, sitting away from everyone else. He beat around the bush, trying to revisit the topic from the theater. As close friends, we had long shared our psychological burdens, but recently he'd been elected to the YL branch committee and was now obliged to tell everything to the Party branch leaders.

He probed and I dodged. Finally, he got to the point. "You must have disturbed Anna. There's a secret between you two, I can see it."

"Please don't chase the wind and clutch at shadows. It was only a casual meeting at the theater."

"You can't fool me. Every time you walk into our office, she glances at you with tender, amorous eyes."

I pretended to perk up. "Really? I haven't gotten any signals."

"I have an eye for these things. I'm sure you could break up her relationship with Yao, but the masses would attack you for sabotaging another man's happiness. They've dated a long time."

"Ethically, I'm in the clear if I chase her before she's engaged. But I don't plan to, because we have nothing in common."

"Anyway, your financial situation can't meet her high demands, but the old professor can. Even if you won her now, she'd be frustrated sooner or later. Cold wars at home would sap your energy and kill your ambition."

The next Sunday afternoon, while jogging along a country road to kill the loneliness, I saw the two guest geologists from Sichuan who worked in our division. Zhao and Chu were married to peasant wives back in their home villages, but they couldn't hide their admiration of the urban style of love and family life, which, in their view, my being a single Beijing resident afforded me. More than once they had urged me to chase Anna, even predicting I'd succeed. Now as I stopped to chat, Zhao gave me a quizzical smile. "Have you gotten close to her?"

"Bad news, an officemate told me that he saw her hand-in-hand with another man at the Wangfujing Department Store."

Chu, a short-tempered guy, said, "We met them too, on the wide staircase. That old man can't compare with you."

"But his wallet can. The old monkey earns five times what I do. Most women are practical."

Zhao waved it off. "You need confidence. A natural woman, even the Moon Goddess, would feel partial toward a guy like you. Believe Chu. When the Lord of Heaven bestows you with a rare chance, you won't win it with your hands down, you have to battle your rival."

I used their Sichuan dialect to feign indifference, "Chasing a woman who's going out with a high-ranking man will make me a rabbit for the hungry political hounds."

"You have to pay attention to ways and means. At least you can secretly keep in touch with her."

Chu threw his hands up in the air. "It's worth it to strike a blow for love. Your punishment will be temporary, but your happiness will last a lifetime."

Moved by their solicitude, I invited them to have a drink at a shabby roadside restaurant. Sitting among the local peasants,

we enjoyed some northern cuisine: eggplant fried with garlic
and casserole-stewed pork. I was surprised by their capacity for
liquor as well as for their forthright talk. Normally, I didn't
touch hard liquor, but that day I lifted the ban.

31

After each hectic day and evening, I tossed and turned in my
bottom bunk. Above me was a member of the Korean
minority, a hydraulic model tester, he played soccer and got
drunk every payday. A researcher of construction material slept
in the next bunk; he carried a defensive look and never spoke
first. My other two roommates were political activists with
chilling glances. Building materials were scarce in the north, so
instead of the relative luxury of a wooden platform, I lay on
meager bamboo strips arrayed between wide gaps, and my
cotton-padded mattress was thin. It was hard on my back, and
I felt every slat.

During the sleepless time, I no longer considered the five
Soviet-trained engineers as my competitors, because they were
unworthy of their ranks. Calling them straw bags was too
caustic. In contrast, Anna's aerodynamics professor possessed
real knowledge and ability. To catch up with him, I had to
struggle desperately. Itching to sharpen my sword for a fight, I
would become fully awake.

To catch the hours escaping through my insomnia, I used a
flashlight to study math under my comforter. However, it gave
me a headache for little gain and a hangover the next day.

My impatience to change my social status began to annoy
me. It would take a long, strenuous, even risky struggle, with
no guarantee of success. Noticing the signs of my impetuosity,
Aiming wanted to have a heartfelt conversation with me.

In the past seven months, as new employees, we'd gotten to

know each other and built up mutual trust. He'd grown up in Shanghai and attended university there. His cosmopolitan upbringing put him in awe of Western culture, he particularly relished Hollywood movies and Beethoven. In contrast, the vacuum of my lonely childhood had imbued my life with Chinese classics and folklore. Our ragged mining region had showed me the extent to which poverty, plague, and superstition dominated the wretched majority who lived there. Our stories, from such different backgrounds, complemented each other's, and we each alternated between narrator and audience.

We found other common interests. He regretted having missed a chance to go to the US when his family situation could have allowed it. I admitted that losing the chance for graduate studies in the Soviet Union had touched me deeply. Like a mirage, the opportunity had emerged briefly, flirted with me, and flitted away.

It was early April. We strolled around a soccer field in a golden sunset. After exchanging information about Stalin's atrocities, recently revealed by certain bold writers, he turned to me. "I'm glad you backed out of the dangerous situation with Anna."

"She's in her proper place. Some coworkers blame her dating an old man on bourgeois desire. They're dogs catching mice. She has her freedom of choice. Our tradition praises the marriage of talented scholars and beauties."

"But you're depressed."

"Not much. The lost opportunity spurs me to become a racehorse. Someday I'll be someone in our field."

Aiming smiled. "The day will come when you can hold your head up. While most people around us are muddling along, we should keep a low profile and move forward slowly like ice-breakers."

"But how great if we could go abroad for training."

"Nice, but not necessary. Look at Zhuquan Cai, the factory worker who invented all those advanced lighting filaments, and Dr Wu, the first Chinese surgeon to reconnect a severed hand. Neither visited foreign countries."

Our friendship and shared professional ambition boosted my morale. As usual, I arose each morning at 4:30 to study math and Russian. I used all my spare time outside of work for that purpose. Tiny slips of paper with unsolved math problems and new Russian words filled my pockets and helped me pass the tedious time I spent on buses. During marathon political discussions, I could find a safe corner to glance at them. Even on my sickbed, I used them to fulfill my self-assigned plan. I wanted to become a specialist in my field, defeating those big eagles without real ability and learning.

Most Party members, including our division director, Old Ma, looked reserved and sluggish about the March toward Science. Maybe they felt they were losing the superiority they built up in the turbulent years, or considered the enthusiasm for professional pursuits as a resurgence of a bourgeois spirit.

At a weekly YL group's self-examination meeting one Thursday night, the Party member in charge of youth work came to listen to our mutual criticism. He raked me over the coals for studying in the lab instead of participating in 'voluntary' labor on the previous Sunday. "Our Party requires us to become *Red and Expert*. We need a correct direction to prevent two kinds of deviations. One is, 'Becoming expert before one becomes red'; the other is, 'Becoming expert without having to become red'. Beware, comrades, they are tendencies toward bourgeois individualism."

I said, "The March toward Science has just begun. We can't give up technical study for fear of swelling individualism. Lenin said, 'Only those who are equipped with the entire culture developed by mankind can become genuine communists.' Measured by that standard, our knowledge is too little."

Knowing my words were useless, even harmful, I decided to study secretly. If there were two or three hours available, I would go to Beijing Library, wasting money and 40 minutes by taking the trolley. In the meantime, I broke a linear algebra textbook into loose pages and folded a few of them into my pocket like a hidden gun. I wouldn't squander time even in the lavatory, equipped with only flushing water and porcelain pits. Reading a page behind the door, my legs became numb from squatting on my heels.

We celebrated May Day, 1957 with exuberance: the First Five-Year Plan for economic development, started in 1953, had been successful. The fireworks would begin at nine, but we had to be in Tiananmen Square before six, waiting for half a million people to sit in an orderly fashion on the ground. The pavement was hard on our thighs.

Against the noises of loudspeakers, drums, gongs, and shouts I shouted toward Aiming's ear, "How stupid it was for me to skip Sunday's *voluntary* labor," I said. "I saved a few hours for study, but my potential loss could be huge."

He sighed. "I'm glad you can solve the maze between professional advance and politics. The two-year intensive training program at Qinghua University is a good deal because trainees get a salary to study for two years, and many famous professors are going to teach them. But without Party membership, you and I can't get into the program."

It hit the sour spot in my heart. "I know. Smiling Tiger is the lucky man selected from our division. He isn't qualified to study solid mechanics."

Aiming breathed on his glasses and wiped them with a handkerchief as he dug into his memory. "It's hard to say. You need Party membership to qualify you for the opportunity of promotion study. On the other hand, to gain Party membership, you have to neglect professional study in order to achieve outstanding political performance. Unlike the KMT, which was like a club that everybody could join, to join the CCP requires clearance of your family through three generations, and you must be battle-tested over many years. So, I didn't struggle to join the Party at university."

"Don't worry. You can board the next train. It'll come soon."

"Who knows?" He put his glasses back on. "The real psychological hurdle is, I'm not ready to become a Party member. I haven't discarded my selfish concerns."

"I think it's better to put personal purification ahead of Party membership."

"In wartime, heroes were tested by the rain of bullets. In peacetime, speculators gain ground by paying lip service. As a result, ever since 1949, the students we have sent to the Soviet Union are mostly good political performers with a less-than-average academic level."

I laughed. "We should be honest with the Party. But don't think we can't become Party members until we've become saints."

He hit his palm with a fist. "Today, *The People's Daily* published the decision of the Party's central committee to launch a large-scale rectification. An opportunity like this comes only once in many years. Let's dive in as activists and establish our credibility with the Party."

32

The Rectification Campaign started the next day, and ideological battles again overrode research. The March toward Science automatically ended.

Up to this point, all the campaigns had targeted people outside the Party. This one seemed to aim at despotic Party leaders and disreputable government officials.

The masses were invited to help the Party get rid of the Three Devils: Sectarianism, Subjectivism, and Bureaucracy. We were encouraged to recount everything we could, with no reservations. Party Central pledged to regard as respectful warnings all criticism aiming at wayward Party members and not to punish anyone who spoke up. Suddenly, satiric essays and cartoons appeared in *The People's Daily* criticizing corrupt Party cadres. Everything seemed to predict the advent of a democratic era. For years, the Party had taught us that in a socialist country, people should enjoy freedom under the leadership of the proletariat. Also, contrary to false democracy in capitalist countries, our democracy, under centralized guidance, was the best. How lucky we were!

Our division Party secretary, Liang, assigned me to take notes at the Free Airing of Views conferences because I wrote faster than most of my officemates. To affirm the Party's sincerity, he also told me not to write the names of anyone who spoke.

For two days, all my coworkers appeared shy or reserved, and our meetings often fell into awkward silence. The third day, a woman receptionist complained tearfully about her not having a salary raise in 1956. Then, a geologist echoed her grievance with the sad story of his family's geographic separation.

I couldn't help laying down my pen to make a remark, "We're learning from the Soviets in every aspect. From their movies and novels, I feel they have the freedom of choosing jobs and moving around. They seem to have no problem with family reunions. Why don't we learn from the Soviets in this aspect?"

Aiming interrupted me by switching the topic. "I'm angry with Comrade Bai, the head of our security office, for beating his wife, a nurse at our infirmary. I happened to be there to see him grab her by the hair and raise his fist. When the bystanders cursed him, he shouted, 'Don't you know whom I'm punishing?' As if he has the right to beat his wife."

A few colleagues giggled under their breath. The revelation lifted the gate of gossip. Everyone tried to contribute tidbits to make a story from what he or she had observed. We laughed heartily, but Party Branch Secretary Liang, presiding over the meeting, was disappointed. "Don't waste time on chicken feathers and garlic skins. Say something important, with social and political significance."

Aiming turned red. "Isn't wife beating a significant social and political problem?"

Liang waved his palm with a superior's smile. "Wife beating is a private problem, belonging to lifestyle. Only class struggle and attitudes toward the Party's policy are important. We can't deviate from the correct line."

The large room turned quiet. Then, once again, he wooed the senior engineers to speak out about what had bothered them the most, even begging them to dispel their misgivings. "Any retaliation from Party cadres for what you say now will be punished. Trust me, please. If, in the future, you find out I've cheated you, you may sue me, slap my face, write my surname upside down, and curse my mother."

No matter how humble and earnest Comrade Liang appeared to be, the seniors who'd been targets in previous campaigns kept uttering compliments to the Party.

The frustrated secretary asked me if I had any good ideas to lure the old fogies into speaking out. I suggested having one-to-one meetings with them. He insisted on my accompanying him. I said, "If I carry a pad to take the minutes for you, the meeting would look like an interrogation."

"No, your role is to represent the masses and show your trust in the Party. Your persuasion would be ten times more effective than mine."

"So, I don't need to bring a pen or a pad."

"No." He traced a circle around his temple with a finger. "Just memorize what they say."

The first target in his mind was Old Bian, a dapper, well-groomed man, who graduated in 1946, with a bachelor's degree in civil engineering. His historical burden, two-year service in the KMT Army's Corps of Engineers, had weighed him down. In 1956, he was ranked ninth, two steps lower than seventh, which he would've deserved if he hadn't had the dark shadow of KMT hanging over him. I guessed Liang knew what Bian was disgruntled about but had difficulty fishing it out.

Bian spent weekends with his family downtown, staying with us in the bachelors' dorm on weekdays. The evening we went to his room, his roommates immediately got out. Liang was born in Shanxi and comported himself with a mild tone, blinking eyes, and a perpetual smile. Tempered by previous campaigns, Bian comfortably told stories, spiced with a mimicked Shanxi dialect, about how Shanxi merchants got rich in Beijing before 1949.

Reaching the end of his patience, Liang repeated the statements he had made at the rallies. Old Bian clammed up, ending the conversation with the pet phrase of the times, "The Party's achievement is primary, shortcomings secondary and inevitable in its progress. I'm very happy with my situation."

Rebuffed by Old Bian, Liang set his sights on Engineer General Qian, with a ranking of second, the highest at our institute. His father was the last chief commander of the Qing Dynasty's capital garrison. With family funds, he'd studied civil engineering in Germany before World War II. He became infamous for his complaint, "The buses in the outer suburbs of Beijing are not as good as the prisoner trucks in Germany." He'd denied the accusation, but most people believed he'd said it because it fit into his overall image. Recently he'd stayed at home most of the time on doctor-approved sick leave.

On a Saturday afternoon, Liang and I jostled along on the

crowded outer suburb bus line. Chewing over Engineer General Qian's notorious remark, I guessed it would be an abundant source of grievance, and our trip wouldn't have been made in vain.

In a quadrangle bungalow, he sat in a rattan armchair, unable to stand up to greet us. I worried the chair wasn't strong enough for his fleshy, Buddha-like body. After Secretary Liang made clear what we had come for, Qian began to complain about his illness. "My blood pressure shot up to 220 yesterday. I feel dizzy all the time." Then, a fit of asthma and coughing stopped him.

His old wife handed him a pill and a cup of water. When he calmed down, Liang gave him a lecture about the Party's policy of opening the door to rectification. Soon, his head fell aside, his eyes half closed, and his snoring made us gaze at each other in despair. I shook his arm gently, but he snored even louder. Embarrassed, his wife put a cold towel on his forehead and slowly woke him up.

Feeling sorry for our leader, I pushed Qian. "Secretary Liang has come personally to invite your criticism. Please do him a favor and let out what's bottled up in your chest. Otherwise, he'll be blamed for returning empty-handed."

He tried to say something in a full sentence, but his throat sounded like a broken bellows. "The Party is glorious, correct, and great."

In our final effort, we talked to Zhu, an expert in groundwater dynamics, in a corner of the mess hall during lunchtime. Normally garrulous, he was quiet in the presence of the Party secretary. Irritated by a half hour of beating around the bush, I noticed the gap left by his two missing front teeth and remembered how children made fun of his faulty pronunciation of certain words. I poked him. "Has the man apologized for knocking out your teeth? How was that case settled?"

He flew into a rage. "No. Five years ago, I was interrogated as a money embezzler. Shao, the fake leftist, punched me during a struggle. I lost two teeth and bled a lot. My name was cleared, but I was forbidden to argue with the son of a bitch, because our leaders want to protect him as a campaign activist. He has trampled the bodies of innocent people to climb up ..."

Secretary Liang eventually gained something to report. I was also satisfied for helping him harvest a vivid example of subjectivism and bureaucracy, which the Party had pledged to get rid of.

33

Though it was an emergent period of the campaign, Old Ma and I were approved to go to Qinghua University twice a week for a course given by a Soviet professor. The class consisted of university teachers and industrial researchers, but the Russian taught undergraduate stuff. Privately complaining about the waste of time, we attended the class regularly to preserve Sino–Soviet friendship. I took it as a chance to see my high-school friend, Jushi Yin, on that campus. He'd invited me several times and complained that my not yet coming to see him was an example of the inconstancy of human relationships. He looked down on his job, which he considered a waste of his talent.

The Free Airing of Views developed rapidly there. Just two weeks after the campaign started, the campus was seething with big-character posters. The walls around the administration center had been fully covered, and fresh articles were glued on the pavement. The striking titles and bold arguments challenging the authorities, not seen since 1949, brought an ominous tension into the air. The thousands of viewers, many coming from other schools and cities, made no sound except muffled coughing. They read the criticisms with rapt attention and stepped gingerly to protect the handwritten papers on the ground. Moving along with them, I sensed my coincidental presence at the center of a big historical and social storm.

Like a volley of fire, the penetrating essays converged on class struggle theory and the political control exerted on the students. They denied the famous Stalin formula: "The greater the socialist cause achieves, the more sever the class struggle will become, and the deeper class enemies will penetrate into the revolutionary camp." From that assertion, China's educational authorities had deduced a theory that 80 percent of university students belonged to the bourgeoisie. The sharp observers also revealed the existence of blacklists dividing students into left, middle, and right, which unfairly determined individual futures. To counter this malady, the writers demanded personal freedom and equal rights for competition without prejudice.

Two months earlier, the Party's secretary general, Xiaoping Deng, had given a speech at that very campus, which had been relayed through phone lines connected to loudspeakers at numerous other universities nearby. He warned Chinese students not to try extreme democracy, such as demonstrations on the streets. He said, "We have three million PLA troops."

Reading such bold posters, I suddenly remembered the warning issued by Ke, the current mayor of Shanghai and later posthumously honored as Chairman Mao's Good Student. Ke's words, published in an inconspicuous corner last winter, hadn't gotten much attention from people I knew but they came back to me then. "There has been an undercurrent in China since the Hungarian Uprising."

Which should I follow, the truth or the Party's top-notch leaders, Deng and Ke?

At this moment, the most emotional and sensational subject was the 1955 Eliminating Counterrevolutionaries Campaign.

Posters put on a wall by Guo Sima, an architecture student born in Indonesia who held double nationality, had drawn the largest crowd. His family wasn't poor, and he'd had the freedom to study in the West. He came home with love and respect for the place where his parents were born. But he was rounded up as a suspected spy. The whole summer of 1955, he'd been jailed by his classmates, often denied food or water, deprived of sleep, and scorched with spotlights in hot weather.

These brutal, illegal actions against the 1955 targets in Beijing were exactly the same as the ones I'd witnessed in Wuhan. Without unified leadership, the nationwide movement couldn't be kept in step.

An author with the pseudonym Rolland, obviously a worshiper of the French writer Romain Rolland, wrote two articles raising a cry defending human rights. When many readers moved their pens rapidly to copy the trenchant critiques, I wished Ziwei Cao could be there, reading them along with me. If only all lovers separated by the storm could be reunited.

To add fuel to the flames, some students set up a Free Forum in front of a dorm near a corner of the large sports field. With a microphone mounted on the lectern, anyone could talk about anything, as if Hyde Park's Speakers' Corner had moved to Beijing, a dream for Chinese liberals. It was open only in the evening until midnight, so I couldn't attend. However, numerous posters saluted Guo Sima, the architecture student who had returned from Indonesia, for his speech denouncing his merciless persecution in 1955. Some articles said, "Guo Sima is an exceptionally good orator, making good use of both logical analysis and strong emotion." Many listeners wrote letters to console him, and some women even went to his dorm to express their sympathy.

Since our lectures were scheduled on Monday morning and Thursday afternoon, two hours for each session, I decided to catch the Free Forum the next Sunday evening and stay that night on campus. My friend Jushi Yin was teaching projective geometry at the Mechanical Engineering Department. He was physically short and unattractive, but had been praised by our peers as a genius during his high-school years. He was one year above me, and we'd belonged to the same drama group.

Besides his good scores and writing skills, he'd impressed me with his cynicism and frolicsome manner. During a debate, when someone held that a man courting a pretty woman must have a bourgeois world outlook, he argued, "I believe that Karl Marx never chased a woman with a pockmarked face." He'd turned in applications 12 times before joining the YL, presenting each fresh one immediately after the previous rejection, quite playfully. He'd persistently chased Hot Chili, our high-school friend who was going to graduate from medical school in 1958, considering her the best fit, and sending her uncountable letters. She hadn't accepted him but liked his flowery phrases, which she quoted and recited to her friends, including me.

He shared a room with another young teacher, who was away, so I had a bed to sleep in. After an early dinner, we walked around the campus and vented our frustration to each other about our lovelorn state and uncertain future. Before graduation, a famous scientist wanted him as a disciple, but the Party members of his class blocked his way. He cursed. "They use Marxism as a gun to deal with others, but for themselves, they calculate everything shrewdly. They're all double-dealers."

"Shut up about that. Some of them are true believers, so don't generalize the problem. For your own safety, you can't afford to piss them all off."

When we passed the Water Resources building, he pointed at its west wall and an article posted there. The author used a pseudonym, MG. It carried the title 'Defending History', which superficially sounded like a tit-for-tat statement against

'Defending Human Rights', written by Rolland. Reading the views on both sides, I found they were different in approach but equally skillful in ripping apart the 1955 campaign. The tone, mood, and opinions of MG were extremely close to those of my friend. I turned to him.

He looked uneasy.

I concluded that MG was nobody else but him. "Whoever wrote this kind of article will get in big trouble. I don't believe you would take such a risk." I said.

A look of surprise passed over his face. Then he softened. "I wouldn't. I have no problem with the Party's leadership."

The street lamps were on. The hubbub of the crowds and the noise of microphones being adjusted from the sports field distracted us. We hurried to the site of the Free Forum. A student in the Electricity Department was condemning the torture inflicted on him in the summer 1955. Then, from the midst of a wrathful audience, a young fellow pushed his way forward and climbed onto the platform. With tears in his eyes, he took the microphone. "I'm guilty. I was the inquisitor in charge of your 1955 case and led the attack on you as a hidden enemy. I apologize and beg your forgiveness."

Although I hadn't seen him in six years, I recognized him as Taizhen Zuo, who'd graduated from my high school the same year as Jushi Yin. He was now a model Party member in the Electricity Department and a member of the university YL committee.

He sobbed. "Comrades, the Party sincerely asks you to help it get rid of the Three Devils. I'm an embodiment of the Three Devils. I condemn myself."

He hugged the campaign victim. "If you forgive me, we can be friends again."

The audience broke into cheers. Following the prolonged applause, slogans roared across the large rally ground, "Down with the Three Devils!"

"Salute Comrade Taizhen Zuo!"

"Learn from Comrade Taizhen Zuo!"

"All conscientious Party members come out to expose yourselves!"

The small room where Jushi Yin and his roommate lived was filled with two twin beds, two desks, and two bookshelves, all narrow. The conditions weren't much better than mine. Before going to bed, he got a basin of hot water for me to wash my face. I found his towel stained like the rag used to wipe tables. The dirty clothes piled in the corners gave off a foul smell, depressing my imagination. That night, we talked in the dark, inquiring about each other's career ambitions and marital opportunities.

He asked about Hot Chili.

I said, "Her former classmate Guo is your competitor. He'll complete his six-year program of applied mechanics at Beijing University in 1959, and probably work in the missile industry. If she can come to Beijing next year, after graduating from medical school, I'd like to see the drama of your love triangle. Ah, I have a question: do you think MG is an admirer of Maxim Gorky, the founder of socialist realism literature?"

"Maybe. What's your opinion of his article?"

"Well-written, but its intention is ambiguous. While Rolland holds up the flag of human rights, MG requests that wronged souls accept their fate, and even those who died of injustice should joyfully close their eyes for the sake of advancing history."

He sounded at ease. "That's what the Party hopes for."

"However, his words, 'To attain their red goal, the rulers often create white terror and resort to blue laws, expelling all stupid talk about human rights or humanitarianism,' are accusing the Party. Does he equate the Party with ancient dictators?"

He paused before answering. "I feel MG is playing the role

of a kind of referee or mediator between the Party and the campaign victims. I hope the article can relieve some of the tension between the two sides. I appreciate his call to forget about the black footprints left by history."

I rolled to face his bed. "Who's allowed to act like a referee, standing between the Party and the campaign victims? Our duty is to listen to the Party, follow the Party, and defend the Party. Some posters accuse Rolland and MG of coordinating by tacit agreement: one coaxes and the other coerces."

"Rolland wants to punish the 1955 campaign activists as a part of the rehabilitation for the victims. MG asks the victims to forgive their tormentors. Judging by the venomous words Rolland used to attack MG, they don't know each other. How can they coordinate?"

"It doesn't matter if they know each other or not. Since the two articles are both written with white paper and black ink, they two authors might be caught or forced to confess."

"Do you think they're going to be severely punished? What could be the worst scenario?"

I played dumb. "I don't know. Our anxiety can't help either Rolland or MG at all. It's very late now. Let's get some sleep."

34

In the bachelors' dorm, the young men were excited about the boiling demand for freedom, democracy, human rights and the rule of law at Qinghua. Though the trip cost two yuan for bus fees and a simple lunch, four of them decided to spend a Sunday there. They asked me to be their guide to the most striking articles among the tens of thousands. I agreed. "Newborn calves aren't afraid of tigers."

As we looked forward to seeing the high tide from the western suburbs, the wind abruptly changed. At eight in the morning, June 4, a Tuesday, no Party members were in their offices. An hour later, they came back with pens and pads in their hands. Like soldiers taking their positions, they scattered to sit among us as if deploying a pattern designed to listen to everything. Secretary Liang said, "During the whole month of Free Airing of Views, some people have kept their mouths shut. Today we should let them have enough time to talk, and they have the obligation to place themselves in the midst of the Party's rectification."

The few reticent people were on edge while the whole division waited for their voices. Unlike in the past month, when I took the minutes in a relaxed atmosphere, I felt an unprecedented pressure and responsibility. As all the Party members moved their pens swiftly, I had to make my records more accurate and complete than their transcripts.

Then a young woman lab worker bashfully raised her hand. "The Party members and YL members in our compound behave like sectarians in a clique. They stick together and exchange whispered comments about us. The worst part is they add color and flavor to what they've collected."

I hesitated. The pen in my hand felt like a knife, but duty forced me to write down her words. Then, a lab trainee, a 19-year-old with a ninth-grade education, quoted a sentence from an article written by a famous artist, which was reprinted in *The People's Daily*. He held up the paper and read aloud. "Intellectuals have both the gift of, and right to be discontent with, reality."

I groaned inwardly for him. That article had been put in a special section for things that editors obviously considered heretical opinions. Perhaps he didn't know the editor's trick or the real meaning of the sentence either. He added, "I'm not an intellectual, but I'm discontented with reality too." Most of our officemates thought he was forgivable.

Two days later, June 6, Chairman Mao launched the Anti-

Rightist Campaign, accusing all the previous month's outspoken people of waging a savage assault against the Party and socialism. The month of free speech, along with the March toward Science, had become history. We automatically canceled our plan to see the big-character posters at Qinghua. Since the teachers from other cities who attended the Soviet professor's lecture had to go back to join their local campaigns, the short course was over.

The university heroes from last month were now under fire as public enemies. Taizhen Zuo, my high-school idol and a model Party member, was denounced as a traitor for surrendering on the battlefront because he'd apologized to the 1955 campaign target. His name was damned in a banner headline of the *Daily China's Youth*. Under the pressure of the thundering masses, Jushi Yin, another talented high-school idol, confessed he was MG and accepted the accusation as a stinking political criminal.

At our division, the last Free Airing of Views had enabled the Party branch to win an easy victory by catching two rightists. Secretary Liang was visibly pleased after his one-month failure to lure the old foxes to talk.

The young woman who cursed the Party and YL members as a sectarian clique was banished to a remote southern mountainous area, where she would clean a public latrine instead of lab glassware. Without a second thought, her fiancé packed to go with her. The 19-year-old lab trainee was sent back to his home province, Hunan, to forced labor as a rightist along with landlords and other enemies. This destruction of a teenage boy broke my heart. Jushi was expelled from school as an extreme rightist and sent to a reservoir construction site as a forced laborer. His salary was cut from 62 to 31 yuan.

One day, during siesta, I sat at my office desk and rested my head on my arms to have a nap. Secretary Liang came in with a dozen blue-covered pads: last May's minutes from the division's Free Airing meeting. He knocked on the desk to wake me. I stood up and leafed through the pages full of my handwriting. "Do you want me to keep them?"

"No." He stashed his normal smile. "Please write the names of all the speakers in the right places." He pulled from his pocket his personal notebook in which he'd recorded what I'd been instructed not to—their names. "Also, you missed some obscene words and sensitive phrases. You need to pull out the full sentences from your memory."

I was stunned. "Didn't you ask me not to write down their names?"

"Yes."

"Now you're breaking your promise and making me a cheater."

"Since class enemies took advantage of our sincerity to attack us, we're forced to change our policy and organize a counterattack."

I slumped onto my chair and rubbed my temples. "This will look like a plot to trap young and simple people. When I helped you persuade the three old engineers to speak out, I genuinely hoped they would help the Party with rectification. But they were shrewd. The young ones felt it was their duty to the Party to dredge up some minor complaint."

Liang's flat face turned livid, and his eyeballs looked frozen in place, like a statue of a fiend in Taoist temple. "Do you want to do it or not?"

"I can't."

"A soldier refusing an order on the battlefront would be shot."

"This is peacetime."

"This is a war, and the rightists are enemies without guns. Once they've defeated our Party and socialism, millions of people will be beheaded."

The deadlock lasted for ten minutes. Then he said, "If you haven't finished the work by midnight tomorrow, you'll get more than you bargained for."

Perplexed and scared, I went to see my former classmate Chenwu Lei, now the only cadre I knew sitting in the Party committee's Office of Rectification. The signboard had been quietly replaced with a new one, Anti-Rightist Office.

Among the five classmates assigned to the institute, Chenwu Lei was the only Party member. Nine months before, we had taken the same train from Wuhan to Beijing. For those 36 hours, he clutched his shoulder bag against his chest even while he was asleep. Through a loose corner of his bag, I spotted five large brown envelopes, which contained our dossiers. Each one was sealed with a tissue strip across the seam of the glued flap, and the red stamp on it gave me a foreboding feeling. I knew my fate was in his hands.

We were born in the same year, but he'd behaved like a didactic older brother, always correcting my point of view during our casual chats. In 1954, when a famous professor gave a speech at the National People's Congress advocating family planning, I talked to him privately, "It's easy to understand his point. Our limited land and food production can't support a rapid increase of population." His eyes enlarged like two bells and the veins stood out on his neck. "That is bourgeois Malthusianism. Listen to what Chairman Mao says!"

Later that year, he had a heart attack during a PE class, I took the lead to carry him piggyback to our dorm, then found a car to the hospital. After that, I felt his criticism of me contained both preaching and concern for my safety.

When the Party chief of our institute used his handwritten records to herald Mao's speech at the Supreme State Conference on February 27, 1927, I was baffled by the Chairman's solution to China's population problem, "Enough food for three people can be shared by five people." I waited for a few days until my friend indicated that he was in a good mood. Then I teased him, "That is not the solution to the problem. If someday, when enough food for three people must be shared by 50 people, what can we do?"

This time, he wasn't angry. He smiled, shaking a finger at me. "Don't distort the instruction of our great leader. What he teaches us is to be generous, to have the selfless spirit of communism."

His political quality and poor health seemed to have fitted him for light work at the Party committee office. The previous May, he had collected complaints and criticism for the Party's rectification. Now he was soliciting and organizing articles for the Anti-Rightist Campaign.

Still panting, I related to him what I'd said to Liang. He pushed the door closed. "Only enemies and morons say our strategy was a conspiracy. We say it was an overt scheme. We had to lure the monsters to come into the open before wiping them out."

"Who said that?"

He raised his hand reverently and pointed to the ceiling.

"I see."

"I doubt that." He took a pamphlet from a desk drawer and turned the pages. "Ah, here. 'By launching the rectification of our own accord, we've purposely created a possible Hungarian incident and broken it down into many small Hungarian incidents, staged for various organizations and colleges to deal with individually.' You know who said that, don't you?"

I nodded. "But it's wicked of me to do it against my conscience."

"Where would your conscience be if Beijing became another Budapest and Party cadres and security soldiers were slaughtered on the streets? Go back and finish Liang's assignment. Otherwise, we're no longer friends."

I'd never seen him so angry. I worried that the sudden rise

of adrenalin might bring on another attack of his congenital heart disease. Holding his trembling hands, I led him to sit down. "Okay, I'll do it, for your health and our friendship. I'll just forget about my conscience."

Writings and artistic works that praised the Party and socialism were called fragrant flowers. With the original hand drafts of wall posters collected and the contents of the blue books fully recovered, the Party committee excerpted key phrases, printed them into mimeograph bulletins with serial numbers, and titled them 'Collections of Poisonous Weeds'. Like flares flashing in the night sky, the collections illuminated their targets like slow-moving blimps.

Every morning, our loudspeaker system relayed the Central People's Broadcasting Station's warning that our motherland was facing a frenzied attack by bourgeois rightists. It seemed to be a fateful moment for the Party and for socialism: they would succeed or fail in China, and everyone had to choose a side, bourgeois or proletariat.

Three weeks after the June 6 editorial in *The People's Daily* calling for an attack on rightists, our compound was rather quiet. The targets pinpointed by the Party committee were isolated and downcast, but not hated by the majority. Like most of my colleagues, I had difficulty in seeing any anti-Party intention in the quoted phrases, which were mostly taken out of context. Party members also seemed dismayed. I could tell they were waiting for guidance rather than daring any personal thoughts.

35

To break the dull, apathetic atmosphere enveloping our compound, Comrade Qin, the institute's Party committee secretary, was forced into a public self-criticism of his poor leadership for the current campaign. At the end of his two-hour repentance, the vice minister who came to oversee the rally declared we must start an immediate overhaul of the Party and YL system within our institute.

In a few days, most Party branches had elected tougher leaders to replace the previous ones who hadn't been diligent enough in their search for enemies. As an exception, Secretary Liang of our division remained because of his catching two young rightists in a single hour. The overhauled Party branches immediately became powerful fighting forces. Under their supervision, all YL branches had to be overhauled.

The division's YL branch secretary, a delicate and well-primped woman, quickly responded to the call to overhaul the branch she led. Her nickname, Mulan, after the ancient female warrior, was a piece of sarcasm earned by her affected militancy, but she answered to it proudly. One evening in late June, she intercepted me outside the mess hall after dinner. "Do you have time to go for a walk?"

We strolled along the brook outside a preparatory school for candidates going to the Soviet Union. Young men passing by on the shaded trail, not knowing I was undergoing a grilling, glanced at me with envy. Soon after the customary questions about my daily life, she started her inquiry. "Many comrades say your attitude toward the Anti-Rightist Campaign is ambiguous and passive."

"Not really. Perhaps my actions have lagged behind my mind."

"Do you think the Anti-Rightist Campaign is necessary?"

"Necessary, important, and timely. I fully support it."

"I'm glad to hear that. However, when someone in your dorm said, 'the strategy of luring snakes out of their haunts is indecent,' you didn't refute his slander."

Her information chilled me. "I hated his remark, but I wasn't able to articulate my point at the time. Actually, I actively helped Secretary Liang lure the three old snakes out into the open. But they're too cunning to be trapped. Now, with Chairman Mao's new instruction, I know how to fight."

"What do you think about the demand for democracy and freedom?"

"It's wrong. We enjoy more democracy and freedom than people in capitalist counties do."

"How do you regard the estimate that five percent of the population should be suppressed as enemies?"

"It's a scientific judgment. In doing so we can unite 95 percent of the people around the Party."

"Why are political qualities more important than professional skills for promotion or selecting candidates to study abroad?"

"Lenin said the proletariat should train and cultivate its own experts."

I waited for more questions. She stopped. Like a customs inspector, she backed up a yard and looked me over from head to foot. "You sound as correct as *The People's Daily*. But where do you really stand? You look like someone watching a fire from the other side of the river."

"I know I'm a little slow."

Her face turned ugly, and her angry grin revealed one of her teeth, wrapped in yellow gold. "Only a little slow? Just to remind you, everybody has to be tested by fire during this campaign."

At a branch meeting. Mulan put on great airs. "The battle ahead is a life-and-death struggle to determine who wins: capitalism or socialism? Today's election has consolidated our organizational structure and leadership. Yet we need to heighten our fighting spirit. How? Let's welcome Party Branch Secretary Liang to tell us."

As if in a time of a national emergency, Liang said, "The Three Check-ups conducted by the PLA were very effective during the War of Liberation. After the soldiers had been checked for their class origin, performance of duty, and will to fight, they fought like dragons and tigers, sweeping away the KMT forces. Now, facing the formidable rightists, we have to check up on certain examples regarding their class standing, performance of duty, and will to fight."

Mulan raised her voice. "We welcome everyone to check up on himself voluntarily. We also encourage cross-examination, not sparing anyone's feelings." Looking around, she glanced meaningfully at her close followers. "We have engaged the rightists within our institute but not yet won the battle. The situation spurs us on. We must start to rectify our ranks now, tonight."

A young man, a lab technician and campaign activist, stood up. "I heard that Dapeng Liu omitted some important words when taking minutes last month. He should make it clear whether he intended to shield the evil speakers."

"At that time," I said, "I considered the recorded words as reminders or references for our leaders to improve their work. Some obscene words, yes, I didn't—"

Mulan stopped me with an upturned palm. "No explaining! Not tonight. Just jot down the questions raised by our comrades for your self-examination. You'll have plenty of time later."

Secretary Liang opened his notebook. "He probably feels lucky that he was taking minutes last May. That fluke helped him to hide his views. But a fox can't hide its tail."

"When the geology guy shed tears for his family reunion difficulties," Mulan said, "Dapeng stopped recording to talk about freedom in the choice of jobs and relocation in the Soviet Union. His admiration of the Soviet Union is a smokescreen. Denial of our success is his true intention."

Liang said, "When we met Engineer Zhu to invite his criticism, Dapeng pointed at the gap from his missing front teeth to inflame his hatred toward the campaign that closed five years ago."

"You wanted to collect complaints from him," I said. "I did that for you and believed in your sincerity."

Mulan yelled, "Shut up!"

Liang put on a false smile. "We've revealed only a few of the errors you've made. I know you spent a night at Qinghua to meet some anti-Party rightists."

"You can do an investigation," I said.

"We will. Today, we just want to let you know how serious your problem is. You'd better exhume all the mistakes you've buried before it's too late."

Liang wrapped up the meeting. "Those we have named for repentance tonight still have the chance to make amends for their faults. We'll settle accounts with them at the end of the campaign."

36

The next day, when I stood at the end of a long line to buy lunch, Old Bian, the engineer who'd served for two years in the KMT government army, approached me. With a suave voice and concerned air, he asked, "Are you okay?"

"I'm fine. Last month, when Secretary Liang solicited criticism from you, your refusal saved your skin. You're an old horse who knows the way."

He grinned widely, plugged his chopsticks into his breast pocket, and clinked his two bowls together. "My younger brother, you've shown your stand too early and too clearly. Sometimes, you have to feign ignorance and play the fool."

"I'll learn."

"Have you noticed the sign for drivers at some intersections? 'Look, slow down, then cross.' I take it as a survival philosophy. No matter how big the pressure when a campaign starts, you'd better watch and move slowly with the crowd. I'm saying this only to you. They won't punish the majority, so there's survival in numbers."

"I don't know how much trouble I'm in."

"Compared to those who charged ahead like bulls, you were rather prudent. Don't worry. Our leaders already have enough targets to fill their quota."

We moved up to the window and got our food. Sitting among the other diners, I quietly bit the buns and did a calculation: besides the young woman banished to Yunnan and the 19-year-old boy sent back to his home village, six other men, all researchers, had been labeled as rightists. The eight criminals accounted for two percent of the four hundred employees. In the meantime, the dozen lesser offenders were under fire and probably going to be expelled from the Party or the YL, or punished with administrative measures. Radicals had invented spiteful tags for them, such as *limit-touching rightist* and *rightist slipping away from the net*. Five percent of our institute's population had already been dug out to corroborate Chairman Mao's estimate.

The kitchen crews started to sweep the floor, and the empty dining hall was booming with broadcast readings of articles assigned by the Anti-Rightist Office. Bian said, "The major targets of this campaign are all clear now. It's time for you to show your talent and speak aloud as the Party's mouthpiece. Once you become an accepted activist, all the minor errors you made last month will be written off by the leaders."

Then came the crisp voice of a woman announcer through the loudspeaker. She read the Party committee's decision to commend three senior workers as honored activists in the Anti-Rightist Campaign for their political sharpness and tenacious fighting spirit.

I sneered at the broadcast. "They all have a bad history of affiliating with the KMT. Do you believe the three old foxes really hate rightists or worry about the restoration of capitalism in China?"

"You should learn something from them. They might've over-performed, but I admire them for their composure, braving irony and satire from people like you. This time, the leaders need them to fight like a squad of daggers to convict the rightists, while most people act with inertia. Therefore the Party treats them as friends and allies."

"People like me," I said, "don't understand the pains people like them have taken to whitewash their pasts. Maybe I should learn how to endure scorn and gossip like they have."

Bian left the table to wash his bowls then turned back. "Don't waste time trying to decipher the correlations among traditional ethics, Marxist principles, and political tactics. Take action to perform shining service and offset what you've been accused of."

"I don't know how to cut into the fighting formation."

He raised his eyebrows. "Isn't Chenwu Lei an old classmate of yours?"

At one o'clock I went to see Chenwu Lei. He greeted me in an odd voice. "Do you think you've done enough just by filling the names into the records? How much did you enjoy the Free Forum at Qinghua University? You think you can get by without touching your soul?"

His all-season, black Mao jacket hung loosely on his bony body. His hollow, disproportionately large eye sockets signaled his limited time on earth and gave him an air of earnest melancholy I'd never sensed before.

"My old classmate, you didn't drop me a single hint last May."

"Nobody gave me a hint about a storm that big. In fact, no Party members or branch secretaries were told about Chairman Mao's strategy. It was a surprise to everyone. For a whole month, your wavering state had me scared to death."

"I sincerely believed in the Party's open-door rectification.

Now that I know what it was really about, I want to catch up.
Can I do something to help you?"

He breathed easier and nodded. "You've come late because
of your slow awakening. But late is better than not coming."
He gave me three mimeographed pamphlets, a series of
'Collections of Poisonous Weeds'. "The campaign at our
institute remains dull. Many people still don't believe the
campaign targets intended to overthrow our Party and
government. To convince the masses isn't easy."

"You need me to write some articles."

"Some articles? You should write day and night to help
masses to overcome their doubts and expel their misgivings.
We need the walls fully covered by posters and our broadcasts
charged with firepower. I'll talk to your division leader to get
you off any other jobs."

My current productive task was to design a large-scale
machine to measure the strength of the conglomerate. Though
I had no experience, I dissembled an instrument made in Japan
for small samples, and copied the components with enlarged
sizes. My officemates laughed at my procedure, comparing it to
drawing a tiger with a cat as a model. Then, I rolled up the
unfinished drawings and put the drawing plate against the wall.

Working directly for the Anti-Rightist Office, I felt I had
strong backing. Even Mulan and Liang appeared milder toward
me. I wrote posters with apple-size characters on colored
paper. My first article targeted Director Zhang of the Structural
Analysis Division, now the number one rightist of our institute,
for advocating the bipartisan system in the US. It was long and
took up three columns on the wall of the dining hall. Thanks
to Father, for forcing me practice calligraphy, and Teacher
Meng, for teaching me composition, my article drew a large
crowd. Chenwu Lei liked it, particularly because I'd imitated
the tone and style of *The People's Daily* and quoted phrases from
Lenin's *The State and Revolution*.

I felt at ease, and justified in repeating Lenin's views: the bipartisan system of the US was designed to maintain a capitalist dictatorship, and the real difference between the two major parties lies in their different philosophies about the most efficient way to oppress the working classes. Since I'd never seen what a bipartisan system looked like, I thought of it as a ghost and then dismissed it.

But as I continued to work on other subjects listed by the 'Collections of Poisonous Weeds', conflicts arose in my mind. While criticizing an engineer who insisted on the US's superiority to the Soviet Union in science, it was hard to say he'd intended to break up the Sino–Soviet friendship and split the socialist camp—especially since it was one of the charges my older brother, Haitao, had been punished for in 1955. To follow that line of abuse would be like joining in on the torture of my own brother.

When a large number of university students protested the cruel treatment of the 1955 campaign targets, a hydraulic turbine researcher at our institute wrote an article to ridicule the estimate of enemies at five percent of the campus population. They were all accused of opposing proletariat dictatorship and inciting Hungarian-type rebellion in China. Knowing the truth, and with Ziwei's fate in my heart, criticizing the turbine researcher would trample my conscience. My sense of betrayal stopped me from writing.

My hesitation delayed production. Fretting, Chenwu Lei came to my lab. I made the excuse of a minor illness and promised to speed up my work. Aiming was writing his poster with a brush pen at the next desk. After Chenwu left with a glum countenance, Aiming, without looking in my direction, said, "Don't squander the opportunity your former classmate created for you."

"Do you feel comfortable quoting words out of context and stretching them as far as you like?"

"You're having another fit of petty-bourgeois sentiment. Our articles have nothing to do with the fate of the rightists. Their future has already been decided by the leaders, no matter how you criticize them or how you rationalize your analysis. Our work is educating the masses not to repeat their mistakes."

"It's brutal. Our accusations and malicious words will make their misery worse unnecessarily."

"It's necessary for the Revolution. The more miserable they are, the fewer the number of people that will follow them. This is a war, and we're soldiers. When soldiers are ordered to shell an enemy position, they just raise the gun barrels and fire. They can't ask the commander whether so much death is really necessary."

Normally we didn't censor our conversation in the presence of Engineer Bian. Now he shifted near us with a mug of tea in his hand.

His pure Beijing dialect vibrated through his thin lips. "My mother-in-law believes all human beings and animals will go to Hell after death. She pities the chicken but has to kill it. Every time she grabs the chicken's neck with its wings crossed and holds the knife in her other hand, she murmurs, 'Chicken, please don't complain, you're doomed to be cooked as a dish in the world of the living.' Our neighbors' little children have learned these words and chant them along with her."

Half-panicked, I asked, "Is it true that Wei Li, the military song composer, was your civil-engineering classmate?"

Perhaps feeling we disliked his uninvited talk, he abruptly walked out.

I struggled to complete the dozens of posters Chenwu Lei assigned me to write, expelling from my mind the image of the old lady praying for the chicken before killing it.

Some young women told me they'd never seen Chenwu Lei smile. It was true. One afternoon in late July, when he was escorting a cadre from our ministry to read the posters in our office building, he smiled as he introduced me to the leader. "This is the highly productive author, Dapeng Liu. He takes his articles very seriously."

The cadre shook my hand. "Xiao."

His dark face, bronzed skin, powerful grip, and bulging muscles boasted of his laborer origin. He wore a pair of cotton army pants and sandals, and his unbuttoned white shirt, sleeves rolled up to the elbows, hung outside his belt. The red words printed on his T-shirt read *Resisting US Aggression & Aiding Korea*, a reminder of his glorious combat history.

Chenwu said, "*Secretary* Xiao is here to inspect the ongoing campaign."

Judging by his age, late thirties, he probably joined the Party during World War II and was currently a small-time secretary at our ministry's headquarters. As a roving observer, his opinion about how the campaign had been conducted here would make our institute leaders nervous, at least different from what they boasted about themselves.

He released my hand and pointed at one of my posters. "At other units, I've seen articles on the same subject. Yours is the best. To defend the Party's top leaders, you don't repeat or entangle them in slander about their private life. This shows you understand Chairman Mao's strategy and tactics: while enemies attack us in their ways, we attack them in ours."

37

Secretary Xiao began to build up a Dragon's Head, a taskforce of 12 speakers he'd selected. He would train them to lead the mass criticism with the goal of liquidating the pernicious influence of rightist opinion.

At the propaganda office of the Party committee, Xiao interviewed me as one of the candidates for the Dragon's

Head. He started with a general instruction. "The rightists are turtles in a jar. We can punish them anytime. The tough problem for us is to make the vast masses know why they're wrong and dangerous to our country."

I nodded.

"We want you on the team of 12 speakers for a big rally. It'll convict the rightists, strengthen the Party's prestige, and make the masses more confident in the road leading from our current socialism to its advanced stage—communism."

"My division Party branch leaders might not think I'm eligible."

Xiao lit a cigarette and pushed his rolled-up sleeves higher. "I found no problem in your personal dossier. You have a good evaluation from the university. During the Free Airing of Views month, you vacillated like many middle elements. This helps you learn from your errors. Your practical actions have proven your awakening and progress. We want you to become a leftist through the struggle and be lifted out of the middle element. Any other obstacles?"

"Some comrades suspect me of a dubious relationship with a high-school friend, Jushi Yin. He's now under criticism as an extreme rightist for his articles written under the pseudonym MG last May. I've admired him for his talent but haven't echoed what he said. I hope you can hold an investigation into this matter. That's the only obstacle I need to remove."

"No problem, we can do that right away. But don't worry too much about a query from the Party branch. Even if you were fooled by his rightist opinions in the past, you can throw it off by self-criticism now. Your performance has won our basic trust in you."

He took one of the books piled on a side desk and handed it to me as if issuing a gun to a soldier. The thick hardcover book, *Corpus of Socialist Education*, was made up of excerpts of classic Marxist theses on socialism, and had collected recent editorials from *The People's Daily*. In deference to his dignified manner, I accepted the book with both hands and bowed to him.

He walked me out. "Like soldiers who go into battle with a light pack, we should have nothing on our conscience when take part in a political movement. I hope you become a proletarian intellectual through a baptism of fire."

Secretary Xiao assembled his 12 handpicked speakers and assigned each of us a specific topic on which to criticize the rightists by categorizing their crimes, such as advocating bourgeois ideas, challenging the Party's policy, or denying previous campaigns. My coworker Aiming was also selected as a member of the taskforce and assigned the topic, 'Why Bourgeois Individualism is the Root of All Evil'. My subject was 'Why Anti-Rightist Struggle is Necessary'. We were all beginners in writing political oratory, but Xiao required us to write convincing and powerful speeches. Though we were released from professional tasks, we had to work overtime to pass every Saturday's group examination.

Since many colleagues didn't believe there existed a specific kind of people called *rightists*, I quoted Chairman Mao's words. "Except in deserts, there are leftists, middle elements, and rightists anywhere on earth where there are inhabitants, and it will be like that after ten thousand years." I opened my speech with this quotation as a mathematics teacher begins his lecture with a theorem or axiom.

Why should the Party and government divide the masses into left, middle, and right factions? I invoked Stalin's famous instruction: 'Depend on progressive forces, isolate intermediate forces, and strike at the diehards.' Mao had modified Stalin's formula by the policy of uniting the vast intermediate forces. Nevertheless, the two great leaders were unanimous in demanding we defeat reactionary forces, the rightists.

In a month or so, the draft of my speech took the shape of

a seemingly tenable argument. To get feedback from our team members, we had a weekly collective discussion on Saturday. A female member made a suggestion. "You have to emphasize Chairman Mao's idea of treating the middle elements as good people, compared with Stalin's strategy of isolating them. It's a brilliant Marxist development by Chairman Mao because to isolate the intermediate forces would isolate the proletariat itself."

To adopt her recommendation into my draft, I wrote:

> Comrades, Chairman Mao recently taught us that the proletariat left wing of the population is a small part at one end, and the bourgeoisie right wing is also small at the other end. Only the middle elements in between form a large central part. Visualize it as an American football, in the shape of an olive, with tiny ends and a fat middle. The Party, vanguard of the proletariat, has the duty to unite with the majority of our population to isolate the rightists.
>
> However, as a class, the rightists won't step down from the stage of history. Once the opportunity arises, they will stage a comeback and try to win the middle elements over. I hope the vast middle part of the masses is aware of the danger and will stand firmly by the Party.

During the next group discussion, in a conference room, Secretary Xiao asked me to read this paragraph again. He sucked his pipe while we all waited for his opinion. Then, he pointed at me with the stem of his pipe. "This part is good, but not strong enough. If you can use your own experience as an example to advise the audience to have faith in the Party, your speech will be powerful and convincing. I mean you have to have the courage to reveal how you vacillated in May, and how you shifted your ground with the help of the Party."

After all the other members had left, he told me, "I interviewed your high-school friend, the infamous MG, in the presence of Qinghua University's Party leaders. He said you disagreed with his opinion on that anti-Party poster and warned him not to write that kind of article. I asked him why you had reservations toward his political stance, was it your pro-Party passion or merely your worry for a friend? He said, 'Maybe both.' He added that since neither of you expected the Anti-Rightist Campaign at that time, it was more likely you didn't like anti-Party criticism."

My friend was already punished and in an impasse. What he told Xiao conveyed his intention to protect me in whatever residual capacity he still had. I was moved by his goodwill but sad to see his ruin. "From your side," Xiao said, "you still need a revelation of your vacillation last May, and how you got back to Chairman Mao's line."

For two months, a new category had emerged but hadn't been clearly defined, *intellectuals*. They were incessantly showered with criticism. When the term was sweepingly applied to all educated people, practically including high-school dropouts, I couldn't keep out of that class. The continuous scolding of intellectuals sounded logical, persuasive, and earnest, making me feel shameful for contributing nothing to the Revolution and taking the victorious fruits for granted. Especially when the broadcasts blamed intellectuals for seeing the moss on the trees but missing the forest, I felt guilty for not standing up to defend the Party until I was prodded to do so.

In the final draft of my speech, I admitted how deeply I pitied the 1955 campaign targets. When my high-school idol and model Party member, Daizhen Zuo, tearfully apologized to the campaign targets, I was filled with veneration for his humanitarian spirit.

Comrades, I was wrong when I believed in my friend out of my admiration for his talent, and when I forgot that a revolution is an act of violence by which one class overthrows another. My petty-bourgeois, tender feelings toward the campaign targets led me to lose my bearings and be carried away by friendship. Thanks to the Party's timely education, I'm no longer a dupe of bourgeois humanitarianism. From now on, in all future storms, I'll firmly stand by the Party.

38

From Tiananmen Square, Chang'an Grand Avenue goes due west about six kilometers, crosses the water-supply canal, and branches off into a northbound avenue toward the zoo. That route, flanked by high buildings, provided Beijing with a new face and was frequently lined by large cheering formations welcoming foreign heads of state standing in convertible cars. Within that scenic setting, our research center built its new compound.

To greet the New Year, 1958, we young men of the institute formed another taskforce, rushing our equipment and furniture from the rural eastern suburbs to the new site in the prettiest section of Beijing. With our southern frontage recessed a hundred yards from the noisy street and the eastern boundary hedged by a line of willows along the canal, the large facility looked like a hidden park.

Within the enchanting landscape of the western suburbs, I remained in a bachelor's dorm organized like a military barracks. Four men shared the room with three double-decker bunks. Without a desk, we used the two vacant upper decks to store our cases, basins, bowls, and shoes.

The political combination of roommates, assigned by the administration, created a solemn air that dominated our daily life. One was a Party member in charge of youth work. He was born in Shaanxi, looked kind, but was secretly nicknamed Smiling Tiger by political laggards. Another was the man with a female name, who accused me of attempting to spark a Hungarian-type rebellion in our institute. They talked almost exclusively to each other. I suspected they were doing an inventory on our private speeches and social contacts. Several times, upon rushing in, I interrupted them by chance. They stopped abruptly and greeted me with phony smiles. Fortunately, I'd learned their provincial dialects. During such embarrassing moments, I would tease them by imitating their native intonations, which were dramatically different from Mandarin.

Dong Long, the geologist who'd graduated in 1956 when I did, and had been criticized for turning the lights off on the poster writers, was the fourth, and the only one I got along with.

He was born in Northeast China, but was physically smaller than me, a southerner. His dry skin made him look older than his age. He'd finished elementary school under the Japanese occupation, which had retarded his native language skills, but he was talkative and made judgments through conscience and intuition rather than by quoting books. One time, when we'd just passed by a group of Japanese tourists on the wooden arched bridge across the canal, he stated his theory: "The Japanese are smarter than the northern Chinese, but less intelligent than people born in southern China." I didn't know if he intended to flatter me. I was sure that he'd pondered the problem a long time.

On New Year's Day, I got up early and jogged in the chilly, fresh air. Near the mouth of the lake, where the canal takes in the water, I heard someone call from behind. "Dapeng, wait for me." It was Dong Long. We ran together along the lakeshore. We walked out of the pine woods and faced boundless farmland stretching toward the east. He pointed at the high peaks in the west. "This area looks pretty much like my home village, a huge plain with a mountain ridge as a natural defense."

"Wasn't the Civil War fought there, around 1947?"

"Yes, in a series of seesaw battles."

"Your area changed hands several times."

He shuddered. "Once, after a battle, I followed the villagers to search for wounded communist soldiers. We carried them to the humble medical field station on stretchers, but left the class enemies, the wounded KMT soldiers, groaning on the slopes and in roadside ditches."

"Nothing like in the movies. How did you feel about it?"

"Heartbroken. Those young soldiers were all conscripted by the KMT from poor families in South China."

Such firsthand information couldn't be gotten from other sources.

The irregular schedule during the moving and setting up offered us snippets of free time, one or two hours, even longer. Whenever a chance came, my coworkers would make off at once to shopping centers or nearby scenic spots. But my zest for sightseeing was dampened by a letter from Chuju with a recent photo of her poised on a balance beam.

In the past year and a half, we hadn't written to each other. I'd thought she'd already forgotten me. Now, 19 years old, a full-grown woman, she surprised me with her grief-stricken and accusatory tone.

Dear Dapeng,

You must be having a good time, or why would you have forgotten us? Ironically, my poor mother always says good things about you. When you were at university, I'd receive a letter from you every semester. Since your visit home 18 months ago, you haven't sent me a single word, especially as one blow after another has hit my family.

In 1949, when the PLA captured my brother-in-law, a battalion commander in the nationalist army, my oldest sister was 17. She was left in a primitive mountain village in Yunnan with her parents-in-law, the entire clan watched her closely to ensure she remained chaste. In 1955, the government notified her that her husband had received a 20-year sentence in a labor camp. Her nightmare was her secret alone until 1957, when a cousin in our home county learned the truth and told my mom. Following the bad news, my father died of a heart attack while on duty in an iron mine hundreds of miles away.

In our financial crisis, my second oldest sister, Minqing, hastily married a senior PLA officer, an honest man whom she couldn't love. Seeing the unkempt groom, who was nearly as old as my mom, the neighbors ridiculed her marriage as, "a flower planted in oxen dung." Minqing certainly could have done better if our father hadn't died. To support Mother, I dropped out of school and enrolled as a trainee in a machine factory near my home. A few months later, the factory manager chose me as an assistant accountant. In terms of my education and career, I'm in a dead lane.

My family's financial difficulties seem to create a void when it comes to attracting single men, especially if they have power and resources. The big pressure came from political cadres on behalf of

their bosses or fellow officials. As long as that
nuisance lasts, slander comes from rejected suitors.
Eager to end the annoyance, Mother pushes me to
write this letter. I used to believe all other men are
fickle and that you were an exception. But I
might've been dead wrong.

Chuju

At first glance, she sounded strange, given how coldly she'd
received me during my home visit in the summer of 1956.
Subsequent readings of the letter brought me heavy memories
of our childhood during the war.

To some extent, at least subconsciously, I'd been waiting
for Chuju to grow more mature, and to nurture her mother's
good wishes into passionate feelings for me. Her letter and
photo proved that she still honored a promise her mother had
made to my family years ago. As circumstances pushed her to
marry, she considered me her first choice. Perhaps my biggest
advantage was my working in Beijing, a chance for her to leave
our hometown, a rather primitive area.

On the other hand, if I couldn't make the decision to marry
her, she wouldn't remain available to me for too long. If I
couldn't move her to Beijing, I would lose my advantage.

In her photo pose, she rested on the balance beam doing
the splits, her waist twisted and arms stretched out like an
actress of the Beijing opera. She smiled amorously as though
posing for my appreciation. Suddenly, I felt it was a spiritual
victory to have a lady's picture in my pocket, I would not let
the other wretched fellows in our dorm regard me as totally
hopeless.

Whenever I was alone, I'd look at it, and a Tang Dynasty
poem came back to me:

Covet not a gold-threaded robe,

Cherish only your young days!
When a flower opens for you, gather it,
Why wait for an empty bough?

During the mild and sunny holiday, I followed other Beijing residents around the scenic site adjacent to our compound, with Chuju's letter and photo in my pocket. The forest extending from our backyard shaded the cemetery, which was exclusively for the princesses of the Qing Dynasty. The ornamental marble columns, stone guards and horses often inspired me to meditate on tales of the ancient royal family. Farther north, the canal connected with Jade Pond, and a platform marked where the late emperors used to drop their fishing lines.

Seeing romantic couples strolling the serene trails and cuddling among the cypress trees, I could imagine Chuju there with me, alluringly turned out in the popular 1956 Beijing style: close-fitting, blue-green blouse, navy-blue, tailor-made pants, and dark leather shoes, the Western fashion that recent foreign leftist movies inspired liberal young women to emulate. In the summer of 1957, they were seen in bright décolleté, their hair coiled into French twists, and their pretty feet in red flats. If Chuju were here, the vibrant urban fashions would showcase her simple beauty and accentuate her supple, athletic carriage, which outshone many of the young Beijing women I'd met.

I believed her mother's betrothing her to me had helped her retain a seed of love in her heart, which could have sprouted and flourished had we been allowed to live near each other.

However, time and distance had alienated her from me, and planning a visit home was daunting. The weeklong railway roundtrip, even on the cheapest hard seat, would cost a month's pay. Getting permission to take leave would be even harder. As the cold weather in the north had forced me to buy warm clothes, a thick blanket, and a pair of pigskin boots, my savings had grown much more slowly than I'd expected. In a year and a half I hadn't accumulated enough money for a home visit.

Everything looked unreal to me. I hesitated. Chuju and I lacked the passion mature people needed to talk about marriage. We hadn't dated like young couples in big cities. We'd had only one private meeting in our whole history, a 40-minute chat in a tiny backyard. When I did make a date with her, she stood me up.

I sent her a friendly letter saying we needed more mutual understanding. If circumstances allowed, I would visit home.

39

One evening, at dusk, the temperature dropped to freezing point. My roommate Dong Long and I walked home from the Military Museum after an hour's hike, following the lampposts along the lakeshore and canal. When we touched on the topic of how difficult it was for us men at the bottom of the hierarchy to find suitable women in Beijing, he said, "Beijing's crowded with lonely eligible men—transferred military officers, university graduates, experts returning from abroad ... There aren't enough educated women. Ordinary men are in a panic."

I took out my wallet and handed him the photo of Chuju. He stood under a lamp and scrutinized it from various angles and distances. "She's gorgeous. If someone like her came to our neighborhood in Beijing, she'd be pounced on by the rich and powerful before you got a chance to know her."

"You think I should marry her anyway?"

"If you prefer beauty to career. If you can't move her to Beijing, you'd have to be happy to give up your career for a family. If you want to keep your job in Beijing, you better marry someone here. You'd have no problem finding a woman with a higher education, but she would of course be less pretty than Chuju."

"I have no social life in Beijing, and hardly any women work in our compound. The few we have are nice coworkers, but marry them? It's hard to give up Chuju."

He handed back the photo. "Who knows what our future will hold?"

"The Anti-Rightist Campaign seems to have come to an end," I said. "What's next? Do you think it's proper for me to have a home visit during the quiet time?"

"There's a new episode starting. In five years, all educated personnel in Beijing will have to serve one year of physical labor with peasants or industrial workers. If you ask for leave, people will say you want to escape the physical labor."

"What if I make a strong statement at a meeting before asking? I can say I'd be very pleased if the Party allowed me to do my term the first year of the plan."

"Not strong enough." He pondered for a few moments then grinned. "We should write a jointly-signed poster demanding the Party committee list us in the 1958 group."

I hesitated. "Don't take chances. If the leaders take your words the wrong way, you might be sent away for a whole year's physical laboring to remodel your mind."

He looked at me with a cunning smile. "If the leaders don't want you to go laboring, your brave shouting won't make them send you. On the contrary, if you fear being listed and keep silent, they can single you out and force you to go. According to my observations, Old Ma needs you to stay here and help him."

I used a brush pen to write big characters on red paper to request that the leaders send us to the countryside for a year's hard farm work as he suggested. At the end of the poster, he insisted on adding the pet phrase of the time, "Without being tempered in the raging fire of the Revolution, our hearts cannot be turned pure red!"

We pasted our manifesto on the front wall of the dining hall, close to the entrance. It stood there for quite a few days before being covered by other posters.

As Dong Long speculated, neither he nor I were included in the first group.

One morning in the middle of January, we had a stylish sendoff for 80 or so of our colleagues leaving for remote construction sites, beating drums and gongs and pinning red paper flowers on their chests.

The next morning, the six engineers and technicians labeled as rightists were sent to a labor camp in the Gobi Desert after being thoroughly berated, and convicted by our ministry Party committee. The young woman banished to Yunnan and the 19-year-old boy sent to his home village were also formally condemned as bourgeois rightists.

Around 6:30 am, all six of them sat on the curb outside our boiler room, waiting for the coal-hauling truck to take them to the Front Gate railway station. One of them, Dalu Cui, had joined the Party's underground in Shanghai before 1949, this won reverence from us bachelor-dorm residents, especially since he'd fought alongside the famous martyr Xiaohe Wang, extolled by the movie *Immortal Fighter in the Raging Fire*. Unfortunately, he had complained about top leaders replacing their old wives with young city girls after the Revolution.

I was in the boiler room with a thermos to fetch hot water, and the line was conspicuously longer than on other days. During the slow minutes, my idol, now a state enemy, raised his head to have a final look at me, showing a numbed expression. He bowed and rested his head on his knees. I was full of sorrow for him, a revolutionary hero punished as a traitor because he'd criticized the corrupt leaders. I felt guilty for what I'd said under the circumstances.

A few minutes later, from my dorm on the fourth floor, I watched him climb aboard the truck and sit on his bedding roll. I watched the earflaps of his cotton-padded hat flutter in a piercing wind until the truck disappeared. A labor camp in the Gobi Desert awaited him. There, in all likelihood, he would be buried along with his knowledge, talent, righteousness, and independent thinking.

Pushing on in the flush of political victory, our leaders publicized a sexual crime, and an illegal abortion associated with it, to stop noxious capitalist influences. The two brothers punished were both 1956 university graduates and had worked in the Hydraulics Division. Their coworkers admired them because of their strong physiques, easy-going characters, and their membership of the Beijing Ice Hockey Team. Unfortunately, they had difficulty finding wives. The peasant woman they hired from the outer suburbs to take care of their ill mother was married, and she had left her husband at home. In their cramped living space, she had an affair with the older brother, and became panic-stricken by certain symptoms of pregnancy. To cover up the scandal, the younger brother and their older sister, a medical doctor recently convicted as a rightist, secretly arranged an examination and an unauthorized abortion.

As the result of the joint investigation by the court, the Party leaders of the hospital and our research center, the two brothers were sentenced to a two-year jail term. The woman involved in the case was deported to her village. The sister, doubly guilty, taking her political violation into account, was sent to a labor camp, ending her lenient treatment of being remolded under surveillance by the hospital personnel.

Their violation contained several aspects, but the long post pasted on the wall of our office building didn't say how much the abortion had attributed to their punishment. In the same period, a woman in our group, who had two children, aborted her fetus without authorization from her leaders. She was punished with a record of demerit and a notice of criticism that was circulated within our institute. I took her case as a reference on the gravity of unauthorized abortion.

The ice-hockey brothers had lost their jobs. After their two-year jail term, they would be regarded by the whole society as *bad elements*, one of the five categories of class enemy. This episode was cheered as a great victory for the proletariat against the bourgeoisie on the political and ideological front. The Party and the YL system called for a lesson to be drawn from the two brothers' moral degeneration and their surrender to an unhealthy relationship in their private lives. But such meetings often ended up in awkward silence.

On January 16, 1958, during the peaceful lull, I passed by Tiananmen Square. Two dozen old men were marching with a banner, 'We Want to Open Our Hearts to the Party'. It looked odd and funny. The next day, I learned from the news media that they were political celebrities, leftovers from the old regime taken in by the CCP as figures displaying a United Front Line. Their slogan sounded like they were ingratiating themselves with the Party while making a courteous suggestion to the whole population. I felt nothing compulsory or threatening.

By February, the flames of the Open Heart to the Party Campaign were scorching any silent individuals who'd been suspected of having a dubious past or harboring heresy. Any deeds, words, expressions, or feelings revealed as harmful to the Revolution were criticized as if they were poisonous weeds being burnt.

Nevertheless, during a break in a senior engineer's confession, I gingerly approached Secretary Liang, who was presiding over our division's rally. "My parents are very sick. I need leave for a home visit."

He looked up at me as if in a dilemma. "I'm willing to help

you, but I can't. The Party committee has ordered, in writing, that nobody is to leave unless declared physically unable to attend meetings by a doctor."

He leaned back and tapped his head. "This is a conscientious revolution taking place here. Cleaning up bourgeois influence means fighting invisible enemies. Nobody can stay out of the battle. Please put off your home visit."

40

The first two weeks were easy and leisurely for us young workers with simple histories, while the fire licked at the feet of Engineer General Qian and Engineer Old Bian. The two were *old-fashioned intellectuals*, an informal title but used by radicals to their faces and in public. They had a lot of bad things to say about their families and themselves. When they were forced to confess, it was like toothpaste being squeezed from a tube; we enjoyed the juicy stories.

Our good times didn't last, and we were mandated to undergo 'voluntary' self-dissection in public. During the rotating confessions, I somehow resisted the pressure and postponed my turn until the last day. Still, I couldn't offer a self-portrait of ugly pictures or sinful desires.

I admitted some minor things, including my admiration of Soviet professionals for their freedom to relocate for family reunions. As a brilliant ending for my self-criticism, I quoted the popular slogan, "My own pledge is to promote what is proletarian and liquidate what is bourgeois."

Secretary Liang sneered. "You've avoided the important and dwelled on the trivial." With an inciting tone, he asked the 60 or so division employees, "Do you let him pass?"

"No," two or three of his close followers responded.

To break the tense silence, Mulan challenged me. "Could

you show us what is in your pockets?"

I showed my wallet, handkerchief, and keys. She laughed. "Everybody has such things. Would you empty your pockets?" I hesitated, but I possessed nothing shameful. As I pulled out the hundreds of flashcards and slips of paper from various pockets, some around the long conference table, and others in the back rows, rushed up to get a piece.

"Wow, Russian words and math problems."

"No wonder he always sits in a corner during political discussion."

Smiling Tiger stood up. "These pieces are evidence of his dream to become a bourgeois expert. Even during the Anti-Rightist Campaign, he evaded Sunday volunteer labor, hiding in a lab to read technical books. He's never shown such enthusiasm in political study. He has chosen a very dangerous road. Chairman Mao recently said, 'To be expert first and red later means to be white first and red later.' Once you've become white, you're already an enemy. Do you know the danger?"

His tough words emboldened the man with a female name. "Last May, you suggested that someone in our dorm attend the Free Forum at Qinghua University. What was your motivation?"

"I've thoroughly redeemed that problem through my speech at the big rally, and Secretary Xiao has endorsed my work."

As the accusations were escalating, my close friend Aiming stood up. He was popular because he had confessed that he had wished to study in the US and that he harbored resentment toward his father for not helping him before 1949, when family money would've made it possible to go abroad. Surrendering such a sinful idea indicated his loyalty.

His morality-puffed airs brought me into a cold sweat; then he shocked me with a high-flown speech.

"I'm your close friend, Dapeng, so I have higher hopes for your improvement than for others'. You're a good socialist worker, but our ancient literature and Western novels have planted a virus in your head. A woman left her motherland to live in Hong Kong, a man-eat-man capitalist society. What are you sad about? Your nostalgia for her seems to be indelible. Such deeply seated, petty-bourgeois sentiments are harmful to you and to the Revolution. I hope you can hold me to the same critical standard. Let's criticize each other, encourage each other, and live up to the Party's hopes."

The young men were galvanized when they learned that I had a desire that would only invite trouble. They tilted forward and moved their chairs closer to our long table. Anna left the room, entrusting her notebook and purse to the woman next to her.

I had an inventory of all the accusations against me in my heart. In summation, they were not at a threatening level, except the relationship with someone in Hong Kong. I answered furiously. "Last year, in our dorm, Aiming and another young man were relishing their romances at university, but I had nothing to brag about. To hide my feelings of inferiority, I told my insipid story in a poetic way to impress them. It was a joke. How can you raise it to the height of class struggle?"

The rapid steps sounding in the corridor reminded them of the dining hall's long lines, and they became restless.

Liang held the impatient audience a few more minutes to smooth things over. He instructed me, "This is a revolution to the depth of our souls. Please take the criticism like a patient takes medicine. Be honestly prepared for your next round of *opening your heart*."

41

One evening in early March, Aiming stopped me in the corridor and invited me to eat homemade dumplings at his place. Obviously, he wanted to patch things up after his political exposure. I also wanted to bring him to his senses and prevent him from further damaging me.

He and his wife rented a place close by the North Sea Park, actually a room in one of the bungalows built at the foot of the high wall of the ancient palace. The gray bricks were poorly laid, the seams between them roughly cemented. Every family had a tap for running water set under the narrow eaves, with the aboveground pipe wound with straw ropes to prevent it from freezing. The public latrine was 30 yards away.

Their full-size bed occupied a third of the space. Between the wardrobe and the small desk sat a pile of carrying cases and cartons. A metal rack with a washing basin stood behind the door, leaving space to maneuver two chairs in the middle of the room. In the winter, they brought the stove indoors for heating as well as cooking. To keep the room warm, the four-inch stovepipe took a U-shaped detour before going out through a hole above the window. Underneath the bed, on either side of a wooden partition, they'd laid in honeycomb coal briquettes and cabbages for the winter.

My glasses blurred with the steam rising from the kettle. When I was cleaning them with my handkerchief, Aiming said, "Before 1956, my family servant had much better living conditions than this." His anger and audacity shocked me, but I felt his trust in me and the threat of his unstable characteristics.

I remembered how the Shanghai newspapers hailed his father, a pre-1949 capitalist, for surrendering his factory to help nationalize private enterprises. To the cheers of the media, he further donated his Shanghai home, a two-floor, French-style villa, to the local government. I was in Shanghai in December of 1956 and visited his parents at their home when a news reporter and cameraman happened to be there. I joyfully helped remove the furniture.

"Your father must be very excitable. The more the local government praised him, the more he surrendered to the state.

Now, his generosity makes you despair."

Yijuan, Aiming's wife, an architect, spoke rapidly in the pure Shanghai dialect. "Exactly. Aiming is also easily excited and easily despairs, just like his father. He often acts on impulse and later regrets it. Like father, like son, it runs in the family."

I faced Aiming. "Your position as a YL branch committee member has the weight of a sesame seed but it has made you behave like a standard bearer. While many people hide their wishes of going to America and say they hate the US, you revealed your desire to go there. Your confession will most likely be used against you. Don't you know that?"

Yijuan aghast. "What? You confessed that? Haven't you noticed Party members rarely expose their true thoughts?"

I nodded. "Like artillery officers hiding behind a thick embankment before ordering a bombardment."

Yijuan clicked her tongue. "A vivid metaphor."

"The secretary praises you now," I said, "but he can't protect you later. His sweet words drove you out of your mind. I couldn't believe my ears when you revealed my broken dream to that tasteless crowd."

Yijuan gasped. "Aiming did that?"

"Terrible." Aiming held his head in both hands. "I apologize for publicly pulling the scab off your wound. I'm so sorry. It was like a religious feeling came over me. I was hoping you'd confess everything to the Party like me."

Moved by his long face, I said, "Let's forget that little episode in the big tragic farce. If someone raises the question again, you have to play it down. Whoever started the trouble should end it."

"I'll do that."

I wanted to leave. When he pressed me to stay for dumplings, I insisted on going. "I'm not hungry, and your promise is better than any delicacy."

Walking me to the trolley, Aiming said, "My younger

brother was 19 and got hit by his army unit as a rightist. What had he said? Stalin is a dictator, and Tito is a hero rather than a traitor of the international communist movement. Now he's in a backwater town mixing coal and clay to make briquettes."

"Sorry for the sad news. How ironic. Your father was cited as a red capitalist and granted Party membership. A year later, his youngest son is hit as a bourgeois rightist."

His face turned red and blue veins stood out on his temples. "My father got his glorious title through the expropriation of his properties. My brother got his disgraceful label with the expropriation of his rights."

I patted his shoulder. "The storm hasn't spared my family either. Last month, when the campaign was extended to high-school students under the name of Socialist Education, my younger brother became a target. He'd complained food rations were too small and YL members don't do anything except tattle. On top of that, he was one of just a few tenth graders who tried to listen to a Taiwanese broadcast at a classmate's home. At only 16, he was expelled from school as an anti-socialist. If he'd been 18, he'd have been sent to a labor camp."

"When the nest is overturned, no egg stays unbroken." He gripped my hand tightly. "Let's protect each other from further damage."

42

As the campaign continued, all young, ordinary workers took turns to open their hearts to the Party. Without fresh energy, the leaders seemed dismayed and waited for new whims from Chairman Mao.

Suddenly, from out of nowhere, the leaders introduced a new program to our institute, Sweeping Away All Evil Trends.

It sparked accusations over improper behavior, manners, style, and speech that anyone considered incompatible with socialism or just an eyesore. Those who'd hated each other for years used it as an opportunity to settle scores. Sometimes, they united to attack the few female colleagues who had good looks, fine dresses, and genteel behavior. Anna became a target as a 'pampered bourgeois lady'.

Staying neutral toward the mutually-hating individuals, I searched for a way to cut the loss of my time that such meaningless fighting caused. I resumed my design job, and memorized some Russian words whenever I was alone in the office. We had two hours to take a nap in the summer. I quickly finished my lunch and rushed to the library, which normally had no borrowers at that time. Sitting on the cement steps of the stack room, I read a book on the functions of complex variables, a prerequisite for studying applied mechanics. I enjoyed the calm place, which was like a Buddhist temple, until the bell. In the afternoon, when the repeated and tasteless speeches buzzed on, making me drowsy, I struggled against falling asleep by biting my lips or rubbing my temples. Nevertheless, I would still doze off, and a friendly coworker would nudge me.

Then, resounding through the skies came Chairman Mao's call to eliminate the four pests: sparrows, rats, flies, and mosquitoes.

On March 20, the unforgettable day, we joined millions of Beijing residents to kill sparrows, a threat to agriculture because they eat grain. At nine o'clock whistles screeched, launching a noise attack. Car horns, bells, gongs, and firecrackers scared sparrows out of their nests to desperately glide here and there, looking for a peaceful place to perch. But human crowds hooted to prevent them from landing. The poor birds, with short wings for heavy bodies, were soon exhausted and fell to the ground, sometimes bleeding. Others sat in the trees awaiting capture.

At night, after ten hours of running and shouting in the fields, we were exhausted too. But the political activists, equipped with ladders and flashlights, continued to search for moribund sparrows under the eaves. I was sad for the birds, not sure whether they were really enemies of the state, and I was obliged to waste three days. In the evenings, I tried to study. Though too tired to focus on the books, I felt better for having salvaged a couple of hours of my youth.

During the third evening, around nine, when I was reading a Russian book on foundation design in the alcove of the lab, someone opened the front door and turned on the lights in the large hall. I tried to hide my book and dictionary, but it was too late, as Smiling Tiger had already turned the knob of my partition. With a wire wastebasket in hand, an extra container for dead sparrows, he seemed to have something to say. But he said nothing. With a meaningful nod, he left.

Within easy walking distance of our place, the Beijing Design Institute of Non-Ferrous Metals was holding a Self-Exposure Exhibition, highly praised by the Party system as, "a creative show of proletarian victories on the ideological front."

Colorful paintings with striking captions covered the walls of two large halls. Sets of pictures told stories of what had gone through the illustrators' minds. Pointing with a lecturer's baton, each narrator somberly narrated his or her experiences of, "the perils of bourgeois individualism." One set of pictures showed a woman at a desk wiping away tears with a handkerchief while glancing at her director, who was talking affectionately with another woman, her officemate. The woman said, "Jealousy represents a kind of bourgeois psychology. It's harmful to revolutionary unity and incompatible with proletarian broadmindedness." Mulan sighed with affected regret, "We all have scenarios like this in our institute every day, but we fail to see them. How ignorant we are."

At the next division rally, Liang said, "The exhibition has enlightened our minds and hearts. It tells us we should fight bourgeois thoughts everywhere and every day. We can and must catch up with our comrades working on non-ferrous metals."

However, there were many distractions. Following the annihilation of sparrows, we engaged in the Patriotic Sanitation Movement. After three full days of cleaning interior and outdoor areas, we were swept into a nationwide automation campaign. While some restaurants used conveyer belts to carry dishes from the kitchen to the tables, we were criticized for not knowing how to automate lab operations.

Then came the biggest interruption. The three water-resources research centers were merged into one large one with one thousand four hundred employees. I moved to the north campus and enjoyed a twin-size bed with a wooden platform to replace the bamboo strips under my mattress. The changes in our organizational structure demoted Secretary Liang to a less important post, and I belonged to a different group from his. His hands were no longer directly on me. Smiling Tiger was no longer my roommate, but his silent nod and accusing air that sparrow-collecting night still lingered in me.

Since the other two institutes had many senior engineers who'd worked in the old society and scientists with advanced degrees from Western countries, the masses expected to hear confessions with historical colors and exotic flavors. As Open Heart to the Party was in its final stages, I guessed the political searchlight had shifted to them. A small fry like me could at last breathe easily.

One mid-July afternoon, our machine shop called me to pick up some accessories I'd ordered. Near the factory, I met Engineer Bian. He gave me a mysterious smile and bent his index finger to lead me off my path: "Let me show you something."

He unlocked a shed near the junkyard fence. It was a storeroom for soil samples and rock cores, and smelled of the wax and asphalt used to preserve the natural moisture of the samples. I asked, "Why are we here?"

He put his finger to his lips. "Normally, only the sample keeper comes here. Now some radicals have taken cover in this dirty place. We better leave as soon as possible."

Instead, he led me to one end of the long, narrow shed, where some sketched cartoons lay on a ping-pong table. Finished ones, pasted on plywood, leaned against the wall with the pictures facing inward. He checked them one by one, then pulled one out. "Please savor this masterpiece."

In the lower part of the tableau, a young man in a four-pocket Mao jacket stood under an aspen by the canal holding a handful of flashcards. The setting bore a strong resemblance to the scenery of our southern compound. Hovering above his head, a coquettish woman in Western attire dominated his universe. And the captions said, 'Living off the fat of the socialist land, I dream of the lady in Hong Kong, the British colony and capitalist hell.'

I threw the picture back to the wall. "Junior Song, the weird chemist, must be the painter."

"Don't blame him, others put him up to it."

"No wonder I saw Mulan and Smiling Tiger hanging around here the other day."

From the pile of sketches, Bian pulled a finished painting, yet to be pasted. It showed a man on the top of a ladder, holding a wastebasket and a flashlight, while his buddy crawled beneath an eave with his legs up in the air. Near the bottom of the ladder and inside the window, the same young man as in the pasted picture was absorbed in books. The caption said, 'When the proletarian masses were catching the enemies to save our agriculture, I kept walking on the capitalist road to become a white expert.'

I grabbed the painting. "Some scientists say sparrows eat more insects than grain. They tactfully recommend substituting bedbugs for sparrows in the list of four pests."

I started to crumple it into a ball, but Bian stopped me. "No. They'll accuse you of sabotaging the campaign."

He unfolded it and flattened it on the table. "I've never seen you so rough and impulsive. You need to be prepared for what they're plotting, and not so reckless that you give yourself away."

"They're copying the exhibition held by the Design Institute of Non-Ferrous Metals. They want to trap me into confessing what I've already denied. It is very strange, Aiming has publicly admitted his dream of going to the US, and the vipers let him off."

Bian hinted with his unique smile. "Aiming left for Wuhan to join the research on the rock foundation of the Three Gorges Dam. The hunters only shoot at nearby targets."

I nodded. "In ancient novels, either a hero or a villain in a hopeless situation would say, 'Of the 36 stratagems, the best is running away.' Aiming finagled a way to leave on time."

43

When, in 1958, Chairman Mao called for the doubling of China's output of steel within the year, the Great Leap Forward injected a mania into every industrial sector. In the mountainous area west of Beijing, on the Yongding River, thousands of workers broke ground to build a waterpower station without finishing its design. The project's chief designer, a female Party member, asked our division to conduct special field tests on the rocks around the tunnel to determine how much support they could give the conduits lined with concrete and steel against the enormous water pressure. Since our group specialized in rock mechanics related to dam foundations and tunnels, we would have someone qualified to undertake the task.

Those of my coworkers familiar with this topic had been dispatched to other provinces. Old Ma, whom the recent merger had reduced from division director to be our group head due to his lower rank, didn't know how to deal with the project. Two days later, when the female designer came again, our division director, Gu, a fearsome Party veteran, ordered, "If you can't find someone suitable to go, you should go. Don't stay in Beijing all year round, drinking tea."

Soon after Director Gu left our office, Ma asked me if I could go. I said, "I only read something about it in a Russian magazine. Like a tiger hungry for the sky, I don't know where to strike first. I need time to study." He continued to mumble about his wife's illness and his heavy management load until I promised to consider his suggestion.

When I recovered from my surprise at Old Ma's request, it dawned on me that this was a great chance to escape the trap set up by Mulan and Smiling Tiger. That night, I composed a 'Written Request for Battle Assignment', following the style created by the PLA soldiers:

> Dear Party Branch Committee,
>
> When people all over the country are excited by the Great Leap Forward, I can't sit quietly in my office. Following the political and ideological triumph of the Anti-Rightist Campaign, and on the crest of our First Five-year Plan's achievement, Chairman Mao calls us to catch up to the US. We are now realizing Marx's prophecy that the revolutionary masses will accomplish in a day that which normally takes 20 years.
>
> I'm ready to undertake the toughest mission you wish to assign me. If you can't find someone more suitable to undertake the groundwork for the

Yongding Power Station, I'd like to go. Though I don't have all the knowledge needed for the project, I'll take our revolutionary forerunners as my example, learning warfare through war. I pledge to be resolute and surmount every difficulty to win victory.

Salutations,

Dapeng Liu

Director Gu received me in his office. Unlike most senior cadres who wore a navy-blue Mao suit, he chose light olive-beige and kept the creases bolt upright. Though short and thin, his protruding face, sharp nose, and piercing eyes hinted at his character, which was outspoken and belligerent. To announce a decision, he had a unique opening phrase, "The Party branch committee, which I head, has decided ..." Because of his grand airs, so far I'd avoided him in the compound.

He waved my written request, which Old Ma had presented to him. "Young man, I like your guts and enthusiasm. When many fresh workers flinch from unfamiliar jobs, you brave the difficulties and hardships."

He lit a cigarette and gestured for me to sit down in the chair opposite him. "I like your posters and public speeches. Now, your written request shows your political progress. I root for you. Go full steam ahead. Do you have any questions?"

"Some activists deliberately make my life hard. They even got excited about flashcards with Russian words on them and slips of paper with unsolved math problems in my pockets, as if they'd captured a great battlefield trophy. I kept those to make use of bits of spare time for study, like waiting at a bus stop. But the—" I tackled the word *morons* before it reached my tongue. "But the activists mistakenly exaggerated them as evidence of my dream to become a white expert."

He sighed. "Such a charge is arbitrary but inevitable during a mass movement. I like your habit of studying. But we can't ignore the public mood and live outside the mainstream. Don't worry, your past is clean and your family background simple. Most importantly, you passed the Anti-Rightist Campaign with a better-than-average score."

"Thank you. I'll do my best to reform myself."

He stood up and shook my hand. "If a soldier fights like a hero, nobody will remember his personal faults. I believe you'll change your public image and political status by good service. If you can meet the challenge at the construction site, I'll sing your praises."

44

Unlike in the past, I wouldn't have a written contract with the local authority. To realize the ambition of having China's industry catch up that of the US in 15 years, we followed slogans as our guideline: 'Long Live High-speed Construction', and, 'Breaking with Convention'. The construction site was chaotic. Deployed to set up a tiny base in an unknown area, I had to work like a guerrilla.

Director Gu showed a fondness for grandiosity and easy glory. While I was relying only on sketchy descriptions from a Russian journal to solve a problem totally new to me, he invited ten geologists and lab technicians from various provinces to "train them." For the first month, working in a five-foot-diameter shaft excavated from the rock, I had only an 18-year-old assistant to hand me tools and parts while our ten guests chatted and smoked at the mouth of the well.

Having to work by trial and error frustrated me. Over and over, I had to disassemble the whole contraption, and once even had to demolish a concrete lining and recast it. Eventually, I solved the problems. Though only 24, I was able to argue with foremen, beg local Party cadres, and coax young workers to meet my job specifications. Still, enormous difficulties with our mismanaged site and motley group persisted.

One storm-filled night, just after the middle-shift crew came back to the shed where we slept, I saw that a sheet of their test records was missing from the folder. Carrying a flashlight and wearing a raincoat, I searched the riverbank around our tent for 40 minutes and finally found the paper behind a rock.

Another evening right after we left for dinner, wastewater and rock debris from unexpected excavations buried the entire facility for our experimental shaft. We could find no-one at fault. A geologist had helped us choose the location from an old, still-authorized drawing; then, without notice, the survey team used a hastily altered design to lay a new branch of their tunnel right through our test shaft.

Bureaucratic mix-ups plagued us, too, and often drove me to panic. Returning home one evening, our testing crew found all of our belongings tossed out of the shack. The administrator, thinking the barracks we lived in was vacant, had assigned it to a concrete work crew, who had emptied it of our things.

I yearned to resume the academic plan I'd started two years earlier, which had been interrupted by the incessant campaigns. I'd stashed my personal agenda but not given it up. For the present, entangled in the Great Leap, I had to prove I wasn't a coward flinching from unfamiliar and difficult tasks. I needed to show I wasn't less capable than the Party members. I believed, finishing this job would give me a good start and, in the next ten years of battle tests, I'd eventually qualify myself to join the Party.

Still, I was exhausted, and the filthy environment had taken its toll. In and around the mess hall, flies were everywhere, even swooping onto the rims of our rice bowls as we ate. No sooner had we succeeded with our first test shaft than I fell victim to diarrhea and dysentery in the middle of September.

During the few hours when I could lie down on the bamboo-structured second floor of our living shed, I often had to scamper down a ladder and run to the latrine. Physical pain, added to the extreme work stress, emaciated me while the Great Leap raged forward.

One evening around six o'clock, a column of off-duty, able-bodied men trudged back to the mess hall past the middle entrance of the tunnel where my crew and I were working. Among the innocent faces of young peasants hired as contract workers, a familiar one, a man wearing a wicker hat and carrying a bowl under his arm, stunned me. I recognized the former political star of Wuhan University, Xiaohou Ban. We graduated from university at the same time. When he was chairman of our student union, his charm and eloquence evoked thunderous applause. Hordes of young women seemed to follow him around.

As I had learned from my fellow alumni in Beijing, he had openly questioned, in May 1957, why a poorly educated veteran cadre should be put in charge of a college, a steel mill, a museum, or an art troupe. Worse, he'd called them, "old dogs lying in the road."

He was around the same age as me, and he'd lost all his pride and his robust youth. Driven out of the Party and the workplace, he faced a society that viewed him as a criminal, bad since birth. To avoid embarrassing him, I tried to slip into a toolshed on the roadside, but he called my name. Certain that the lines in the mess hall would be long at that moment, we converted our wicker hats into cushions and sat on the dump of excavated rocks outside the branch tunnel. When I looked around nervously, he said, "The young peasants are simple. They don't give a damn about a rightist. None of them will report our meeting."

I pointed at his one bare foot wrapped with a towel. "You

hurt yourself?"

"No. The slurping concrete sucked my shoe away. You can hardly imagine what new procedures our crews followed."

"I know you cut the specified amount of cement for every cubic meter of concrete and add more water for easy handling at the cost of strength."

He stretched his bare foot forward. "And we don't use vibrators to guarantee density. Instead, we dance Yangko, a farmer's dance from Shaanxi, using our body weight to compact the concrete. Such monkey business is our way of realizing Chairman Mao's principle of building socialism with greater, faster, better, and more economic results."

"Big trouble ahead. We're ordinary people, but our tradition tells us, 'Every man has a share of the responsibility for the fate of his country.' We should let the leaders in Beijing know the mess here."

"I'm a rightist, lower than, even outside, ordinary people. Any opinions from my mouth are poison. My salary has been cut in half. I don't want the remaining 31 yuan to be cut."

At the bottom of the canyon, it was cold in late October. The evening wind carried the musical prelude of our primetime newscast blaring from a loudspeaker at the site. "Socialism is good. Socialism is fine. People safeguard the state's socialist power. Rightists want to overthrow it, but in vain."

The booming chorus dominated the space, and the furrows on his face contracted as if he was being whipped. I said, "Sorry about the propaganda song."

"Never mind, my nerves and ears have turned numb to curses." He put his wicker hat on and clutched the bowl under his armpit, pretending to be at ease. "Still, I feel sad whenever I hear kindergarten children singing this song while walking hand-in-hand with their nannies. With hatred for rightists like me planted in their hearts, I'm becoming an enemy of the next generation."

Gazing at his receding figure, I listened to the male announcer recite a long article from *Beijing Daily* under a special column entitled 'Why Should Communist Party Members Be Docile Tools of the Party?' Thanks to the new criteria for Party members, Xiaohou Ban was a victim of his own independent thinking. He now served as a walking reminder.

Away from my boss and political supervisor for four months, I had worked hard. When my shifts stretched to 17 hours a day, though my salary covered only eight hours, pride welled up in my heart. I was striving to possess the communist spirit—namely, working without considering compensation.

The next moment, standing in the shortened line at the mess hall, shame overrode my pride. As one of the powerless, I was silently watching the destruction of my country by maniacal mobs.

My diarrhea and dysentery lasted for three months, until December when all the flies died. Remaining weak, I struggled to finish the last test and presented the results to the chief designer. The next afternoon she sent a young man to find me when we were packing up the equipment in the tunnel. I went to the designers' shed, where a Russian geologist sat by the designer's desk. With a fierce face, she said, "The parameter you measured from the first shaft is too low for the hard rock. It will force us to use a thick steel plate and concrete lining for the high-pressure conduit."

I answered in a humble but firm tone. "Yes, the small rock blocks are hard and rigid, but the whole rock mass is weakened by cracks, joints, and fissures. The low value of the parameter makes sense."

She scowled. "Are your measurements and calculations correct?"

"Of course."

Women with both a high level of education and Party

membership were rare in China. She was also a chief design engineer. Almost in an authoritative tone she asked, "Can you find a way to make it higher?"

"The only way is to consolidate the rocks around the test well with high pressure cement grouting. A month later, I can repeat the test, and the number should be higher."

She flipped my report with the back of her hand. "We have to install the steel conduit right away, and your suggestion would delay the whole schedule by two months at least."

"Sorry, I can't change the facts to help cut costs."

Moved by our lunatic Great Leap, the Russian geologist beat her drum through an interpreter. "Young man, your academic style doesn't fit the boiling mass movement."

"We can't achieve the Great Leap by jerry-building. A revolutionary should have a scientific attitude."

The interpreter refused to translate my words, and the group left in a huff. I shouted after them, "You don't have the right to alter any numbers in my draft. A valid copy must be formally typed, signed by my supervisor, and stamped by our institute."

They pretended not to hear me.

A few days later we found a truck carrying logs to the site, and the driver agreed to take us back to Beijing. This time I'd have better chance to get permission for a home visit and to meet Chuju. I would have a haircut and a bath, overdue for half a year.

As we were loading our equipment and luggage, a security clerk and three burly men with red militia armbands rushed up. "You can't go."

The administrative arrest made me angry but not hopeless. I shook hands with the ten guest workers and my young trainee. "Please tell Director Gu the whole story."

I turned to the security bureaucrat, "What kind of power do you have to restrict my physical freedom?"

Pushing his sleeves up, he announced, "In the name of the Revolution. We give you an opportunity to repent and turn over a new leaf."

Before I could argue more, he tilted his head to signal the three burly men. They acted simultaneously to twist my arms and grip the nape of my neck, pushing me to a hilltop a kilometer away from the site. They detained me in a small temple for a mountain god. Inside the barbed-wire fence, a storage bunker of explosives occupied most of the yard. A PLA soldier guarded it with a shiny bayonet fixed on his rifle. The big characters on the horizontal board under the temple eaves read 'Red Ideological Clinic'. A couplet ran vertically on either side of the door: 'Dampening Bourgeois Spirit', and 'Boosting Proletarian Morale'.

Terra-cotta statuettes of Taoist gods were piled in a corner, and two of the wooden altars had been shoved together as a table for detainee study. Unlike the three armed sentries who enjoyed a heated brick bed, we anti-Great Leap suspects slept on the ground on wheat-stalk hay.

The security clerk gathered the other detainees, asking them to turn in their written self-criticism, which was due that day. Then he announced the charge against me. "You skillfully created poor data to waste precious materials and slow down construction, you're a saboteur of our socialist cause." He turned to the soldier. "Please tell your comrades to pay special attention to this man. He doesn't belong to our construction bureau."

Master Zhao, one of the three other prisoners, was a talkative young man, slim and nimble. He approached me warmly by revealing his past and the history of the Construction Bureau. After finishing fourth grade, he became an apprentice in a watchmaker's shop and spent ten years there, then taught himself to be an electrician. When he helped me to unfold my sleeping roll alongside his spot, I couldn't help asking him why he was there.

He answered rashly. "The electric meters produced this year are rubbish. When I tested them with voltage or current a little bit wider than the specified range, many of them burnt out. Those morons accuse me of damaging state property on purpose. They don't blame the factories that make such crap for the Great Leap."

"Shut up!" howled the middle-aged man sitting on the threshold stone.

Zhao whispered, "He's the former chief of an engineering district. He came here because he said the Great Leap is an outbreak of petty-bourgeois fanaticism."

I jerked my head toward the yard. "Who's that guy pacing back and forth over there? He looks like he's from Fujian and well-educated."

"He used to be an inspector for safety and quality control. Two months ago, he forced the concrete crews to stop working in the tunnel, waving the shoes and helmets he'd found in the section that had been already cast. Now he's accused of attacking the Great Leap for a single fault and denying its overall picture."

"How long will they keep me here?"

"Who knows? Even though you're a guest worker, they'll find some strange ways to punish you. I've been here four months already. Once you're in their hands, it's not easy to get out of here unless you buckle under their demands."

The inspector walked in. "When the dam collapses, that's when we'll be let out of this hell."

Life was unbearable at the improvised detention center. For every meal at the mess hall by the riverside, we had to hike down the slope for half an hour and then back up again. Without hot water to wash with, we stank. The sour stench of human bodies pervaded our universe.

At night, as the gusts from the northwest desert swept over

the peak, I huddled up and chattered with cold. Rolling on the brick floor, cushioned with a thin layer of wheat straw, I was consumed by the horror of being isolated by my own compatriots. However, I had an advantage the other detainees did not. My personal dossier, residence card, and payroll were not in the hands of local tyrants. I began to plot.

45

On New Year's Day of 1959, the security clerk and a soldier escorted us four political suspects to the railway station to transport explosives. After the driver parked the truck at the western end of the platform, we began to fetch bags of TNT, boxes of detonators, and spools of fuse from a carriage stopped far away, crossing two lines of track to load the stuff on the truck. The soldier watched us vigilantly from the truck bed, gun loaded and aimed. The security clerk counted the items again and again, incessantly checking his invoice.

A passenger train headed to Beijing started to move eastward along the platform as a westbound freight train was passing on the next track. For a moment, I was sure neither the clerk nor the soldier could see me, and all my cash, saved from the previous months, was in my pockets. An idea struck like a flash of lightning. Instead of picking up my next load, I jumped the second track, and walked along behind the tail of the freight train, which shielded me perfectly from the truck. When I reached the middle of the passenger train, I grabbed the handrails of a car and pulled myself in.

The conductor greeted me with a roar and followed up by checking my ID card and giving me a lecture about the discipline a technical cadre should have observed. Finally, after I paid the fare with a 50 percent surcharge as a fine, he allowed me to sit down. In a corner seat, with the flaps of my winter hat dropped, I tried to see if anyone from the construction site was following me.

A few minutes later, the train left, approaching the western suburbs of Beijing. The carriage became crowded. A familiar young man stood in the aisle, holding a seatback in front of my row. He was the warehouse keeper on the construction site. Leaning my head against the window, I pretended to take a nap.

"Hey, Dapeng, where're you going?" His tone and stretched neck conveyed an air of friendly inquiry. The hen in his basket began to cackle. He was on his way home with something bought from a mountain village.

I took the chance to surrender my seat to him. "I'm going to pick up some equipment at the terminal. Please sit down, I'm empty-handed."

He seemed grateful. "You've really learned the communist style of helping other people."

As soon as he took my seat, I squeezed all the way to the end of the carriage. Standing by the lavatory and facing the door, I had found the shortest escape route.

Before noon, I arrived at the West Gate Station, Beijing. The security clerk must have been stamping with rage by now, but I figured he had no way to catch me. I laughed, "He's not smart enough. Instead of my pockets, he searched my mind for anti-Great Leap crimes, leaving the money for me to live on. I slipped into a narrow street away from the busy area and had a haircut. In the barber's mirror, my sunken cheeks and shriveled face were records of lessons learned from real society, and I felt a temporary escape from the mobs fighting in the dark.

I dawdled in the stores awhile and ate a late lunch, especially enjoying the hot tea that I'd craved for half a year. Chewing the fried eggplants with garlic, I did an estimate for the security clerk, and concluded he'd be unable to get any authorization for hunting me in Beijing in the next two days. I sneaked back to my research center through a side door, and found everything normal in the bachelors' dorm. Dong Long and a few other moderates treated me nicely, as in the past, and put their spare bed sheets, quilts, blankets, and pillows together to make my bare bed a warm nest.

The next morning, our group leader, Old Ma, assembled all the members to listen to me. When I walked toward the office building, Director Gu was making his way across the front yard. His words came back and knocked at me, "If you can meet the challenge at the construction site, I'll sing your praises." I hid behind a billboard to avoid the hard-to-explain disgrace.

The hearing began after Ma's brief. Since they all knew the case from our ten guest workers, I just talked about the Red Ideological Clinic and how I escaped. Some political laggards laughed at the name Red Clinic until they saw the others' solemn faces.

The radicals called me an anarchist or accused me of disobeying the local Party committee, and breaking a public relationship. I said, "Comrades, I'm on the correct side of history. Today is January 2, 1959, please mark it down. No matter what you say about me, I won't budge. Sooner or later, when the tunnel collapses, you'll apologize to me."

"Bravo, you have guts." Director Gu spoke behind me. I didn't know when he'd come in. I turned to see him sitting by the door. He stood up, holding his notebook like an imperial edict. All the listeners turned their chairs or bodies to focus on him.

He turned to a page and read his handwritten notes reverently. "About 18 months ago, Chairman Mao exhorted the chief of *The People's Daily* not to be afraid of the five punishments for sticking to the truth: being removed from a leading post, expelled by the Party, divorced by one's wife, imprisoned, and beheaded. Only when you've spiritually prepared yourself for all five do you dare to seek the truth from facts and hold firmly to the truth."

"Could you read it again?" My officemates requested and tried to take notes.

After the hubbub subsided, Gu assumed a lofty tone. "Dapeng Liu has shown great courage, which many of us lack. Though he's neither a Party member nor a married man, he's risking three of the five dangers. He's a good example of holding firmly to the truth."

The others quickly trimmed sail, "Dapeng has remarkably enhanced his political consciousness through the Great Leap."

"Without the leaders watching him, he worked in the tunnel 17 hours a day."

"True communist spirit, working without thinking about your pay."

"I have some extra words about Dapeng," Gu said. "He has the courage to undertake an emerging task even if he hasn't heard of it. This is a special feat in our Party's tradition—learning warfare from war because the Revolution cannot afford for you to study military skills before war breaks out. I'm proud of him."

The next day in Director Gu's office, I met the security clerk who'd come from the Construction Bureau to ask me go back to the Red Clinic. He presented Gu with a letter stamped with the seal of their Party committee. "I'm doing official business according to the official principles. If Dapeng refuses to go back with me, I'll be punished."

Gu overawed him. "Your bureau and our research center are two parallel units under the Party's unified leadership, neither is subordinate to the other. How can you put a guest worker in custody? Dapeng Liu hasn't done anything wrong."

The clerk, around 30, used to be a carpenter and had been recently promoted to a security cadre. His servile smile at his Party bosses and his fierce look at innocent targets revealed his worship of power and position.

As he dejectedly left our compound, I walked him to the street. He asked me, "What's Director Gu's rank?"

"Thirteenth."

"Wow, our bureau chief is only fifteenth."

"The number-one leader of our center is a ninth-level cadre."

He gaped, standing at the sidewalk without words. I took the time to compose my own parting words. "You and I don't have any old scores to settle. Believe it or not, the high-pressure section of the tunnel will collapse as soon as it's put into service. Then, everybody will know that I'm correct and the chief designer is wrong."

"I hope that won't happen."

"Me too, but just wait and see. Please take care of my belongings. Sooner or later I'll come to pick them up when your leaders bow their heads to accept the blame."

46

In the corridor near our office, two women whispered that Anna was getting married. The wedding was two weeks away. For many reasons, I'd already retreated from her, but the news still hit me hard. It reminded me of that missed chance, so hard to come by in the shortness of youth.

On the eve of her wedding, the first Saturday of February, we workers of the institute went to see Beijing's Municipal Great Leap Achievement Exhibition at Sun Yat Sen Park. Toward the end of the day, Anna handed me a folded note asking me to wait for her at the florist near the southeast corner of Tiananmen Square at six o'clock.

As I walked toward the square, chilly gusts of wind made me shiver and blew away my illusions. I was haunted by a scene from a Western story, when the bride changes her mind at the altar and escapes from the church.

The street with the florist's shop was lined with embassies; it was the cleanest, quietest district of Beijing. A row of lamps on the central median was already lit, casting soft light on the evergreens. Cozy recesses contained curved, well-made benches. In the cold weather, white steam arose from young couples' prattling words of love. The whole setting mocked me.

Anna sat by a lamp, dressed entirely in black. Her black overcoat, scarf, gloves, and shoes made her look as if she were going to a funeral. Perhaps she'd intended to create such a sorrowful air for me. As I approached, she put her purse on her lap to make room for me to sit beside her. For 20 minutes or so, with feigned casualness, she talked about our mutual friends.

The temperature was below freezing, and so was my mood. Listening to the irrelevancies, I endured the renewal of my faded pain and wasted time and energy. I patiently waited for her to come to her reason for meeting me.

In a plaintive voice, she suddenly said, "I feel guilty about walking away and leaving you in the cold after I lit a flame in your heart. For two years, your lovelorn state made me sad, but I can't help you at all. Please don't hate me."

"I've never hated anyone, let alone you."

"Your frustration and smoldering anger tell me the opposite. I hope you understand my difficulties."

"I understand you deeply. I couldn't do anything when the state blocked my road and you'd been compromised. If you hadn't asked me to come today, I wouldn't have uttered a word. Being here just opens old wounds."

"Staying away from me and keeping resentment to yourself doesn't mean you understand anything."

"Soon after we watched *Twelfth Night*, I saw that your relationship with Professor Yao was already cooked rice. What's done is done. Still, I tried my luck."

With a trembling voice, she interrupted me. "Don't think I'm cold-blooded. I've cared about you for a long time. In the summer of 1957, I was constantly afraid for you after I heard that activists had collected quotes from your private conversations, especially your praise of the Free Forums on university campuses. At the end of the year, when Smiling Tiger read the list of YL members who had to go through another public hearing, my heart jumped into my throat. I was so relieved your name wasn't included. I was still worried until the end of the year, when I could be sure you weren't in trouble."

I touched her arm, "Thank you. I really appreciate your compassion, which is so rare these days."

She sniffled, "You have a chance to find someone better than me. On the other hand, if I gave up Yao, he'd never find someone like me."

She was on a boat in the middle of a rapid river, and I was a man left on the bank. She couldn't stop for me. It was time to wave goodbye to her and to watch her sail recede from sight.

I waited for my throat to relax. "Don't worry about me. I'll be fine, and I take your reassurances as a blessing. I wish you well."

Silence fell between us. I was gathering the strength to leave when a gust from the west blew through the street. I shivered, and a spasm seized both my hands. I rubbed them with my gloves still on, but no feeling returned.

She removed her gloves and helped me to take off mine. Massaging my knuckles, her warmth and patience eased the cramps away. She seemed to be searching for forgotten words, but I was ready to go. Her right palm covered my left hand as she teased me. "Look, my fingers are longer than yours, but your palm is wider."

Unable to reply, I tried to capture her transient tenderness. I held onto her final touch to offset my dreary desolation.

I stood abruptly, "Congratulations." I turned and ran doggedly to the bus station.

47

The Great Leap made people feel it was time to realize
Chairman Mao's dream of making the mountain goddess
marvel at the world, changed by the people he led. His poem
carried his imagination of the future Three Gorges Dam,
"Walls of stone will stand upstream to the west, to hold back
Wu Mountain's clouds and rain, till a smooth lake rises in the
narrow gorges."

The research center in Wuhan asked our institute to send
more people to work on the rock foundation of the Three
Gorges Dam that remained at the stage of conceptual design. I
got the opportunity to join the team. It let me go farther away
from the Yongding River, beyond the reach of the Red Clinic's
hand. More enjoyably, I'd meet the elites from all over the
country and have the chance to visit my alma mater.

However, I stayed there only a month. Then, Director Gu
passed through Wuhan with a group of Russian experts and
received me in a fancy hotel suite. We sat on the couch and
sofa, facing each other. He started the conversation with a
personal question. "Do you have a girlfriend?"

"No, I haven't met an ideal one."

"A female chemist, just graduated from Nankai University,
is single. She's 25, same as you."

"Thanks, but I have a childhood friend, still in our
hometown. She works as an accountant-in-training, without a
university education. Is it possible to find a job for her in our
institute?"

"How old is she?"

"20 next month."

"Aha, you prefer them younger. And she's pretty, right?"

"Sort of, but definitely thrifty and disciplined."

He leaned back and flipped the ash of his cigarette into the ashtray. "Last year, our research center recruited over a hundred lab assistants and machine-shop trainees, all young people just out of high school. You should've told us earlier. Now the hiring has ended."

"I missed the chance last year because I was working on the Yongding River. But our organization is big, one thousand six hundred employees now. It wouldn't be too hard to place one more person on one of our two large compounds, would it?"

In a flat tone, he said, "I'll keep your problem in my mind. If any new openings come up, I'll put in your request as a top priority." Abruptly he sat straight up. "Now, the Great Leap preempts anything else. It's not the time for your personal agenda. Go back to Beijing and get ready. There's a group in Fujian Province that needs your help working on high-speed tunneling."

"I don't know how to dig tunnels."

He laughed. "Young man, you looked brave last year, and we've given you the credit. That's why I picked you. It's good for you, a tough trial will promote you fast. As for your personal matter, let me put it in this way: if you're eager to help your leaders, your leaders will take care of you."

I stood up to leave. "I'll undertake the task. Please don't forget my request."

He patted his chest. "If there's only one new residence permit available for our division, I'll give it to your girlfriend to move to Beijing. If there's only one for the whole institute, I'll snatch it for you as fast as I can."

In early April, I spent a day in Shanghai on my way to Fujian Province. Walking along a street, I suddenly remembered that Chuju's twentieth birthday was a few days away and I should send her a gift as a token of my affection. I'd had an income for two years, so a gift was overdue. Perhaps

Chuju already felt I'd left her out in the cold. Nevertheless, a late gift was better than none.

Searching store windows on the busiest street, I found no red leather shoes, the height of fashion just two years before. The image of a gaily-dressed Chuju no longer fit our nation's mood.

It began to drizzle, typical of southeast China, reminding me that the gloomy Jiangxi weather, where the rains could last six months, as they had in 1954, was again upon us. I decided to buy her something that fit both the natural and political climates, a pair of green-gray rubber boots. She would probably be pleased by their practicality, especially on her muddy country road.

Attached to the parcel, I sent a note about Director Gu's promise.

From the small railway station, Gukou, in Fujian Province, I took a charcoal-powered bus to Gutian Waterpower Station. At the Construction Bureau's headquarters, a woman on the technical staff, Junior Chu, received me. After I put my belongings in the hostel room, she led me to a nearby tunnel branch. Antiquated pneumatic drills, 1930 and 1938 Soviet models, were the only equipment available. The explosives were also primitive. Able-bodied men loaded broken stones into skip carts with hand tools, then pushed the carts along the small-gauge rail tracks to dump them in the creek outside the tunnel. As the excavation went deeper into the mountain, the steel conduit for ventilation was extended with woven-bamboo piping wrapped in oilcloth, it was rough and leaky.

The shabby picture depressed me. I asked Junior Chu, "Do you think we'll be able to create a world record for high-speed tunneling?"

She spoke slowly, as if censoring her words. "Now, miracles appear everywhere. Last year, *The People's Daily* reported a high grain yield per acre, one hundred times higher than most peasants could believe. Excited by the Great Leap, sophomore students at Beijing University have collectively written a book, *History of Chinese Literature*, which they will use in their senior year. They claim it's better and more correct than earlier ones written by individual bourgeois professors."

"People in every trade are trying to please Chairman Mao with miracles," I said. "Everybody seems able to launch a Sputnik to shock the world."

She lowered her head to avoid further comments. From her sheepish and jittery manner, I decided she was one of the 1957 political targets.

"I'm the coordinator for the research group," she said. "I'll join your work later. Now the whole thing remains on paper. Much has been said, little done."

I smiled, "The headquarters of our ministry have been exuberant about your plan and slogans. And my leaders are waiting for me to launch a satellite from here."

At the first group meeting, I proposed adopting certain Western ideas and procedures in line with local conditions. The Party secretary of the experimental tunnel section burst into laughter. "You intellectuals always worship foreigners. Don't forget Chairman Mao teaches us to respect the masses' initiatives."

The slogan of the time, 'Let the Party Secretary Resume Command', no doubt had invigorated him. One of his followers jeered at me, "You've drawn a colorful cake to satisfy our hunger."

Master Fong, the head of a 14-member drilling crew and a former PLA platoon leader, didn't say anything to support or oppose others' opinions. With a strong Shandong accent and a soldier's determination, he said, "Chairman Mao led us to defeat eight million KMT troops in just three years. Surely we can break the world record for digging a tunnel."

He'd fought all the way from North China to the

southeastern coast, where he was transferred to be a construction worker. After the meeting I chatted with him and found his towering physique combined oddly with an easy, amiable disposition.

Two other researchers had come from the Institute of Construction Technology in Beijing to join us. We took turns working on various shifts, getting familiar with the current tunneling process. We made reasonable suggestions that enhanced efficiency gradually but not much.

As the news media bombarded us with victories from all the provinces and all sectors of our economy, the secretary became more and more reckless. He slept little and didn't allow the workers much sleep, while pressuring us to contribute new ideas and implement the masses' initiatives.

One of the initiatives for blasting was deploying electrodes on a record turntable to control the ignition sequence. I expressed doubt. "The Americans and Swedes can make the ignition interval between two groups of detonators as short as thousandths of a second. Our turntable rotates at 78 revolutions per minute, so the shortest interval we can achieve is tenths of a second. Most likely the first explosions would cut the wires to the next groups of holes."

Nobody listened to me, but a test in an open area revealed that some detonators didn't ignite. The drillers were scared. If that happened in real excavation, they would have to drill new holes close by the old, charged ones. Other construction sites had tried this and reported a high death toll. Quietly, they gave up this idea.

Then came another mass initiative, which said adding lime to the TNT would enhance explosion efficiency. Junior Chu, who graduated from university two years earlier than I did, one of the few women on the staff, undertook this experiment. Physically weak and with glasses, she must have had difficulty working under the harsh conditions. I wanted to help her and we formed a team. The tunnel, lacking adequate blowers and air conduits, had little ventilation. To help us determine whether carbon monoxide levels from the explosion would rise to life-threatening levels, we took two white mice into the blast site. Equipped only with gauze masks, we rushed into the smoky chamber immediately after the explosion and deposited the two caged mice. Three days later, I felt dizzy and nauseated.

Resting on a log near the tunnel entrance, I asked Chu, "Any changes in the mice?"

She hesitated. "They're still running on their exercise wheels, but seem less energetic than before."

"They're not the only ones. How about you, do you feel dizzy?"

She stammered, "Not much … only a little."

"Perhaps women can endure more carbon monoxide than men. Is that true?"

She lowered her head, aimlessly hitting the log with a piece of rock. "Both my husband and I have gotten into trouble for our big mouths. He was labeled a rightist, and I was expelled from the YL. We were separated in January 1958."

"I apologize. I don't mean to bring up sad memories. We can stop this stupid test. Let me find a way to deal with the bureaucrats."

My taking on the thorny problem seemed to touch her. With traces of tears on her dusty face, she asked, "Do you have a fiancée now?"

I showed her Chuju's photo. "I have a candidate in Jiangxi, but I can't make the decision. The biggest hurdle is how to move her to Beijing. Also she has only a high-school education."

"Wow, she's cute. I can assure you, you won't find a beauty like Chuju in Beijing, the VIPs would grab her up. What are you waiting for?"

"I worry about living separately after we've married."

She snorted. "Don't look too far away. We could die anytime in either a political campaign or construction disaster. Enjoy what you have now. The earlier you marry and the longer you've been geographically separated from your wife, the higher priority you'll have on the waiting list for a family reunion. How about asking her to come now and have your wedding here? I can help you to find a humble place to live for one or two months."

"Thank you for your concern and offering. Heaven will reward you for your tender heart."

In the meantime, I started to lobby the high-ups to notice the looming disasters. Most of them didn't read foreign journals. I decided to develop my few pages into a long report, introducing Western technical information to my coworkers.

48

Junior Chu lived in a loft above the technical staff office, a bamboo structure at the bureau's administration center, near the residential center. Her warm, caring character and university education helped her to attract women technicians around her. And many of them spoke the same Shanghai dialect as hers. When they met her in public, they would talk in it loudly, showing their identity and superiority to the Fujian natives. All those phenomena gave me confidence in her ability.

Seeing her actively searching for a nest on the construction site so that Chuju and I could marry, I wrote my idea and plan down and sent them to Chuju asking her to be ready to come. She immediately wrote back to me, "... Mother and I are overjoyed by your decision after one year's waiting. Let me tell you now, I was almost determined to be single all my life. I'm so happy to have you as my husband that I smile waking up from my fancy dream. Fujian is next to Jiangxi. I'm waiting for your telegram."

The unexpected development energized me. In high spirits, I walked above the ground.

One Sunday morning in late September, a truck driver gave Junior Chu a ride, and she arrived at our working place earlier than normal. With her safety helmet in hand, she smiled broadly and told me, "Good news! An operator at our bureau's telephone exchange is going to deliver a baby in Shanghai, where her mother can take care of her during her maternity leave. Her husband, a purchasing manager, has a chance to handle his business there. The couple has agreed to let you live in their home for the two months."

"I'm touched by your generous help, especially during your own difficult time."

"Their living shed is humble, but has everything for a simple life. They trust in people I've referred, but, to let them feel at ease, you'd better meet them before they hand you the key. How about this evening, after work?"

Overjoyed, I said, "Heaven will bless you!"

Going to meet our excavation team, we met Master Fong at the tunnel entrance. Seeing my flashlight was dim, he insisted we swap batteries, his new ones for my dying ones. Such a show of generosity, making a sacrifice to help other people, put him in rare company. As the Party required me to learn, his gesture gave me an example of the noble quality of the working class.

A sudden power failure cut the lights and ventilation. The workers shut off their pneumatic dills, and the compressed air kept shrieking through the worn valves. The Party branch secretary shouted, holding his flashlight, "Comrades, we can't stop. The air compressors outside the tunnel are still running on diesel engines."

The on-duty engineer said, "The air blower needs electricity. Without ventilation, the silica dust will ruin the workers' lungs. And we don't have kerosene for the lanterns."

Ignoring him, the secretary ordered the 14 drillers to continue working and to use gasoline to fill the three lanterns.

The engineer cried, "No, that will cause a fire!"

"You bookworms always fear hardship and danger. Get out of here. If Heaven falls, we working class can prop it up."

The engineer stormed off. I felt sorry for him, but even more so for the drillers who were forced to inhale the rock powder and diesel exhaust.

Junior Chu looked at me with an inquiring air, as though asking what we should do. I whispered, "The secretary is the commander here. If we leave, the drillers will see us as pampered intellectuals."

The lanterns emitted a dim light. The drillers were groping in the thick cloud of rock dust and the mist of cooling water. I took a lantern off a steel rod in a boundary hole and held it over a driller's shoulder. He shouted through the deafening noise, "It's very kind of you."

About ten minutes later, a hose from the air compressor burst and detached from the drill, swaying like a rearing snake. Before the driller could catch the free end of the hose, it knocked my lantern. The raging sound of igniting gasoline engulfed me. I dropped the lantern, but the flame had already spread over my body. I tossed my rattan hat instinctively, but the piercing pain on my face exasperated my panic. Someone yelled, "Roll on the ground! Get rid of your raincoat!"

I sloughed off my raincoat easily, but not my melting rubber pants. Master Fong pushed me to the ground and rolled my body to put out the fire. Junior Chu helped me stand. The melted rubber stuck to my legs, and the pain paralyzed me. She held my arm and led me, staggering, for about 20 steps.

Then I heard an explosion. The other two lanterns must have caught fire. Coughing and screaming replaced shouting, and dense smoke billowed behind us. Junior Chu dragged me to a skip cart and helped me stand on its rear edge, "Hold on tight."

She unplugged the manual brake pin and desperately pushed the cart. As it gained speed, I bent over the empty container and gripped its frame, enduring the pain to keep my trembling body balanced. Though the tracks generally ran downhill toward the entrance, the uneven stretches were tough on Chu. The one kilometer ride was unbearably long.

When we reached the open area, Junior Chu ran to look for the Party secretary and section chief, wailing all the way, "Fire, fire! Our drillers are trapped in the tunnel!"

Few people were around. The man who operated the air compressor carried me piggyback to the field meeting room and laid me down on the rough table. Soon he brought in a trainee nurse, a girl who had finished ninth grade and been recruited for first-aid work during the Great Leap. She cleaned the right side of my face and dressed the burnt area with anti-inflammatory powder and some ointment. When she tried to peel melted patches of rubber from my legs, beads of sweat welled up all over my body, and I fainted.

Whistles and gongs woke me up. People shouted, "Fire in the tunnel! Comrades, rescue our class brothers!"

The impetuous secretary cranked the telephone, crying to the bureau's headquarters five kilometers away, "No lights, no ventilation in the tunnel! The flame must've spread to the wooden shoring by now. The barrels of diesel fuel could blow up any second, and we still have 14 drillers down there!"

Junior Chu stopped the trainee nurse and used the phone to call the bureau's clinic to send an experienced doctor. Through the window, I saw only the dense crowd desperately pushing and squeezing toward the tunnel entrance.

The wailing wives arrived one after another, "Let me go!" they screamed, and desperately wedged into the front lines, trying to get into the dark hole. The first rescue team had nothing but wet towels to shield their noses and mouths. They couldn't get far enough to reach the victims, and some passed out just a hundred meters or so into the tunnel, which was now full of carbon monoxide.

The doctor arrived two hours later. He gave me a shot of morphine before he treated my wounds. Soon after he had bound up my legs with gauze, my two colleagues from Beijing transported me to the sleeping shed I shared with them.

The frustrated rescue crowds lay on the ground, and female workers attended to the fainted wives of the trapped drillers. The leader kept cranking their telephone and shouting to the operator to connect the line to Beijing and Shanghai for help. The next morning a medical group arrived from Shanghai, but their gas masks were useless because they lacked oxygen bottles. The third day, the navy's East Sea Fleet arrived and retrieved three drillers who'd stayed alive by breathing compressed air. There were only three hoses, however. The eleven others, including Master Fong, had given their all to the Great Leap.

Work halted for a belated safety check, and sorrowful silence reigned for miles around. Local workers believed that the spirits of the dead would haunt the site, and fear intensified their grief. I missed Master Fong, hardly believing he'd died. I felt his spirit following me, most strongly at night when I was using his batteries in my flashlight. One of the survivors said that at the life-or-death moment, Fong surrendered his hose to him.

On the long weekend of Tenth National Day, my two colleagues from Beijing went to Fujian's capital, leaving me alone in our rundown shack. In the middle of one night, sleeping with my face toward its shaky door, I saw a vague shadow sweep over a window to my right. My mosquito net rippled. Suddenly, the door sprang open, and the dead Master Fong stood before me calling for help. I sat straight up in bed, by then fully awake, but saw nothing. The door was still latched. My back and hands were drenched in cold sweat.

When our race against the Western imperialists brought a fever like that of a war, an officemate working at a site in Yunnan Province wrote to me that a drilling crew had tried to drill parallel holes about six inches away from charged ones that had failed to explode. Without a guiding device to control the direction of the new holes, the drill bit hit one of the detonators. Seven of the eight crew members were killed, and the one survivor got uncountable rock fragments driven into his flesh, disabling him permanently. It was the disaster I expected from the suggestion of using a record turntable to control the sequence of detonation at the site.

Accompanying my physical pain, the possible aftermath of my burns haunted me day and night. I couldn't walk and endured tremendous difficulty. If I'd become permanently disabled, my whole future would have been ruined. The disaster had foreclosed the planed wedding with Chuju in Fujian. Looking ahead, if I developed a limp and carried an irremovable scar on my face, Chuju might change her mind and end our engagement. However, I was lucky to be alive, as excavating workers died everywhere at that time. We lost 11 drillers, and a gas explosion in a Shanxi coal mine killed hundreds around the same time. I determined to do something to help stop other calamities caused by ignorance.

The full commitment had eased my physical pain and encouraged me to overcome the inconvenience of daily life. Snatching free moments in my reckless life of the previous months, I'd read a recently published Russian book on underground excavation. I was surprised by the author's great respect for the technical developments in the US, Japan, and Sweden. Following the Soviet author's references, I found the

English originals and asked our institute library in Beijing to send me the pertinent issues of those magazines, mainly a journal published by the American Society of Civil Engineers.

The disaster had hushed all sound from the hundreds of workers. Out of respect for our dead comrades, the ping-pong room next to our thatched hut was quiet. In the pressing graveyard silence, the specter of Master Fong and the innocent faces of other dead drillers flashed around me, spurring me to write down what I had learned from the magazines.

I began to reproduce the contents in Chinese with neat handwriting and standard graphics. The former ping-pong players occasionally peeped in, curious about me and my desk piled with books.

The few teenage boys who'd worked as able-bodied men after finishing middle school would walk in gingerly to watch me write and draw. Gradually, they began to ask questions and took an interest in the glossy photos of construction machinery and sites presented in the American magazines. They admired the smooth surface of an excavated tunnel with the halves of the exploded holes left on the rock walls like the perforations between rows of stamps. More often, they pored over a manufacturer's ads where a delicate blonde girl posed elegantly, holding a pneumatic drill as nimbly as a tennis racket.

They seemed to value what I was doing and quietly took care of me. A carpentry apprentice even made a chamber pot, which I could use either in the latrine or at home. Whenever I needed to go to the bureau's clinic, they would improvise a stretcher with bamboo and ropes to carry me from the valley to the highway, halfway up the hill, where I could hitch a ride on an engineering truck.

Their warm support helped sustain me through the adversity until I finished the report, which I titled 'Catching up with Western Tunneling Technology'. Following the ritual and custom of the time, under the title, I added, 'My Gift to the

Party for the New Year of 1960', hoping it could gag the mouths of some xenophobes.

Over the previous two months, Junior Chu had persistently urged me to go back to Beijing for better medical treatment. Now, she declared, "You have no reason to stay here for one more day." With her initiative, my two colleagues from Beijing forcefully packed my belongings and escorted me on a bus to the railway station at Gukou, about 20 kilometers away, where they seated me on the train to Shanghai. That was the shortest route for returning to Beijing.

Prompted by Junior Chu's telegram, her father was waiting for me at Shanghai station, holding a carton flap with my name written on it in large characters. The old man, smiling like a Buddha, patiently accompanied me for half a day until I boarded the express train to Beijing.

49

Going north from Shanghai, at every railway station, passengers jostled against the crowds to buy some junk food, but found the peddlers' baskets empty. Beggars raised their palms to the windows of the train. The tension on the platform foretold the coming starvation. Everywhere, crops had been left to rot in the fields for two years, while peasants were mobilized to melt steel, build reservoirs, and participate in militia drills. From then on we had to pay grain ration coupons for food in restaurants in addition to money, a tough measure which had not been seen since 1953, when the ration system had started.

I returned to Beijing without the triumph my leaders had expected me to carry back from Fujian. Instead, as a casualty of the Great Leap, I had to use a pair of crutches to support my burnt legs. The stinging pain, the swollen muscle around the wounds, and the ominous fluid seeping out from the bandages worried me that my legs were infected. The padded dressing on my face, reflected in the mirror hanging in the train vestibule, reminded me once again that I might be permanently disfigured.

With my string bag and knapsack slung over my shoulder, I hopped along behind the crowd leaving the railway station. The express bus on Chang'an Grand Avenue took me due west to the water-supply canal, where I transferred onto a trolley along the northbound avenue toward my research center.

The majestic façade of Beijing, new high-rises, in the stately Soviet style with classic Chinese roofs of glazed tiles, had been added during my absence. These showpieces of architectural achievement, flamboyantly celebrating the tenth anniversary of the New China, amazed me. They diverted my mind from my inflamed wounds for a moment. Then I noticed the black rubber propane bags fully covering the roofs of some of the buses, trembling in the cold wind like the bloated bellies of patients on stretchers. The ugly bags silently announced a gasoline shortage, and painted a sad picture to frame my personal disaster.

While approaching the trolley terminal, I pulled a large persimmon out of my pocket, which Junior Chu's father had given me. Before I could take my first bite, starving pedestrians mobbed me, "Comrade, where did you buy that?" The human wave would have knocked me down if I hadn't leaned against a concrete power-line pole. First, I gobbled the persimmon. Then, I explained, "Sorry, I brought it with me from Shanghai." They sighed and scattered.

When I entered the office with crutches and thick bandages, all division employees were gathered in groups to criticize Director Gu's anti-Great Leap sin. My coworkers surrounded me, taking my bags and helping me sit down. Anna stood outside the circle, her rueful countenance holding some sympathy for me.

During a break in the group meeting, I thumbed through

The People's Daily while she knitted a sweater in a far corner. With no preamble, she suddenly spoke as if to a distant passerby, "Did you hear the good news?"

I looked around – there was no-one but us in the office, "About what?"

She stood and passed me heading for the door. As she passed, she bent close and whispered, "Big Sister Cui, in our division office, types confidential Party branch documents. She told me that you recently got an excellent evaluation. I was amazed, but you're in second place on the list of leftists or advanced elements, just below Old Ma."

I thanked her without turning my head. Then I said, "That's a secret, please keep it to yourself."

The campaign to denounce those who'd criticized the Great Leap and the People's Commune Movement was drawing to an end. Except for Minggui An, my coworker, who sat in a corner of the office nursing his psychological wounds, and Director Gu, who kept writing his confession in isolation, all my colleagues were talking about food. In the evenings or on Sundays, they hurried to reach Dong'an Market near Tiananmen Square, the best shopping center in the capital, which was even frequented by foreign tourists. So far, it had been a presentable façade for our faltering economy. But only the earliest of early birds had a chance to buy groceries, especially cooked meat, which wasn't available in the suburbs.

In the first week of 1960, we got the good news that everyone with a Beijing residence registration would receive a half jin, about nine ounces, of pork for the New Year. Following the excitement, everybody became anxious about how to get an equal share with enough weight. By consensus, a committee was formed with representatives from all divisions to help and supervise the kitchen crew. Though clumsy with my crutches, I was elected for the job on behalf of our division.

On a fixed date, two weeks before the Chinese New Year, we had the feast during lunchtime. To guarantee fairness, every share of meat was put in a separate bowl on a bed of a few pieces of cabbage. After a half-hour steaming, the other committee members served the bowls to regular diners in the mess hall, where we had our rations managed collectively.

The institute's Party committee secretary turned the occasion into a briefing. He stood on a stool in the central aisle to give a lecture while everyone finished the pork, cabbage, and the sauce in a few minutes. Before the tables at the far end were served, the diners near the kitchen already longingly stared at their empty bowls or hit them with chopsticks. The din drowned out the Party secretary's voice. I finally heard him say,

> Khrushchev has betrayed the Soviet Communist Party, founded by Lenin and Stalin, and betrayed the Soviet people. Now he colludes with Kennedy to oppose us, taking advantage of our natural disasters. Reactionaries of other countries, especially India's Nehru and Yugoslavia's Tito, join their anti-China, anti-communist chorus. They're doomed to fail, I guarantee it. Comrades, believe me that hardship and challenge regenerate a nation. Difficulties don't scare us.

This marked the start of the famine, officially recorded as the Three Years of Natural Disaster, 1960–62.

During group discussion, my officemates behaved like sensible children sparing their parents' dignity. They attributed the famine to bad weather and put as much blame on Khrushchev as they could. As they expressed their determination to save our country from the crisis, I declared along with them, "Our difficulties are temporary. The revolutionary path twists and turns, but our future is brilliant."

At night, my lofty sentiments and aspirations receded, and

my stomach rumbled with hunger. While mourning my school idols, now wasting their youth in labor camps for what they'd said, loneliness gnawed at me. Dreams of my student days replayed in my mind, ridiculing me. In my adolescent imagination, life would by now have been infused with love, happiness, and success.

In the desperate peace imposed by starvation, I couldn't help worrying about the future—my country's and mine. I might succumb to disease or disaster, but I didn't want to die before I married. In the dark, listening to the north wind wailing like the wives of the trapped drillers in Fujian, I feared dying without a wife to cry for me. If so, my dwelling in Heaven would be an unbearable extension of my earthly celibacy.

Ahead, my love horizon was bleak. The nature of my work would continue to force me to move from one wilderness area to another. We would never have the freedom to choose job or relocate. After the famine, no doubt another round of campaigns would start. A new mania would interfere with my personal plan. Director Gu had promised to help move Chuju to Beijing, but now, he was hardly able to save himself.

Ever since Chuju sent the letter expressing her eagerness to marry and that she was still available for me, the Great Leap had kept me from seeing her. She and her mother, waiting for my final decision, might've lost, or would soon lose, patience as suitors in our hometown kept pestering them. Given our inevitable financial problems, our marriage wouldn't be a happy one. Our combined salaries would be only 96 yuan a month, part of which we'd have to give to our elderly parents. What if we had children? The threat and consequences of poverty could not be clearer.

Another worry, more critical than financial plight, already haunted me, but only in the back of my mind. Now it rose up like an insurmountable wall. Since 1953, every change of domicile had to be approved by the local authorities. Without official residence cards, households received no rations of grain, cloth, or cooking oil. All organizations, factories, hospitals, and universities adjusted their hiring plans based on allotted quotas for new resident permits.

From the eastern suburbs to western Beijing, I had lived in bachelors' dorms alongside married men forced to remain separate from their wives. I saw their suffering, the pride they swallowed trying to obtain home-leave permits, and how they had to squeeze travel expenses out of meager stipends. Mostly, I saw their crippling loneliness.

Anyone who wanted to relocate his job to reunite with his family got only the standard Party answers: "The Revolution needs you here," or, "Individual interests must remain subordinate to those of the nation." Sad husbands' heartfelt pleas were sometimes quoted by Party leaders as examples of bourgeois individualism hindering revolutionary work.

Night after night, my secret worry about our future geographic separation kept plaguing me until my head became heavy and stuffy. I would quell my surging thoughts by returning to my burns. The egg-sized scar on my right cheek had a copper color, and the edge of the patch shrank pulling the lower eyelid down. *All nonsense, all moot. All such anxiety comes from the assumption that Chuju will value you as she did in the past. The accident has devalued you and changed your world. Be ready for an all-is-lost situation.*

50

Freight trains clattered along the east–west rails just a hundred yards from my dorm. In the past, without wounds, I ignored the noise, even in the middle of otherwise quiet nights. But on this frigid January morning, when the muscles inside my bandaged legs twitched with sharp pains and my toes remained numb, every train rattling my frozen window would wake me.

As our jobs always required us to work in places away from Beijing, my two roommates were in other provinces, one laboring in the countryside of Anhui, and the other doing field tests in Yunnan.

As I tossed and turned, the slight warmth I'd accumulated during the night escaped, and constantly pulling the comforter up to cover my neck made my shoulders ache. Better to get up.

I put on my two sweaters, long johns, cotton-padded jacket and pants, and a Russian-style felt hat. The rope tied around my waist stopped cold air from rising up under the hem of my loose jacket.

I poured myself a mug of hot water from my thermos, savored its heat with both hands, and blew its steam on the window to melt a patch of ice. With my sleeve, I wiped it clean, and watched an eastbound bus pull up. It was Sunday, a week before the Chinese New Year. Young women, hurrying to reach Dong'an Market before it opened, ran along as the bus slowed to a stop.

I turned away from the window. Sitting at the three-drawer desk, which I shared with my roommates, I couldn't distract myself from my plight. Three months after the disaster, I wasn't fully recovered. Though the doctors in our contracted hospital saved me from the infection and I avoided gangrene in my legs, I couldn't hide the aftermath of the burns from Chuju. Long pants would cover my discolored legs in public but not from her.

I held the pocket mirror my roommate, Old Ye, left on the desk, and raised an edge of the pad on my face. The skin under the soothing ointment remained whitish pink and showed no sign of new skin, and its ragged contour predicted a nasty scar. No trace of the former high-school, drama-group star attracting letters from admiring girls would remain. I wouldn't be the grown-up version of the attractive eighth-grade boy, predicted success by many when a rich local family invited me to be best man at their son's wedding.

So far, I had told Chuju little about my misfortune. I couldn't imagine the enormity of her turmoil if we met now. I decided to wait until my wounds stabilized, and then tell her the details. In the meantime, I hoped some new medical technology developed in China could cure me and keep the damage to a minimum.

One Thursday afternoon, a week before the New Year, I tossed the crutches aside. Without calling first, I went to see Hot Chili, my high-school friend, who was now working at the high-ranking cadres' healthcare center as a cardiologist. I found her in an office of the Outpatient Department.

In a white robe, she was slight as a child, while an old man, fat and stately, was condescendingly listening to her explanation of his cardiogram. His armed bodyguard and a gentle attendant became wary, turning their heads to follow my every movement. Hot Chili nodded to me and pointed at a chair. After they left, she held the next patient outside the door, "Do you know who he is?"

"At least a governor of some province."

"Bigger than that. The king of Northeast China, a cadre of sixth rank."

"Then you must be very important, too."

She didn't smile at my school-chum banter, "At this moment, what I am is very busy." She hastily checked the scars on my face, legs, and hands.

She stood up, "An expert has recently come back from the West and now is doing skin transplant experiments at the Chinese Academy of Medical Science. Let's wait for his success. I'll definitely find a connection and get him to examine and treat you."

I counted on her ability at manipulation and her strong provincial loyalty. Her reassurance warmed me for a while. But by the time I got back to my room, I couldn't see any miraculous way for me to recover my previous health. Whenever sitting alone, I would mournfully stroke the coppery glossy patches around my legs and especially the one on my face. A certain loss of agility in my hands also made me worry I'd be butterfingered with sensitive devices. I had to prepare myself for living with physical impairment and accepting its consequences. I decided not to hold up on telling Chuju the bad news.

On a Saturday evening, I walked to the nearest photo shop to have two pictures taken, one full-length and one of my face. While waiting the three days to pick them up, I tried to figure out how to write the letter to Chuju. I couldn't put down a single word on the blank paper. After I picked up the photos, I wrote:

> Remembering the horrible image of your father in 1945 after he was burnt in an accident, I'm sure you must be on tenterhooks about my possible situation. I've been waiting for my wounds to stabilize before showing you.
>
> From these two photos, you can see I'm still in one piece. My hands are okay, though my fingers aren't as sensitive as they used to be. However, my legs are ugly with strings of burnt patches, and the scar on the right side of my face has especially disfigured me. As the photographer adjusted the lens and asked for my attention, I imagined you were peeping through the camera with your head under the black cover. He suggested I turn 45 degrees to the right, obviously intending to hide the scar. On the contrary, I turned left to let the damaged side of my face be fully exposed to you.
>
> Since I received your warm letter and charming photo two years ago, I haven't been allowed to leave my post for a home visit. Plunging into the Great

Leap Forward, I couldn't grumble about personal inconvenience. Now I have the time and can easily get the permit for a leave, but I don't want to meet you with my ruined appearance. I no longer look like the man you remember.

If we'd been married before the disaster, that would be another story. Your mother would have persuaded you stick to tradition: 'a woman sticks to the man she's married even if he is a dog or a rooster.' But now, you have no obligation to accept my disfiguration as a condition of your marriage, or to compromise your happiness because of our old good wishes.

I've been honored by your mother's goodwill and your choice of me as your future life partner. Since disaster has changed my fate, I have to accept it. For the sake of your wellbeing, I sincerely propose that I release you from your early promise of betrothal. Please don't feel bad. The mutual affection we've enjoyed since our childhood is unforgettable, and the friendship between our two families forged by the war will endure forever.

51

Unlike in the past, when my coworkers started leaving for construction sites in late January, all the employees stayed idle together in Beijing. To occupy our office hours, our boss told us to study a document drafted by the Party's central committee. It was briefly called 'The Sixty Directives', and focused on how to rescue China's agriculture and consolidate the People's Commune system.

During a break in a political lecture at the auditorium, I left for the lab to take some readings from a rock sample undergoing tests. The main building was quiet except for the sound of doors opening and my own footsteps. The walls on both sides of the corridor were fully covered by big-character posters, with newly written ones pasted onto old layers. Articles attacking Director Gu were made prominent by their sheer number and outrageous words. He was kept in his office to write a confession. The repeated accusations had become known to all.

"Gu's anti-Chairman Mao stance is all too clear from his vicious assertion that having the whole population make steel caused more loss than gain."

"Gu's ugly reactionary features have been thoroughly exposed by his slander that the cadres of the People's Communes are worse than landlords in the old society."

The title of a freshly plastered article attracted me to stop in the middle of the corridor, not far from the men's room. No sooner had I read the title, 'Gu's Impure Motives to Join the Party and his Speculation with the Revolution', than the door of the restroom banged open. It was Gu, the former cocky leader, returning to his office to write his confession. He averted his eyes and stepped aside. I couldn't change my habit of addressing him as 'Director Gu' quick enough. He replied with an uneasy glance and a wan smile, as though he accepted my respectful tone like a fresh breeze to a suffocating man.

Right in the midst of his political quarantine, neither he nor I dared to talk. I watched his back as he dragged his feet toward the staircase. He wore a warm peasant coat dejectedly, like a prisoner.

Suddenly, he came back and stood in front of me, "Sorry about your injury. I apologize for squandering your best time to meet your fiancée." He raised a hand to point at the article I was reading, "Heaven didn't know that would happen. Sorry."

In mid-February 1960, while Director Gu and other

dissidents remained in disgrace, people still waved the Great Leap as a sacred banner, inviolable. However, pragmatic leaders quietly operated to clean up the industrial mess left by the manic two years. Right then, the steel conduit of the Yongding Power Station burst during its test run. High-pressure water spouting from the cracks in the concrete-steel lining caused a landslide. Rocks of various sizes rolled downhill and hit the plant. Some of them were stopped by the wall, but others shot through windows and landed on the generator-room floor.

The accident called for a field conference to find its cause and remedy. A vice minister from our ministry, who presided over the discussion, introduced new jargon, *dissecting a sparrow*, "The sparrow may be small but it has all the vital organs. Now, we're analyzing the disaster as a typical case, just like dissecting a sparrow, and our purpose is to discover the common and intrinsic problems existing inside our waterpower construction system."

As one of the witnesses, I was assigned to attend the conference. I met two of my three fellow detainees at the Red Clinic—Master Zhao, the electrician, and the safety-quality inspector. They'd been rehabilitated now and welcomed me like their bosom friend as opposed to a fellow anti-Great Leap inmate. As they rattled on about the details of building code violations in the past two years, I admired their extensive investigation and diabolic memory. Local leaders seemed to tolerate their publicizing the bureau's domestic shame, perhaps due to their plain language, which didn't deny the Great Leap as a whole.

Besides the burst conduit, the two-day hearing also revealed other major faults and hidden dangers in the overall project. As the flaws were identified, the cadres, engineers, and administrators responsible for them made sweeping self-criticisms one by one, addressing themselves as sparrows accepting dissection. Then, the fire was concentrated on Shen, the chief designer.

To introduce Shen as the major sparrow for the third day's analysis, the vice minister stood up. The slim old man looked like a gentle professor. Besides his seniority inside the Party, he had been revered because of the glory of his father, one of the founders of the CCP, who was killed by a warlord. He turned to face the window behind him, and everyone followed his finger to look at the hillside, where the landslide had buried one end of the plant.

He spoke slowly and deliberately without looking at Shen, as if dictating to a typist, "Such an ugly scene saddens our own people, but gladdens the enemy. As the chief designer, you, Comrade Shen, disregarded experimental data, cut specifications for lining materials, and ignored the consolidation of rocks around the high-pressure conduit. So, the disaster was bound to happen. Now, experts suggest building a new, high-quality steel conduit to closely fit into the old one. In the meantime, you've underestimated peak flood levels to design the dam and bridge. The impish young workers have composed this doggerel: 'What silly things are happening on Yongding River? Old tube sheathes new tube, old bridge piggybacks new bridge, and old dam jacks up new dam.' Isn't it shameful?"

Shen sobbed, "Two years ago, when the crazy masses forced me to break free from building codes, they were more ferocious than you are now. At the beginning, I held my ground as stubbornly as I could. Then, after my leaders and coworkers had all been silenced by the storm, how could I stand alone? Without magic means, the only way to achieve high-speed construction was lowering standards and cutting specifications. I admit I'm a weak woman."

A bureau chief stopped her, "You're not an ordinary woman. You're a Party member and a chief engineer. Unfortunately, you lack the backbone of a revolutionary. At the critical moment, you abandoned the Party's fundamental interests to follow the street wisdom: 'A clever man knows how to avoid being beaten.'"

She stopped crying to grumble, "Two years ago, people pressed me to alter the design in the name of the Revolution. Now, you blame me for lacking the very least attitude of a revolutionary. I wish I could have a zipper mounted on my chest. Then, any time the leaders and masses needed to dissect me as a sparrow, you could just pull it open."

Laughter burst from the audience while the leaders kept straight faces. I couldn't help standing up, "Frankly speaking, I hated Chief Engineer Shen's guts when she colluded with the security cadres to put me in the Red Clinic. But now, I feel it's not fair to put all the blame on her. My comrades and leaders, I want to remind you of the three one-line slogans painted on the front wall of the bureau's office in 1958. The wall has been whitewashed, but the lines have lingered in my mind: 'What can we do without procedures? Everyone talk freely! What can we do without materials? Rig things with whatever we have! What can we do without manpower? Rush headlong into action!' When such guidelines overrode engineering manuals and building codes, anything that could go wrong did go wrong. Anyone stronger than her would have been crushed."

She smiled through her tears, "Your words are the fairest. I apologize for what I've done to you. The chaos and disaster have proved you're tougher than me."

When the aide to the vice minister announced a break, Shen walked around the long table to shake hands with me. I said, "I'm not tougher than you, I just had less to lose. I'm not a Party member, not married, and have a low position, so there was space for me to fight."

During the break, she led me to the security office to collect my changes of underwear, books, washing basin, shoes, and my bed sheets and comforter wrapped like a loaf with a blanket. Such gear was shabby and worth little, but it composed my major property, all a Chinese person could possess. After I left them in the Red Clinlic, I felt a part of myself was missing. Worse, it could be held as evidence of an unsettled political case against me. Carrying it toward the railway station, where I'd slipped away like a fugitive 13 months before, I felt elated, as if liberated from an evil spirit.

52

Two weeks had passed since I sent the two photos to Chuju, and I expected her reply by now. As soon as I dropped my luggage at the dorm, I ran to check my mail at the reception desk at the front gate and the division office. Nothing from my hometown. I immediately wrote to my high school friend, Kai Tao, because he lived in the same block as Chuju's family, and his wife, Huiwen, was close to Chuju.

Ten days later, after they'd visited Chuju's mother, the couple replied, "Chuju's mother hasn't wavered from her promise. But Chuju was moody and refused to appear in public. We haven't talked to her, but will keep trying."

Chuju's moody reaction boded ill, and I felt ready to terminate the dream with her. Then, after another week, her letter came.

> Your photos darkened my sky and made me cry. Mother groaned, "Why is Heaven so unfair to our family?" In past years, big shots from Beijing and the provincial capital have come to our county hunting for beauties. During the negotiations, the young brides all insist on the same condition, that they don't have to appear in public with their senile husband-to-be. Unlike them, I've been proud of my

handsome young man. Out of the blue, these ruthless pictures and your grim words have shattered my dream.

My sorrow can't be hidden from the YL leaders of our factory, especially because I'm a seed for them to cultivate as a new member. They've taken turns nagging me until I've admitted their opinions are correct. They blamed my infatuation with your past appearance on bourgeois taste and say it is incompatible with the proletariat revolution. More importantly, they say, your physical damage demonstrates a noble spirit—conscious sacrifice for our communist cause, which I should take as an honor. However, the high-sounding words didn't seem to come from their hearts. I loathe their didactic tone, and their easy manner carries a gloating flavor.

The only one who really understands is Comrade Gong, the director of the women's association at our factory. She considers my agony and pain as a normal human reaction, and enlightened me with a Soviet novella, *It's Just for Love*, by Lieboshinskaya. It's about a Russian couple, an amorous nurse and a handsome engineer, who have a happy romance and marriage. Then, when Nazi Germany invades, the husband joins the Red Army and is burned beyond recognition. When peasants' wives welcome their disabled husbands home, they cry and smile but show no hesitation. But the nurse flinches from her husband and for many days is unable to extricate herself from her mental turmoil.

After reading it, I felt I was passing through the same journey as the nurse, though disfigurement is much less than the Soviet engineers'. At the end of the book, the pure, innocent, peasant wives put the nurse to shame for forsaking her vow of eternal love. By the time she goes to pick up her husband, Director Gong said, the proletarian spirit had expelled her petty-bourgeois ideas. I began to doubt my pain and dismay. Do they come from my petty-bourgeois sentiment?

Meanwhile, Mother keeps reminding me how nicely she treated Father after he was burnt out of shape by the gas explosion in the iron mine in 1945, and how you protected my sister Minqing and me from Coyote Tian, who called us Charred Man's Daughters. Now, I'm gathering the courage to face what happened to you, actually to us. No matter what idle people say, the leaders of the YL and the women's association are guiding me to follow the patriotic nurse depicted by Lieboshinskaya.

Please come home to meet us, both Mother and I are anxious to see you. We love you the same as we did in the past. We are proud of your bravery and noble deeds.

53

The windy season began at the end of February 1960. It was another lonely Sunday. Husbands living away from their wives uttered sad sighs: as one fell, another rose. The waves passed through our narrow corridors, unsettling me more than ever. Through the window, I watched sandstorms blasting the farm fields and overtaking cars. Whenever a bus slowed at the nearby stop, young women braved the dirt cloud and ran to jump aboard.

Among the early birds rushing to downtown Beijing, the appearance of a new nanny at our institute's kindergarten intrigued me. She used to be a maid at a fancy state-owned hotel in Hunan Province, and recently moved to Beijing, a year after marrying a Russian language interpreter at our institute. That was unusual after the hiring of 1958 had stopped.

The previous summer, when I was in Fujian, our institute got one residence permit from Beijing's Public Security Bureau. All the lonely husbands in this bachelors' dorm got together every day to guess who'd be the lucky guy. There was a big battle among the division leaders, a real dogfight. Every division head claimed that his protégé had suffered the most from family separation and that his wife was the most eligible to move to Beijing. Finally, the golden opportunity was given to the interpreter and a hotel maid. The other despairing men, without a hope of moving their wives to Beijing, were still feeling unfairly treated and aggrieved. There had to be some secret behind the decision made by the institute leaders, and I couldn't help searching for it. Perhaps Minggui An, a Party member familiar with the interpreter, knew something about it.

Carrying my mug of warm water, I knocked on the door of the southern room where he lived. Still in disgrace, he rarely had anyone to chat with. Fortunately, my stay in Fujian let me avoid my obligation to curse him, nor did I see him under fire.

He greeted me with a humble smile and yielded the only chair to me. I got right to the point, "Do you know how that woman got transferred to work at the kindergarten?"

He sat on the edge of his bed rubbing his hands together, "You bet."

"What confuses me is that senior engineers should've gotten priority, but a green interpreter got the permit. What happened?"

Minggui paused for a while, "At the time, the Soviet experts in our institute were still busy, traveling around with the interpreter. They liked the guy and wondered why he couldn't live with his wife, and they kept asking our leaders why this was the case. The Party committee decided our international image was the most important thing. So, the lucky couple had their paperwork done before the winter of 1959 when the Soviet experts left."

"In Soviet movies and novels, married couples never seem to have problems with family reunions."

He looked startled, "Please don't stretch our chat that far. Are you going to marry someone who is not in Beijing?"

"Please keep it confidential. She's my childhood friend, and—" I gestured to my face and legs, "She's the best I can do. But if I get married, my rank is too low to get any help from the leaders."

He shook his head, "Not really. You're indispensable to Old Ma. Everybody can see that. I also feel Jiang, the new division Party branch secretary, considers you one of the emerging mainstays in our division."

I sighed, "But he isn't a man who fights for his assistants."

"Don't be so sure. After graduation in 1950, he worked for several years in the Public Security system."

"He seems like a tough guy with a suave look. So my fate depends on if, or how hard, Jiang will lobby his higher-ups for me. Meanwhile, my credibility isn't strong enough for him to beat my competitors from other divisions, and all this assumes residence permits will become available."

With his hands on his knees, he spoke unhurriedly, "I see an opportunity coming up for you to make new contributions, but it's risky."

"What's that?"

"A field conference at Yangwumiao, where they're planning a large dam, up the Yuan River in western Hunan. So far, all the eligible workers have refused to attend the conference, and each of them came up with a plausible reason."

"What is the real reason?"

"Simple: hardship and death. Jiang has pointed it out sharply, but only at our cell meeting. Once you attend this conference, you'll probably be tied to the project and stuck in the mountains of western Hunan."

"I'm supposed to have Chuju moved here as a reward for the assignment that got me burned. How should I fall for that again?"

"You can't blame Director Gu. He promised you sincerely. Now, he's knocked down, anything he's promised will be invalid and denied by the new leaders."

The room was warm, but I shivered all over, "The living conditions and transportation in western Hunan must be hideous. In the early fifties, many PLA soldiers died there mopping up residual KMT forces. I heard all the native men now older than 25 joined the insurgents back then. The Party pardoned most of them so they wouldn't keep fighting. They must be desperate now because of the famine."

He nodded gloomily, "Highest murder rate in China. If you could represent our institute at the conference, I'm sure Jiang would be happy to work for your reunion with Chuju."

I shook my head, "I did this already. If I took the risk again, it is very likely that I would get injured again, and that the new leader who's promised to help me has been ousted or relocated when I come back. Do you know something else I can do that is safer?"

He looked depressed, "Nothing ventured, nothing gained. You might make it through all right, if you're careful enough. Meanwhile, Secretary Jiang is a judicious man, popular and rising now. The chance for him falling is very, very slim."

The next morning, at our group meeting, I offered to undertake the task. Two coworkers, who had feigned ignorance of the public pressure, now shook hands with me as if I'd pushed them out of the path of machinegun fire.

Secretary Jiang received me in his office before lunch. Blinking behind his glasses, he spoke solemnly as if measuring the correctness of every word, "Your name was the first to come to mind when I received notice of the field conference. Considering you need time for rest and medical treatment, I'd hoped other members of your group would show their sense of obligation. But they haven't. As in the past, you outshine them."

"I just do what I can. I think only infrastructure development can bring peace and stability to that poor region."

He nodded, "I'm proud of you. Do you have any requests or personal difficulties needing the leaders' help?"

"Last year, Director Gu promised to help me to move my fiancée to Beijing."

He tapped his desk with two fingers, "Don't worry, there'll be another chance once the economy gets better. I'll support you, if you keep working as hard as you have so far. I believe the other division leaders won't be unconcerned regarding your difficulty."

His rain check set my mind somewhat at ease, "May I meet her in Changsha after the conference or take a couple of days off to see her, plus a Sunday? The delegates will assemble in Changsha, not far from my hometown."

"Either way is okay if it's convenient for you."

54

I wrote to tell Chuju the details of my tight schedule and invite her to meet me in Changsha after the conference. By the etiquette of our small town, a man returning from Beijing should present gifts to his close friends and relatives, but I didn't have the money and time to save face. So, I chose the quieter and cheaper way. And Chuju would like to see a city much bigger than Pingxiang.

In early March, I met the other conference attendees at Changsha, the capital of Hunan. The presence of a provincial bureau chief, an engineering general from Beijing, and a famous professor recently returned from Europe spurred local cadres to arrange a comfortable trip for us during difficult times. Thus, small fish like me benefited from our association with the big shots.

A Czechoslovakian-made tour bus took us to the highland city, Yuanling, four hundred kilometers from Changsha. The gasoline shortage had reduced the number of buses, and local passengers waited fretfully at every stop, gazing enviously at our fancy bus with red paint and green curtains. Then, the 304th Geological Survey Brigade, our host for the conference, used their only motorboat to take us downstream to the dam site. During the six-hour voyage, we passed one dilapidated junk after another, leaving each bobbing in our wake. Seeing their sizable sails, patched with rags of every color, and listening to the creaking of their oars and masts, I felt guilty for having an easy ride in a motorboat.

When the boat anchored for a rest, we climbed up the steep bank and found a piece of flatland where a tall monument commanded the vast view. Above a two-tier base of cemented rocks stood a granite monolith. A vertical line of characters was carved into it and painted red; 'Eternal Glory to the PLA Martyrs for Eliminating Bandits.' The pillar, the like of which I'd never seen elsewhere, marked the bloodiest battlefield of the Revolution. A woman traveler stroked the inscription on the granite with emotion. I moaned for the victims of the massacre, all of them from poor peasant families.

The 304th Geological Survey Brigade had set up camp in the deep mountains with worksites on both banks of the river near the dam's axial line. As soon as we arrived that afternoon, the brigade's security cadre warned us that the famine had upset life in western Hunan earlier than in most places and now threatened travelers' safety, "Two weeks ago, when our carpenter was at evening group study on the other side of the river, a thief broke into his home, snatched a bag of rice, and beat his wife to death."

The county government allocated some meat and delicacies to treat the guests; the amount was scanty. The brigade's administration selected the most self-restrained young women to be kitchen helpers, believing their spirit would help them resist the temptation of the exclusively supplied food. When those hungry volunteers delivered aromatic dishes to our table, they averted their eyes and swallowed hard. I doubted the conference was worthy of their selflessness and strong sense of discipline.

Except for a geological tour of the future dam site and a presentation of the design concept, the major technical discussions were fruitless. The main presenter, Professor Cheng, was a buffoon. As a Chinese person born overseas and a famous scientist returning from Europe, he was a personage of the Party's United Front Line at the central government level.

We rank-and-file people felt funny about Cheng's arrogant show, but it hurt Engineer General Hu of the Changsha Design Institute, a big eagle in Changsha. I felt sorry for him when the crowd flocked to Cheng, leaving Hu out in the cold. Hu had practiced since 1935 and visited the US Bureau of Reclamation after the war. Now, his status was that of a personage of the Party's United Front Line in Hunan Province, normally the central figure surrounded by his assistants and local cadres on field trips. In terms of privilege and prestige, he ranked lower than Professor Cheng, who was the center of the conference.

The conference lasted three days. When it ended, the

motorboat took us upstream to the city of Yuanling. When Cheng's bragging speech on the deck carried nothing instructive, I chose to sit next to Hu in the cabin. I took the idle time to ask him questions, especially about the foundation treatment of Hoover Dam and Shasta Dam.

Hu wasn't at ease, and did not want to be left out. When our boat was passing a section with a wide river bed, filled with enchantment, he gingerly shifted toward Cheng and said, "The scenery around here is like the Tennessee Valley."

Cheng turned to look the other way, deliberately insulting him. I suppressed my smirk in relation to Hu's message about his study in the US. It was a childish way to beg respect. As for Cheng, a pet of the central government, his rudeness was barbaric.

While Hu sulked, I heard Cheng tell a bunch of his fans, "My PhD adviser is as famous as von Kármán, adviser to Professor Qian."

With a wry face, Hu asked me, "Why doesn't he say he's as famous as Professor Qian, Father of China's Missile Technology?"

I made a dismissive little wave toward Cheng, "He knows he can't be weighed on the same scale as Qian. He's a typical example of what Marx called a merchandized personality. The problem is the political cadres; they've spoiled him like a prince."

Hu grinned with his thumbs up, "Sharp, sharp, you hit the nail on the head. Young man, study hard and overtake him."

Ever since that episode, Hu chatted with me like an old friend, dropping the bossy airs he used when he talked to his aides.

We arrived at Yuanling in the early afternoon, and the first striking scene in the highland city was the starving peasants lying on the ground by the bus terminal and within a circle formed with straw ropes. Immovable and waiting for deportation, their spiritless eyes still rotated in their grimy sockets, as if pleading for help. The stores on the streets were closed. Many houses had yellow paper with mourning couplets pasted on their doors, indicating a high death toll.

We had a dinner at the hostel of the Yuanling County Party Committee. It was a near feast, for which we paid only a small token fee. The ten courses of gourmet food filled the large round table to its edge. Roasted duck, steamed bass, and shark fin soup, which I'd never tasted before, weren't affordable for ordinary people even in good years. Sitting at the table, I wondered if the banquet had been subsidized by the county's public-relations budget.

At the dining hall gate, hungry locals poked their heads in and stared at the dishes and at us, but guards hooted them away. The greasy food quickly filled me, then made me feel sick. All night, it seemed to have frozen in my heart as well as in my stomach, keeping me awake. I thought of the peasants starving in the cold. I imagined that the next time I came here, I would be alone and only able to stand outside the dining hall and poke my head in. But no matter what the future world would look like, I would carry out my present personal agenda and meet Chuju in Changsha.

The next night, after a long day's ride of four hundred kilometers, we returned to Changsha. As I'd done on my previous trips to Hunan Province, I considered the Changsha Waterpower Design Institute my host and stayed at the hostel affiliated with it, located within its large compound, the former campus of Hunan Agricultural College. It was a humble lodging, but quiet and inexpensive, an ideal place given the limits imposed by my low rank's per diem.

The manager of the hostel had kept my mail during my few days' absence from Changsha. A long-awaited telegram from Chuju told me she would arrive just as I'd asked, around eleven the next morning.

55

The railway station was crowded. As trains came and went, the platform seemed forever chaotic. I jostled with others at the gate, trying to spot Chuju through the mass of humanity. An hour later, I could only assume that I'd somehow missed her. I blamed myself for my stupidity. Now what could I do?

Suddenly, I saw her leaning against a flagpole watching the busy street next to the plaza. A large handbag lay at her feet, her sole luggage for the two-day visit. I rushed up to reach her from behind, "Welcome, Chuju!"

She didn't turn to greet me. Instead, she hunched her shoulders and clutched her arms to her chest. I held her shoulders and apologized, "Sorry, I've been looking for you for an hour. I lost you in the flood of people."

She shook my hands off, "I'm unattractive and easily overlooked. As you've done for years."

I picked up her handbag, "I didn't know you'd gotten so thorny, my dear. For all these years, you hid yourself from me. Do you remember how coldly you treated me in the summer of 1956?"

She turned to me. Her eyes darted to the scar on my face and turned away as soon as they caught my eyes. She twisted away from me to hide her expression but couldn't muffle her gasp. My heart sank, but I composed myself to lead her to the bus terminal.

Maybe a hundred people were lined up there, more kept joining, and frustrated passengers ahead of us often gave up and left the line. I asked her, "Are you too tired to walk to the hostel?"

"If you, a delicate scholar, can walk the distance, why

should I have a problem?" This sounded more like the Chuju from the old days. I tried several times to carry her vinyl duffel bag, but she wouldn't let me.

She had a badge on her chest, a medal awarded to people who passed the Standard Exam II of Physical Readiness for Labor and National Defense, a nationwide program of military significance that flourished in the mid-fifties. Participation was voluntary, but peer pressure ensured that all high-school and college students took the training and the test. I was embarrassed at not having passed even the Standard Exam I. In the 1955 general exam, my hundred-meter and one-thousand-five-hundred-meter runs and rope climbing met the requirements, but I failed grenade throwing and box vaulting. I didn't mention it to her.

As we walked along the side road skirting the commercial area, our steps fell in sync and calmed me. Her tender, eggshell face and vivacious, dewy eyes made her seem even more feminine and alluring than before, while her voice had ripened with mellow charm.

She peered around, as if not shocked by my disfigured face. I could tell she was searching for something happy to say. After quite a few minutes of silent walking, she asked, "What sports facilities do you have at your institute?"

Not many, in truth: "A full basketball court, a tennis court, and a small field with horizontal and parallel bars."

"Have you been to a recital by the soprano Lanyin Guo?"

"Not yet. I prefer Beijing opera to modern vocal music."

"Why don't you join an amateur chorus?"

"No time. And my singing probably isn't up to Beijing standards."

Like other young women in our hometown, she held a fanciful picture of life in Beijing and yearned to live there.

Each time she tilted her head to glance at my scar, she immediately averted her gaze. Perhaps she was assessing me with a sense of loss and misgiving. Finally, our eyes met, and we smiled quizzically without words.

I said, "Sorry for your father's death. He worked hard without enjoying life. If it hadn't have been for the crazy Great Leap, he wouldn't have ignored his heart problem and worked around the clock in the mine."

She stopped to face me, "I owe a big thank-you to your parents and your brother Haitao for their help. They took care of my mother, brought my father's coffin from Hubei, and gathered volunteer laborers and gift money for the funeral. They helped us through the crisis. Otherwise, I don't know if we could have survived it."

As she dabbed her eyes with a handkerchief, I felt the longtime compassion between our two families and between us. I took her handbag and patted her back, "I know how hard the disaster hit your family."

"In 1957, I graduated from high school and entered a three-year program for a pharmacist's certificate. Just as I finished the first year, I had to quit studying. I don't see any chance of going back."

I held her arm to lead her down the path, "University study doesn't add up to better wages. My friend Little Tiger, who doesn't even have a middle-school education, now makes more money as a lathe operator at your factory than I do. Even worse, university students are politically classified as intellectuals and considered unreliable."

Chuju smirked, "I get it. University study has no advantages at all. Now I feel so much better."

"No, I don't mean that. It helps you get skills and a better understanding of the world. I just want you to know that the fate of university graduates isn't as fancy as you imagine. Anyway, I hope you can go back to school someday."

We passed a pond rippling in the breeze. She picked up flat stones from the ground, skipped them across the water, then lifted her chin and looked at me, "Can you do that?"

I tried several times, but the rocks only plunked into the water, "I humbly admit defeat."

She pursed her lips, "That's just a kid's game. But our general situation makes me feel inferior to you. Without a university education, you won't respect me."

I raised a hand, "May thunderbolts fry me if I look down on Chuju."

She stamped, "Don't say that. Who wants you to die? I only need your respect."

I pulled her hand and started walking again, "I already respect you. If my finances get better, I'll support you in going back to school. If we don't get that lucky, we shouldn't be frustrated. Chairman Mao didn't go to university, yet we accept his instructions as the golden rule and infallible law."

Around two in the afternoon, we arrived at the hostel and met Chuju's roommate. From her round face, home-cut hair, all-season blue blouse, and rural look, I guessed her to be a county-level political or administrative cadre.

To make the place more agreeable to Chuju, I asked the manager to change the bed sheets and fetch hot water in a thermos and a washbasin. Chuju announced she needed a nap. I said I'd come back in three hours.

The hostel consisted of two parallel brick buildings a few yards apart. They were like two-story barracks, with the windows facing north, the doors south. The kitchen and dining hall formed an annex to the east. I was staying upstairs on the north row, and from there everyone in the south building, especially on the ground floor, was visible through the hallway banisters. When Chuju washed her face in the center of the room, I took the opportunity to appreciate her profile and gestures, she was quite different from the girl I'd seen almost four years before.

Under her warm jacket, she wore a hand-knitted sweater,

light green and close fitting. When she stretched up to hang the towel on a string, her sleeves slid down to expose her white arms, and the hem of her sweater rose above her slim waist. Her supple features reminded me of the local big shots poised to swoop down on her.

Comrade Dai, a former classmate and currently a division colleague, happened to be in the same hostel, and the manager assigned him my room to share, where a vacant bed was available. His appearance was nothing but a nuisance for me. I would have no privacy at all, even a thousand miles from my workplace. He must have glimpsed Chuju with me, because he asked if he could greet her and have a friendly gathering. I agreed that we could all walk to the mess hall together for Sunday's second meal.

While Dai, Chuju, and I sat at a table waiting for the lines to shorten, a woman with a familiar face appeared in the crowd. I lowered my head to dodge her, but she bustled to my side, "Why don't you introduce me to your pretty girl?"

I groaned. The other guests all turned to stare at us. Chuju blushed. The energetic lady, Fu, was an instructor of engineering geology at Beijing Waterpower School. I'd met her at a construction site a year before. Teacher Fu was physically petite but equipped with a sharp tongue and she was well connected to the gossip network.

All during dinner she loudly regaled our table with rumors about prominent women in Beijing. Nothing in her freckled face suggested intelligence. Her tart mockery annoyed me and served mainly to make me appreciate Chuju, who, by contrast, seemed gentle and fair.

As our meal ended, dusk fell. The air was brisk. Dai suggested we stroll in the compound's vegetable garden. As soon as we walked outside, Chuju and I lagged behind, leaving Fu with Dai.

The agriculture school had moved two years earlier, leaving

experimental fields unattended. Wooden placards, with both Chinese and Latin tags, were scattered along the fence, relics of sample species that used to grow there. Now, as the designers and staff of the institute engaged in farm production to supplement food rations, the fields had become gardens of cabbage, turnips, sweet potatoes, and more.

The trails were flanked by plowed patches and racks for holding pumpkins and tripods for long beans. I stopped under a bamboo frame where the winter melons had been harvested, leaving dried vines woven like an awning. I faced Chuju, "This is the first time we've walked together without your mother. Have you ever left home for longer than a day?"

She stepped toward me and rested her forehead on my cheek, "Never. This is the first time my mom let me go out alone. She doesn't think you're a kidnapper. But are you?"

I pulled her toward me, "If only I had a place to hide you. If only we had the right to move around freely, we could go wherever we wanted under the sky."

She looked into my eyes as I clasped her tightly. The scent of citronella hair oil drew me closer and I rested my forehead against her temple. Standing on her tiptoes, she raised her head and put her lips to mine. We had our first kiss as if we were in a scene from a Soviet movie.

When Fu's haranguing voice grew nearer, we pulled apart and looked into each other's eyes. Fu and Dai interrupted us for the walk back to the hostel.

It was only about seven in the evening, too early to let Chuju go back to her room. After the other two left, we continued to walk, looking for a place to sit. A dim light gleaming among the willows drew us. We left the vegetable garden, walked in another direction, and came to a large pond. Weeds along its shore rustled in the chilly breeze. At one corner of the pond, a pump hut sat among shrubs, its inlet hose lying exposed in the early spring. Chuju seemed frightened at the wilderness, and looked around nervously. I said, "Nothing to be afraid of. The robbers and murderers are flocking downtown and at the railway station. The place belongs to a government unit. We're safe."

I pushed the thorny branches aside and led Chuju to the shabby shed, its wobbly door held shut with a single wire. In the faint light cast from the streetlamp, I peered through its cracks and saw only a pump on the floor and a switchbox on the wall. The room smelled dusty, but she seemed not to mind. I grabbed a bamboo stick from a side fence to knock spider webs from the ceiling and walls.

I pulled the door closed, "Sorry I don't have a decent place to entertain you. If I were rich, I'd invite you to visit Beijing and take you on a tour of the city."

She sighed softly, "If I had the freedom to change residence, I'd come join you in Beijing and work at any job I could find."

The closed door let dim light spill in through the crevices around its edges and its frame. I gazed into her dark, gleaming eyes, "That would be nice. We have many hurdles ahead. I don't know if you're willing to live a poor life with me. I also worry that if we can't move in together for many years, you may not be strong enough to stand being alone."

She stepped closer and put her head on my shoulder, "Believe in me."

"I do believe in you. But the world is tough. A man who wants to change his status has to work hard for decades with no guarantee of success. But a pretty and smart woman can achieve that goal through marriage. I love you, but I want you to think it over before you make the big decision."

I felt her warm breath on my neck. She whispered, "I'm not a snob and can't imagine being happily married to a powerful old man. I want to be self-reliant, work hard to support myself, and have a young, handsome husband like you."

I wrapped my arms around her, "I'm lucky. But I'm no longer handsome."

"Your scar isn't as bad as I imagined. People in our town remember your previous good looks. Like your comrades in Beijing, they'll see it as a badge of brave service to our country."

A load lifted from my mind, "I appreciate your noble thoughts."

She laid her head on my chest and wriggled as if settling in to sleep. I hugged her with all my strength until she gasped for air. Our faces pressed together on their left sides. She pushed away for a moment then pulled closer again so that our faces were now touching on their right sides, silently declaring her acceptance of my wound as an inseparable part of me. I sank into the trance her open lips offered, obliterating all else from my mind, the heat of her kiss bringing me bliss I'd never known.

In a dreamy state, she asked, "Will you always treat me so nicely?"

"Of course. No need to ask."

She studied my face as though searching for the truth. I stroked her hair, "Now it's my turn. How long will your love for me last?"

"If you don't marry me," she said, "I'll never marry."

"In a recent letter, you wrote, 'We love you the same as we did in the past.' I want to hear you say that."

"I've only heard that in foreign films. We Chinese keep our warmth inside, like a thermos. It would be creepy to say the word *love*."

I embraced her, "Then how about this? Just shake your head or nod. Do you love me?"

She banged my chest twice with her forehead. After a moment's silence, she whispered, "I love you."

So, in the simplest way, we were engaged, and Heaven

witnessed our pledge.

Through the crack above the sagging door, I saw night vapors rise from the pond as a thin fog drifted toward us, surrounding the tiny shed like a capsule and carrying just Chuju and me into another world.

56

The next morning, we got a ride in the van that took all the conference participants to the trains. From the railway station, Chuju and I walked toward the city center. Jostled by window-shopping crowds, we browsed the stores in the busy commercial area. The market looked less depressed than in Fujian, but most items were rationed. We saw few smiling faces among the customers.

In the late afternoon, we entered a small restaurant for an early dinner. Sitting together, eating noodles, we ordered pork fried with green beans, steamed eggplant, and authentic Hunan hot-and-sour soup. We ate everything, enjoying the food and the first chance to share such a meal in a restaurant.

We explored a large department store. Among its luxurious goods, clerks idled, watching Chuju and me saunter by the glass counters. When she stopped at the embroidery counter, hands on the edge of the glass, I could tell she wanted a silk quilt cover. I asked which she liked best. She pointed to a pink one, embroidered with a large white phoenix. While the clerk was counting the 16 yuan I paid, Chuju bent over the silk fabric, caressing it tenderly. I could tell she was quietly ecstatic to have the first article for our future household.

In a small, tidy shoe store, where most customers flocked around the counter holding cheap footwear with cloth uppers and plastic soles, I found a plain pair of good-quality leather shoes for 18 yuan. I asked the saleswoman to take them out for

Chuju to try on. She pulled my hand off the counter, "No, they're too expensive."

"In the old days, even poor families struggled to buy their future spouses one ring each as a symbol of their engagement. Now only foreign visitors wear rings and exchanging them happens only in movies. I feel better buying something practical and affordable as a token of our engagement."

While the saleswoman tied the shoebox with string, Chuju held my upper arm with both hands. With this bravest public gesture, she let me know how much she was touched.

When we returned to the hostel, Chuju's roommate had gone. Around ten o'clock, Comrade Dai and Teacher Fu came to Chuju's room for a farewell visit. They would travel back to Beijing when I did, the next evening. Chuju's train to Jiangxi would leave six hours ahead of ours.

All four of us chatted casually for an hour. Then Dai and Fu shook hands with Chuju, "We'd like to come to your wedding." It seemed natural for me to remain in the room. In the meantime, the ideology-oriented characteristics my compatriots had acquired in the previous decade, required that they must be concerned with where I'd spend the night.

The moment Chuju shut her door, an invisible, mysterious blanket enveloped us. Suddenly Chuju and I were alone in the room. The room was our private cell, a world temporarily ours alone. Dai and Fu couldn't watch, though they'd keep speculating.

It was 11 o'clock, and half the hostel's rooms were dark. None of the windows had curtains, and anyone could see into the still-lighted rooms. I sat on the stool by the desk, which shielded my lower body from being seen from outside. I took a deep breath, "The wounds on my legs aren't pretty, but I can't hide them from you."

I untied my belt and pushed my long johns and pants down

to my ankles. In the shadow of the desk, the discolored patches on my legs were visible, like the disconnected islands of Japan. Chuju squatted down, stroking and examining them, then slipped down to sit on the floor, "What awful pain you suffered. I hate it that I wasn't by your side when it happened."

Her shoulders jerked, and she sobbed, "I'm sorry for wavering after your photos came. I'm immature and selfish."

As her tears washed my knees, I pulled her up from the dank cement floor and stretched my arm to pull the light cord dangling from the ceiling. It was midnight, and no other lights were on.

In the darkness, I urged myself to ignore the outside world, but an inexplicable fear seized me. As if looking for support from her, I asked, "May I stay here tonight?"

"If you want."

My dream had come true, after years of craving. In the darkness, with Chuju in my embrace, I was frozen by fear. A dog barked in the distance, perhaps at a lurking voyeur. I whispered, "Listen, is that a voice?"

"You're hearing things."

Perched on the edge of her bed, we held each other's hands and enjoyed the lingering moment. As time spun out, the swishing of bare willow twigs dominated the night sounds. I knew our highly vigilant fellow citizens were sleeping. The dim light of the streetlamp further thinned as our breath fogged the window and a haze veiled us, bringing me a sense of safety.

Chuju snuggled into my arms. I pulled her to sit on my lap. Slowly, we slid down onto the narrow bed. Around 30 inches wide, it was cramped, and, with four bunks and two narrow desks built into the small room, it was impossible to push two bunks together to make a large bed. The rough, cotton-filled comforter prevented us from lying flat. I threw it onto the vacant bed, making the narrow space fully available for us. As we rested our heads on the same pillow, I propped up my chin with one arm and, from inches away, fixated on the glint in her eyes. I cherished her face, no longer as removed from me as a painting in a museum or an actress's photo on a poster. I threw myself on her. With our lips pressed together and our arms binding us like hoops, we rolled wildly as one, struggling not to fall off the bed.

I moved my hand down to her tender, silky belly, my fingers creeping up under her shirt. She closed her eyes, willingly waiting for my advance. I sensed that the greatest moment, which I'd so long waited for, was right now. I tore off my shoes but dared not take off my layers of clothes in case we were interrupted. During my clumsy movements, Chuju watched me, eagerly and nervously, while my virile drive rapidly shrank. Cold air and fear doused my desire, which had been so untamable during my years of solitude. I tried to command myself to be excited, but a profound mental barrier forbade me to act.

Baffled by my sudden inaction and frustration, Chuju assessed me with somber eyes. I retied my belt, put on my shoes and lay beside her, "We better wait for the day we have the marriage certificate as our permit. I can't do it like a thief now."

I got up and spread the comforter over her. She sat up and started to unbutton her jacket, "It's cold. Take off your clumsy clothes and stay warm with me under the comforter."

I held her face and kissed her forehead, "If I go back to my room too late, Comrade Dai will memorize the exact time and make up a story against us." Still reluctant to part, I squatted to untie the laces of her running shoes and helped her take off her jacket, "Sleep well. I'll come early tomorrow and walk you to the train station."

As if resigned to let me go, she continued to undress, one layer after another, and her outfit became a mound of cloth on the chair. Chuju revealed herself to me, almost nude, before she slipped under the comforter. Her tender skin, rising bosom, and shapely buttocks rekindled a fire inside me. I found new resolve to act, to release my dammed desire for the first time.

I pushed my long johns and cotton-padded pants down to my knees so I could respond quickly in case of interruption. The large lump of corrugated pants held my legs together like a shackle, hindering my effort to sink into her. I hit a warm, wet spot in a crevice and pushed in, enduring the pain of friction. Besides my physical awkwardness, wild thoughts plagued me. I imagined Dai watching me from his high window, and Teacher Fu, next door, putting her ear to the wall to detect any incriminating noises. The hellish sound of the creaking bed drove me to even more frenzied motion. The more nervous I got, the longer my ejaculation was delayed.

Finally, it was over. All in a sweat, I had no joy, but felt something monumental had happened to mark our mutual commitment. I hastily fastened my belt and put my warm jacket on.

Chuju was still aroused and didn't want me to go. Breathing heavily, I pulled away from her. My hands and feet were numb with cold, "Teacher Fu, the rumor mill, is in the next room, ready to target anyone within shooting range. Comrade Dai loves revealing anything he thinks is wrong."

"So, what? Our relationship is perfectly justifiable."

"You're too green to know how murderous tongues can kill people."

"But Teacher Fu doesn't have a way to hurt you directly."

"Maybe yes, maybe no. If she wants, she can find one. A while back, a man visited her colleague in the dorm for single women teachers. The colleague's husband was a rightist banished to some remote outpost. Eager to cook up charges of possible illicit sexual activity, Fu tiptoed to her room to eavesdrop and peep through the keyhole."

"How do you know that?"

"I know several teachers in her school, and they all hate her. If we spent a night together before the wedding, it would be a great chance for Fu to spread the news as a scandal. It's better not to give either of them any ammunition."

Chuju looked down and slowly nodded.

That night, lying in my room on the second floor of the north building, I couldn't sleep. Looking out the window, with my sweaters and pants bolstering my pillow, I could easily see Chuju's window on the first floor. I waited, watching, in case she turned on the light.

Dai's snore, steady and somehow menacing, irritated me. I was fully awake. With Chuju so close, I felt myself a hostage, captive to the vigilant eyes of my comrades even as they slept. I blamed my bad luck for springing Dai and Fu on me that important night.

The sleepless night left me exhausted and, in the morning, I nursed a terrible headache. On the way to Chuju's room, I pounded my chest. *Coward, you flinched from the busybodies. To dodge their poisonous tongues, you ruined the best time of your life.*

After breakfast, I walked Chuju to the station, tortured all the way by regret. On the platform, I said, "We should get married in a few months. The sooner we do, the earlier I can ask my leaders to put our names on the waiting list for family unification."

A furrowed brow shadowed her tender face, "We don't have the money for a wedding."

"Never mind. I have some savings. If we hold a revolutionary-style wedding in Beijing, we only need to buy you a train ticket."

"My mother and your parents will want to be there. And they could help a lot with the preparations."

"We can't afford it. People in small towns have stuck to old customs. If we get married there, no matter how poor we are, we'll at least have to hold a banquet. Our guests would include relatives and friends from both sides, from two generations. How could we afford to feed such a large crowd?"

She bowed her head, "A few days ago, restaurants in our town suddenly inflated their prices by a factor of five. If we hold our wedding in Jiangxi, no matter how humble it is, we'll carry the debts forever."

"And picky guests will complain and make jokes about us if the banquet isn't fancy enough."

Chuju smiled, "You're right. It's much simpler and cheaper to have the ceremony in Beijing. And my dream of seeing the great capital would come true."

No matter how much I wanted to hug her, in public we could only shake hands to say goodbye. Upon the conductor's gesture to shut the door, Chuju secured her bag with one hand and climbed into the car.

Puffs of steam escaped the locomotive like a deep sigh for my poverty. Was I just bragging? I didn't have enough money for even a shabby wedding.

The largest expense would be the train fare. If I were going back to Jiangxi, a one-way ticket for a ride on a hard-wooden seat in an express train would cost 30 yuan. For Chuju, I felt obligated to pay another 18 so she could have a berth, because the 'express' train ran took 32 hours to cover the one thousand seven hundred kilometers. A roundtrip was 96 yuan. I also wanted to dress Chuju like a bride. My entire savings amounted to 80 yuan.

57

On the way back to Beijing, around four hundred kilometers north, I stopped over in Wuhan for a day. I walked to my uncle's rented place, a room in a shabby house near the railway station, where my mother was working as a house keeper for her younger brother, Jixi. Uncle Jixi was a college English teacher without the slightest aptitude for managing a household. Since his wife had died six years earlier, Mother had spent more time in Wuhan than in Jiangxi, leaving Father and my brothers at home.

Since the Liberation, I'd never seen a smile on Uncle's face. His oldest daughter, Jinhua, had married an engineer in the KMT Air Force and fled to Taiwan. To make his public image worse, he'd never praised the Party aloud, nor denounced his daughter publicly. As a result, he was picked out for laboring at a tea farm at this bad time, though he was over 60, and had weak bones and muscles. Now, Mother took care of his home as a family center for her nephew and two nieces.

When I arrived around nine o'clock, Mother wasn't there. An old lady from another family living in the house, whom I met a year before and called Aunt, came out from the kitchen to greet me, "Your mom went to the tea farm yesterday. Normally she comes home at noon the next day. You may wait here and have some hot water."

She led me into the shared kitchen and pointed at a corner with a stove and a pile of honeycomb briquettes, "Your mom cooks here."

The weather was chill and humid. I opened the little door at the bottom of the stove to clear the coal ashes and let the air in, then added a fresh briquette. While waiting for the water in the kettle to boil, I gnawed the bun I brought from Changsha.

A large column of tattered, listless peasants was passing by the front door and window, "The peasants are too obedient," I murmured, "Two policemen can round up a thousand men. Nobody tries to run away?"

"They're too weak to run." Aunt continued her cooking, "Cadres in the countryside report high grain yields to look good. Then the government levies taxes and makes grain purchases according to those false high numbers. Too little is left for the peasants to eat. They're starving."

"Where are those peasants being sent?"

"To their home villages, but they'll flee to the big city again. The People's Communes give them written permits for begging. Officials call them blind migrants."

With a large bowl of boiled water to wash down the cold, dry food, my body warmed up and I got sleepy. Then I heard heavy steps, followed by a throaty voice, "Anyone without a residence permit must be evicted from the city."

I rushed to the front door. Mother, shivering in wet muddy clothes, was there with a bamboo walking stick and a basket hung on her arm. A policeman, a head taller than her, impatiently gestured for her to hand over her ID. Her hair was falling about her face, her shoes were drenched, and strips of rags bound the soles of her shoes to her insteps.

She searched every pocket of her multilayered clothes, "I have a temporary residence permit. I have to find the key to my room first."

I took the basket and stick from her. Ignoring the policeman, she gazed at me, "You're much thinner than last year. You've eaten coarse, mess-hall food too long."

Crying, she held my waist and put her head on my chest. The policeman thrust the tip of his baton between us to separate us, "No stalling tactics! Where's your key?"

The brass key was tied to her belt, which was actually a rope. "Here it is," I said, "Where's the household registration book?"

She untied the key and pointed down the hallway, "The end room. Under my pillow."

After I showed the policeman Mother's temporary residence permit, a red slip stamped with a recent six-month extension, he left without a murmur.

Aunt urged Mother, "Hurry, change your wet clothes."

Mother turned to me, "Father and I are happy you've decided to marry Chuju." She smiled with chattering teeth, "Chuju is the best girl. I've watched her grow from this tall." She spread her hands a foot apart.

I held her arm and led her to her room where a vacant bunk awaited Uncle Jixi. She asked me to have a nap, but I carried warm water in a basin for her to wash the mud from her face, hands, and hair. Without spare warm clothes to replace the wet ones, which I hung on two stools to dry by the coal stove, she roughly cleaned her feet and cuddled up in her bed. Leaning against the wall with the thick comforter pulled up to her neck, she sighed, "The tea farm is about 120 kilometers south of Wuhan. From the railway station, I have to walk two hours. Uncle Jixi and several other troubled teachers are toiling over there." She began to weep.

I tried to stop her crying, "Uncle is not alone. He'll be okay. You're keeping the family together: he has a nest waiting for his return."

She cheered up a little, "I go to the farm every month and bring Uncle some food. Otherwise, he can't survive. I also mended his clothes and cleaned the room he shares with the other teachers, messy as a pigsty."

"It's dangerous for you to go that far into a rough area."

"With my walking stick and the few characters I know for the signs at the railway station and on the streets, I can make it."

"But you fell on the road and rolled in the mud. Your blood pressure is high."

She smiled, "With my feet, I've gotten used to stumbling. In Jiangxi, where I washed diapers in the pond for my grandchildren, I rolled on the slopes countless times." She dozed off.

I stayed in the kitchen, holding her clothes close to the

stove so they would dry more quickly. An hour later, the clothes still not yet fully dry, Mother said they were warm and bearable to wear. She cooked a large bowl of noodles for me, with fried eggs and green onion on top. She sat beside me. No matter how hard I pushed her to share the food, she refused.

She relayed regrets from my cousin Yinhua, "She has classes and meetings, and coming here is a four-hour roundtrip by bus and ferry."

Yinhua, about ten years old than me, got her English degree from a Canadian missionary college in 1949. Since 1952, after a crash course, she had been teaching Russian at a high school.

"I know how busy she is," I said, "A woman always trying to compete with men."

"She was elected 'model teacher' last semester. Not easy, with a sister in Taiwan."

I finished the late lunch and helped clean the dishes. Mother borrowed a comforter and a blanket from a neighbor to make a bed for me. While stuffing clothes into a pillowcase, I said, "Judging by the situation in Beijing with people similar to Uncle, he might be there another year. You'd better go home soon after he returns to Wuhan."

She walked to her bunk, a door plank set on a pair of sawhorses. From under the mattress she pulled a brown envelope wrapped in a handkerchief, "It's 50 yuan, Yinhua's wedding gift to you."

I was shocked, "That's a lot, a young high-school teacher only makes this much in a month. Her big gift actually repays your wholehearted service to Uncle Jixi."

Mother gingerly opened another envelope, "This is all I've saved for a year from what Uncle and Yinhua have given me, also 50 yuan. Now I give it to you."

"No, Mom, I can't take your sweat money."

Sometime in 1947, Father had asked a friend to bring her ten silver coins. After several months without income, she was thrilled. I had watched as she sat in a corner, counting with her fingers, "One coin to buy rice ... two for rent ... three to reserve pork for the New Year ... ancestor worship on July 15 ... can't be covered by three coins. No, we need at least 12. Ah, how dumb I am—I haven't counted school registration."

Since my silent observation of her murmuring calculations I had always kept track of her budget. I pushed the envelope back into her hands, "You need this money badly. I remember the things you were eager to buy when I last came. Wool to knit Father a sweater. A military blanket from the secondhand store for my younger brother. More important, the coffins for Father's and your final day are still a pile of lumber air-drying. More money to pay the carpenter and painter. I hate it that I can't help you more."

"Nice boy, you know everything." Mother smiled and pushed the envelope back at me, "I would feel selfish if you didn't take it, because marriage is the most important event in life."

In the end, I took 20 yuan from the envelope, leaving 30 for her. Then I tried to give her some grain coupons, but she refused. Because I didn't want to eat up her rationed food, I suggested skipping dinner.

The sky turned dark. She fell asleep before me. In the dark, I listened to the sound of her snoring, it was much weaker than ten years before.

The next day, she saw me off at the front door, drying her eyes on her apron. Her snow-white hair and stooped back confronted me with how much her aging process had accelerated. I hated that I didn't spend enough time with her.

PART TWO

1

On the way from Wuhan to Beijing, I worked out that the minimum budget for my wedding should be no less than three hundred yuan. I had only half enough. Since all moonlighting sidelines had been banned as capitalist paths, there wasn't a single way to make the money I badly needed. Then, the anguish pressing my brain squeezed a nugget from my memory.

In May 1958, following the initiative of activists at the Beijing Institute of Waterpower Design and Surveying, every YL member in our system donated five yuan and spent Communist Sundays in 'voluntary' labor, as Lenin had advocated. For several Sundays, we had to dig and move earth to build a tiny YL Power Station, an educational exhibition for children.

Feeling fierce competition from their peers, the radicals in our research institute also demanded that we engineers and technicians assigned to construction sites 'voluntarily' gave up our fieldwork allowance, "It will save the government money and enhance our communist spirit." As nobody dared argue, I raised my hand with the others.

Now, empty stomachs forced people to drop their vanity. I risked sounding out a few colleagues. They all said they were no longer volunteering to give up their allowance.

But nobody dared to take the lead. Dong Long even warned me, "The standouts usually bear the brunt of attack. The bird that leaves the flock gets shot."

"I'm desperate, I'll take the risk. I'll be careful to make good use of the Party's new policy."

"People cheer the circus acrobat because, as the saying goes, 'Boldness of execution stems from superb skill.' I'm not sure you have the skill to deal with political danger."

"I have no choice. If I fail, or succeed now but later get hit, I'll accept my fate."

I composed a report to lead the petition effort. Six of the

ten who were eager to get the money back signed their names after mine.

The head of our accounting office received me with her well-known poker face. Rumor had it that her husband was a bureau chief at our ministry's headquarters, which might have been a source of her air of superiority. She read my report aloud to her officemates, deliberately exposing my private action, which would be held as selfish by the public.

She clicked her tongue, "You intellectuals know how to pursue personal gain in the name of Party policy, eh?"

"Come on. A veteran cadre shouldn't taunt a small fish like me. I know you're reluctant to help me, but I have to start worshiping at your office before I kowtow and burn joss sticks to other idols."

She put on a false smile, waving me away, "Let me ask the finance and accounting bureau of our ministry for instructions."

For three weeks she kept telling me, "I haven't a word from the bureau."

The third time I left her office, a female accountant, for whom I'd once helped carry a large parcel to her mother in Changsha, followed me into the corridor, "The money withheld from fieldworkers like you remains in our ledgers. Nobody knows what to do with it."

The tip inspired me to contact the bureau chief in charge of finance and accounting at our ministry's headquarters, a few blocks away from our hospital. The lanky old man spoke with a benevolent tone and a strong Hunan accent, "Ai-ya, your institute hasn't sent your report to us. It's a common problem for many people like you. I see it can be straightened out, but not immediately. Please wait with patience."

I hung around the staircase, not knowing what to do and reluctant to leave. Suddenly, I remembered the phrase from *Dream of the Red Chamber*, "Tolling a gold bell once is more effective than hitting brass cymbals three thousand times."

Some ancient stories talk about oppressed people who couldn't find local officials to redress an injustice but finally got help from an imperial envoy during their tours of inspection. They block the way, intercept the sedan chair, and plead their case to the highest authority. Finally, they get what they've wanted. That was the only option left to me.

Secretary Yao, the king of our ministry, would be my gold bell. He didn't know me, but I had seen him in public many times and believed him a broadminded man, much wiser and magnanimous than the small-time cadres at the bottom of the hierarchy.

A female cadre in the corridor pointed out his office at the east end of the third floor. It wasn't marked with a sign. As I approached to the door, the bodyguard stopped me. A young aide came out and skimmed my copy of the report, then asked me to leave it there. I said, "Giving you the report is like throwing a rock into the sea. I want to talk to Secretary Yao, just for two minutes."

"No."

With neither side willing to budge, the guard grabbed his pistol and yelled, "Get out of here!" I glared at him.

His spine stiffened.

A booming voice with a mild tone spoke from deep inside the office, "Let him come in."

The guard retreated two steps. The aide tilted sideways and stretched out an arm to usher me in. Secretary Yao was reading something on his desk with a magnifier. Though bald, obese, and limping, his witty remarks and fatherly manner created a majestic impression. Standing a yard away from the large desk, I felt how paltry my status and motives were when compared with the legend of his career: a university physics major in the early thirties, a leader of the 1935 mass movement in Beijing, a tough communist fighter jailed by the KMT, and then commissar of the Northeast Anti-Japanese United Army in the forties. And now, leading a large ministry of the state council.

"I like your handwriting, young man." The irrelevant

comment caught me off-balance. "It's vigorous and graceful. What calligraphy do you emulate?"

"The Liu style of the Tang Dynasty."

"How old are you?"

"Twenty-six."

"Most people of your age don't give a damn about handwriting. What a shame." He took off his glasses and tapped his teeth with them, "Let's come back to your report. Normally, I don't touch such problems. I've already heard complaints about me meddling in administrative affairs." He leaned back in the swivel chair, put his glasses back on, and looked at the ceiling, "Now, tell me how you can make your case with the Party's new policy."

I weighed his words while tensely watching his expression. His aide, standing behind him, gave me a cruel smile and gestured, with his palms up, for me to speak out.

Pressed by limited time, I spouted the phrases I'd composed in my mind, "Your recent speech is instructive and enlightening. In the past two years, many peasants were mobilized to build roads and reservoirs without pay. Family-raised poultry and hogs were freely turned over to the communes. Now, those actions are blamed as *the blowing of the communist wind.* When that wind blew over Beijing, we were pressed by some coworkers to give up our fieldwork allowance."

The secretary cut in, "So, you pretended to be a voluntary donor, but didn't want to. Now you're riding the Party's new policy to get the money back. Am I right?" His flat, neutral tone showed neither approval nor denial.

"Yes, I need my money back, but the accounting system doesn't seem to respond to the new policy. It also still holds the withheld fieldwork allowances." He looked at me sharply. I pressed on before he could ask how I knew that, "In my desperation, I was bold enough to bother you. I'm sorry for my audacity."

The old man pulled his fountain pen from his breast pocket

and wrote a short line in the upper margin of my report. I stretched my neck but couldn't read the words. He said, "I won't hold it against you this time. But you'd better watch out for the red lines."

Knowing it was approved, I bowed slightly, "I won't trouble you again."

The aide held the report and led me to the head of the finance and accounting bureau. The lanky old bureau chief picked up the phone to call our institute's accounting office, "Refund the withheld fieldwork allowances to the workers who 'donated' them. Later, I'll show you Secretary Yao's written instruction."

"What?" He turned to the aide, "She said, if everybody tries to fool the top leader and act in his name, there would be a great disorder under Heaven."

Yao's aide took over the receiver and joked, "If the emperor doesn't worry about the situation, what is there for a eunuch be anxious about? Do it now, no more questions."

My two-year total came to about 120 yuan, all saved for me by the accounting office. The unexpected rebate was handed over to me in a lump sum, almost making up my minimum budget for the wedding.

2

I sent Chuju the news of my financial readiness at the end of March, and she wrote to tell me her boss had given her nine days' leave. She would arrive on Saturday, May 7, 1960, and stay until the following Friday. The hostel manager at our institute helped me buy the express train ticket, which I sent her by registered mail.

She was coming to marry me. Holding the telegram, I realized I didn't know where to begin. I sat down and made a list: a place for us to live for a week, the wedding ceremony,

bride's dress, how to treat my coworkers as guests ... it threw
me into a panic.

I visited two renowned clothing stores for women, Blue
Sky, which was due east of Tiananmen Square, and Every Inch
Refined, in the western district of downtown.

I looked at displays and watched shoppers, women
apparently from the south by their manner and appearance,
trying on gowns or suits in front of mirrors, admiring
themselves. After the 1957–58 criticism of the bourgeois
lifestyle, close-fitting and off-shoulder styles had disappeared,
but fine, solid-color fabrics and subtly elegant designs still
dominated showrooms. I didn't know if women took political
preaching as seriously as men did, but I admired their ability to
express natural grace. Even with the current severe restrictions,
many women were 'every inch refined'.

Seeing a few young customers with bodies like Chuju's, I
resolved to find the right wedding clothes for her. Perhaps my
years spent observing young ladies in public or in museums
and art galleries would help me.

I bounced between the two stores until I bought what I
needed and exhausted my small budget. Those few clothes
would create a distinguished Chuju. The sapphire-blue,
cashmere sweater and navy-blue, wool-blend pants would
show off her lovely, pale skin. A pair of thin-soled, leather
shoes would suit her brisk, girlish stride, one that struck me as
somehow like a lotus dancing on the waves of a gentle pond.

I thought of classical-looking women in Russian art prints,
specifically Repin's *Lady under the Sun,* one of the color plates in
the notebook I used as a diary. I imagined Chuju, in a turquoise
silk blouse and skirt, holding a parasol, which would transform
her into Repin's character.

On the morning of her arrival, my group leader had yet to
find a room for our nuptials. Negotiations with the
administrative office had failed. Not one room was available in
our residence compound. My female coworkers held a women-

only meeting. They announced their solution on Saturday at noon. The night before the wedding, Chuju could have a vacant bed on the women's floor above my dorm.

Meanwhile, Big Sister Wen, a senior chemist, promised to find a place for the two of us. Wen's family shared a three-bedroom apartment with a divorced typist's family. Wen and her husband had the largest room, measuring just 16 square meters, and their daughter had the smallest one, 12 square meters. The typist and her tall teenage daughter squeezed into the middle-sized, 14-square-meter room. Wen assured me we could have the smallest bedroom, letting their five-year-old daughter spend a week with her grandmother in a southern suburb.

Initially grateful, I became consumed by regret. I usually avoided Wen, with her sharp tongue that constantly spewed sarcasm. But now I realized that her heart was warmer than those of many women with sweet mouths.

Chuju arrived on Saturday morning, and I met her at the new railway station, one of Ten Great Buildings finished in 1959 to celebrate the People's Republic of China (PRC)'s tenth anniversary. From wall to ceiling to floor, everything was shiny.

According to traditional etiquette, further fortified by the Revolution, we declined to show our emotions at the station: no hug, no kiss. After shaking hands, we walked side-by-side.

As we passed through the tunnel toward our bus stop, the white ceramic lining under the fluorescent lights shone brightly for Chuju. Dressed in a pale-green, cotton blouse and black-and-white, checked pants, she looked like a demure peasant girl. With her sweet profile and graceful bearing, she was a pleasant contrast to the human mob jostling us.

Compelled by sudden urges, I seized the moment to put my arm around her waist. She twisted away and shook me off, frowning delicately: "Not in public."

In less than an hour, we arrived at our institute. Without hesitation, I led her to the Personnel Department, where a political cadre wrote the standard letter proving that Chuju and

I were both single. When I urged Chuju to accompany me to the residence committee for our marriage certificate, she laughed, "Why are you so impatient?"

"Well," I said, "it's almost lunchtime. Everyone will detour here to have a look at you. That might be fun."

She grimaced and dashed out of the compound. I detoured to put her duffel bag in my dorm, letting her wait for me at the bus stop.

The district residence committee office was an hour's walk away, but having official proof of our single status quickly paid off. Five minutes after arriving, we had our marriage certificate.

Walking back, neither Chuju nor I had much to say. In a quiet mood, she walked ahead of me, kicking pebbles. Perhaps she was trying to comprehend what marriage would mean. Maybe she was comparing me to what she'd first imagined, or to other men. Maybe she was dismayed for reasons even she didn't understand.

I didn't know what was on her mind, but I found myself dreading our pending separation; it would happen soon after we had a chance to sleep together. I touched my bag to reassure myself I still had the certificates. They suddenly weighed heavily, like invisible arms holding us into a married relationship, yet forcing us to live apart.

At the end of the willow-shaded road, we reached the bus terminal, where Chuju broke our silence, "What have you been thinking?"

My answer startled even me, "I wonder if, in 20 years, our daughter will be as lovely as you are now." She glanced at me with feigned reproach.

We took a bus and transferred to a trolley, each ride for a few stops. Then we ate a late lunch at a humble restaurant near our compound.

While we'd been out getting our paperwork done, the few young women in my division had moved into action, happily preparing the room for our wedding and no doubt enjoying a rare break from their tedious lab work.

They'd also taken up a collection for gifts. Except for my closest friends and immediate boss, everybody in our division contributed half a yuan. That token of comradely congratulation was the established convention at our institute.

With the resulting 46 yuan, the women bought us a window curtain, a tablecloth, a bed sheet, and two pillowcases. My group leader gave us an enamel thermos, and from a close friend we received a tea set. All that, plus a five-tube Panda radio that Big Sister Wen had left for us to use, made the tiny room look like a stage set.

Though no guests would expect to have food or drink at the ceremony, candies were essential. However, ordinary candies had been rationed, and the price for tasty ones with gorgeous wraps had been inflated fivefold. Minggui An persuaded a dozen coworkers to donate their candy rations for May, saying that as it was early in the month, many people hadn't bought their candies yet. Seeing the large heap of cheap sweets under the few fancy ones, I knew how much embarrassment An had taken from those who'd rejected him, and how patiently he'd talked the reluctant ones into surrendering their meager buying opportunities.

That night, lying in my bed on the second floor, I endured one more day's wait, while Chuju was lying two flights above my head on the fourth floor. As I rolled restlessly, my fantasy about her gradually shifted to scenes in early Soviet novels, when red guerrilla soldiers made love with wild peasant women in barns and wheat fields. Now, with our marriage registration done, we would have no chance for wild sex like the Soviets. Was it tradition that made us more priggish than the Russian revolutionaries? I dozed off without reaching a conclusion.

The next morning, I knocked at Chuju's door. Alone inside, she was trying on the wedding clothes I'd bought. They fit her well and suited her. Before I could offer my praise, she urged me to hurry over to help the two female lab workers voluntarily decorating our wedding room. They'd risen early, and she was humbled by all their efforts.

When I got to our room, they'd already cut out large characters from red paper. The words 'Double Happiness' were pasted on the window. On either side of the door, vertical couplets read, 'Carry the Revolution through to the end', and, 'Grow gray together as a devoted couple'.

Multicolored, paper ribbons festooned the ceiling, and around the light hung a handmade palace lantern. The women had managed to create a warm, festive atmosphere in the otherwise drab room. There was nothing I could do to help. The two comrades suggested I take a rest and get dressed. The ceremony would begin at seven o'clock.

3

At last, we were alone. Chuju started to get dressed while I arranged candy, cigarettes, melon seeds, and other treats on a desk, then washed the apples, plums, apricots, and peaches.

I couldn't help casting my eyes on her as she moved about slowly and deliberately. Forgetting even to dry my hands, I impulsively embraced her from behind. Supple and lithe, she bent into my embrace but quickly pushed me away with a stage whisper, "The guests will be here any time now. How many years have you waited? Do you mind another few hours?"

I returned to washing the fruit and put it all out on plates. The kettle on the coal stove hissed weakly. I waited for the water to boil, then filled the thermoses while Chuju put away her belongings in the chest of drawers.

Chuju asked me to button the back of her skirt. As I did, I was struck by our humble reality. No wedding photos, no rings, no banquet, and no drinks. All those formalities, and the expense, had been dismissed by the Revolution. Our wedding was more like a child's make-believe, a small, simple gathering of a few leaders and colleagues.

A hubbub on the staircase interrupted my reflections. Chuju and I greeted the first wave of guests, mainly people from my research group.

Junior Mu, a former PLA soldier transferred to our group in 1958, offered to preside over the ceremony, a unique chance for him to act like a leader among the educated folks. Many others arrived, and they had to borrow more chairs from the neighbors. Some had to stand by the door and in the kitchen.

The ceremony was brief. Chuju and I began by bowing first to Chairman Mao's portrait, then to our guests—the masses—and last to each other.

Our division Party branch secretary, Jiang, gave a political speech, even repeating the same couplet pasted near the doorframe: "Carry the Revolution through to the end," and "Grow gray together as a devoted couple." Following him, Lanyu Rong, the female vice secretary, offered congratulations, "We hope the newlyweds see Karl Marx and his wife Jenny as a brilliant example, encouraging each other, going through hardships together, and striving for the common, noble goal of realizing communism."

The event took only 30 minutes, during which thick smoke from cigarettes filled the room, making the nonsmokers cough. The leaders soon left, and our senior engineers and scientists stayed another half hour, just long enough to express their good wishes. Without those solemn faces around, the remaining crowd lightened up.

Junior Mu subdued the hubbub with his loud voice, "Now it's time for the bride and her groom to tell their story!"

Other men echoed it, "Let the bride speak first. Who took the initiative?"

With everyone eager to question Chuju, I wanted to deflect the brunt from her: "Our story is simple. The Japanese invasion drove our two families together, and her mother promised her to me in marriage when we had grown up.

Then—"

My answer was interrupted by several guests. One of them said, "No, that was only the external cause. We want to know when and how your passion was sparked."

My voice faltered, "As long as I can remember, I wrote letters to her, at least once a semester, keeping up our friendship."

Junior Mu stopped me: "Those are trivial things, not worth mentioning. So far, the bride hasn't opened her mouth. We welcome her to speak."

Chuju looked at me: "What should I say?"

A young man shouted, "No discussion between you!"

Others cheered, "Say what you want! Just tell the truth."

Chuju giggled nervously, "In the summer of 1956, in the tiny backyard of my home, Dapeng and I watched the stars in the sky. When my mom went inside and closed the door, he tried to kiss my cheek. I panicked and pushed him away."

Someone asked, "How old were you then?"

"Seventeen."

The crowd hooted, "Seventeen!"

"Oh, Dapeng, you're quite daring!"

"A saint doesn't chase a girl so young."

A female technician asked Chuju, "Did you report his behavior to your mom?"

The fussy woman was well known to us. Several men made faces. She had turned a male coworker's courting letter over to the Party secretary and accused him of unhealthy bourgeois ideology. Some guests, with hands over their mouths, even smirked.

Knowing nothing of this, Chuju answered sincerely, "Yes. But my mom said it was no big problem. 'Men are like that,' she said, 'and I've betrothed you to him. You're right to keep your self-esteem, but next time, be nice.' So I waited for his second try."

The crowd applauded, "Now the bridegroom! Dapeng,

when was your second try?"

I gently slapped Chuju's arm: "You've talked too much." I faced the crowd, "Her behavior hurt my self-esteem, and it was a setback."

Minggui An, battered in the 1959 campaign, seemed to dislike the newlyweds' stories, as if they encouraged an unhealthy tendency. He shouted, "How about welcoming the couple by singing the musical dialogue from the folksong, 'Gui Wang and Xiangxiang Li'?"

"Good idea!" The conservative faction applauded while the others looked disappointed.

The groom is supposed to sing first, but I hadn't sung in public since high school. Nervousness led my voice out of tune, and the guests laughed. Eventually I sang all of my part.

> Contending in beauty and fascination,
> Flowers line the roadside;
> Even the one called "celestial plant"
> Can't compare to my sweetheart.

Without hesitation, Chuju followed gracefully, with real feeling.

> Sorting the horses from the herd,
> Not easy to find a steed;
> Selecting a man from the world,
> I have found the best.

My performance embarrassed me, but at least it amused our guests. Then we had yet another folk ritual to endure. While standing on a chair, one of our guests held an apple on a string, insisting Chuju and I bite it at the same time. Having seen this at other weddings, I knew the trick was just rough horseplay to make fun of us. After a brief attempt to decline, we accepted the inevitable.

As we lunged at the apple, he yanked it away. Everyone knew what he was up to. Finally, his perfect timing made our lips meet, creating a scene our guests never got to see in public except in Soviet films.

The guests' hearty, satisfied applause marked the conclusion of our wedding ceremony.

4

After the guests left, Chuju swept the floor of melon-seed shells, candy wrappers, and cigarette butts. I opened the window to air things out. It was already 11 o'clock.

No sound came from the two families who lived in the unit. They must have been asleep. I left the front door ajar, though there was little likelihood more guests would arrive. I took a deep breath of fresh, spring air, and watched the night scene outside the window while Chuju brushed her teeth in the lavatory we shared with the two families down the hall.

Suddenly, I heard a familiar voice accompanied by the creaking of the door, "Congratulations, young couple!" It was Director Gu. I quietly let him in and offered him a comfortable seat at the center of our small room. His late visit disappointed me, but I understood why he hadn't come until the other guests had left.

When Chuju walked in, I introduced him, "Dear wife, this is Director Gu of our division."

"Just call me Old Gu." In fact, he'd been stripped of his titles, Division Director and Party Branch Secretary, six months before. Now, after a rough phase of public denouncement, he had begun to lick his psychological wounds. He looked less miserable than last winter when I returned from Fujian and his denunciation was at its peak. His humble manner now suggested something like gratitude, a kind of closeness I'd not sensed from him before.

Chuju served him tea and a cigarette, then returned to stand by my chair. She suddenly whispered into my ear, "He's the spitting image of Yaobang Hu," while staring at him with amused eyes.

Gu looked confused and uneasy. I pushed Chuju, "Please say it aloud." But she was too shy.

"She said you look like Yaobang Hu," I said. Hu was secretary general of the YL's central committee.

Gu relaxed, "Many people say that. Short, skinny, and a fast talker. I like him, an honest man, always. That's why he had trouble in every inner-Party struggle."

The leisurely atmosphere restored his outspokenness. Stretching a hand toward me, he talked to Chuju, "You're lucky you married a nice man, he's smart and righteous. He doesn't bend with the wind, and never hits a person when he's down."

I offered him a new cigarette, which he lit from the burning butt. Then he looked at Chuju again, "How old are you?"

"Twenty-one, just last month."

"Just the right age to marry." A leisurely plume of smoke drifted out of his mouth, "My wife was 21 when we married in Yan'an. At that barren, guerrilla war base, there were too many men craving the few women. An old sow might look delicate to them. You can't imagine how lucky I was."

Chuju added hot water to Gu's cup. He took one noisy sip after another, "Soon, I'll be head of the Construction Technology Institute, under the General Bureau of Waterpower Development. Please keep this news secret. It's only a ministry decision so far."

The Party had a common practice: after each rectification, the disgraced cadre was to leave the place where he'd lost face and credibility. I congratulated him in my heart for his assignment to a new place, where he could restore his dignity among new faces.

He sat up as if an idea had just struck him. He looked at

Chuju and pointed to the floor with the two fingers holding the cigarette, "This is a rural area. I'm bored here. You must be, too. Come work in my institute, only two kilometers west of Tiananmen Square. Our office building is two blocks from The Auspice Theater, where our famous Beijing opera actors perform every night."

His casual 'rural area' barb had nothing to do with dusty roads or the poor public transportation serving our compound, but reflected his aversion to our division, where he'd been so deeply tormented. He wanted to let me know that, at least in terms of rank and power, his new job was equal to his former post.

Clapping with her hands above her shoulder, Chuju bent over to face him, "That would be wonderful! Are you sure?"

With a proud face, he said, "A veteran cadre won't swallow his words. I'll have hiring power. First chance I get, I'll allot you a residence permit, and you can be our file-keeper, accountant, or receptionist, whatever we can arrange."

I put my palms together like a Buddhist, "If that comes true, you'll be our savior."

He stood up to leave around midnight. I took Chuju's hand and walked him to the apartment door. When we returned to our room, Chuju asked me, "Is he serious?"

"Yes. He has the goodwill too. But I don't know if he'll get the power and opportunity to make good on his promise."

5

Twenty minutes later, while Chuju lay in the dark, I sat by the window, holding up a corner of the curtain to enjoy the moon, almost full on the thirteenth of the month by the lunar calendar.

Chuju rose and slid quietly closer to me by the window, resting her chin on my shoulder. No longer children on the threshing ground during harvest season, we shared the moonlight for the first time, letting it flood over us as it did the roads and fields as far as we could see from our nuptial room.

Listening only to her breathing, I looked out the window, down toward my bachelor's room on the second floor of the building across from us. It was dark. Old Ye used to be there, but now he was enduring the hardships of the famine-stricken countryside in Anhui.

Chuju interrupted my pensive state, "It's late." She held onto my back, "You have to get up early for your militia drill. People will laugh if you're late." A train passed, screaming ominously.

"Tonight we enjoy the moonlight together. Next month we must watch from two faraway places."

Her tears fell on my neck.

I whispered, "I'm sorry. I shouldn't say that. Let's look on the bright side. We both have stable jobs. I'm doing well at work, and I believe the leaders will help us. Director Gu is serious. Just be patient."

Our parting, five days away, loomed over our tiny space, pushing me to undress her. Chuju yielded sweetly to my caresses. I prolonged our kisses as if to release years of desire, to feed an insatiable hunger, to soothe future longings in advance. Assuming she sensed my passion and urgent wish to hold on to this fleeting moment of happiness, I savored her willing participation as an expression of love in inverse proportion to the short time we had.

Apart from occasional coughing and snoring coming from the other two families through the thin walls, all was quiet. Chuju's breath synchronized with the rippling sound of the breeze coming through the window as if counting how fast time was slipping away. We were two guests in a borrowed room. Even the fragrance of magnolia trees had escaped from the room when I tried to smell it again.

Chuju snuggled up in my arms. I held her naked body tightly as if to make time stop flying. But her jade-like skin and carefree mind offered me no peace, instead they reminded me of her vulnerability in a rough world.

"Do you remember what you vowed," I said, "in the pump hut by the pond? If I didn't marry you, you'd never marry?"

"Don't you believe it?"

"What if someday I say something wrong and am banished?"

With a determined voice, she said, "I'll wait for your return, or join your exile, no matter where I have to go—Gobi, Tibet, anywhere."

Warmed by her passionate pledge, I fell asleep.

6

The next morning, I woke almost an hour later than usual. The daily militia drill was no doubt over. I'd never before been absent from any collective activity. I felt shame and regret. I should have borrowed an alarm clock.

To my relief, the drill had been cancelled. The Beijing Municipal Government was organizing a demonstration to condemn the Treaty of Mutual Cooperation and Security between the US and Japan, which Japan's Prime Minister, Kishi Nobusuke, was trying to push through parliament. To help ensure a procession of a million marchers, personnel from our institute were to walk ten kilometers to join the rally at Tiananmen Square.

On the sports field, our normal drill ground, Old Ma was busy preparing flags, placards, and banners along with other Party members. He approached me and said, "I've already asked Secretary Jiang to let you take the day off."

I felt uneasy being detached from such a significant movement. A senior engineer came to persuade me, "Go. One-day leave for a honeymoon is reasonable by any standard. Most people understand. All the downtown parks are closed today. Go to the Summer Palace with your bride."

The human tide surged into the streets, and all public transportation around our institute halted. We had to walk through Purple Bamboo Park to find the day's temporary bus terminal while endless lines of trucks and buses, densely packed with people from far-off suburbs, rolled east to assembly sites.

Our ride on the nearly empty bus was comfortable. I acted as tour guide for Chuju, "The elm trees and aspens along this avenue were specifically planted for Empress Dowager Cixi around 60 years ago so she could ride her sedan chair through the shaded gallery all the way to the Summer Palace."

"My history teacher said that the Empress used up all the money raised for the empire's navy to build the palace."

"She controlled the Imperial Court for 47 years and died in 1908. She was powerful, but her life wasn't as happy as yours is going to be."

"How's that?"

"Her husband, Emperor Xianfeng, died when she was in her early thirties. By royal family law, she couldn't marry again. Instead, she was plagued by court conspiracies, foreign invasions, and revolution. But you have me. I love you, and I'll protect you."

She moaned, "Cixi was the richest but the loneliest."

She gazed intently at the glazed roof tiles of the Friendship Hotel, the towering red-brick building of the Agriculture Academy, and the exclusive, exquisite villas in the distant woods. The landscape obviously appealed to her, and I enjoyed watching her enjoy it.

Entering the Summer Palace, the serenity enveloping the vast lake and exquisite buildings was a huge relief from the daily boredom and the scene at Tiananmen Square, where my coworkers must be busily shouting. A dearth of people left the setting in its proper, regal splendor. I felt privileged to have the picturesque resort almost to ourselves. I nudged Chuju, "We can imagine ourselves as royal family members of the Qing Dynasty."

She showed little excitement about the scenery and architecture. Instead, she hid in rockeries, jumped out from a concrete conduit stored by the roadside, and played other tricks. On a wooded peninsula, we reached a secluded convent, obviously a Buddhist sanctuary for the royal family. Repairs were underway, and a wide ditch had been dug in front of the entrance. When I gingerly walked across the narrow plank bridge, Chuju followed me closely, bouncing to make it buck and vibrate. She giggled when I got nervous.

Once across, I hugged her and tickled her neck with my nose, "Why did you scare me—for fun?"

She kept giggling, "I'm training a gentle scholar to be a rowdy sports guy."

The sun was high in the sky now. Near the northeast corner of the lake, the golden sunshine had brightened the emerald roofs of the palace. Its centerpiece, the Tower of Buddhist Incense, sat on a stone foundation 70 feet high. It had four levels of octagonal eaves and was surrounded by pavilions at various elevations up the hillside. A slender, seven-story pagoda stood alone in the far background. I told Chuju, "They built that hill by hand with the dirt dug to make the lake. They called it the Mountain of Ten Thousand Years Life Expectancy to flatter the empress."

The southern slope had a huge vertical wall lined with mosaics. At its foot, two staircases went east and west, leading to the hilltop's architectural complex. With reverence for the royal villas sanctified by Buddhist priests, I started climbing the marble steps slowly and steadily.

Chuju said, "Let's have a race to see who climbs the hundred steps first."

I wanted her to win, but said, "No problem, you don't stand a chance."

We were even for the first third of the race. Then she shot ahead. When I straightened to look up at her, she'd already reached the head of the steps, the finish line. With 20 yards to go, I stood panting for a moment before finishing. I found her standing on the marble pedestal of a human-size, bronze crane guarding the bronze pavilion, where the late empress used to chant scriptures and pray to Buddha. With one hand clutching the crane's neck, Chuju, victorious, swayed with joy like a child.

Walking down the hill, we entered the long colonnade built along the northeast side of the lake, where a few Western visitors also strolled. Having never before seen a foreigner, now she was at close range, Chuju looked the women up and down, from head to toe. I squeezed her fingers, "That's not polite."

She laughed: "No problem. They smiled at me."

I pulled her out of the narrow passage and away from the tourists, "If you keep watching them like that, they'll want to talk to us, and we might get in trouble."

She pouted but followed me, "I like their high-heeled shoes. And their outfits, they're so colorful and well fitted."

"I like them too. But our leaders call it bizarre and bourgeois. It's just too far from the traditional Chinese dress with broad sleeves and long skirts."

"Why?"

"I don't know, but here's a thought. For thousands of years, powerful men possessed their wives and concubines as their private assets. They didn't allow women to express themselves in public, all the while indulging themselves with innocent young girls."

She nodded, "I hate those men."

We found a state-owned photo booth in a corner of the waterfront museum. The cameraman had us sit in a carved marble boat, fashioned to look as if it were floating on a calm lake. The sky turned cloudy, and the light wasn't optimal for a picture, but we wouldn't have another chance. So I paid for a standard, two-inch-square photograph. With postage, the whole thing cost only 1.2 yuan. It might be the one picture we'd have of our honeymoon.

We had a simple lunch at a tiny restaurant. The deep-fried, twisted dough sticks smelled wonderful and made my mouth water, but we would need a grain coupon and a cooking oil coupon, which were issued separately by Beijing Municipality. I had only national grain coupons, which contained certain oil rations, although the ratio of oil to grain was unknown. I calculated with a piece of paper. Every time I went to the field, the manager of our dining hall would withdraw my next month's ration: 30-pound grain and 7-oz oil to exchange for 30-pound national grain coupons as my next monthly ration. That meant the ratio of oil to gain for Beijing was about 0.23. Now four twisted dough sticks cost a one-pound grain coupon and one-ounce oil coupon; the ration was four times higher than what the official determined. Unfair! I bargained with the cashier, but she jeered at me, "Go argue with the police station in charge of your district!"

Chuju lost patience, "We can live without dough sticks."

We compromised with boiled dumplings and spicy soup.

At the next table, a man in his late sixties was feeding himself with difficulty. His hands trembled badly, maybe from Parkinson's disease. I spoke to Chuju quietly, "Life is short. Forty years from now, I might be like that."

She gently touched my arm, "Don't worry. I want to help you in your old age."

"I'm lucky."

By the middle of the afternoon, I was tired but felt our half-day tour wasn't stylish or memorable at all. Craving a romantic interlude, I suggested we rent a rowboat. It would be a lovely, inexpensive way to continue courting my bride on our short honeymoon.

After the boatman pushed us out onto the water with a long pole, we discovered that neither of us could handle the oars well. The breeze in the morning had now become a wind rippling over the water. Away from the pier, our boat drifted against our will. Our course became almost entirely directed by the wind. We gave up all hope of crossing the lake. In half an hour, a hundred yards from the pier, we began to worry.

I had an idea: "If we can't row back, we better get to that retaining wall. Then we can pull ourselves along and inch back to the pier."

Chuju laughed, "Are we that useless?"

Suddenly, a gale whirled around us. Waves rose, and the sky grew turbid yellow. Chuju sat on the crossbeam, bending over facedown to avoid the dust. I fumbled to button up my sweater, "Don't be afraid. I'm here with you." But I found my own voice trembling.

In desperation, I paddled with my hands while Chuju frantically rotated the oars, not even touching the water. The boat pitched, rolled, and bobbed. A few other boats swiftly passed ours. A man shouted, "Don't be afraid. If you keep calm, you'll be fine."

I knelt behind Chuju and took one oar, trying to synchronize my stroke with hers, "If the boat capsizes, you hold onto it, I can swim while pushing it and yelling for help. If the water isn't deep, I can stand on the bottom."

My words helped me relax. To entertain my bride, I sang the tune to a 1939 song, 'The Boatmen of the Yellow River', improvising my own lyrics as a parody of the original. Although my singing was rough, my spontaneous enthusiasm calmed her, and our coordinated rowing worked better than before. We learned how to row and steer a boat. When we were about three yards away from the pier, a worker hooked us with a pole and pulled us to the wharf.

Once on land, I said, "That was just a miniature test of how well we can work together under difficult circumstances. It should make us happy."

On the way back to the bus, we had to walk against

ferocious winds and swirling sand. I recalled old stories I read
in my childhood about ancient astrologers using the weather as
a predictor of military outcomes. I couldn't shake the image of
a tornado snapping an army's standard just as it is on the verge
of conquest. The general loses the battle and dies.

I remembered Chuju's sweet wince the night before and the
bloodstained patch on the cotton blanket I discovered in the
morning. This evening promised leisurely ecstasy for us both,
and I passed the hectic hours in a haze of erotic anticipation.
When everyone else had fallen asleep, I reached for her
shoulder and traced with my fingers the line of her collarbone.

She pulled away, "Where's the woman who played the fox
in your fairy opera at high school?"

"I told you before," I said, "She joined an army
performance troupe then married a division commander. No
further news."

I caressed her neck and tried to take off her underwear. She
gave a start and writhed away from me, "It's late."

"I know." I kept smiling, "I've been waiting all day."

When I reached out to her again, she pushed my hands
away. I stared at her in shock but couldn't get her to look into
my eyes, "What have I done wrong?"

She frowned: "I can't."

My bewilderment only grew. *Had last night been bad for her?
Was she afraid?* "Chuju, aren't you happy to be with me?"

"Of course, but I can't ... not tonight."

"Tonight is all we've got. Are you afraid it may ... um, still
hurt a little?"

She shook her head: "It's just not a good time."

I stood up, "What do you mean? We just got married, didn't
we? Isn't that a good time?"

Her voice fell to a whisper: "I, ah, I got my period ... an
hour ago."

I suddenly felt totally deprived of my conjugal rights.

Through the common knowledge of all the people I knew, sexual intercourse during a woman's period would harm her body, and hence it was indecent and should be forbidden. Stunned, I suddenly remembered a tidbit of physiological knowledge that had been carried by a magazine, probably *Women of China* or *Public Health*, during the relaxed year of 1956. The 'Letters to the Editor' column replied to a woman that she'd done the right thing to resist her husband, who'd tried to force her to have sex during her period. Disregarding the damage it could do to her health, her husband's behavior was selfish and barbaric, stemming from the ideology of the exploiting classes.

The ethical authority of the editor descended on me like a mental gate. I had only my misfortune to blame.

What she saw in my eyes made her reach for my hand, "Please, Dapeng, I'm sorry. There'll be time." Her voice cracked: "I'll make it up to you."

I exploded, "How can you do this to me? You know your cycle. Why didn't you plan around this? I can't believe you could be so heartless!"

Her mouth was tight, but there was fear in her eyes, the misery of a child who has broken a bowl, "When I got my permission for leave and the train ticket you sent to me, all I could think about was how happy we'd be, how great this was. It didn't occur to me that … I didn't know. I'm sorry."

I took a deep breath and closed my eyes, "I can't blame you. It didn't occur to me either. But your mom should've told you. When I was in high school, two old women whispered under our eaves about how a mother taught her daughter—a bride-to-be. It was all hush-hush and code words, but I could tell it was about sex and they didn't want to be heard. But I thought that's what old women did for their daughters."

She took both my hands, "All mothers aren't the same. My mother was a bit prim with her children, she never talked about it. Otherwise, I would've planned for it."

I slapped my pillow and looked up brightly, "Ask your factory leader if you can stay six more days in Beijing. Let's see if we can salvage our honeymoon."

She struggled not to weep, "You don't know how I had to beg just to get five days. I had to cry in Vice President Wang's office. Anyway, it's too late. If I write to them tomorrow, I won't get an answer for ten days, and then I'd return to work late and be punished."

I covered my face with my hands, "I can restrain myself for the next few days. But then our separation will begin with our depressing honeymoon. I'm scared. What did I ever do that Heaven should play such tricks on me?"

She fell into my arms, "Dapeng, forgive me. There'll be time for us to make up for this fiasco."

Through my fuzzy vision I glimpsed how hard this was for her too, "Someday," I held her close but not too close, "someday."

7

On Tuesday, after the torment of our second night, I got up about six o'clock for militia drill. Chuju couldn't bear to see me so stressed, "You don't have to go. Nobody would blame you."

I lay down for a few minutes before leaving and stroked her hair, "A few days' absence from militia duty wouldn't cause me trouble, but I need more political credibility than I have now if we hope to live together in the near future."

"It's too tough for you."

"These days, when people are tough and mean to each other, we have to be tough on ourselves. During the 1958 steelmaking campaign, one of my former classmates hid his heart problem to join the race, and on the second day, he was hospitalized. I won't go that far, but I have to grit my teeth."

She sat up in bed and wrapped her arms around my waist, "You're very thin and tired. You might collapse." I kissed her forehead then dressed. She buried her head under the pillows.

I arrived at our usual drill ground, the basketball field, earlier than most militia members. When the others arrived and began to stand in formation, I shouldered my Russian rifle with its bayonet and joined them. I believed nobody had spotted my dejection.

After a meager breakfast, I listlessly led a group discussion. After days of denouncing the revival of Japanese militarism, we were returning to the Party's central theme of the moment: criticizing contemporary revisionists, namely Khrushchev and other leading European communists. I dawdled away the day, half-heartedly taking some notes, while my officemates repeated one another's speeches, drank tea or smoked.

That night, I was determined not to touch Chuju, and fatigue kept me sleepy for one or two hours. Then, in her sleep, she rolled over into the space I'd deliberately left between us and rested her arm and leg against me, electrifying me. In my overexcited state, I tried to mobilize my willpower to refuse temptation. In desperation, I thought of Hui Liuxia, praised by scholars as one of the four greatest sages along with Confucius.

The legend said Hui Liuxia once lived by a city gate, and, one cold and stormy night, a pretty homeless woman knocked at his door asking for a shelter. To warm up the woman, almost frozen to death, he opened his robe to bundle her body. Even with a beautiful woman sitting in his lap, he'd maintained his presence of mind and sexual restraint. For two thousand six hundred years, he had been upheld as an ethical model.

In my terrible fix, the lofty image of the ancient saint retreated, making way for an ordinary man, a biologist I knew, who told me that his wife, a musician, had refused to have sex with him for eight months after their wedding, insisting on its

sinful nature. Where had he found such willpower? He was a
contemporary saint. I was the same order of human being as
he was, so I should be able to do what he'd done.

Chuju was in a deep sleep. As soon as I'd gathered enough
mental strength, I gently shook off her arm and leg, turned her
to face the wall, and regained the clearance between us. I
cooled down and fell asleep.

Before long, I startled awake and found myself holding
Chuju from behind. Again in a fretful state, I recalled a
conversation with semi-illiterate soldiers I'd met in 1955, who
understood much more about sex than I did.

That year, during our three months of practical training at
the Meishan Reservoir, I lived in a bamboo hut with some
soldiers that had recently transferred to the site. In the rainy
season, those working night shifts had no place to go in the
daytime. They would gather in threes or fours in a corner and
have a long bull session. Sometimes, their lowered voices and
ambiguous language made me suspect they were talking about
sex. Since Chairman Mao had instructed us to learn noble
qualities from soldiers and workers by living with them, I felt
indecent listening intently to their obscene tales.

Nevertheless, some of their slang would hit me, distracting me
from my textbook to decipher their coded meaning. Squad Head,
a senior technician recruited from Shanghai to lead a drilling tower
team, was a keynote speaker rarely absent from these discussions.
To boast about his virility, he would narrate his performance
graphically and conclude with his wife's praise, "You're old but
amazingly vigorous, just like a treasured dagger."

Before I left the site, Squad Head was denounced at a series
of struggle meetings for, "stirring up base passions to erode the
revolutionary ranks." His avid listeners were also forced to
make self-criticism as captives of rotten bourgeois culture. Still,
some of his slang remained incomprehensible to me. Once he
said that when he demanded sex, his wife answered tenderly,
"Which way, by water or by land?" Like a cow chewing its cud,

I'd tried to digest the meaning of those obscure words, but wasn't sure if I'd understood them. Now, with Chuju in my embrace, they stealthily prodded me to look for an alternative solution.

But I couldn't forget the premature, infamous end of the star student at our high school. He became popular by participating in the Party's underground movement before 1949. Then, in 1950, he took the lead to join the Land Reform Working Team as a fresh cadre. Unfortunately, while organizing the peasants to beat and evict landlords, he was revealed as a suspected homosexual and discharged by the team. He was allowed to return to school, but his schoolmates treated him as a dirty man who'd committed rooster raping— the Chinese term for sodomy. On the way to school, girls would speed up to pass him or even take a wide detour. Soon, he disappeared, removing himself as a campus eyesore.

His wretched looks the last time I saw him, displayed in the darkness like a ghost's, interrupted my wayward thinking about alternative solutions. I felt guilty for being influenced by Squad Head, who'd been accused as a bad element hiding in the working class. More seriously and uglier, if I tried, Chuju would curse me as a pervert, a hooligan, or even scream into the deep night. I let go of her and rolled away.

At the end of my restless hours, with my clothes on and a blanket under my arm, I whispered into her ear, "It's a torture for me to stay here. I'm going to rest for a few hours in my dorm."

She sat up and hugged my waist, "Don't go. Stay. You can do what you want."

"No, I'd be guilty of damaging you. I'm fine."

I helped her to lie down comfortably and kissed her cheek, "See you tomorrow."

A few lonely bachelors were chatting on the balcony. They rushed to my room, "What's the matter? Did you have a fight with your bride?"

I laughed as if nothing had happened: "I just came to get some books."

In my office with two books and a cotton-padded jacket, I laid my head on my arms at my desk. I couldn't sleep for a long while. Then, in my stupor, I heard someone snore faintly. My own noises seemed far away, and drool trickled onto my sleeves. My arms turned numb, but fatigue prevented me from moving them. When daylight dimly showed on the large window, I struggled to sit up straight and stretch my arms.

Returning to our nuptial chamber, I dragged my feet along the staircase. Chuju's swollen eyelids told me how she'd fared during the hours of my escape. I sat next to her on the edge of the bed and held her shoulders. A half hour later, she broke the silence, "Do you loathe me now? I hate myself for bringing you this pain."

"Don't say that." I tried to smile.

She started sobbing. I embraced her, wiping the tears off her cheeks with my face, "Sorry, don't cry. I'll stay with you from tonight. It's time to train for living alone. I'll tame myself to be a strong man."

8

That Wednesday I stayed in the office, as dejected as I had been the previous day. Some young idiots crowded around to goad me, "You newlyweds must be as hot as dry kindling in a stove."

"Look at you, you can hardly stand up after your wild night."

"You must've pounced like a hungry tiger."

"Better see a doctor before you drop dead."

The two Party members, Junior Mu and Minggui An, shooed them away.

Night fell. I was nervous about my promise to stay with

Chuju for the remaining nights of our honeymoon. In my drowsiness, I recalled how Hot Chili had mocked the senile dignitaries with young wives.

The communist Revolution emancipated women from polygamous marriages. However, the new marriage laws recognized polygamous unions that had begun before its effective date, May 1, 1950, as long the women involved didn't request a divorce. Some former warlords, who'd been preserved by the Party as showpieces, still kept concubines. One of them frequently visited the clinic. He was otherwise healthy, except for low testosterone due to aging. Whenever he came, escorted by his youngest woman, Hot Chili knew what they needed. Sometimes, she didn't ask him anything, just gave him a prescription for androgens. Once, in a bad mood, she tossed a gibe at the concubine, "Please hold your grandpa carefully."

When she proudly related that joke to me, I raised a thumb, "You're still earning your nickname."

By intuition, I thought that there must be a way to do the opposite, suppress male hormones. Now, after working hours, no doctors at our contract hospital would treat me as an emergency case. It was also extremely difficult for me to broach the problem with a stranger.

After dinner, I braced myself to see Hot Chili at the dorm for the hospital's single employees, where she shared a room with two nurses. Skipping any small talk, I told her about my hasty marriage and immediate misery. As usual, she had to criticize before helping, "You should've done better. Chuju is a nice woman but uneducated. You went for good looks as a top priority. Now, how are you going to get around all the problems ahead?"

"The rice is cooked. Please help me first, slap me later."

She led me up to the third floor to meet her fiancé, Dr Cai, a Party member who graduated from the PLA's Medical University. As the director of the radiology lab, he had a whole bedroom to himself. Before knocking on his door, she said, "Your problem is rare and I don't have any clinical experience with the related medicines. Please wait here. I'm going to consult a professor of urology at his home."

During her absence, I tried to chat with Dr Cai. Physically small and wearing a faded military uniform, he looked like a mature professional. Scanning the titles of the books on the shelf, more Marxist than medical, I hesitated. Since he was born in southern Jiangxi, a place that bred many great writers and philosophers in the Song and Ming Dynasties, I praised his birthplace. Such topics helped me hide my worry and embarrassment, but I could tell that he was tolerating me as a task assigned by his fiancée.

After waiting for a long hour, Hot Chili returned with a little bag in her hand. Dr Cai asked, "What's that?" She waved to stop him.

She shoved the bag into my hands, took the thermos from a corner, and poured some hot water into a cup, "Take a pill now."

On the bag, the Chinese name under the Latin words was Female Stimulating Agent. The dosage instruction said one per day. Inside it were three pills. I swallowed one and put the bag in my pocket.

Hot Chili said, "Chuju is home alone, so we won't keep you. Be our guest any time. We'll invite you to our wedding, probably on the eve of the upcoming National Day."

Dr Cai walked us downstairs to the ground floor and said goodbye. On the way to the front gate, Hot Chili told me, "The professor wasn't comfortable prescribing this drug. A certain American clinician, he said, uses it to chemically castrate sex offenders. These three tablets, a small dose, aren't likely to cause permanent damage to your body, but I feel sad using them on a friend during his honeymoon."

I sighed, "People normally see inequality in the disparity of income and living standards. I see it in the classification of sexual freedom. Old men like the warlord use androgen to satisfy their concubines, but I use estrogen to kill my natural need."

Her face froze, "Don't stretch your personal problem too far. Keep a tight rein on your mouth. Remember Jushi Yin's tragedy."

Jushi Yin, her former suitor and our mutual friend, had been in a labor camp for almost three years. If he hadn't been labeled a rightist, she would've accepted him. I couldn't help saying, "Jushi's a very talented guy. He tried to defend history, but history tossed him in the garbage."

She shook my hand, "You have a sharp tongue but a cloudy head. I worry about you."

I tried to smile, "You're sharp in both. But don't turn Dr Cai into a henpecked husband. Thank you for your help."

I passed the night with sweat, dizziness, fatigue, fretfulness, and nausea. I didn't know whether those symptoms were side effects of the drug or the results of my general depression. Nevertheless, I was peaceful with Chuju, and she was careful not to touch me.

With the famine deepening, we had neither meat nor eggs for the whole honeymoon. I treated Chuju to overly boiled cabbage and spinach, no better than hogwash. On Thursday at lunchtime, there were long lines at our mess hall waiting for egg custard, and everyone was allowed to buy one share. The manager knew that my bride was here and told the kitchen crew to sell me two shares. I was excited to at last have something tasty for Chuju.

Those ahead of me in the line carried away bowls containing a single yolk diluted with water and steamed with salt. They started to complain.

"Where have the whites gone?"

"Exported."

Dong Long whispered to me, "Foreigners select the

essence, and we accept the dross."

I winked at him, "Egg yolks have many nutrients we need."

I carried our food from the mess hall to our little borrowed room and found Chuju doing a handstand, trying to touch the light bulb hanging from the ceiling with her feet. The radio was on, spewing platitudes from *The People's Daily*.

I put our bowls on the desk, "What are you doing?"

Still upside down, she said, "I'm bored."

I held her body and gently lowered her to a standing position, "Time to eat."

She laughed: "Am I living like a chicken, released from my cage just for feeding?"

I sighed, "You may go home now, if a train ticket is available."

Her smile suddenly disappeared, "Are you driving me away?"

"No. I want to set you free from the cage."

We both stopped eating. She gazed at me: "That would cut our six-day honeymoon by one third."

"Added to the uncountable days we'll live separately, parting two days early won't make much difference."

She lowered her head and scratched her nails against each other. I put my hands on hers, "The damned drug might make me a eunuch. That's cruel and unfair. I want to save my body for our future. We'll have lovely children."

She began to pack up her things. I pulled her back, "Please finish your lunch first. Let me check with the hostel manager if we can get a train ticket for today."

It was too late to get a ticket for the same day. But the manager ordered one for the express train the next afternoon, and I could pick it up from his office that night.

When I came back, Chuju was sitting on the edge of our bed, her bags at her feet and the silk mantilla tied on her head. Everything was ready to go, but her lunch remained untouched. I took off her mantilla and pushed her to finish the food.

She started sending the coarse rice, salty egg yolk, and tasteless spinach down her throat, "You must know the famous story. A guest wants to stay longer and uses bad weather as a pretext: 'The rain keeps me from leaving.' The host replies, 'The rain does, but I don't.' Now the train schedule keeps me here, but my host doesn't."

Standing by the desk, I petted her until her sobs stopped. Tears drenched the front of my jacket.

I was embarrassed for not having enough gifts for her mother and siblings, and they were short of everything. Many stores in Beijing had empty shelves, or filled them with bamboo baskets, pottery, and porcelain vases. Still, I had some cotton ration coupons to buy four yards of print for her mother and a shoe coupon for a pair of tennis shoes for Minqing, her sister. After that, I used all the ration cards I could get from my coworkers to buy cigarettes, soaps, toilet tissue, detergent, etc. In those times, they were all valuable gifts. Chuju said, "The cigarettes are for my stepbrother, the rest are for my friends and neighbors."

That afternoon, I got a small bag of barbital pills from our institute's clinic to help me sleep. I took two of them at bedtime and had a stuporous sleep all night.

9

Chuju had to go on Friday. Her train would leave at 2:25 pm.

After working for three hours in the office, I returned to our room, where Chuju was sewing my old quilt covers. She'd removed and folded the new embroidered silk ones; they would await our next use. Her face was tear-stained.

We embraced silently. I sighed into her ear, "We've had a five-day honeymoon but only one joyful night." She began to sob. Instantly, I regretted my words, and it took a while to calm her.

With tears still on her cheeks, she quietly said, "My period ended early this morning."

I hurried to undress her, but we couldn't fully enjoy that last chance. Worried she might miss the train, she squirmed impatiently. But I needed release. As she hurried to double-check her bags, a trickle of my viscous fluid ran down her thigh. She wiped herself with a towel and urged me to get dressed.

On the trolley to the station, we sat on a rear bench with our thighs tightly pressed together. The pressure of her leg against mine silently conveyed her sorrow for squandering our second, perhaps last, chance to make love. My smothered desire still burned.

Travelers at the railway station plaza looked aimless, lost, animated only by the arrivals and departures. Each must have had pain, joy, hope, despair, but each meant next to nothing to anyone else in the crowd. If the travelers saw me at all, I was only a particle in the human waves, no matter how severely tormented by a truncated honeymoon and the looming separation from my bride.

She walked across the plaza with me, and we took the escalator to the waiting hall. The slick leather soles of Chuju's new shoes lost traction on the marble floor, still wet from being mopped, and she fell. When I reached my hands under her arms and pulled her up from behind, her buttocks pressed into my groin, and my passions surged again.

I controlled my emotion and walked her to the platform, searching for parting words, but could only say, "Please write to me often."

Standing at the entrance of a hardwood bunk carriage, she silently fondled the tip of her long braid. Before boarding, she buttoned my sweater uneasily, "Sorry I didn't bring any money to help with our wedding. You struggled to arrange everything, and we stayed together only five days, one day being cut off our originally planned honeymoon."

I held her hands, "We're in a small boat on a stormy sea. We should struggle together with one heart."

The locomotive whistle screamed. She stood behind the conductor, waving to me with her white handkerchief. The conductor closed the door, and the train jerked into motion. Picking up speed, it grew smaller, until it disappeared around the bend. My hands and feet felt frozen in the sunny mid-May afternoon.

10

I came home from the railway station trying to blot out the universe.

Moving like a robot, I packed my belongings and cleaned the room. After taking the final load back to the bachelor dorm, I returned the key to Big Sister Wen, the outspoken chemist, and thanked her for her great kindness.

She brushed aside my thanks. At the staircase, she stood a few steps above me, "What a pity: only five days. The comforter hasn't even been warmed up."

The crowd in the men's dorm greeted me with mixed expressions. The single men welcomed me like a friend back from a journey. The married men, whose wives lived far away, treated me like a former patient returning to a hospital ward with a relapse.

That night, as I listened to the deep, rhythmic breathing of my roommate just back from Yunnan, my honeymoon was already a mere memory, a stage play now over.

I had to pull myself together. The research paper I had to do was challenging my inadequate scientific knowledge, writing skills, and ability to read foreign languages. From the daily morning militia drill to evening meetings, I participated in the usual activities. During political study, while my peers sat quietly or were lost in daydreams, I continued to take notes.

The other staff took the two allowable breaks each day, officially ten minutes at ten in the morning and ten more at four in the afternoon, but most spent at least half an hour for each. I often used such time to weigh persimmons, slice soap bars, or distribute other rationed items, which our resourceful cadres bought through their own connections. I took pains to be accurate, giving everyone in our group an equal share.

During the absence of our group leader, petty conflicts arose among our 39 members, and the aggrieved parties started coming to me. I tried to pacify them but, failing that, hurried to the second floor to find our division authority. The hectic activity diluted my loneliness and kept Chuju off my mind much of the day. Soon the young workers were treating me as their deputy boss, while cynical seniors called me First Group Vice-Leader, as if bestowing a Soviet title upon me.

One day, the Party branch committee member in charge of propaganda, Guodong Zeng, called me to his office, "Recently, you've done a lot of volunteer service, showing your enhanced socialist consciousness. We're happy about your progress and see more political potential in you."

At that time, every division had been publishing a monthly blackboard newsletter. Now, the Hydrology Department, on the third floor, had increased their publication to twice a month. Thus, a new competition sprang up. Since the Party branch interpreted my voluntary work as an indication of high socialist enthusiasm, its propaganda chief required me to write our newsletter once every week to help our division get ahead.

I had to align four blackboards in a row then fill them with words on behalf of our leaders. Except for the heading, which someone skilled in art created, I composed the whole content and wrote the text in white chalk, with the subtitles in color. The short articles were intended to show how warmly people in our division responded to the Party's call, and how the communist spirit had brought a fresh mental outlook to the masses.

One Sunday, I spent hours writing the articles on the boards. The building was quiet, and all the offices on the second floor were closed except the one in which Dihua Fang, a soil engineer, was studying.

The consensus of the fellow sufferers living in the bachelors' dorm was that Dihua was our current number-one miserable man. He had married in 1954, and his wife remained in Xinjiang, close to the border with Kazakhstan. Every two years, one of them got a leave permit. Traveling back and forth to see each other, even so infrequently, used up all their savings. The railway hadn't yet reached the remote area of Xinjiang, so their weeklong truck ride exhausted at least one of them to the point of illness. Despite these hardships, Party leaders deemed each indispensable to their post and refused to transfer either.

As I was squatting to write the lower lines on the board, Dihua stood behind me with a teacup in his hand, "Silly work. Who reads such nonsense?"

I grimaced, "Please spare my face, big brother. It's a formality, but it counts for our division's honor."

"I see only a waste of your time."

"It kills my lonely time and buries my sadness."

"Don't take my joke seriously." He nudged my back with his shoulder, "I don't blame you. You do something to please our leaders, they'll return the favor."

"I hadn't known your pain until I married and was separated from my wife."

"You're a discerning man, but wisdom can't substitute for experience."

"We're fellow sufferers. Your case makes the rest of us lose hope that we'll ever be allowed to live with our wives."

"Heaven have mercy on us."

One morning at the end of June, I counted the five weeks since Chuju had left. How could I stand being solitary for the months and years ahead? Since it was difficult to do anything that required deep concentration, I decided to check the group members' job progress, a weekly routine I did for the division administration. As I entered the office on the other side of the corridor, Anna turned her head and looked up at me, "Do you miss her?"

I shrugged and feigned coldness: "A little."

"The man in my family couldn't live a day without me."

I was deeply hurt by the truth she told, recalling the spark that had transiently flashed between us three years before when we were both single. Now, while her man enjoyed an endless honeymoon, I was living like a widower.

She didn't attend my wedding, which I was glad about, but her question revealed her knowledge of my dire situation, and her light-hearted complacency left an aftertaste of gloating.

When all my officemates had gone to the mess hall for lunch, I stayed in the office, chewing on Anna's words. She was certainly not sensitive enough to know how much pain such a question from her mouth would inflict on me. Recalling the embryo of love that briefly lived between us, I found no reason to be mad at her. As an artless speaker, she simply didn't know how to express her solicitude properly. Her kind heart wouldn't allow her to gloat over my misfortune.

On my way to the mess hall, Anna was going back to the office at a slow pace, her fingers busy knitting a sweater. The three rapidly moving knitting needles drew wool thread from a ball in her shoulder purse. In previous weeks, she had stripped and washed a worn-out sweater then wound the yarn around the back of a chair to straighten the curls and dry the wool before making it into balls. This tedious, painstaking work had occupied all fragments of her free time and tested her patience. Like an enduring peasant woman, she was struggling, with little to keep life going on.

Though her husband had a high salary, she no longer showed off new clothes as she had before her marriage. Meanwhile, as some female coworkers gushed, she had urged her husband to spend a large portion of their income to feed his many young siblings. All these merits had proven her a thrifty and virtuous woman, utterly different from what I'd predicted three years ago. Her delicate physique and fancy clothes had led to my excessive apprehension.

It was useless to cry over my lost opportunity. Whether she was sympathetic or gloating, it made no difference to me.

11

In mid-July 1960, I went to the Yangwumiao Dam site on the Yuan River to meet its local research team. We spent a week discussing the details of our joint field test. This time, not traveling with VIPs, I had to climb three peaks of a mountain to get there. From early morning until evening, I hiked for 13 hours, just as the local workers did.

I found a vacant bunk in a room with its young workers. The peasant family who leased the room to my host, the 304th Geological Survey Brigade, had left a coffin stored there, expecting sooner or later to need it for their aging grandmother. It rested against the wall, forming the inner boundary of my bunk. At night, the smell of the oil paint made me feel sick to my stomach. I'd roll toward the wall, and my face would touch the coffin's lower edge. Nausea overwhelmed me.

The nights were hot. In the dark, humming mosquitoes hovered, taking every opportunity to attack. My roommates all had mosquito nets, but I'd only been able to borrow a blanket. I tried burrowing beneath it, but too quickly it created suffocating heat, and I had to take it off. Then the insects attacked again, they were unrelenting. Unbearable itching tortured me and forced me to hide under the blanket again.

When at last the mosquitoes withdrew in the dim light of daybreak, I was exhausted. But I had to get up. All that week I worried about relapsing into malaria, which had tormented me most of the time between the ages of ten and twelve.

I worked in a narrow tunnel under the river where the future dam was likely to be positioned. Although a sump pump worked all the time, the humidity stayed at one hundred percent, and the tunnel was chilly. The meals consisted of rice dressed only with fermented soybeans, it was rinsed free of worms, but rancid.

The day I was to leave the survey brigade, I felt feeble, dizzy, and nauseous. It would be impossible to climb the big mountains with two bags. A local geologist helped me bargain with a peasant to take me to catch a freight boat. After I paid him one yuan, he rowed his canoe toward a large cargo junk. As I threw my bags onto the deck and clung to the gunwale, a sailor stamped and yelled, "No, no! We don't carry passengers. Damn city slicker, get lost."

The geologist had told me, "Don't be scared by the boatmen's intimidation. You've got to be tough around here. They're nice people, though crude."

With my arms hanging over the sideboard, I kicked in the air to gain upward momentum, and the canoe owner lifted my legs to help me roll over the hurdle.

The junk owner and his wife treated me as a persona non grata, grumbling that I was in their way no matter where I sat. But a few hours later, the sailor's elderly mother began asking about my family and allowed me to buy their cooked rice and stale pickles.

For two days, without wind, the boat drifted slowly. The scorching sun turned the tiny space beneath the low canopy of reed mats into an oven, especially with the coal stove burning nearby.

I couldn't find a place to spend the night when I arrived at

Changde, the harbor city to the west of Dongting Lake. All the hotels were reserved for a local cadres' conference. I sat on the wharf for 14 hours waiting for the steamboat that would cross the lake to Changsha.

The day I returned to Changsha, I was sick with fever. For two days I lay weak and ill in the hostel, eager to visit Chuju who was only 120 kilometers away. When my fever faded, my head cooled too. I couldn't afford to visit her. Instead I wrote to her:

> I'm virtually penniless, yet my two poor brothers would certainly expect my financial help. And now, your mother is my new mother-in-law, and I'd have to give her money as the customary first-meeting gift. Friends in our hometown would expect to celebrate our marriage, not knowing we haven't the means. We have no place to borrow the money, and no ability to pay it back. Under the circumstances, I can only go north, hoping we can live together soon.

> It is brutal not to see you when my trajectory has taken me so near you. Before boarding the train, I looked to the southeast and moaned, "Chuju, you'll never know the pain mosquitoes and poverty have inflicted on me!"

I mailed the letter to her at her mother's address. Every Sunday she walked home from her workplace for supper, hoping for a letter from me. This time she wrote, "Reading of your trip to Changsha, I cried the whole long walk back to the factory without eating the supper Mother prepared for me."

12

After I returned to Beijing, we were mobilized to provide for
ourselves by engaging in agricultural production, as the old
guard did in guerrilla bases. We used office hours and our
spare time to reclaim lots around our buildings. The vegetable
seeds would grow in months, but it was too late to plant corn
or wheat that year.

Instead of waiting, we tried to find food by digging up reed
roots from the sandy banks of the Yongding River. They tasted
slightly sweet, much better than purslane and other edible wild
herbs. Young men wielding hoes and spades dug up the roots,
while senior engineers and women transported mounds of
them to a truck. Our respected institute director, an intellectual
who'd joined the Party's underground struggle, removed his
good shirt and long pants to make cloth carriers. That roused
our spirits for a while, and many of us were inspired to take off
our jackets to help carry too.

Under the scorching sun, there was no shade on the wide
riverbed, and the beach was heated like the Mongolian
Desert. Toward sunset, the breeze was soothing, but we were
staggering from fatigue and our lips were parched. The three-ton
truck was only half-full after the intense effort by our institute's
several hundred laborers. We'd surely expended far more energy
than we could possibly gain from the day's harvest.

In late July, Fuchun Li, the Director of China's National
Planning Commission, announced that all state-owned
enterprises and government organizations would be drastically
cut down.

The leaders of our institute racked their brains trying to
fulfill the State Council's layoff quota while keeping our
research units functional. First, mobilization meetings were
called to prepare everybody to leave his or her post and to see
it as a rigorous revolutionary trial. At the ensuing group
discussions, everyone was pressured to pledge that he or she

would willingly obey the Party's arrangements.

Without any worries about being laid off, Party members and senior engineers comfortably said they were, "pleased to share the nation's difficulties and volunteer to go where conditions are the hardest." The less-skilled workers, political laggards, and those who had committed misdemeanors were on tenterhooks.

Like all my officemates, I solemnly parroted the proper words: "I'll voluntarily accept the Party's arrangement." Deep down, I felt myself between the two categories but on the safe side. With my good evaluations in both academic work and political study, it was unlikely the leaders would let me go. However, it was immediately clear to me that our institute wouldn't be hiring anyone in the foreseeable future. This new development, unexpected before my wedding, shattered my dream of bringing Chuju to Beijing.

In early September, Party branches finalized their layoffs, which were officially called "transfer to grassroots levels." Without murmuring, our group's ten trainees, recruited in 1958, left for the provinces whence they had come. Three young technicians with wives in the countryside had to go back to their home villages without a salary or the right to live in the city.

In our group, there were two who refused to leave Beijing: Anna, whose husband had a secure, high-ranking position with the military; and a man with sick parents. Both had been born in Beijing and, per current public views, were longstanding backward elements. Despite their feelings being roughed up by pressure and criticism at group meetings, the two stuck it out. They entreated the division's Party branch to let them remain in Beijing, even if it meant demotion. Finally, they left the institute, a branch of the central government. A shopping center owned by Beijing Municipality accepted them, assigning the young technician with sick parents to a bicycle-repair shack, and Anna to a cookware department.

During my absence at a conference in Wuhan, Anna left

without leaving a note. Her vacant desk in the cold, empty office called to my mind our old friendship and made me regret that, for the chance to have a family in Beijing, I hadn't resisted the political and administrative pressure in 1957 and reached out to chase her.

13

By the end of October, 19 of our 39 members had been dismissed. At a division rally, Secretary Jiang announced, "The campaign of transferring personnel to the grassroots has been completed." Like my colleagues in the half-empty room, I was enormously relieved.

Jiang continued, "Those who've left us are happy. Now we must take over their unfinished projects and work with double effort."

Old Ma entrusted me to preside over our group's political discussion, a proposal endorsed by the Party branch. It would be a bigger job than taking minutes, and let me feel more optimistic about my job security and career prospects.

When a North Korean engineer visited us, Old Ma appointed me as his escort on a tour of our lab and instructed me to answer his questions, even accompany him to view a drama in a famous theater. It was common knowledge that only politically reliable persons were eligible to contact foreign guests.

I appreciated his trust and benevolence, but my future would be determined by the long-standing, prestigious Party members, who often displayed sanctimonious faces to me. Among them, the most fearsome was my former classmate Yonghon Huo, who seemed to know every thought I'd had since college. Rumor had it that his strong principles, fighting spirit, and organizational powers had inspired a secret plan among our ministry's top leaders to promote him to deputy director of our institute.

In his school days, he had scared us by quoting Julius Fučík's *Notes from the Gallows* to measure our political deficiencies. We felt compelled to learn all the noble qualities of the Czechoslovakian communist leader. Recently, he had updated his demands by referencing PLA training regulations, which emphasized the command: "Refuse to leave the front for minor wounds ... don't even cry from severe injuries ... dare to see a bayonet turn red!"

One day, an officemate was caught hiding in a locked bachelor's dorm during work hours, studying math. With Old Ma out of town, I had to preside over a meeting to criticize my colleague, but I pitied him for having been hospitalized as a mental patient when he was 15. He confided his history to me while claiming perfect current health, which I didn't believe. After his self-criticism, during which he touched only lightly on his problems, the large room fell silent.

To fulfill my duty, I fired the first shot, "You've looked down on practical work, especially lab tests. How can you spend office hours in your bed studying math? You have to study Chairman Mao's article, *On Practice,* seriously. Also, you have to strengthen your discipline."

"Stop!" Yonghon hit the desk with his mug, and water spilled over the day's newspaper, "Is this a tea party or a serious criticism session? For years you've stayed on good terms with everyone, disregarding Party interests. In fact, you've shielded this man and his bad behavior. In ideological struggles, we have to fight like PLA soldiers. 'Dare to see a bayonet turn red!' Can't you do that?"

I grew flustered. A moderate Party member, a senior engineer, tried to smooth things over, "Dapeng is a good worker, but not yet a good fighter. As our leaders groom you to take a responsible position, you need to stand up against all harmful tendencies without sparing anyone's feelings. Yonghon's comment is sharp because he sets a high standard for you, like the saying, 'wishing iron could instantly turn into steel'."

After the meeting, Dihua Fang, the soil engineer whose wife was in the Gobi Desert, privately said to me, "I know you put up with extra hardship to impress the leaders, hoping they'll help you with a family reunion. From my experience, I think you might have to give up."

After years detaining Fang, our division leaders at last allowed him to move to Xinjiang. Although they regretted giving up such a skilled man, his departure helped them meet their downsizing quota.

He was the last to leave. The evening before his departure, he came to my room with his box of books. Due to the scanty book supply in the Gobi Desert, he wanted to get some practical engineering books in exchange for his copies of theoretical ones. I presented all I had and let him choose what he liked.

He shook my hand, "It's hard to leave Beijing and abandon the credit I've built up here. The place and job waiting for me aren't good trades. But life is short. My wife and I have lived almost as if the other were dead for years. You don't know what that means. It's only been six months since you saw your wife."

"I'm scared to think about the future."

"I tell you, the years of separation ahead will be unbearable. Please do everything you can to go back to Jiangxi. The sacrifice of your career will be paid off by your reunion. Life is short, my younger brother. You shouldn't have to suffer so much when you're so young."

The truth, etched in his caring words, kept me awake all night. Director Gu had promised to help us, but that could take years, and it would not happen before the nation's current economic situation improved. So far, my requests either to move Chuju to Beijing or to relocate me south hadn't even reached the Party branch. I had to take action.

The next afternoon, my colleagues and I walked Dihua Fang to the front gate of our compound. As we all waved, the jeep taking him to the railway station accelerated and soon disappeared. Our crowd dispersed. Winter's first cold spell came in the middle of November that year. I paced around our building, one lap after another, ignoring the piercing north wind.

Finally, I reached a decision. I vowed to accept any reproach possible from my boss, and demand a family reunion. At present, my relocation to Changsha was the only logical request. Having steeled myself, I went to talk to the Party branch secretary.

14

I knocked on the secretary's office door, "Come in, please." Comrade Jiang was seated in the leather chair that used to be Director Gu's.

He put down his pen and raised his head from his writing. I blushed. Even my earlobes felt hot. He smiled and asked me to sit in a chair opposite his desk, then waited for me to speak. Looking at me with a quizzical air through his glasses, he seemed to know what was on my mind and already have an answer. I wanted to ask him about anything else and even considered talking about the budget for machine repairs.

My embarrassing silence continued, fueled by Dihua Fang's parting advice. At last I blurted, "I hope the Party branch will allow me transfer to Jiangxi or Hunan Province, where I can be close to my wife."

His smile disappeared. In a voice soft but authoritative, he said, "During our downsizing, we did consider everyone's specific problem, such as the arrangement we made for Dihua Fang. Your request is understandable, but your situation is different from his. He married in 1954, and his town in Xinjiang is remote. Besides his family reunion, we have a higher purpose, to consolidate our northwest frontier. The reason for you to stay here is the importance of our research. You have to put your personal difficulties aside for the needs of the Revolution."

"If I joined the provincial working forces, I would still work for socialist construction."

He restlessly rotated the pen in his hand, "As I said at the division assembly, whoever must go ought to be happy, and the remaining comrades should sit tight at their posts. Those aren't my own words, but a call from the Party."

I nodded and considered one last appeal, but Jiang continued, "For the last two years you have performed quite well. Your coworkers and leaders are happy to see your progress. Don't let personal problems drag you down."

All the courage I'd garnered to answer Dihua disappeared when I was dealing with Jiang's words.

I stood, and he walked me to the door of the anteroom. As if trusting me with a secret, he said, "Everyone here considers you the key member in your group, and we want to cultivate you as a top player of our national expert team. If the opportunity arises, we'll select some comrades like you to study abroad."

I was confused by his coaxing strategy. 'Abroad' meant the Soviet Union at the time, and the chances of studying there were growing dimmer by the day as the divisions between the USSR and the PRC came out into the open. I smiled, "Don't make fun of me. All Soviet experts in China have gone home, and all Chinese people studying in the Soviet Union have returned. No matter what the possibility is, the idea doesn't attract me at all. Moscow is no closer to Chuju than Beijing."

"In the long run, we should believe in the people of the first socialist country, they won't let Khrushchev stay in power for long. For the current struggle, we're expanding our cultural ties with Western Europe, Japan, and many other countries. More opportunities will appear than you can now imagine."

I was ready to go. He raised a hand and tilted his head,

"Wait a moment." He fetched a letter of invitation from the PLA Corps of Railway Engineers, which required a politically reliable person to represent our institute at a discussion on Beijing's first subway design. He gave me the letter in a cordial manner, "The meeting is in two days, it's a great chance to get familiar with some experts in underground structure."

Charged with the project's significance for defense and its connection to world revolution, I attended the meeting at the military compound. Unlike our own office, the well-heated conference room was comfortable. Snuggling in an armchair among the 20 or so participants, I soon felt sleepy. Since none of the responsible designers showed up, we knew nothing about the subway layout or surrounding geological materials. The discussion went on like a lecture in a classroom, based on hypothetical conditions. Why did the participants need to be politically reliable?

When a professor from the Beijing Mining School delivered a long paper digressing from engineering applications to show off his math, many listeners got bored. I couldn't help pushing my chair backward on the terrazzo floor with a sharp creak. All heads turned to watch me. I bent over the handouts and kept quiet for the rest of the day. As other speakers took turns, one after another, to present their tedious articles, I chewed over my conversation with Secretary Jiang and found that what he'd promised me would never lead me close to Chuju. I'd suffered enough from our separation. The whole situation wasn't showing any sign of ending.

That evening, I turned in, to the administrative secretary of our division, the 11 handouts I'd received from the meeting. Since all the covers of the pamphlets were stamped 'Confidential', she registered them one by one and stuck an index number on each. After that, I formally borrowed two of them and signed my name in her ledger. The two papers, 'How to Consider Shockwaves on Underground Structure Design' and 'The Influence of Geological Characteristics on the Attenuation of Explosive Impact', touched on areas in which I lacked basic knowledge.

Returning to my office, I cleaned my drawers, full of messy odds and ends. I determined to meet Chuju and lobby my prospective boss in Changsha for help, casting all caution to the winds. Finally, I gazed at the last line of my savings passbook. The balance of 72 yuan, resulting from a severe cutting of expenses since our wedding, was remarkable, but barely enough for a frugal trip, "Heaven never seals off all exits." With a decisive sigh, I withdrew all I'd saved, leaving two yuan in the book like a root.

Without a permit to leave, I left Beijing early the next morning carrying a shoulder bag and a small handbag. As I walked out the front gate of our institute, acquaintances greeted me as usual, showing no suspicion, but my heart beat fast.

The railway system looked stretched to the breaking point because a large portion of its capacity had been mobilized to deport hungry peasants back to the countryside. All tickets for the express train passing Changsha were sold out. I bought one for a slower train to Wuhan, where I would transfer to another slow train. It was also jammed with passengers at every door. Holding the vertical handrails, I couldn't get my body inside. I noticed two soldiers standing by and talking in a Jiangxi dialect. I shouted to them, "Comrades, give me a hand!" My native voice prompted them to help wedge me into the crammed car and assist the conductor to close the door.

The pressure kept increasing at the next stations, with passengers being stuffed like sausage meat into a casing. Meanwhile, the cars vibrated and jerked like jackhammers, constantly jolting the already stressed human bodies. Gradually, the collective pressures squeezed and pushed me to the middle of the carriage. In the evening, the rumble of the train crossing the Great Yellow River Bridge reminded me that Zhengzhou, the capital of Henan Province, was ahead. I snatched a seat from a passenger who was getting ready to alight. Soon the conductor serving the only meal reached my place. He took my 0.35 yuan, marked my ticket with a black circle, and gave me a shallow aluminum box half-full of water-saturated rice topped with a few pieces of cabbage and pork skin.

I'd been hungry for many hours, and I had food and a place to sit. But I was seized by a paroxysm of anger at my leaders in Beijing. They must have started searching for me. Gossip and speculation about me must have been spreading throughout my division and institute right at that moment. Wednesday night was our weekly meeting for criticism and self-criticism, which I loathed but felt to be indispensable. At this moment, my officemates would put me on trial in absentia. My voluntary assistance to our group leader, performed as if I was his deputy, and my semi-Bolshevik self-discipline, would be reinterpreted as bourgeois hypocrisy. Now, I'd become an extreme individualist, a bourgeois liberal, even a deserter from the Revolution.

Since childhood, I'd never disobeyed my parents or teachers, nor missed a single class or one day's work. In recent years, I'd never dodged difficulties or flinched from danger for the sake of the socialist cause. My tongue felt numb, and guilt permeated my whole body. Without knowing when or where my next meal would come from, I swallowed the rice, cold and coarse, along with my grievances.

15

The next morning, I reached Wuhan and waited at the railway station for a train going to Changsha. It wouldn't come until late afternoon. My nostalgia for the place where I finished university propelled me to walk all the way to the city center. I wanted something warm to eat, but, after spending 21 yuan for the slow train from Beijing to Wuhan, the 49 yuan in my pockets were needed to cover the expenses for my travel to Changsha, visiting my hometown, and going back to Beijing. I had to save money by enduring hunger.

Two blocks away from the station, at a street corner, I saw a starving man snatch a package of cakes or cookies from the hands of a shopper walking out of a store. Then, 50 yards farther along, an old man slapped the package into the dust. The shopper, a young man, more angry than hungry, surrendered the contaminated food to the robber while repeatedly punching him. The old man screamed, "Stop! You've hit me enough!" How starvation had stripped people of their dignity.

For the four years I'd studied here, my student aid had been only enough for meals in the mess hall, and I'd had nothing to eat at a restaurant. In the years since, remembering the glorious variety of inexpensive cuisine sold in Wuhan, none of it available in northern China, I had savored the memory of the aromas: baked chestnuts, sweet rice mixed with eight kinds of seeds and nuts, and fish steamed with ginger and onion. Those scents had lulled me into a sweet, secret ambition. Once I had a salary, I'd return to Wuhan and taste the specialties sold on every street, one by one.

In normal years, the area around city hall and the major commercial centers bustled with people. But now, with the whole nation in the grips of famine, the Land of Fish and Rice was graveyard quiet. Malnutrition had caused epidemics in the city. Standing at the entrance of several restaurants, I was scared off by huge signs hung above certain tables: 'Reserved for Customers with Hepatitis'.

I revisited a famous ice-cream stand, where customers stood eagerly eating chunks of sweetened, flavored ice without cream. They used chopsticks instead of spoons, which had probably all been stolen. The customers rolled and shredded their ice balls in their bowls with bamboo chopsticks, blackened from being handled by scores of customers and undoubtedly an effective means of spreading hepatitis. I declined to eat the ice. Better hungry than deathly ill. Instead, I bought a large, baked sweet potato for two yuan, five times the price it had been the year before. I sat in the public library's garden to eat it.

Like a fugitive, I arrived at Changsha around daybreak. Under the dim starlight and facing a chilly wind, I hurried along a back street, which ended in farmland and a trail through paddies. I tried to stay at the hostel affiliated to the Changsha Waterpower Design Institute, as I did in the past. However, the female manager who knew me wasn't there. Her substitute, a young man, refused to check me in. Besides my ID card, he insisted on seeing an official letter to verify that my current travel was authorized: "For the sake of public security, I'm obliged to stick to the rule."

To my surprise, I found Dong Long at the mess hall finishing his breakfast. He'd just completed six months of fieldwork in western Hunan and had arrived at Changsha by bus the day before. He exchanged some internal food tickets with me for money and national grain coupons, and I had my first real meal in three days. The green vegetables fried without cooking oil tasted like grass; still, I enjoyed the fresh color, available only in the south.

He led me to his room, where two of the three beds were vacant, "You'll have no problem sleeping here for two nights. Most construction projects are shut down and travelers are rare. The manager won't check."

I lay down on a bed and stretched my body. He rubbed his hands together for warmth. At the end of a long period of silence, he asked, "How could you forget to write an introduction letter? You're usually smarter than that."

I decided to tell him the truth: "I'm absent without leave." I sat up, "Nobody in our office knows where I am. I want to see my wife and meet Hu, the engineer general of Changsha

Design Institute, and ask him to help me relocate here."

"Stupid! You're throwing away your good reputation and the trust of our leaders. If our leaders treat you as a deserter, you'll lose your job, and your marriage will collapse like a sand castle. I can't bear seeing that. Go back to Beijing right away and beg forgiveness. You might be saved."

"I've already paid the price. It would be stupid to surrender with nothing to show for it. At least I want to stay with Chuju for a few days and get a promise from Hu to lobby my case."

Dong Long lowered his head. Then he poured hot water from the thermos into a metal basin, "Please clean yourself before going to meet anyone. I'll get another bottle of hot water."

When he returned from the boiler room, he handed me his comb, "Now that you've taken the loss, you should talk to General Hu. But no matter what answer you get from him, you'd better go back to Beijing before Monday. Go see Chuju, but just for one night."

After washing my face, I scrubbed my chest and steeped my feet in warm water, which refreshed my mind, "Hu is busy. I might wait for him the whole afternoon outside his office. Could you talk to Lab Director Yan? He knows me. I'm not choosy about job assignments, I can do anything he needs a hand with, as long as I can live with Chuju."

He hit his palm with a fist, "Good idea, let's work along both lines. Yan's a nice guy, easy to approach. Later, you can push him to remind Hu of your case." He put his hands on his hips, "How can you be so sure General Hu will help you?"

"I met him ten months ago at a field conference when Professor Cheng stole his show. I saved his face by keeping him away from the snobby crowd."

He blinked, "I remember the story you told me."

"It's amusing to see the big shots quarrel like children out of jealousy or fight for the affection of the authorities."

He asked, "Did you take the opportunity to tell him about

your possible future need? He must've seen you as a comrade-in-arms."

"I mentioned it. He answered positively but informally."

16

General Hu was somewhere in the building when I went to his office. His secretary jotted down what I told her. She went out for a while then came back, "General Hu asked you to wait for him."

I hung around on the second floor. Watching the dam and power plant designers smoke and sip tea and the draftswomen chat leisurely with needlework in their hands, I found two former classmates and caught up on their situation. Two hours later, Hu returned to his office and received me, my piece of paper in his hand, "I definitely need you. At the field conference, I found you had clear concepts on engineering problems, and you read technical articles in English and Russian. None of my assistants can do that. But I doubt your institute will let you go."

His secretary said, "Only if your institute surrenders your personal dossier to our institute can we proceed with the transfer."

"We can negotiate with your leaders," Hu said, "but have no leverage with them."

"I'll toughen my hide and nag my boss. Are you sure you'd be able to move my wife here?"

The secretary opened a palm to her boss and said coyly, "There must be a way if General Hu needs you."

"I can't guarantee to put your wife in this building. But we have hydrometric stations and survey brigades around the province. Worst case scenario, we can register her residence in one of our subsidiary units, and let her work here in Changsha."

I wanted to make his oral promise a binding treaty, "May I take your words as an official decision?"

The woman secretary got irritated: "You can't push our leader so hard. General Hu has never dishonored his words."

Hu smiled and stood up, stretching his arm as a gesture to let me go, "What has been said cannot be unsaid. So, go pester the bureaucrats in Beijing."

Walking to the corridor, he said in a lowered voice, "Young man, you need more worldly wisdom. Several of my aides have their spouses living in other provinces. I can't promise you, as you wish, and upset them. But take it easy. I'll help you to the fullest extent of my power."

I returned to the hostel, where Dong was waiting for me, "Good news. Director Yan said he'd like to put you in charge of one of his four test groups. He also promised to forward your future letters to General Hu and do whatever he can to help you."

I relaxed: "This trip was worthwhile."

On Saturday morning, after a sound night's sleep, I was ready to go home and tell Chuju about the new development. I thought my money was enough for the journey but nevertheless Dong Long loaned me 20 yuan as a reserve. He also offered to walk me to the railway station for a look at the commercial area.

We were astonished by all the people hanging around in the streets, thrashing about like a swarm of flies. Although the stores had almost nothing to sell, people idled between bare shelves, and one argument after another broke out. Often, after customers paid money and grain coupons, their wrapped packages of food products were snatched away by thieves lurking as bystanders.

Dong Long looked unkempt, having gone months without a haircut. With gum in the corners of his eyes and dressed in grease-mottled clothes, sales clerks looked at him with suspicion. Approaching a counter for a closer look at some glass jars, he was suddenly blocked by a clerk intent on safeguarding a package of crackers a customer had just paid for. Instead of taking it as an insult, Dong Long laughed.

As we strolled farther north toward the city center, I was shaken by a piercing alarm issuing from inside an empty store packed with aimless, moneyless shoppers. An illuminated glass box on the wall displayed a red notice: 'BE ALERT FOR PICKPOCKETS'. Next door, a man with a tin megaphone shouted over and over, "Comrades, be cautious! You must be responsible for any lost money or grain coupons because this store will not be!" Alarms rang out every few minutes.

We turned east toward the large square where the railway station was located. Policemen pushed and yelled at thousands of peasants to form a three-column line before deporting them in boxcars. Most of the waiting hall was roped off as a temporary detention center where policemen confined the hungry peasants they took from the streets. Whenever the area filled up, detainees would be led to the square, and then the boxcars.

We stood near a holding pen pitying the feeble, bony peasants. They were all dressed in tatters. Dong Long sighed: "Our people are so obedient. A rope of rice straw works like an iron wall."

He had hardly finished speaking when a policeman swaggered up to him, "Show me your ID card."

While the policeman was scrutinizing it, I groaned inwardly. Dong Long had once shown me this card. The female clerk at our personnel office had issued him a used one, torn off the photo of the previous holder, then glued on Dong Long's photo, which was smaller than the standard. The scratched base and rough edge around his picture would make anyone doubt its authenticity.

"You're too smart to make a counterfeit ID."

"Not his fault, Comrade," I said, "The woman in our personnel office produced this tattered card for him."

Holding his club at the ready, the policeman asked coldly, "Who are you?"

"I'm his colleague in the same working unit. I'm his witness, proving him to be a technical cadre of the state, a good citizen." I showed him my ID.

"Yours is no problem. His is a fake."

He returned my ID and tapped Dong's bulging pocket, "What's inside?"

"A camera."

"Take it out!" The police officer opened the leather case and smiled at the Leica label like a hunter at a shot bird, "Where'd you steal this?"

Dong got angry: "I didn't steal it, I borrowed it from our research center."

The policeman grabbed Dong's shoulder, "What's all that money in your pockets? How much is it?"

"I don't know. Some is borrowed from our accounting office for travel, and the rest I saved from my salary for the past six months."

"Liar, you're under arrest!"

The policeman tied Dong's hands behind his back with a rope. I said, "Comrade, don't do that. He has a good class background. His father is a poor peasant, and his brother is a PLA officer. You're hurting a revolutionary, which only pleases our enemies."

He raised his club: "Stinking intellectual! You dare lecture me? Shut up or I'll arrest you too."

Dong Long shouted, "Dapeng, stop! It's just a misunderstanding. Find Lab Director Yan. Have him ask local leaders to help me."

17

As a host of our joint research program, Director Yan took on the problem as if it was his own. He asked the institute's security office to contact the Changsha Police Department (PD). They sent a telegram to Beijing asking our institute's leaders to act. After lunch, I stayed in the lab until news came that Changsha PD was communicating with our home office in Beijing to verify Dong's ID and ensure that he wouldn't be abused.

That was all I could do in Changsha, so I decided to go home and meet Chuju.

It was 2:30 pm. Pressed for time, I adjusted my load, tied the long strap of my shoulder bag to the one on my handbag, threw both bags over one shoulder, and started to run.

For the hundred-kilometer distance from Changsha to Pingxiang, the express train took one and a half hours but it was too expensive for me. So I spent four hours on a slow train. I arrived at Pingxiang around seven o'clock, the time Chuju's evening political study would be going on. Alerted by Dong Long's arrest, I tried to keep a low profile. Taking darkness as my cover, I followed the railway embankment to skirt the west and south sides of the old city, then took the hill-path shortcut to reach the factory.

I moved gingerly around the large workshops. Standing by a tree or under the sill of a high window, I asked the passing young women, "Have you seen Chuju Wu?" Before I found anyone who knew where she was, two young men approached me from either side, one dressed as a mechanic, the other in the faded green uniform of a former PLA soldier.

"Are you Dapeng Liu?" Their hostile tone was ominous.

"Yes. Is something wrong?"

"Please come to our security office and wait for Chuju Wu there."

"I want to see her first."

"We make the decisions, not you."

They escorted me to a room on the ground floor of the administration building. Three desks were aligned at one end to face the large space and two long benches stretched along each side wall. I put my bags on the cement floor and sat down. The former soldier cranked the telephone.

"The man you want is here ... Don't thank us, he took the bait ... No, he wouldn't be able to escape, even if he had wings."

The other guy showed me a sheet of paper with the letterhead of Pingxiang's Public Security Bureau on it.

> Be vigilant. If Dapeng Liu appears in your
> factory, arrest him immediately, and keep him
> in custody until our armed policemen arrive.

I asked, "May I see my wife now?"

"We can let her come and have a look at you. But don't try to pass on any secret words or signals to her. For your own sake, behave yourself."

He walked out. Ten minutes later, Chuju had not yet shown up. I heard the sound of a motor vehicle, and through the window I saw the shadow of a Russian-made three-wheel motorcycle with a sidecar. The two policemen, in blue, cotton-padded uniforms, had handguns on their belts. The tall skinny one seemed to have a higher rank than the burly one. As soon as they walked in, the burly one pointed a finger at me, "Stand up, bow your head!"

I couldn't make heads or tails of the situation: "Is something wrong?"

The tall policeman moved to the back of the central desk, waved me to stand facing him, and puffed up like a pigeon, "Bow your head. I'm declaring the Party's policy. It is consistent and clear. We'll treat leniently those who confess their crimes and severely punish those who refuse to. Do you understand?"

"I don't know what all the fuss is about."

The burly policeman pounded the desk, "Don't play the

fool. Where are the two secret documents you stole? If you confess now, we'll give you a light sentence. If a foreign agent has carried them out of our country, you'll be shot."

I couldn't help laughing, "The two pamphlets have nothing to do with state secrets. They're summaries of published theories. You can find their content in foreign textbooks and technical journals. I borrowed them from our division just because they're easy to read."

He loomed closer: "Anything written or drawn for the Beijing subway is a state secret. If you're playing for time to let your foreign boss escape, you're killing yourself."

I sneered, "Please don't make a mountain out of a molehill."

He gripped my collar like a vise, rotating his wrist to squeeze my throat, and lifted me up, "Where are the documents?"

I was almost retching from the chokehold.

The door creaked open. My collar was loosened a little amid the distraction. Against his knuckles I turned and saw Chuju come in. She dragged her feet, inching forward along the wall. With a hand over her face, she was afraid to look at me. The factory's security clerk, who'd ushered her in, walked up to me, "If you don't confess, you'll never see your wife again."

Suddenly Chuju rushed up and tried to pry the policeman's paw from my throat, which was almost suffocating me. He shoved her away with his left hand. She dodged him, darted forward, and bit his wrist.

"Ouch, you poisonous snake!" He released my throat and threw her into the far corner like a bundle of millet stalks. Chuju landed on the floor and bumped her head on the leg of a stool.

"Fuck your mother!" the policeman yelled, "I'll smash you into pulp!" He rubbed his fists and took a step toward her.

"Don't assault a woman!" I shouted, "If you're a hero, go to liberate Taiwan instead of bullying unarmed civilians!"

He abruptly turned to roar at me, "Now I'm beating up a

Taiwan agent." He slapped me, which sent me staggering to the wall. I struggled not to fall. Following the shock, my face was burning and my ears ringing. The violence and insult caused a rage that I'd never experienced before in my life.

I couldn't hear my own voice, but I meant to shout, "You behave like a KMT bandit from Taiwan!"

Like a shot putter, he rotated his body counterclockwise for momentum, bounced back clockwise, and hit my right jaw with the back of his hand. I tumbled and lay on the ground as the earth spun under me.

My face felt swollen and feverish. I wanted to get to my feet, but my arms and shoulders refused. I heard a dull thud followed by a piercing shattering. I propped myself on an elbow and saw a thick glass ashtray in pieces on the ground, and the policeman wriggling his back and shoulder in pain. Chuju, strands of her hair stuck to the tears on her face, scuttled away.

The policeman pulled his gun and rushed out after her. His tall comrade helped me stand up and led me to a stool to sit on. With a gentle manner, he said, "It's meaningless to argue whether the missing pamphlets are secret material or not. Just tell us where they are."

"Locked in a drawer of my desk at our office in Beijing."

"If you lie to us, the punishment will be doubled. Can you swear?"

"Yes, I swear, I've told you the truth."

The phone rang. He answered it, "Yes, I'll do that."

The two security clerks helped him run a long rope from my neck to my shoulders, under my armpits, and around my arms, and then to tie my hands behind my back. The two clerks searched my bags one more time and put them over my shoulder.

Outside the building, a large crowd flocked around the Russian motorcycle. The burly policeman held Chuju's arm twisted behind her and brandished his pistol, "Anyone attacking a people's policeman is a counterrevolutionary!"

A group of cadre-looking men was trying to calm him down: "She's young and ignorant, forgive her."

"By Chairman Mao's teaching, the trouble between you and her belongs to contradictions among the people, even if her husband is an enemy."

After he'd thrust me into the sidecar, the tall policeman pulled rank: "Leave her alone. Settle the score with her later."

I shouted, "Don't worry, Chuju! The whole matter is chasing wind and shadows. Don't tell our parents what happened."

The tall man started the motorcycle. His buddy sat behind him, pointing the pistol at my back. Then, I heard the discussion of the watching crowd.

"What a luckless woman Chuju is for marrying a traitor."

"I don't know, he looks gentle and decent, not like a bad guy at all."

"It's hard to tell. Chuju knows his face but not his heart."

"Class struggle is too complicated to imagine."

18

That night I was detained in a cell with a metal grid door at the county detention center. Before untying the rope, a woman in a blue uniform came over to question me. The sheet of paper in her hand looked like an urgent, post-office-cable form. Pointing at my nose with her pen, she tilted her head, "Do you dare repeat that the two confidential documents are locked in your desk at your office?"

"Yes, I repeat and I swear."

Playing the pen like a drumstick, she tapped my head: "Do you know the consequences of not telling the truth?"

"Double punishment."

As if in a narrow cage at a zoo, I stood all night in the cell, its brick floor and walls stained by mud, shit, snot, and unidentifiable crud. At first, I leaned against the iron bars of the door, trying to hold that position for a catnap, but my legs gave way, and I startled awake on my haunches. I struggled to stand up and had to stamp to regain the feeling in my numbed feet. Then I changed position, holding two vertical bars and resting my forehead on the icy metal. The distant crowing of roosters reminded me that it was past midnight. I began to worry. Tomorrow would be a Sunday. Could the Beijing security force work overtime to break into my office desk and prove my innocence?

I couldn't stop shivering. My stomach was rumbling with hunger, and the stench of the foul air made me vomit, but only bitter, colorless fluid came up. The pain of my parched throat echoed the throbs of my battered face. Some of my teeth felt loose where that bastard had hit me, and I tasted blood oozing from my gums. Never in my life had I been treated that way. Never in all my life had I been so furious and sad. My whole being was overtaken by rage.

The next morning, a jailer handed me a bowl of rice porridge strewn with salted mustard greens. It alleviated my hunger and thirst a little. Then I sat on the dank ground behind the metal grid and dozed off.

Around ten o'clock, the two policemen took me to an interrogation room where a senior officer sat behind a desk with the female telegrapher who'd appeared the night before. Adjusting his glasses, he opened a pad and smiled at me: "Young man, don't ruin yourself so stupidly. A one-hour delay in confession means an extra hour for our enemy to escape." Then he pounded the desk, "Where are the secret documents?"

"Locked in my desk at our office."

He waved a telegraph: "An hour ago, our comrades in Beijing unlocked your desk and found nothing there. Lying to the people's security force; you're guilty of monstrous crimes."

He glanced at the burly policeman, who then slashed his whip, the kind with metal wires wrapped in rubber, all over my body. Accompanying every whistling blow, he roared, "Where are they?"

I gritted my teeth: "In my desk." His diabolic strength made the impact of the whip hurt more than a stick. I held my head with both hands and turned my back to him, hoping my padded jacket and sweater would offer some protection.

To inflict more pain, he whipped my legs, which were protected only by pants and long johns. That crippled me. Besides his brutality, he had an evil marksmanship with the whip and accurately hit the unprotected spots between my shoes and the cuffs of my pants. I shrieked and rolled on the floor, "Locked in my desk!"

The woman telegrapher kept taking minutes. After a pause, the officer threw a pen to the ground, "Sign your name on our record to pledge that you've told the truth."

When I crawled to pick up the pen, a final lash fell on my head. Following the sparks and lightning behind my eyeballs, I lost consciousness.

When my senses came back to me, excruciating pains returned to my hands, legs, and jaw. My skull felt like it was cracking. Still faint, I found myself lying in a train, hands tied behind my back and my head under a flap table between two berths. During my unconscious state, intensive communication must've been conducted within the police system. I didn't know when or how I was put on a train.

It was dawn. I didn't know the time or location. Whenever I wriggled to raise my body and have a look through the window, the burly policeman stomped me down with his boot. From the accents of the boarding passengers, I knew we were in Henan Province. No doubt, the train was going north, "Comrade, would you please untie the rope for a while? I need to go to the lavatory."

"Who is your comrade? You're an enemy."

"No matter what I am, I can't pee here and pollute the car."

"My duty is to hand you over to the Beijing police in one piece. I don't care where you pee."

I had to withstand the internal pressure for another ten hours.

When the train entered Hebei Province, a glamorous young lady came into the compartment. She must've been an actress, I thought at first glance. Her yellowish-orange woolen overcoat and fancy earrings were not seen among ordinary people. She looked around 30, but her face was well preserved, more tender than that of most girls. Following her numbly and submissively was an old woman with a leather carrying case. They must have been rich; otherwise, for the half-day ride, they would have taken two seats instead of the middle and lower berth opposite us.

The burly policeman was spellbound by the star-like woman. He watched her every move, revolving his head like a set of searchlights. I took advantage of the distraction to sit up straight on the floor and rest my back against his berth. He tried to strike up a conversation by flattering her: "You must be an artist. Am I right?"

She looked pleased: "I work at the Wuhan Opera House."

"What do you do there?"

I raised my head, "You fail to recognize a great star. She's Qiang Hua Li, a leading figure of Chen-style Beijing opera. *The Journal of Chinese Drama* used her stage photo as a cover last year. I forget which issue."

"The April issue," Li said. She stretched her neck to look at me over the small table, "You must be a Beijing opera lover."

I forgot my physical pain and assumed a sophisticated air, "I had the luck of watching the performance of your master in 1957, a year before his demise. In *Dream of the Red Chamber* he successively played the parts of two sisters with completely different characters, just phenomenal. I express my heartfelt condolences to you for Master Chen's passing." I bowed my head.

The policeman pulled his leg up and tried to trample me, "Who allows a criminal to interrupt our conversation?"

Li frowned and shook a finger: "A people's policeman should be civilized."

He grinned cheekily, "All right, I'll humor you. But don't be fooled by this man's gentle looks. He stole state secrets and probably gave them to foreign spies."

I shook my head: "A groundless charge. I borrowed two pamphlets of teaching materials, signed them out properly, and locked them in my desk. Because I left Beijing to visit my wife without their permission, they trumped up this case and beat me half to death."

I twisted my body to present the wounds on my hands, jaw, and skull, and opened my mouth to display the blood and swollen gums. The singing star threw up her hands to express her delicate compassion, and tears rolled from her pretty eyes. She pulled out a silk handkerchief to cover her face and leaned against the window frame.

The policeman seemed quite dismayed. He leaned forward and, in his pungent Jiangxi accent said, "Please listen to me, artist. I know you have a kind heart, but class enemies are cunning. Our mercy to them means cruelty to the people."

Li's attending maid, the old woman, acted swiftly. From her bag she pulled some soft tissue, the kind for stage makeup, and wet it with the hot tea they'd just ordered. Like a hospital nurse, she cleaned away the dried blood and saliva from the corner of my mouth, "It's heartless to torture such a nice young man. If my son had survived the Japanese bombardment, he would've been your age and as handsome as you are." She dabbed her eyes with the tissue, "Without the scar on your face, you would be a much-needed actor to play our great Party leaders on stage."

When I stretched my neck to reach the teacup, she held it

to let me drink like a water buffalo. Her boss nodded: "We have some crackers left in our case."

In the leather case on the luggage rack, she found a slender pack of vanilla crackers along with the magazine with Li's stage photo on the cover. Holding the cover up to the policeman, she pushed it forward to confront him. He stretched out both hands to receive it with respect and reverence.

The conductor came by with a large tin kettle of hot water, refilling every cup to its brim. Piece by piece, she fed me the vanilla crackers. This time I sipped her tea gently.

The policeman was clearly annoyed by her sympathy toward me, an official suspect. His anger and savage nature must have been subdued by his fear and awe of the Beijing Opera star.

I grimaced at the two ladies, "Could you kindly be my guarantors and negotiate with this people's policeman? Please ask him to untie my hands temporarily. I must go to the lavatory. I've been stressed to the point of explosion. Another minute's delay will make my body blow up like a dirty bomb, damaging public hygiene."

Li impatiently waved her handkerchief like a flag at the policeman: "Go, free him. If he escapes, we two guarantors will go to jail."

The policeman made a bitter face, "If my leaders find out I've broken the rules, I'll be finished."

Li slapped the air to deny his apprehension, "Don't worry, I know the police chief of our central government. He can save you."

He smiled in disbelief: "Are you kidding? It's a serious matter."

The old woman took out an album from her bag and turned to the page her boss indicated. Li held out the album so it faced him, and ran a finger across the photo: "See, this is the national Minister of Public Security, your paramount leader. He's presenting a basket of flowers to me after my performance in the auditorium of your headquarters in Beijing."

Her maid pointed at the photo: "Look carefully, you must know the Party big shots standing on both sides. They're even above your minister."

The policeman sheepishly went over the other photos. Quietly giving the album back to Li, he untied the rope without a murmur.

I had a few hours' ride with my hands untied until the train arrived at Beijing. I gave thanks to the Beijing opera star and her maid. They asked me to write to them after my trouble was over.

19

Instead of a rope, the Beijing policeman greeted me with handcuffs. At daybreak, a jeep took me to a heavily guarded compound, where the policeman escorting me from Jiangxi talked to a woman on the graveyard shift and signed some papers. In spite of my confusion, I found out it was November 29, 1960, a Tuesday.

At eight o'clock, regular office hours began, and the building filled up with blue-uniformed officers. I was pushed onto the bed of a Volga jeep. One of the two armed policemen sat with the driver, the other faced me with a handgun dangling from his hand. Though it was rush hour, civilian drivers and bicyclists respectfully yielded to the police car. In half an hour, I was taken to my office, where the security officer of our institute and Secretary Jiang stood. Onlookers were gathering and chirping in the corridor. The lock of my desk had been smashed and its drawers were sealed with long strips of white paper bearing the red stamps of our security office.

His face livid, Jiang asked, "In which drawer did you put the two secret documents?"

I could tell how much pressure he'd sustained, and he knew the documents weren't secret. I was eager to find them to relieve him as well as myself.

Immediately under my humble desktop, a wide drawer

occupied the left and middle two thirds of its length. Under the
right third, four narrow drawers were set vertically. With my
cuffed hands, I touched the top right one: "Here."

Our institute's security officer peeled off the paper strips,
pulled out the drawer, and scattered everything on the desktop:
"No documents. There's no way for you to continue lying."

Panic-stricken, I said unsurely, "I left in a hurry. They might
be in another drawer."

The two policemen pulled out all my drawers and emptied
them on the surrounding desks. One of them gripped the back
of my collar and dragged me around to look at my stuff:
"Where? Tell me!" Then, with suffocating force, he pressed my
head against the wall, pushed his gun barrel against my temple,
and gnashed his teeth, "You sneaky rat, what can you say now?"

I quietly panicked. What had happened? Had a personal
enemy set me up? Recalling the case of a colleague in Yunnan,
my body broke out a cold sweat. He misplaced a topographic
map before going to visit his mother in Guangzhou, where he
was arrested and jailed for six months until the map was found
by his officemate. Had an   actual KMT agent stolen the
pamphlets?

"May I help you with the search?" Dong Long, who had
been arrested as a burglar in Changsha and released the next
day, came up. Flashlight in hand, he squeezed in through the
watching crowd. The policemen and our Party leaders looked
at one another in blank dismay. Only Secretary Jiang recovered
from the confusion quickly: "Go ahead."

Dong Long looked flustered. Under their glares, he moved
nervously, checking everything in the open. While I was
holding my breath and waiting for the moment of his disgrace,
he hit his forehead with a palm, "Stupid."

He kneeled on the floor and twisted his body to check if
anything had been stuck on the bottom of the desktop, but
found nothing. Then he stretched his arm into the box that
held the column of narrow drawers. The front wooden dividers

of the frame prevented him from touching the backboard. Still he tried to get his hands in as deep as possible, using his flashlight again. His fingernails scrabbled against the gap between the desktop and the drawers' guide plates. He was straining to reach something. Then he smiled. He pulled out some crumpled papers and flattened them out on the desktop.

The familiar typesetting of the two covers electrified me: "Here they are!"

The onlookers wandered off. The policeman made a phone call to his boss, whispered to my leaders, and set me free. I took the two pamphlets upstairs to the file clerk and carefully watched her sign her name in the 'returned' space.

During the lunch break, Dong Long and I went to the nearby public bathhouse. Seeing me hobbling, he held my upper arm to help me get on board the trolley car. There were few people in the pool at that time. I enjoyed the hot water while he related his ordeal in the long, cold night after he had been arrested as a suspected burglar. He slept in a pigsty with two bricks as pillows. He held no grudge against the police or the clerk who'd issued him a shoddy ID card.

The next day, I had to face collective criticism. At the group meeting, I argued with those who labeled my leaving my post without permission as deserting the Revolution. I also described the brutal treatment I'd received in Pingxiang, which was turned around as an effort to damage the image of the people's policemen. As a result, the scale of my public humiliation was escalated to division level.

Minutes before the division rally on Friday, all my other officemates had gone to the conference room. Dong Long lingered behind to warn me, "To make life easier, don't try to save face. Believe me, our division leaders still like you even though you've brought trouble to them. After you've accepted all the stinky words from the foul mouths, Secretary Jiang will have reason to say that you've hated your own misconduct."

I followed his advice, swallowed my pride, and accepted all the malicious blaming. As usual, Secretary Jiang said my self-criticism was not profound enough, but he let me pass.

That evening, Dong Long and I went out to have dinner, a silent celebration of my release. The market in downtown Beijing had begun to lose its graceful face, as the famine finally engulfed the whole nation. As we stood in line at a low-priced restaurant, disputes broke out one after another, customer and server arguing over whether, say, the amount of rice was enough for the coupon charged. A scale was provided on the counter to let customers weigh their rice, but nobody knew how to convert the weight of steamed rice into that of the original raw grains. Then, an angry buyer grabbed the scale to beat the server with.

Although the high death tolls from starvation in Anhui Province and the Gobi Desert were kept secret, we knew how lucky we urban residents were. Chuju, an industrial worker, enjoyed certain food rations, and wouldn't be severely starved. Nevertheless, our leaders euphemistically asked us, "to keep a proper balance between work and rest." That order during this emergency was meant to preserve skilled people for the state's future recovery. Most of my coworkers felt they had permission to work as little as possible, thereby reducing caloric burn.

As a violator of discipline, I couldn't have that privilege. As a prescription to treat my ideological illness, the Party branch assigned me to physical labor at a farm in Daxing County, around 40 kilometers south of Beijing, starting Saturday, December 3, 1960, for an undefined period.

20

From the train station, 40 kilometers south of Beijing, to the center of the farm, it usually took 40 minutes by foot. With all my belongings bundled into a bale on my back, like the big shell carried by a snail, I was constantly left behind by other hikers. As every step implied my being moved a step farther away from Chuju rather than closer to her, the grief further slowed down my pace. After two hours, through cycles of perspiration in the freezing cold and shivering because of the north wind, I eventually arrived at the farm office.

Our institute owned the farm and built it with government money, so its production was deducted from our operating costs. But, as with any farm of this kind, the results were unpredictable. Almost all the chickens and pigs, expected to reproduce rapidly, died prematurely from disease and cold weather.

Our supervisor at the farm, Old Wei, was a demobilized PLA soldier, rough but innocuous. Besides me, three other men were left under his command. Though in the slack season, the workload for the few hands was heavy, employees without political debts wouldn't be sent there at this bad time. Old Wei received me in his office with a straight face, and said, "I know your problem. Just be honest with the Party and work seriously to remold yourself. You still have a broad road ahead."

When lunchtime was over, Jiaqing Fan, one of the three laborers, helped me to exchange some meal tickets for money and grain coupons; then asked the cook to sell me a bun and some cabbage soup. Fan was a senior draftsman who got in trouble in 1957 for copying satirical articles authored by others into big-character posters with ink and brush. Later he confessed that his motivation was to show off his fluent calligraphy, but officially he was convicted of anti-Party sentiment. I admired his handwriting on some blueprints, they were no different from machine printed notations.

It was time to work in the field. My former classmate, Huihe Lin, came up to carry my bale of bedding and ushered me to a room that had been rented from a peasant family. Shifting their mattresses on the long brick bed, he made a space for me to sleep. He was once a stellar student. But, due to his submitting a jointly authored letter asking for more time from the 48 office hours per week for technical study—which was interpreted as a rebellious move incited by the Hungarian Uprising—his YL membership had been suspended since 1957. Recently he'd counterfeited some mess hall food tickets with a mimeograph and been caught when he tried to use them for a few pieces of steamed bread. He had been expelled by the YL two weeks earlier. He didn't say a word to me, perhaps because he was in the shadow of his new disgrace. I felt our college-time fraternity returning to us but with a sour and bitter taste.

That afternoon, sitting on inverted round baskets, we quietly selected seeds of corn and sorghum for next year's sowing. Occasionally we stared at, or nodded to, one another. However, my third coworker, Keguang Luo, averted his eyes from me. He was one of the only two curly-haired Chinese men I'd ever seen in my life, and used to be a Party member. He was expelled after privately admitting to the Party branch secretary that in his heart he'd agreed with some of the opinions expressed at the 1957 May Free Airing of Views meetings, which he'd been assigned to preside over. I suspected that he was holding a grudge about my speech at the Anti-Rightist rally, which had been concocted with Secretary Xiao's hands-on help and praised by him.

Both Fan and Luo were labeled as sixth-grade rightists, but their salaries weren't cut. That was mild treatment compared to how first-grade rightists were punished: they were arrested and sentenced as counterrevolutionaries.

From morning to evening, we struggled to finish Old Wei's assignments, such as fetching water from the well, burying the chickens and pigs that had died of pestilence, and feeding the live ones. The most difficult part was digging up the peanuts and sweet potatoes overlooked by our hundred coworkers during the harvest. Our ministry bought the land and we spent labor and money on the products. But hunger propelled the villagers from the People's Commune to deny our ownership. We were outnumbered by the women and children, who were quick of eye and deft of hand.

We didn't have gloves and our hands looked like bark, with blood seeping from the cracks. Everyone tried to fulfill his tasks as a way to atone for his sins.

One day in the middle of December, when the wind blew hard, Old Wei assigned us the task of opening up a piece of wasteland to enlarge our cornfield. Hoeing the frozen soil with our backs to the wind, we made slow and steady progress in the morning. I was worried about how long I would do this, whether it was a temporary correction or a permanent punishment. Tired in the afternoon, I frequently stopped, propping my hand and chin on the handle of the hoe. At one point, I told the story about a peasant in western Hunan who found a wild boar that had fallen from a cliff. He began to carry the huge stroke of luck home on his back, but, on the way, it woke up and tore his throat out.

Huihe Lin said, "He was obsessed by the windfall."

Jiaqing Fan argued, "Men die for fortune just like birds die for food."

While I was waiting for a comment from the curly-haired man, Old Wei approached me from behind and pulled me aside, "Why do you laugh and joke with these anti-socialists? You need to keep a clear line between us and the enemy." He was saying what the Party leaders in our home office had told him. He wanted to let me know I'd been distinguished from the rightists. I sensed there wouldn't be any further disciplinary measures against me.

That night, under the kerosene lamp, I wrote a short letter to Chuju. The last paragraph read:

> Please forgive me for my naïve adventure, which led to our disgraceful fiasco. I didn't even have a

chance to talk to you or touch your hand to make our ordeal worthwhile. Nevertheless, we haven't lost our case. At least my struggle for our union has impressed the Party leaders, though in a negative way. Engineer General Hu has turned on the green light for our relocation to Changsha. The ashtray you threw at the scoundrel gave me a great boost. It declared with thumping and shattering that, in adversity, we join forces. Cheer up, Chuju, we'll win eventually and in a smarter way.

On New Year's Eve, the last day of 1960, curly-haired Keguang Luo caught, killed, and skinned a hedgehog. He shared the meat with us as a treat, and we found it had a thick layer of fat under the skin. On a whim, the cook contributed tiny fishes he'd caught and dried in the autumn. He fried the dried fishes in the hedgehog fat, boasting, "From Beijing to Shanghai, you can't find any restaurant that serves such special cuisine." The other diners praised the taste while I found even the smell of it sickening.

By ration, everyone could buy a hundred grams of hard liquor. We four laborers didn't drink alcohol, and hence surrendered our ration to Old Wei. He bought a whole bottle of sorghum wine. To return the favor, he offered us a tray of peanuts, which should have been turned over to our institute.

We collected enough cornstalks as fuel for the heated brick bed, on which we sat around a short-legged table. To complement the hedgehog meat and gamy fishes, Old Wei drank like a pirate. He drained the bottle in ten minutes then began to curse, "It's not fair. I fought bravely the War of Liberation for three years, and for another three in Korea. I remained a platoon leader. But the fancy talkers were promoted over me. I hate that I had only an elementary school education."

Face red and eyes bloodshot, he wagged his finger to point

at Lin and the two sixth-grade rightists one by one: "You intellectuals went to school by exploiting the working classes then used your knowledge to attack the Party. Do you still want to overthrow socialism?"

Then, he turned to me: "Your problem belongs to contradictions among the people, but your bourgeois individualism is serious. Watch out and don't let it drag you to the enemy's side."

As his words rambled unintelligibly, I held his arm and helped him lie down on the warm bed. Soon he was snoring. The room turned quiet. The cook tasted his rationed wine in small sips, trying to make it last.

In the sullen atmosphere, Fan, the draftsman, began to sob, "With this hat on my head, my daughter isn't eligible for college."

At the end of 1957, the Party Central had exempted sixth-grade rightists from the criminal label of rightist. Two weeks later, in January 1958, the amended order stressed that the Hat of Rightist would be necessary to expedite their remolding.

Luo, the frank man with curly hair, sighed, "At least you have a family. Without a university education, your daughter can still work. My Hat of Rightist scares women away. I can't even find a wife."

Coughing and sniffing, Huihe Lin wailed, "I'm ashamed I faked the tickets. But the letter I wrote was a sincere response to the Party's March toward Science. I wasn't born a bad guy. Dapeng, you're my witness."

"You were an honored student. Your recent mistake isn't unusual. A female student in the college near our center stole two loaves of steamed bread from the mess hall kitchen at midnight. The cooks chased her until a passing train blocked her escape. She threw herself under the wheels."

"Ah, Buddha!" Fan put his palms together.

"When stories like this reached the secretary general of our YL's central committee," I said, "he asked the cadres to stop meting out severe punishments for such minor infractions. He even quoted Lenin: 'During starvation, the proletariat will defy everything.' So, your trouble should stop here."

Luo shook his head: "Huihe's problem is complicated by his 1956 record. His margin of error is narrow now. One more misstep will trap him in my category."

Fan seemed frightened by such talk, "Let's recall our favorite foods, the best we've tasted or heard of."

"You go first," I said, "you're the oldest."

He swallowed salvia before speaking: "I grew up in Shanghai. As I remember, the salty duck and freshwater rockfish are the best."

With craving in his eyes, Luo looked into the darkness enveloping the dim lamp: "A French roll with cream filling."

I passed on something a fluid-mechanics professor had told me: "In the US, turkeys grow so tall their heads are higher than our desks." I stretched my thumb and middle finger to show the length, "He also touted Cuban frogs, with legs more than eight inches long."

The cook born in the northern countryside tempted us with apples picked near a place called Willow Green, a suburb of Tianjin. He struck his palm to mimic a knife cleaving an apple, and shook his head with craving, "The faint, fresh scent, the delicate fragrance." Everyone was drooling.

We spent our New Year's Eve at an imaginary banquet.

21

On New Year's Day, 1961, a Sunday, we wanted to sleep longer than usual and give up the first of the holiday's two meals. Mischievously, Old Wei connected his six-tube radio to the loudspeaker system, barraging us with high-volume rhetoric. From morning to night, the announcer of the Central People's Broadcasting Station read the same article over and over: 'Striving for World Peace and the New Victory of Domestic Socialist Construction', an editorial from *The People's*

Daily.

On Monday, we rested like the other employees in our home office. On Tuesday morning, when we were grading a newly tilled patch of land, a young worker from my division came with a letter written by Secretary Jiang requesting that Old Wei release me for an emergency task. After lunch, the young man shouldered my bale with my comforter, mattress, and bed sheets inside. I carried my other things on my back, for the 40-minute hike to the small railway station.

Old Wei walked with me for a long stretch. His parting words were, "You see, I was right. The Party still trusts you. You'd never lose your belief in the Party."

That afternoon, I returned to our institute. After unloading my stuff in my dorm, I immediately went to see Secretary Jiang. Before talking about a job assignment, he asked in a somber voice, "Do you know what the Party's consistent policy toward erroneous comrades is?"

I answered with the formula everyone could recite: "Learning from past mistakes to avoid future ones, and curing the sickness to save the patient."

He nodded, "Your attitude toward the tough security investigation was basically correct, and you labored well at the farm. Here's a chance for you to redeem yourself by good service."

Along with me, he'd appointed two other researchers, both specialists in underground hydrodynamics, to work on the Haizi Reservoir Dam, 60 miles to the east of Beijing. It was an honor to be chosen when most coworkers were in a state of hibernation, lacking work to do. For me, it was a token of the leaders' forgiveness.

Chen, a bureau chief from our ministry, took three of us in his jeep to meet Pinggu County's party secretary at the dam site. The poor road and cold weather made for a tough three-hour ride. Chen's presence carried weight, keeping us three non-Party members quiet with fear. He had been the 1950 military supervisor for New China's first large reservoir at Guanting, west of Beijing. Before his service in the PLA, he'd orchestrated the Party's underground movements on the campus of a famous university in Shanghai.

Upon my arrival, I noted the barren, ragged terrain and realized the name—Haizi, baby sea—reflected the peasants' craving for water.

The project had been designed by an engineer familiar only with residential structures. Now, water was leaking underneath, threatening the cottages downstream. We knew the physical parameters of the structure and its foundations, and the preliminary evidence suggested that the dam would likely collapse in a heavy rain or flood.

The designer was already there, and the presence of the two officials made the gravity of our assignment clear. To undertake this pressing task, we needed to gather our findings and write our proposal before the Chinese New Year, about six weeks away. Four thousand peasants from the county had already been mobilized, and were ready to repair the dam immediately after the traditional festival. After the rally, we marched to demonstrate our determination to complete the glorious mission. Along the trails on both sides of the river and around the villages, the single-file column stretched for miles. Though hungry, the peasants shouldered hoes, spades, sledge hammers, and red flags, shouting "We must liberate Taiwan!", and "Long live Chairman Mao!" I couldn't see the head or tail of the formation of peasants.

Jiang put me in charge of stability analysis. The first step was to test the strength of the shale and marl under the dam. On-site field experiments would take too long to set up, and in any case, the freezing weather made them impossible. So we lugged samples back to the lab.

I uncovered four identical large machines in the second-floor lab. Alone in that room, I kept loading and unloading the weights and logging all the dial readings. On an empty stomach, I found it difficult to handle the ten-pound iron disks, and I sometimes got dizzy. But this poverty-stricken county couldn't afford a flood, and four thousand peasants awaited my proposal with the results of lab tests as its basis.

Then, on January 17, when I was poised to dash through three final days of testing, news came that the premier of the Republic of the Congo, Patrice Lumumba, had been murdered by other African forces colluding with the US. Three million Beijing residents were mobilized for demonstrations with the rallying cry, "Down with the US imperialists' running dog, Mobutu!" I had to stop my test work to participate in the protest.

While the senior Party members weren't in Beijing, Junior Mu and Minggui An, the two rank-and-file members, and I were entrusted with the security of our marching group; we were to prevent any enemies from penetrating our ranks. In an emergency, we three would keep the group in order. I knew nothing would happen among our purified and disciplined ranks. Nevertheless, entrusting me with security duty, alongside Party members, was a political honor.

I hastily ate a bun and a bowl of porridge before starting the march. As we reached Tiananmen Square, even before we began shouting our slogans, all my breakfast calories were depleted. It was difficult to resist eating the cold cake jiggling inside the aluminum lunchbox in my shoulder bag, but I had to reserve it for the return march, ten more kilometers.

That night, weakened by fatigue, hunger, and cold, I remained spiritually intact, feeling on the verge of real success in my career. With the leaders' trust in both my political reliability and professional promise, I would stride along a brilliant road, Chuju at my side.

The next day, I continued the test. Around ten o'clock, as I was pouring hot water into my cup, a coworker brought me a letter from Youzhi, my younger brother.

It makes my heart ache to tell you that Chuju has been caught in an affair with Huaizhong Wang, the head of the personnel office at her workplace, Jiangxi Mining Machinery Factory. He is also one of the few vice presidents of the factory. Now, as the scandal becomes the talk of the town, I can't hide the bad news from you. Otherwise, you'll be further cheated, and soon ruined by that whore. You are an inspired man, it is not worth keeping such a rotten woman. Please cast away any illusion about her, and prepare to fight against Wang, that two-legged beast. I really worry if you're strong enough to suffer this blow. So I've sent a letter to the leaders of your division Party branch, with the hope that they can take good care of you.

I smashed my thermos against a table, "US imperialists haven't harmed a single hair on my head, but my wife and a Party cadre have stabbed me in the back!"

I sat by the window, unable to believe his news. It couldn't have happened. Chuju wouldn't betray me so soon, so easily. It seemed even less likely that a Party cadre for personnel control could be so ethically putrid.

Our personnel office was a vital part of the Revolution. Besides managing labor needs and assigning jobs, it connected the far-flung branches of the national security system and functioned as an extension of the police. The warning painted on its doors, 'Important, Office of Personnel Affairs: Unauthorized Persons Not Allowed', always prompted me to hurry past.

Anyone working in such an office, so full of secrets and power, must be a Party member with an impeccable record. In the eyes of the public, the head of any such office must be pure, decent, and of the utmost trustworthiness. How could Wang, from such a sacred bureau, have become so great a destructive force in my marriage?

I reread the letter. My brother, who had always been loyal to me, alleged the affair firmly, factually. Chuju and Wang must've created a scandal in their factory.

Youzhi's wife also worked there, in the turning shop, and she told Youzhi that the factory's Party committee had held a closed-door meeting to criticize Wang, and had interrogated Chuju, pressuring her to confess the affair. My wife! Her loose, wild behavior with her boss was a sign that she hadn't loved me from the start.

As the hours wore on, I read and reread his letter. The emotional content was unmistakable, and I was forced to conclude that something bad had indeed happened.

With no appetite for dinner, I passed the mess hall, plodding through a misty dusk back to my dorm. That night, I didn't undress, but just sat on my bed, leaning against the desk next to it. I pulled the comforter over my aching shoulders, wrapping it so tight that it kept my numb legs from moving. I felt as if I'd been bound with rope and dropped into a deep well.

22

The next morning, my stomach hurt and my tongue was numb. Unable to eat, I just drank hot tea the entire day. In the lab, looking at the last set of shale samples sealed in wax, I tried to pull myself together, to concentrate. My body and brain refused to obey my will.

Anemic rays of sun piercing the translucent clouds warmed the room slightly. I pulled my brother's letter from my pocket and read it yet again.

Stapled to his letter were four ration coupons he'd saved, enough for me to buy two kilos of grain. News came from Jiangxi, the major porcelain producing area with rich kaolinite deposits, that famine victims had begun to eat the white clay to appease their hunger. I suspected my brother might've suffered from the pain of malignant constipation as a result of saving the coupons. If that was truly what had happened, accepting them would make me guilty. At least, they made me feel ashamed for not having treated him as a cherished younger brother 15 years earlier, and of neglecting him in his recent disaster. For a while, my anger and grief were overridden by sorrow for my miserable brother.

The 1945 scene of my slapping his buttocks when he begged for a snack on the street came back to haunt me. Thirteen years later, in 1958—when he was expelled from high school as anti-socialist and became a social pariah—I believed in his innocence, but persuaded him to repent nevertheless, like many other timid men, and justified my advice as a pragmatic way to avoid further blows.

I accepted the dirty and worn-out coupons, which he must've bought from the black market at a high price, as a souvenir. In a short note, I asked him not to do anything on my behalf to confront Chuju, and told him I'd come home soon.

I was only two days behind schedule, still able to catch up. I struggled to finish the tests for the dam's foundation and my proposal to reinforce it. In the meantime, the two hydrodynamics experts had given me their findings on buoyancy pressure and seepage. I put all the data and analyses together and sat down to write my report on how to strengthen the dam.

With only a few revisions, the chief engineer from the Beijing City Planning Bureau accepted my report. During the group discussion he led with the other planners, Secretary Jiang endorsed my presentation and conclusions. Unlike many of the other leaders, he always pushed me to the front in order to enhance my reputation. His support helped distract me from sadness for a few hours.

Finally, with my mission completed, I could make plans to go home—only to confront my wife on her marital infidelity instead of for the romantic reunion I'd long anticipated.

Telephone was not available at my home county. Also, I didn't calculate the cost of the trip until I went to buy my ticket. The roundtrip was 68 yuan, just for a hard seat. And I needed to bring gifts.

I should give at least 40 yuan as a one-time token of brotherly assistance to my elder brother and his wife, who were supporting four children and our aged parents. In the meantime, before revealing Chuju's problem, custom also required me to give her mother a sizable gift of money on our first meeting as in-laws.

I calculated I could give her only 20 yuan, no matter how shabby that meager amount might seem to her. Such a small amount would likely irritate her, maybe even provoke her to despise me, and worsen the awkward, bitter situation between Chuju and me.

By happy coincidence, our research group requested that on my way back to Beijing, I stay a few days at Changsha and Wuhan. I could gather valuable information from the local engineers, who had experience with dam-foundation reinforcement. That meant the institute would reimburse my hotel room and public transportation at the two cities. Thus, I could borrow a little money from the accounting office, pay it back later from my salary, and, temporarily, slightly ease my financial woes.

The day before I left Beijing, Secretary Jiang said to me, "In difficult times, we should depend on the Party organization and have faith in the masses. That's the way you won't get lost."

On February 12, 1961, three days before Chinese New Year, I headed home. The express train arrived on time in the evening, but I had no hope of finding a seat. For two hours, I stood jammed into a vestibule, leaning against a doorframe, cushioned only by my bags. Soon my feet had grown numb from a freezing draft creeping through gaps in the car's joints, and I had to stamp them to regain any feeling. I alternated standing and sitting, mustering my mental strength for the tough trip ahead.

Little by little, newcomers pushed me deeper into the car. The next morning, I sat on the wooden floor, resisting the pressure of bodies on all sides, and got used to the thick tobacco smoke and acrid human odors. With my head bobbing to the train's rhythms, I dozed off, and frequently woke up with a start. I didn't know how to follow Jiang's instructions. Yielding to drowsiness, I would say, "Just wait and see."

The second night, I heard my belly rumbling above the rattling of the train. In 30 hours, I'd had two meals. Each one consisted of a small box of rice dressed with a few shreds of cabbage.

Around daybreak, I got off at the railway station in Zhuzhou to transfer to a local train for the last 45 kilometers. From a food joint outside the fence, I bought a bowl of noodles. But the moment I turned my back to get a pair of chopsticks from a nearby table, a shaky young man scooped all the noodles away. Since his grimy hand had dipped into my bowl, I abandoned the dirty hot soup.

Still hungry, I returned to the platform to await the 'slow train', as the locals called it. It stopped at every tiny town, making the 45-kilometer ride almost two hours long.

23

At long last I arrived at Pingxiang, the place of my youth, where Chuju lived. My current tragedy overrode any sense of intimacy with my second hometown.

Father called to me before I saw him. He had just dumped the used household water into a ditch along the street. Holding a rusted enamel basin, he said, "Mother has been muttering all the time, I know she is worried about you because her eyelids keep twitching."

His face startled me. His eyelids were swollen, leaving only a narrow seam, which he could barely see through. His puffy face was yellow. Accumulated fluid under his skin had turned it the color of sick silkworms. An ominous feeling hit me. His waxy yellow complexion reminded me of a young girl who'd lain dying next door to us in 1945, wasting away from edema— nobody could tell why—soon after the Japanese troops withdrew. Her skin looked the same as Father's. He was hit by both poverty and sickness more fatally than ever.

He tried to take my bag. I stopped him by gripping his hand, which was bony and calloused, no longer nimble with the brush pen and abacus, "I didn't know you were so sick. You should've told me you suffered from edema, I could've brought you some medicine."

"I didn't want to add to your burden. You've already had enough."

He led me to his room on the top floor of the rundown building, an abandoned hotel annexed to the slum. With one hand on the rail, he waited until his two feet were steady before ascending another step.

When he gasped for air and strength on the staircase, I said, "Life is too tough on you. I can't even think of you pushing a wheelbarrow on a muddy road."

He waved a hand, "The problem is my age, 64 now. The weight of coal or sand I can carry is less and less. But neither of your brothers is making a good living. Haitao is still a porter, and his wife struggles like a slave to feed their six mouths. They're all my offspring. As long as I can move, I have to struggle to help them. I have no complaint. I only hope you three brothers will do well and be safe."

He used the kitchen towel tucked into his belt to clean his eyes, "Who could expect the disaster of your younger brother being expelled from school as an anti-socialist at the age of 16? It's heartbreaking."

I held his upper arm to help him climb the rest of the steps, "The Revolution doesn't leave many families intact."

"Is that Dapeng?" Mother asked. I found her huddled in the bamboo chair as though more with fear than cold. Five months earlier, when famine made Wuhan a ghost city, she had left Uncle's family and returned to Father.

Under her sagging eyelids, her gaze reminded me of when my two younger brothers, aged four and one, died of smallpox two weeks apart in 1941. Before that, overhearing her talk to our neighbors, I had learned that my three sisters had all died before I was born, but I was too young to understand her pain. After the two small coffins were carried away, one after the other, she wailed and sobbed until she lost her voice. For a long time, she mostly sat in a corner, wiping her tears with her apron or sleeves. Sometimes, she was frightened by her own hallucinations, awaking from her torpor and crying. One summer night, the cooling air made the wooden roof shrink and creak. She said, "Ghosts are coming to steal another child from me." She held me tightly, "Buddha bless us!"

All the tragedies had hammered at her struggling spirit. Although she took every disaster as retribution for sins committed in a previous life, she often secretly prayed to Buddha for peace and safety for us all. Now, as she greeted me with a forced smile, she seemed like a whipped animal expecting another lash.

I hated that my troubles added to the family misfortune. Father, for his part, never complained about society or the people in power. A beaten man, he blamed us only for not being cautious enough to avoid pitfalls.

He talked about Chuju, his words interrupted by gasps for breath: "You shouldn't have urged her to go to university in your letter last year. It's not realistic. Worse, it made her feel like you loathe her poor education. That might have started her disloyalty."

No doubt he'd heard that complaint from Chuju's mother. As the victim, it was difficult for me to accept his criticism. In despair, I thought her going to university would create a chance for us to move in together upon her graduation. At any rate, suggesting her go to school didn't justify her infidelity, yet his opinion lingered in my mind.

Mother sat beside us, alternately gazing at Father and me. Finally, in a weak voice, she said, "Divorce causes too much trouble. Of all the generations of our family, no-one has ever divorced. If Chuju can come around, let it pass."

Father and I kept silent.

To end our chilly talk and lift them a little from their depression, I said, "I'm lucky compared to my two high-school idols, labeled as rightists and dumped into labor camps. I've passed the storms, one after another. I'm respected by my coworkers at the institute. My situation isn't hopeless."

24

Later that afternoon, I went to see Chuju at her workplace. Just walking the two kilometers from my parents' home to the factory wore me out. I paused at the stone bridge where I used to see Chuju stroll through aisles of vegetable vendors. The river flowed quietly as in the old days, but Chuju's innocent smile existed only in the remote past.

As I approached the valley and could see the red brick machine shops down its slope, my strongest feeling was that Chuju had become a stranger. Apparently, she had only pretended to take me as her partner; now she was revealed as a traitor. What should I do or say to her in the next moment? Embrace her or punch her?

I stopped by the factory fence, watching a small formation of ducks on the nearby pond seemingly lost in their cozy world. I hoped my mind would clear.

I spotted two young women, one in her mid-twenties, the other maybe 19, whispering together and staring at me. The elder came over and asked, "Comrade, are you looking for somebody at the factory?"

"I've come to see Chuju Wu."

The younger woman clapped, "We guessed you're her husband. Are you? You have the air of someone from the capital."

The older girl introduced herself: "My family name is Zhang, and hers is Xiao. She's the youngest comrade at our factory. We're good friends of Chuju's."

According to current custom, I called them Junior Zhang and Junior Xiao. Warm and lively, they walked me toward the factory kindergarten on the first floor of a two-story building. There, we heard an orchestra of traditional Chinese musical instruments. Zhang told me, "Chuju is rehearsing with the propaganda team. On New Year's Day, they'll give a performance for a People's Commune ten kilometers from here."

Zhang and Xiao went into the kindergarten's large playroom, it was full of amateur singers, dancers, and musicians. I heard a flutter of commotion at their entrance, and the music abruptly ended. They returned with the head of the propaganda team, who was also head of the factory's trade union. After apologizing that Chuju was right in the middle of rehearsing a short revolutionary opera, he ushered me to his office for a rest.

I said thanks to the two young women. Before leaving, Zhang pointed to the door of a building next to the kindergarten, "We live on the second floor, the third room on the western side. You're welcome to find us anytime you need help."

The trade union's large office had three bookshelves against one wall and a full-size bed in one corner. The area in between was cluttered with piles of red flags, drums, and gongs.

I sat on a stool by a porcelain heating vat, mulling over what to do. A chill feeling seeped into me. I put my hands close to the charcoal embers in the vat, but their warmth was gone. I hadn't written to Chuju about coming. What might she feel about my sudden arrival?

About 40 minutes later, the door was pushed open. To my surprise, Youzhi and his wife, Haiyan, walked in. The two lively young women, Zhang and Xiao, had lost no time finding them.

I'd known Haiyan since she was a fourth-grader, and had in fact first seen her crying after the body of her father, a pre-1949 landlord, had been recovered from a well. But it was the first time I'd met her in the presence of my brother. Their marriage was logically matched in terms of social and economic status as Haiyan, according to a new education law, was forbidden to enter college due to her family background.

They'd rented a room at a peasant's house nearby and already had a baby. I could only imagine how hard they struggled. Their three mouths depended on the 27 yuan Youzhi earned each month, plus 34 more, his wife's salary as an entry-level mechanic.

My brother pushed up his sleeves, "That woman brazens it out. While her scandal spreads like wildfire, she has the face to play a role in a lousy opera. Huaizhong Wang, a pig in human clothing, still swaggers around."

I was too tired to respond. His tone got edgy: "Public opinion is on your side. You have to fight. Don't dream she'll turn into a decent woman. Chuju isn't the only slut in her family; their roots are bad."

"Don't attack the whole family," I said, "Her oldest sister is a model of chastity, and Auntie Wu is an old-fashioned woman. She kept her daughters from any contact with men before marriage."

"Auntie sold her oldest daughter, at 16, to a KMT army officer almost as old as she is, then the second one, Minqing, to a PLA commander, also an old monkey. Doesn't that make her a moneygrubbing pimp?"

"Auntie's illiterate. In 1946, how could she predict the KMT government would be overthrown in three years? Don't attack their whole family."

Youzhi smirked, "Just mentioning her second daughter with

the hooligan, Coyote Tian, will nauseate me. Chuju and she are birds of a feather."

Coyote Tian, the street guy, was now a somebody around our hometown. In 1958, he'd climbed to the position of trade union chairman of a major mining branch under the Pingxiang Coal Mine Bureau. I was stunned: "How can Minqing fool around with that creep?"

Youzhi ground his teeth, "Tian, the toady, has a powerful umbrella."

"Minqing, Chuju's sister, quit college in 1958," Haiyan said, "and began as a staff worker under Tian. It was the crazy time of the Great Leap, when all employees were under pressure to work overtime. Tian kept her in his office every night. At first she hated his harassment but swallowed it because he's her boss."

Youzhi snorted, "A decent woman would've sued him. Anyone who sexually assaults the wife of a PLA soldier can be accused of sabotaging national defense, and the normal sentence is two years. What does Minqing do? When her husband came to see her, she refused to sleep with him. The poor man returned to his barracks crying."

I sighed, "It would be difficult to get the evidence to convict Tian. Especially since he's under the shield of local power."

Youzhi sneered, "Her husband often brags about himself as a Korean War hero, but he's a spineless worm. Now, Minqing has been relocated to an elementary school downtown and her husband has been transferred to a civil office in our county, she's still fooling around with Tian. Can't you see what a rotten woman she is?"

Haiyan said, "Her husband hates Tian but hesitates to beat him up. Tian's like a rat perching on a fancy flower vase, and he's afraid of smashing the vase."

Youzhi glared at her, "You don't know what's right and wrong."

"No more arguing, Youzhi, please." I tossed a piece of

charcoal into the embers and hit the vat with the tongs.

Both of them stopped talking. Silence filled the room.

I tried to relax the tension: "Let's not waste time on the situation with Chuju's sister, we don't have the energy. What's Huaizhong Wang's profile?"

Youzhi said, "He's a frog in a well, shortsighted. But he knows how to suck up to bureaucrats. Now, with ration coupons and special supplies in his hands, he gives their wives whatever he can chisel from ordinary workers."

Haiyan nodded, "He finished only fourth grade, then become a foot soldier during the War of Liberation. He has thick, hardcover books by Marx, Lenin, and Stalin on his desk, but they are just decorations. Whenever he gets bored, he hangs around the factory, flirting with young female trainees. His wife is 12 years younger than he is, but he's insatiable."

Youzhi shook his head sadly, "Master Yuan, a model laborer, worked here two years ago. When he went to a Party training school in Nanchang, Wang snared his wife, a tool keeper at Haiyan's machine shop. Most model workers are gentle and submissive. Even if humiliated, they don't fight."

"Wang counted on Yuan's docile character when he dragged his wife down?"

"He had it all figured out. As soon as Master Yuan got wind of the dirty affair, the leaders quietly moved him and his wife to another factory miles away."

"Wang knows how to take advantage of women's weaknesses," Haiyan said, "He raped some women, but they later denied it. They don't want to stir up public disgust against them."

I chewed over the information, "Is he handsome?"

Youzhi sniffed, "He's taller than average. The steep back of his head looks like a shovel. His face is flat, dark brown, and riddled with pimples. His eyes are small and dull like a rat's."

"No," Haiyan said, "glittering like a thief on the stage."

Chuju walked in. At our first eye contact, she stopped and

fidgeted. She was unchanged physically—still as pretty as ever—but her lack of composure led me to be more suspicious of her infidelity. She looked daggers at Youzhi and Haiyan.

Haiyan greeted her with a feigned smile. Since Youzhi and Haiyan sat face-to-face on either side of me, the only stool left for Chuju was opposite me, on the other side of the vat. Youzhi turned his head, deliberately looking away from her. The silence embarrassed us all. My brother led his wife out of the room without a glance toward Chuju.

The porcelain vat between Chuju and me separated us, and I had no desire to touch her. Using the tongs, she picked up a few pieces of charcoal from a crate under the bed and added them to the dying embers. Walking back and forth at her task, she gradually slowed her pace.

With the casual, friendly air I used to see in the old days, she asked, "Did you just arrive today?"

I kept all emotion from my voice, "Yes."

"How long can you stay?"

"Two weeks. Maybe less."

"I'm sorry. I need another hour or so to finish today's rehearsal. After that, we can have dinner in the mess hall. The cooks will fix better food for the propaganda team than what most diners get. Take a nap or read one of the books here. See you soon."

At the door, she meekly looked back, and our eyes met. I didn't move.

25

The empty room left me only with my restless thoughts. My brother's presence had opened the dreadful wound sooner than I'd anticipated, and Chuju showed no natural grace as she had in the past. Before broaching the problem with her, who could I consult? Where could I get guidance for my actions?

It occurred to me that my childhood friend Tang—nicknamed Little Tiger—was working here at the same factory. I hadn't seen him in 13 years.

Two years my elder, he'd been an outstanding acrobat and created handicrafts for children in our little town. For the yearly Lantern Festival, he would decorate a pomelo, a large citrus fruit, with bamboo strips and colored paper to make a dragon's head almost as good as the ones they sold in the town's stores. I missed those dragon heads and his loyalty to me. In 1945 he provoked Coyote Tian into a fight and left a big lump above Tian's left eye. After that, in the protective aura of my strong ally Little Tiger, I suffered no further threats from Tian.

As if finding my way through a dark forest, I now took the road toward my old friend, the only path my feet could follow. A young worker hurrying to the mess hall answered my query about him.

"Master Tang? Everyone knows him. He's the handiest one on the factory lathes, and the Party branch secretary for the turning shop. He lives in a bungalow near the compound's eastern wall."

When I walked into his tiny place, he was adding coal briquettes to his stove. Hot cinders fell on the wet dirt floor, making instant steam. He rubbed his hand on his pants to rid it of coal dust before shaking mine, then offered me a cup of tea.

I called him Secretary Tang, but he waved it away with some annoyance: "Old friend, call me Little Tiger."

Although he didn't address me warmly or express surprise at seeing me, he quietly waited for me to talk. Like a student facing an oral quiz, he answered my questions one by one about his wife, children, and sister. I was impressed that he remained simple, plain, and respectful. Unlike glib-tongued cadres, he didn't use political jargon at all.

Staring at his wrinkled face and thin body, I tried to see in him the hero of my childhood. But now he was a totally different person from what I'd remembered. I couldn't expect Little Tiger to take sides or beat up Huaizhong Wang now.

He put two low stools by the stove and waved me to sit down. When I was sipping the tea, he kept examining the palm and back of his hand, patiently awaiting my inquiries.

I finally asked, "Do you know the facts of the scandal between Chuju and Huaizhong Wang?"

"You should forgive her. A great man must be magnanimous." His answer stunned me.

I wanted to know the details, but he seemed disinclined to further discussion. As a man of principle, he wouldn't leak anything the Party thought secret.

I stood to leave. He walked me a few steps, "If you want to know more or get the correct opinion, talk to Comrade Du, the vice secretary of our factory's Party committee. He's in charge of Party discipline."

Our brief meeting shut down my childhood nostalgia. As the Revolution overrode human relationships, he'd been reborn in the class struggle, and now it was second nature to obey the Party and parrot his boss.

Returning to the trade union office, I heard no sound from Chuju's group rehearsing. It was dark, and the propaganda team members must have been in the mess hall. I walked out to look for her there, but stopped, picturing the shame I'd feel if she were having dinner with the group and ignored me.

I turned back and saw a human shadow hurrying up toward me. It was Chuju, gasping for air: "My mom is sick. I ran home to check on her after we were dismissed for the day, but then I couldn't find you. You must be very hungry."

She took me to the mess hall, where her team stood around three tables, laughing and joking. When Chuju and I walked in, two young women nudged each other, and the rest pretended not to see me. I chose to stay alone at a separate table, three yards away from the crowd, while Chuju got our food.

The late dinner was a special treat, bowls of rice dressed

with stir-fried mustard greens and a few pieces of pork dredged from skimming fat. Except for the team leader, none of Chuju's colleagues came over to talk to us. I sensed an emotional boycott of Chuju, or perhaps her teammates just wanted to avoid a troubled couple. The depressing atmosphere made my tongue numb and stomach ache. Chuju ate slowly, as if counting the grains of rice in her bowl. She glanced at me several times, then asked in a casual tone, "Where did you go?"

"I went to see Master Tang, the Party branch secretary of your turning shop."

"Did he recognize you after so many years?"

"Of course. We're close friends from elementary school, and I was best man at his wedding. He won't forget me as soon or as easily as some other people."

She blushed and dropped her chopsticks, one onto the table, the other onto the ground. I picked them up and washed them with tap water. I asked, "Is it possible for you to withdraw from the propaganda team or ask for a two-week leave of absence? Otherwise, this visit will be pointless."

She scowled, "It's impossible to find someone to replace me now. We perform at the People's Commune in a couple of days."

"I've come at the wrong time. Did you see how none of your team welcomed me? If you visited me in Beijing, my coworkers would throng to you."

"We factory workers can't be as suave as you big-city intellectuals. People around here are shy. Your urbane, scholarly look, especially your glasses with their chrome steel frame, must've kept them away."

I knew she was just stalling, but I didn't want to argue with her in public.

After dinner, I asked her to go to my parents' home with me. Carrying her comforter, she walked quietly alongside me on a hillside trail, a shortcut from the truck road. At several open places, she pointed out new buildings. I asked about our mutual friends in town. Both of us spoke mechanically.

We kept our distance just as we had last May when I'd walked with her outside Beijing Railway Station. Back then, my desire to hold her made me hate the Chinese tradition of reserve. Now, alone on a country road at twilight, we could have embraced, but no mutual attraction compelled it—certainly I had no such desire.

Whenever Chuju glanced at me, I looked back at her with a steely stare until she turned her head away. I could hardly see the woman I'd married only nine months earlier. I could no longer see her pure, innocent smile.

26

Mother sat in the bamboo recliner awaiting us and would have stayed there until daybreak if we hadn't shown up. Surrendering their room to us, Father agreed to spend the nights at the home of my older brother's wife's uncle, two blocks away. Mother would squeeze in with the grandmother of another family downstairs.

Our arrival relieved her from her watch that cold night. Still, she hesitated to leave. In the dim light of the kerosene lamp, she scrutinized our faces as if she had something to say. I held her arm and urged her go to sleep. Stopping at the door, she turned her head to look at Chuju one more time, "Be patient and nice to each other."

I escorted her downstairs, worried about her unstable footsteps on her old, bound feet. But she safely made her way in the dark, touching the railings, the ceramic water pot, the dining table, and other objects. They were her guides, and she'd developed this skill, saving lamp oil by it, over half a century.

When we got to our temporary bedroom, Chuju sat on the edge of our bed, her head bowed. I told her she should go to

sleep right away, but that I wanted to read for a while. I pulled
out a technical report on a recent conference on large dams.
But the light was dim and the report so boring and irrelevant
to my immediate life that I couldn't concentrate. Although I
held the paper close to my eyes, I paid more attention to Chuju
making our bed.

She was unfolding our two comforters, putting one above
the other. Then she undressed and slipped into bed.

I turned down the lamp wick, keeping the flame to a
minimum. The stingy light leaking through the sooty glass
chimney made the room gloomy.

Chuju lay with her face turned toward the wall, leaving the
outer half of the bed for me. Through the mosquito netting, I
could make out her profile. The comforter was pulled up to
her neck, her breathing deep and gently undulating. But I
doubted she was asleep; she'd only just closed her eyes. She
was no doubt composing answers to my probable questions. I
didn't know what to do.

I remembered vividly the story my mother told other
women under the eaves of the memorial temple, where we
took refuge in the summer of 1944. Her village patriarch had
ordered the family men, acting as the clan's ethics police, to
drown a widow in the river with a millstone tied to her because
she reportedly had had a secret love affair. Her audience
clicked their tongues in support for the patriarch's tough
measure. Chuju's mother had said, "In the old days, everybody
knew, compared to losing her chastity, starving to death is a
trivial matter for a woman."

Following the revolutionary slogan 'Down with Confucianism',
the one-sided, feudal ethics imposed on women had been set
aside to a great extent, especially in Jiangxi, the old base of the
Red Army.

Later, from our hometown in Jiangxi to a construction site
in Anhui, a county near Beijing, courts posted verdicts against
adulterous women who'd resorted to brutal means, be it an ax

or rat poison, to get rid of their husbands. All the tragedies I'd read about ended in roughly the same way: the husband murdered, the wife executed, and her accomplice in adultery and murder sentenced to 15 or 20 years in jail. If divorce were easier, or if people could be open about their love lives, such crimes would have been far fewer. *No, Chuju isn't that kind of woman ... and our marriage would've been a happy one if we could've lived together.*

Still, Little Tiger's words that afternoon triggered in me wild, pained imaginings. Why should I forgive her or be magnanimous? So far, I'd never considered becoming a great man. In our culture, one was remembered in history only for extraordinary merit, bravery, or wisdom. Before I had the whole truth, I didn't know how much anguish I could absorb, or how far I might be from being a great man, capable of fully forgiving.

A gust of wind swept the roof, dried leaves rustled on the clay tiles, and the temperature in the room abruptly dropped. I fetched my overcoat from a stool to cover my aching knees. As I turned, my head blocked the lamplight, its shadow extending to the comforter's edge along Chuju's shoulders.

I blew out the lamp and lay down beside Chuju, careful not to touch her. Old newspapers my parents had pasted on the window to replace the broken glass had ripped in places and vibrated in the wind. The plaintive rustle sounded like my own crying.

All that night my feet were cold, chilling my whole body. Several times Chuju and I rolled face-to-face. Her bodily warmth soothed me from my silent torments, but only briefly. Suddenly my sense of pain, loss, and humiliation would return, startling me from sleep, and I'd roll away from her.

She got up early. Before leaving, she stood by the door, apparently searching for words. Finally, she said, "You need more sleep. If you'd like, you can come to the factory anytime. The office you were in yesterday is vacant. I'll find a way to get some charcoal there for you."

27

Soon after she left, the dilapidated, hive-like building teemed with daily life again. Children's cries and parents' scolding seeped without pause through the cheaply constructed, thin wooden walls. I couldn't sleep any longer.

My sister-in-law invited me to have breakfast, but I answered, "Not hungry," when I saw their pot of porridge, more water than rice. In the center of the table, the salty turnip strips that had been put out in a small dish were all gone. My eldest niece exhibited tremendous self-restraint, feeding her youngest brother, who was two years old. The other two children, a boy of eight and a girl of five, were noisily sucking porridge from their bowls, hoping for another serving before the pot was empty.

I guessed that my parents and sister-in-law had all skipped breakfast.

My feet found the path toward the factory, and I absentmindedly detoured across the East Gate Bridge, maybe just buying more time to make up my mind. When I touched the bridge's ice-cold stone rail, my legs felt too weak to carry me. For a few minutes, I leaned there, trying to regain my strength.

At the other end of the bridge, a familiar-looking man was selling steamed green cakes. After so many years of peddlers being banned as capitalist elements, he was brave to reappear at such a difficult time. His utensils, tiny stove, and bamboo steamer looked like the same ones I'd seen in my high-school days, but they were now darkened and worn, as was he.

The cakes, made from rice mixed with mugwort and coated with soybean powder, no longer had their traditional flavor. Too much mugwort and too little soybean gave them the taste of pure grass. Still, four of them refueled me enough to continue walking.

On the last stretch of the road, I slowed, stopping several times to try to figure out what to do. I strode to the Party committee office on the second floor of the administration building.

Vice Secretary Du left his meeting and led me to a private room with a desk, chair, and twin bed. Sitting on the edge of the bed, he motioned me toward the chair, giving our prospective conversation a comfortable, informal air.

His face, paler than those of most factory workers, with greenish stubble, gave him a sharp, genuine, working-class look as opposed to that of a political hack. He was serious but amiable, and had obvious seniority.

After we exchanged greetings, I asked about the scandal. In an authoritative voice, he replied, "Our first response to the report was to keep the unhappy news quiet. When I interviewed your wife, she was sobbing and said she'd be desperate if the rumor reached you. Much to our disappointment, we failed to prevent the information from leaking out."

"So, she was guilty."

"It isn't as bad as all the flying gossip. I hoped you won't be burdened. We're taking the case seriously. I discussed with other committee members the possibility of having you work here or moving your wife to Beijing. Both are unrealistic. The only thing we can do is to help the two parties repent for their mistake and to make sure they don't fall off the precipice."

Having been stressed for days, I suddenly had an excruciating headache. I waited for the buzzing in my ears to ebb, "How far have they gone?"

Vice Secretary Du looked into my eyes, "No-one's discovered them together undressed. Still, we held a special meeting to deal with Wang and forced him to offer a written self-criticism. Secretary Hong, our factory's number-one leader, lectured Wang harshly, calling him 'a degenerate element of the Party'."

I'd get no more information from him. I stood, saying I was

sorry to have interrupted his meeting. He walked me to the staircase. Shaking hands with him, I asked if I could write to him if I needed to. He nodded.

I found the trade union office unlocked. Fresh charcoal in the heating vat told me Chuju had been by, expecting to see me. Soon she came in with a small pack of crackers, which she'd won drawing lots in the accounting office. That would be my late lunch.

She asked, "How about letting me have the yearly reunion dinner with my mother?"

"By tradition and custom," I said, "you should have dinner tonight with my parents and me, because it's the most important holiday for family reunions. By our custom, a daughter already married off is a member of her husband's family. But my parents live with my older brother, and our home is too shabby; you'd probably feel uneasy with all of us. Hence, I have no problem with our having dinner separately tonight. But I hope you'll come to my place afterward."

"It might be quite late."

"You'll still have legs on your body. Come or not, it's up to you. If you still consider me your husband, you should come."

She blushed: "Since when have you learned to put thorns into your speech?"

"I'll wait for you until tomorrow morning."

My younger brother, Youzhi, ate New Year's Eve dinner with his wife and mother-in-law in their home. Thanks to my elder brother's wife, the reunion meal for the rest of us, three generations, looked good enough for a holiday celebration, it was even sumptuous for the times. For the previous several months, she had cut a portion from every rationed item to create a reserve. Her steely discipline protected it from her famished children. Her smoked pork, salted eggs, and mustard greens substantially supplemented the scanty holiday supply distributed to each resident. Otherwise, the rationed food for the New Year's Eve dinner would have been meager indeed.

After dinner, my sister-in-law retreated with her children. The other families in the shaky building had already turned off their lights. The air in the dining room grew dull and chill.

To urge my parents to go to bed, I told them, "It's sensible to let Chuju have dinner with her mother on New Year's Eve. Later, she'll stay the night with me."

They left the room with hesitant steps, turning several times to look at me with doubt.

My older brother, Haitao, remained seated opposite me.

He rotated the empty wine bottle on the table, staring at it longingly. Its original cough-syrup label was still visible, but the expensive black-market hard liquor he'd stored in the bottle was gone. He opened an aluminum cigarette box, took out a cigarette, tapped it on the table, and lit it. I'd brought him the right gift, which pleased me.

He puffed leisurely, "Listen. In Beijing, you can get the best supplies. Please ask the nonsmokers in your office to give you their cigarette ration coupons, and try to get Grand Front Gate and other good brands. A pack of cigarettes is a passport with unimaginable power. Too bad you don't care about practical things."

He blew a lopsided smoke ring and admired it for a moment, "You should change your bookish ways. Only I can give you such sincere, helpful advice."

"No problem. I'll get them for you."

He squinted and tilted his head, "Father and I misjudged when we pushed you to marry Chuju." He suddenly pounded the table, and the liquor bottle fell flat, "Now, the crow has invaded the nest of a phoenix. Kill him!"

"Are you drunk?"

As I held his arm and urged him to go bed, he mumbled, "Wait, wait. A gentleman retaliates, sometimes waiting years. Ten years isn't too long."

I returned to my parents' room and sat in the bamboo chair,

waiting for the front door, which I'd left unlatched, to creak.

Unlike in years past, children didn't cheer in the streets on New Year's Eve, and I heard no firecrackers.

28

I frequently shivered while sitting in the bamboo recliner. Every minute was too long to wait. Two hours later, I heard the front door creak open, then the wooden latch slide shut. Chuju had arrived.

As she entered the room, the frail old floor shook. I lit the kerosene lamp. Chuju gave me a polite smile. I didn't ask about her dinner or her mother. She sat on a stool in front of me. In the silence, she looked up at me questioningly while I gathered my courage.

"What's your relationship with Huaizhong Wang?"

"Nothing."

It seemed obvious she'd prepared herself for exactly such a moment. To stop the quarrel before I could begin it, she stood and unbuttoned her blouse. I got to my feet.

"There's a storm raging around you. How can you say you did nothing?"

"I've done nothing to betray you."

"Everybody in your factory knows your secret with Wang. I'm the only one kept in the dark. There're no waves without wind."

In a voice softer than before, she said, "Idle people make things up. I went to him only because he's in charge of personnel. You have to pester whoever's in a position to help."

That was how they'd come in contact, but it hadn't stopped there. Telling me truthfully about the affair would be a touchstone of honesty. Then maybe …

"If it's official business, you should only talk to him during working hours. Why did you meet him at his office at midnight?"

She slashed the air with her arm, "Why are you asking people? Do you want to destroy my reputation? I haven't done anything to betray you. Maybe I wasn't firm enough in stopping his harassment, but that's my only fault."

I sat on the edge of the bed, "Don't you know how desperately I've worked to win the Party branch's favor to move you to Beijing? Getting a residence permit is a merciless competition. When the leaders put my qualifications on the table to compare with the others', they'll look at your records too. Any dirty marks at all on your reputation will ruin our chances."

She turned her back to me. I continued, "We've known each other since we were kids. In the summer of 1956, I was frustrated you wouldn't let me to touch you. I fooled myself into seeing your coolness as willpower and virtue, believing that you had self-control and could resist men who wanted to corrupt you. I expected you'd maintain that during our separation." I paused to catch my breath, "I never had a whiff of doubt about you. How naïve I've been."

She fell to the floor and plunged her head into my lap. With her hands covering her face, she sobbed, "I'm sorry!"

I caressed her hair, pulled her up from her knees, and kissed her lips.

That night, lying alongside her, I felt the warmth of her body but no intimacy. When I imagined another man occupying my position over the last few months, I would roll away from her.

She left early on Chinese New Year's Day, February 15, 1961. With the propaganda team, she would spend the day performing for the East Wind People's Commune, which frequently supplied the factory with vegetables and meat, evading the state's monopoly.

Before leaving, she said, "If you'd like, you can come too. It takes an hour and a half to hike there, and the road is rough. Or you can meet me tonight after we come back to the county hotel. Our team has reserved enough rooms. We can have our own."

It thrilled me that we'd have a nice talk and be intimate that evening. And staying with the young team members would let them get to know me. Their support and sympathy for me would act as a psychological fence, preventing her from harming our marriage further.

"I don't have hiking shoes. The road is paved with sand and gravel, and the last rain left puddles and wet ruts in it. Anyway, I'm an outsider, I'm not invited. I'll wait at home."

"Yes, you need rest. I'll come this evening and take you to the hotel." Her swift agreement told me she was glad I wouldn't be there.

I remained in my parents' dim, cold room, trying to read the books I'd brought from Beijing. Minutes, then hours, dragged on. The day didn't look like New Year's at all. The famine had suspended all our customs. No families near us had visitors. Good wishes and auspicious words couldn't remedy food shortages, so people stayed at home to preserve calories.

In the past, New Year's Eve's dinner meant that there was a lot of food left over for the next few days. But all the dishes on our table after the previous night's dinner had been wiped clean of any scraps. My sister-in-law kept her children in bed almost until noon to keep them inactive. From a collective-owned restaurant, Father had bought a bowl of rice covered with cabbage for my breakfast. With both hands cradling the bowl, he entered the room complaining, "The cook at the restaurant is abusing his power with the ladle. Every time I go there, he'll shake the ladle to give me less rice than the coupon and money are worth. Still, it's better than letting my ration be eaten up by my grandchildren."

Until then, I hadn't known that Father was handling his own grain ration. The silent tension between Father and my sister-in-law was worse than I thought.

I tried to share the food with my parents. Father said, "I've already eaten." I didn't believe him.

When I asked Mother to have some, she said, "I'm no longer helpful to the family. It would be a waste for me to eat."

I ate half the rice, covered the rest with paper, and left for a walk. All the stores were closed. Some of my high-school friends still lived in and around town, but to visit them would be odd after so many years without correspondence, especially now. At last it seemed all I could do was return home.

I sat with Mother awhile. We looked at each other as if regretting each other's pain and helplessness.

Finally, I decided to hike to the commune and join Chuju.

At first, I stepped only on relatively dry spots, but in less than 20 minutes my worn leather shoes were completely coated with mud. Water seeped through the seams, so I no longer watched my step. As mud covered the bottom of my pant legs and got into my shoes, I trudged faster, oblivious to the discomfort.

Two hours later, I saw a large camphor tree with red flags posted around it, the headquarters of the East Wind People's Commune, just as Chuju had described it.

The propaganda team filled the commune's headquarters, a house confiscated from a pre-1949 landlord. Some of the team tuned their instruments; others prepared slogan posters. The commune's cadres and the factory performers would feast later that afternoon. A peasant in the front yard was scraping the hair off a pig he'd just slaughtered. Children held back by a fence stuck their heads through the gate to peer at the lively scene, and women with babies stood in a second line, gossiping about what their leaders would eat and drink.

The parlor was boisterous with rushing commune cadres and rehearsing propaganda-team members. I looked for a place not in anyone's way but found only the corner behind a desk, on which was spread red paper peppered with slogans: 'Down with US Imperialists'; 'We're Determined to Liberate Taiwan'. Soon, Chuju noticed me from a distance. She glared at me and immediately turned her back to me. I was nothing but an embarrassment to her.

I watched two women push her in my direction, and she walked over to meet me, "You told me you wouldn't come. Why did you change your mind? Are you checking up on me?"

"You're oversensitive. I'm lonely. I want to be with you."

She lowered her voice to a whisper: "We won't have a chance to talk here. The banquet will be held late this afternoon. We should insist on paying for your meal, even though the leaders would like to treat you as a guest."

Without another word, she returned to her rehearsal. I remained behind the desk. The chorus sang in another room: "To reach the communist paradise, the People's Commune is building a bridge."

Being neither guest nor host, I felt awkward. I could find no place to sit down for a rest among the expectant diners. The same thought kept haunting me: although the propaganda team and commune leaders no doubt had good reason to hold a free banquet, the food and liquor for these privileged diners were certainly wrung from starving peasants.

I approached Chuju. The team members around her retreated a few feet to give us a chance to talk. I said, "You're a guest, and I'm your dependent. I feel ugly staying here as if only for the feast. It's also terribly boring waiting the long hours until night to watch your performance. My feet are frozen in muddy, drenched shoes. I'm going home."

Chuju made no attempt to dissuade me: "You can do whatever you want."

According to what Chuju had promised earlier, I was to stay with her at the county hotel. At ten o'clock, when she still had not arrived at my place, I began to worry. As despair dragged me down, I realized that my sudden exit from the People's Commune had probably hurt her feelings. If so, she might be intending to stay at the county hotel with the team that night and leave me alone.

Another hour passed. The bamboo chair seemed made of thorns. I paced back and forth outside the front door, hoping her shadow would flit across it.

Fretting, I ran to the end of the street and rushed into the hotel. A girl, one of the propaganda team, said, "Chuju's already in bed. You'd better talk to her yourself."

Her room had three beds. Her two roommates were still amusing themselves in the lobby. Chuju lay in bed with her comforter drawn up, her arms outside it. Her eyes were open but she looked away. I asked, "Would you go home with me?"

"I'm too tired."

"It isn't far to walk, less than a hundred meters."

"How about tomorrow?"

"You have no excuse to stay away from me on New Year's night."

Without answering, she turned her face to the wall.

Through my teeth, words popped out: "You've gone too far. You're insulting me in public."

She kept ignoring me. Blood rushed to my head, I tore off the comforter and dragged her out of bed, "Go convince your team members of the reasons why you have to stay away from me. Otherwise, I don't have the face to walk home alone."

She jerked backwards onto the bed, and I fell to the floor and hit my head on the wall. The pain fueled my rage. I hooked her neck and tugged her away from the bed, but we both lost our balance. Our falling bodies toppled the clothes tree, which hit a chair and slid to overturn an enamel basin full of dirty water. The harsh, terrible noises summoned Chuju's teammates from the parlor and other rooms. Amid their splashing footsteps, they all asked, "What's happening?"

In underwear and barefoot, Chuju cried, "I'm exhausted. I

can't go home."

A woman with sharp looks interceded for her: "We hiked on the muddy road, and everyone carried an instrument or prop. Without a rest, Chuju rehearsed and performed for six hours."

Acting like an older sister, she urged the crowd to get out, kept a young woman to clean the floor with a mop, and led Chuju to sit down on the bed. She helped Chuju put on her warm clothes as if dressing a child. Then she held Chuju's calf in her palm to draw my attention, "See the blisters on her instep?"

Her subservient manner and excessive care for Chuju made me suspicious. Was she a secret agent Wang had planted in the team or just a snob trying to please Wang with tacit understanding?

I put on a stern countenance, "Sorry for the disturbance. I came here to discuss something with my wife. Would you leave us alone?"

She left in a huff.

Chuju and I sat on the bed with a gap of two feet between us. Ten minutes later, she asked, "What do you want to do now?"

Already exposed in a sexual scandal, she wasn't frightened. Rather she seemed to be secure in the knowledge that she had strong backing. I felt mystified rather than angered by her tough manner, "I no longer want you to be with me. But I must get to know where the line of battle is. Please show the alignment of your forces. Whoever is standing behind you should come out to the front. I'm all by myself, but the righteous workers of your factory are on my side. Let's fight it out."

"Okay, we can meet at our factory tomorrow night."

I stood up to leave, "Today, you broke your promise. I'll be there before eight o'clock tomorrow evening. I hope you're sincere this time. There won't be another chance if you don't show up."

29

The next morning, I went to see Youzhi. His wife, Haiyan, told me, "Secretary Hong's wife is a member of the Party committee and in charge of the women's association at our factory. We call her the Women's Director, or Big Sister Gong. She remembers you as a fellow member of your high-school chorus. I met her yesterday, and she asked about you."

I remembered two sisters with the surname Gong. One looked open, the other reserved. I didn't know which one had married Secretary Hong, but either would treat me as an old acquaintance. My boss, Secretary Jiang, said to me before I left Beijing, "In difficult times, we should depend on the Party organization and have faith in the masses." The women's director represented the local Party organization. Since no-one in China openly wrote nonfiction about anything involving sex, she would be an experienced person in dealing with family feuds and marriage problems. I decided to meet her.

Later in the afternoon, in the residential area, a girl around seven led me to her home, a second-floor apartment. A woman answered the door, holding a girl around eight or ten months old. I recognized her as the older Gong sister—the open one, luckily.

"Director Gong?"

She waved her hand, "Don't call me that or I'll feel treated like a stranger. We're school alumni, aren't we?"

"Yes. The year I graduated, you were a junior. You and your sister joined the chorus, and we rehearsed the *Yellow River Cantata* for months. Every time the music teacher called roll, he said both your names in one breath."

She burst into laughter, "You have a good memory. Time goes fast. I'm a mother now."

Except for a few pieces of new, handmade furniture, their home was sparsely furnished. Though she did not have a college education, she spoke proudly as a Party member and the first lady of the factory. As her husband was in Nanchang, the provincial capital, I felt less restricted.

After serving me a cup of tea, she sat down and let her daughter stand on her lap. Following a few minutes of casual chat, I began to talk about Chuju.

The girl kept grasping her mother's mouth and nose, so Gong had to dodge the little hands to talk with me, "As a woman, I understand why Chuju thought she had to put up with his flirting. She compromised herself only out of hope of being reunited with you. The head of the personnel office has the power to help or to kill job transfers. Don't blame her too much. Huaizhong Wang should be held primarily accountable."

Her tone, quite different from that of Youzhi and those behind him, confirmed a possibility I'd thought about earlier, one that had partly relieved my pain. I could now imagine how Chuju might have given in to Wang.

I asked, "I heard he previously enticed the wife of Master Yuan. Is that true?"

"I've heard the rumor but haven't checked the facts. For sure, Wang isn't a decent man. He's always grinned suggestively at young female workers or deliberately dragged out conversations with them in his office."

"How far did Chuju go with Wang?"

She hesitated, then spoke with determination, "A security clerk convinced us they'd gone beyond the boundaries of comradeship. But they were fully dressed. We can't punish Wang further than issue him with severe criticism from the Party committee."

Except for one more detail, she answered the same way as Vice Secretary Du had. They seemed to be reiterating the Party committee's conclusion as a standard answer. I wanted to know if they'd deliberately stopped further investigation, keeping silent about major charges while admitting minor ones against Wang.

"The security clerk must've reported the details to your Party committee. I need the information to judge whether Chuju is being honest with me or lied about it."

"It's an internal Party matter, I'm not authorized to release it. Also, as director of the women's association, my duty is to help the troubled couple make peace, not to provide one side with ammunition."

"I respect you as a representative of the local Party organization. Like you, I want to reconcile with Chuju. But to do that, I need the facts. If I don't know, I'll always wonder. I won't misuse any information you give me. I swear."

She paced up and down, holding the baby and speaking disjointedly, "The security cadre crashed into Wang's office late one night and found Chuju sitting on his lap. Having brought another man as witness, he made a fuss at the scene and came here to wake Secretary Hong. We've criticized Wang for his corruption, warned Chuju not to contact him again, and ordered the security cadre to shut up."

I stood transfixed, recalling Chuju's attitude toward me since I'd come home. It was now revealed that she'd indeed had physical intimacy with the pig and lied to me. That was all I could swallow.

I asked Gong, "An order is only an order. How do you know if they're complying or not? Who enforces it?"

She shrugged, "They pledged to obey the Party's decision, and we're checking what they say against what they do. We don't need a team to enforce it, because all the Party members are on the alert."

I found myself rubbing my fists and wiping my palms, "They might keep meeting in more covert ways."

"Trust me, we'll watch them closely."

I sighed, "You can neither control Chuju's heart nor lock up her body."

"If they don't come to their senses, the eyes of the masses are discerning. Wang should know the masses are just biding their time about him. If a rectifying campaign were launched, he'd be targeted like a rat running across the street, everybody yelling, 'Kill it!'"

Dizzy with anger and hate, I rose to leave, "He's not a rat now, and Chuju is in the mouth of a tiger, especially after I leave."

She stood by the door: "I'm duty-bound to be a counselor to Chuju and you. With the Party's principles in my heart, I won't be partial. Please come to see me anytime you have a problem. Calm down, I still have basic trust in Chuju."

On my way back to my parents' place, I tried to simmer down and take stock of myself. Seeking guidelines about how best to proceed, I reflected on everything I'd read about extramarital affairs. My knowledge came only from novels. Many Chinese people had admired the wife-killing heroes in the popular novel *Sui Hu, All Men Are Brothers*. However, the Russian author Chernyshevsky's celebrated book, *What Is To Be Done?*, told me of a gracious way through the character Lopukhov. If Lopukhov had been in my current position, he would have released Chuju to go with whomever she liked. I read the book because Lenin had praised it as a masterpiece; now I found it odd I'd ever accepted such an illusion.

Father was sweeping the hall and shared dining room, while Mother huddled in the kitchen by our brickwork coal stove trying to get warm. Father met me by the front door, obviously wanting to say something. For quite a few minutes, we faced each other without words. Quietly watching his wax-yellow face, I worried about the devastating effect my tragedy might have on him. His poor education and advanced age were such that he had learned only Song Dynasty philosophy, and tales about the murder of unfaithful wives.

Finally, his eyes so swollen he had to turn his face upward to look into mine, he pointed trembling fingers into the air to emphasize his words, "To arrest a thief, you need to catch him with the loot. To convict an adulterer, you have to catch them in bed together."

30

Chuju was hiding from me now. I didn't need her but was eager to catch her in wrongdoing. At dinner on the second day of the New Year, I used hot water and salted turnips to send the rice down to my stomach. Then, in the mist-filled twilight, I hurried to the factory. I decided not to expose myself unnecessarily, so detoured to Youzhi's home on the other side of the pond. Haiyan took the trouble on my behalf to look for Chuju.

As anger and sorrow welled in my heart, I found a long poker by their coal stove. It was sharpened at the tip and had a metal ring as its handle. I used all my strength to practice stabbing a piece of firewood. I punctured it and split it. The poker couldn't become a bayonet to thrust into my enemy, but it was heavy enough. If I hit his head with it, he would be done for.

Around nine o'clock, Haiyan came back after having checked everywhere Chuju could be. The trade union office was locked. The mess hall, the machine shops, and the office building were all dark. The members of the propaganda team had taken the day off.

I went to Chuju's dorm to look for her. It was as large as a classroom, with 15 double-decker bunks in three rows, reminding me of a fourth-class passenger cabin in a boat on the Yangtze River. The girls used a few vacant upper berths to store their belongings, and everyone had a mosquito net that doubled as a curtain in winter. The roommates belonged to various units of the factory. That night the dorm was quiet, as most of the women had gone home. During busy workdays, with the factory operating in shifts, sleep must have been difficult.

One of her roommates led me to Chuju's bed and asked me to wait for her there. Chuju had left her comforter at my parents' place, so only a thin cotton blanket covered the bed. A round mirror lay next to her pillow, along with a comb and scattered rubber bands.

An hour later, the few women at the other end of the room stopped chatting and went to bed. They left two overhead lights on. The mosquito nets screened me from them, so they might not have minded if I'd stayed there all night, but I fretted about being there at an improper hour. Then the thought hit me: was Chuju with Wang right now? *Perhaps they're discussing how to deal with me.* Their most likely rendezvous spot would be Wang's office, because most people were away and would avoid it anyway because of its political sensitivity.

Father's words came back to me, bringing me new resolve. I rushed to Youzhi's residence and woke him up. In the dark yard of the peasant's house, I asked, "Could you help me catch the diabolical pair?"

He smiled, "That's what I've been hoping for."

I took the poker. He said, "No, it's too long to hide."

With a flashlight, he found a hammer and a short crowbar. I whispered, "We need some quicklime powder."

He felt his way to the shared kitchen and gripped a ceramic jar that contained lime powder, a drying agent to preserve food. He sprinkled some into a towel and wrapped it up.

Marching toward the factory's office building, Youzhi said, "You've never done much hitting and kicking. Don't be scared. Trust me. I've learned how to fight in recent years. In my sideline as a peddler, I often hop a freight train with a sack or basket, and punching and kicking is a must. Just calmly attack and dodge."

"Don't take the enemy lightly. Wang was an infantryman and has battle experience."

He was excited: "As soon as we pry the door open, I'll

throw the powder to blind them, and you hit the bell by the front gate. Then we both shout, 'Catch the criminals!' Before Wang can see anything, workers in the dorm will arrive. Then neighborhood people will show up."

All the windows of the two-story office building were dark, and no guard was on duty. We shuffled on tiptoe to the second floor and pinned our ears to the door of Wang's office. For ten minutes, I heard only my own heart pounding, and nothing stirring inside the room.

Above the solid door was a glass transom. Youzhi held my legs to lift me, and I peered in at the interior, shining a flashlight here and there. The office and its furniture were simple, offering no nooks for the wrongdoers to hide in. I continued to sweep the light for another minute, but found nothing.

A sudden thought: why hadn't we checked the accounting office? Chuju would have the key, and her officemates wouldn't go there at night. Youzhi started to hurry, scanning the signs on both sides of the corridor. He found the office at the far end. Seeing the metal door and brick-sealed transom above it, he paused, "There's cash in this office. We might be arrested as burglars. Our hammer and crowbar would be seized as criminal tools. You wait here, I'll hide them in the side gutter."

He rushed downstairs and soon came back with a cobblestone as large as a goose egg, "You can use this to hit the bell. Now, let's climb the parasol tree outside the two windows of this office."

Before I could climb to the level of the second floor, Youzhi had already perched on a high bough and peeped into the office. I followed the beam of his flashlight and saw Chuju's blue hand-knitted shawl on a desk. Besides that, there were only desks and two safes. I whispered urgently to Youzhi, "Let's get out of here. Militiamen will patrol here anytime now."

"No problem, we can explain why we're here."

"No, don't wash our dirty linen in public. I've already drawn enough humiliation. We don't need anymore."

"Okay, don't be too frustrated. All the leaders are lying to you and shielding Wang. Keep watching them. The time will come for us to wreak vengeance on the evil couple."

He went home with the hammer and crowbar. I gingerly returned to the large dorm and sat on Chuju's corner bunk. The three other bunks adjacent to hers were vacant. Ten minutes later, I stood by the window next to her bed and watched the road running by the building. From that position, I wouldn't miss anyone coming in.

Surrounding the factory, the rice paddies and pine woods, dotted with peasants' huts, were pitch dark and deadly quiet. Where could she go in the cold night? Maybe they had a hideout. For most of the year, when I was a thousand miles away, they must've been cheating on me freely. *Now I'm here, and they still do it.*

Already emaciated by hunger and cold, my body trembled at the thought of their secret meetings. I rested my elbows on the concrete windowsill and let my forehead touch the chill glass pane, trying to quiet down.

Gradually my shuddering ebbed. Perhaps she'd not gone as far as I imagined, I shouldn't let the worst scenario drive me crazy. I needed to preserve my energy for the fight.

Eventually, around one o'clock, Chuju's shadow emerged on the road, heading toward the dorm. I listened to the sound of her footfall on the stairs. She opened the door and approached her bed like a furtive cat. Unnerved by my presence, she tugged my sleeve and pulled me toward the door. She was afraid I might flare up right there and create an ugly scene.

I followed her downstairs. She feigned ease, playing with a braid, "I didn't know you'd come."

"You didn't know I was still alive."

"I don't want to argue on the road. Let's find another place."

The propaganda-team chief had offered his office to Chuju for a few nights, a good-will attempt to help us reconcile. That arrangement also fit Chuju's wishes, freeing her of any obligation to go to my parents' home.

The key in her hand told me that she had a place for me to stay but hadn't let me know, "If you don't want me here, why did you accept the key? If you feel I'm in your way, you don't need to hide from me and sneak around like a thief. Just announce publicly that I'm not welcome, and we can go to the court."

She grouchily unlocked the door and yanked it open. I turned on the light and grabbed the two sides of her unbuttoned jacket, "Are you still hanging around with that bastard Wang?"

She wriggled to free herself, "Suspicions create imaginary fears. The real problem is you regretted marrying me because I don't have a university diploma."

"Aha, he's taught you how to blame your victim. Last year, I suggested you go to university, hoping you might get a job assignment in Beijing. Now you take it as a sign of my loathing your insufficient education. A handy excuse for you."

She seemed to calm down: "Is that really your intention?"

"Yes. I can see how the misunderstanding might have upset you. It gave Wang the opportunity to drive a wedge between us. Am I right?"

"This trip you haven't seen my mother. She hates you for despising her."

"If she doesn't know why I didn't call on her, you should explain it to her. Your scandal threw me into a rage. Should I smile at her and pretend nothing has happened? You're still treating me badly."

She slid under the comforter.

"Your mother is just a side issue," I said, "It can't justify your fling with Wang."

She pretended to sleep. I shook her shoulder, "You can't keep avoiding me. Tell me now, do you want to keep our marriage or divorce me? There's no third way."

She twisted toward the wall and huddled herself up like a fetus.

I bent over her and spoke softly: "If you deliberately annoy me to push me away so you can keep your affair with Wang going on as usual, you're wrong. You're sitting on a volcano."

She remained silent. The sighing wind in the surrounding pines made me feel terribly lonely and helpless. With her back to me, her steady breathing sounded far away. As frustration replaced anger, I thought that a milder approach might work better.

I turned her neck and waist to face me. Her passive response to my kisses and stroking increased my impatience. I began to demand her answer, "Do you still love me?"

She pushed me away, "All right, all right. That's enough."

I rolled on top of her and held her head with both hands. By seeking intimacy, I was trying to counterbalance our toppling marriage with sex, or at least to test if any residual love remained between us. With closed eyes, she frigidly followed my moves like a large soft doll. The scene of her sitting on Wang's lap came back to insult me, dampening all my desire. I raised her head and dropped it with loathing. She rolled the comforter away from me. I put on my coat and sat by the heating brazier, waiting for daylight.

31

Chuju got up early and left the room on tiptoe. I tried to have a sound sleep, but anger and hunger kept me awake. It was the third day of the Spring Festival, and the propaganda team's agenda was Chuju's excuse for not spending time with me. Plagued by dismay over my unfruitful homecoming, I thought it was meaningless to stay in Jiangxi for another day. Before leaving, I wanted to meet Hao Ding, my childhood friend.

A few months earlier, he had been transferred from the PLA and appointed Director and Party Branch Secretary of the department store at our county center. My parents and brothers had met him on the street. They all had an affinity for him and said he was yearning to see me. I believed him to be different from Little Tiger, whose brotherly passion had been overridden by the Party's spirit. I suddenly felt myself no longer isolated.

I went to the department store. Though most workers were on vacation, Hao Ding was leading a few clerks to rearrange their stock. Still in his faded green uniform with the sleeves rolled up and a wide belt around his waist, he didn't behave like a boss. I greeted him, "You've kept the true qualities of a revolutionary soldier."

"Don't flatter me. It just bores me to sit all day in an office."

He looked much the same as before, but enlarged; taller, broader. Even the crescent-like scar between his nose and the lower edge of his left eye seemed to have grown in proportion to his body. I'd never asked him what caused that scar— birthmark, injury, or skin ulcer. In any case, it identified him as my unforgettable friend.

He gripped my shoulders from behind and steered me to his office. After making me a cup of tea, he grinned without words. I said, "I still have the photo you sent me from the Korean battlefront in 1951. The black and white have faded into grayish purple. The cuffs of your pants were rolled up. How tall are you now?"

He puffed out this chest, "One hundred and eighty centimeters."

"Amazing, eight centimeters taller than me. The day you left our hometown, the rifle slung over your shoulder almost dragged on the ground. You're finally showing your family genes."

We both laughed.

I said, "I'm glad you're home in good shape after all those battles."

He was a fighter rather than a talker, just as in our childhood. He smiled, "You know what? I was on the east coast of North Korea. US bombers and gunboats showed off their power. Several times, all my buddies in the same trench were killed."

"I met a Korea War veteran in Fujian. He told me the rocky hilltops along the thirty-eighth parallel were exploded into heaps of crushed stone, like the ballast under railway tracks." With two bent fingers I showed the size: "Is that true?"

"Exactly."

"Were you wounded?"

"By flying rocks, not bullets or shells. Once I was thrown from a crater by a shock wave and buried under debris."

I was struck by his humble and calm manner, "You're not destined to die."

"My mother said that when I visited her in 1957."

"I knew how upset you were in 1949 because I didn't join the army. The second letter you sent me on your march toward the Taiwan Strait made me worry you wouldn't consider me your friend anymore. In university classrooms, I often imagined you stuck in a trench defending our people and, specifically, me. I felt ashamed for not joining the army."

"I was a child back then." He tilted his head shyly, "The war dragged on for three years. The last year, we spent most of the time in a tunnel. I got used to the thunder of enemy salvoes. Sitting on the ragged floor, gun handy, waiting for a close-range fight, I was bored. I would daydream, of the summer of 1949 for instance, when we swam in the pond with the water buffalo."

"We shouted to hear our voices echo off the mountain."

"Small things like that often came back to entertain me until the bugles blared to charge."

I heaved a heavy sigh, "The war hasn't killed our good memories. I have to ask you … why did you stop writing to me from 1953 to 1959?"

He stared at the concrete floor, "The ceasefire agreement was signed on July 27, 1953. The few months before that day, the front line was quiet. We kept checking each other's class origin and current thinking. My political director was reading my mail. He said your petty-bourgeois sentiment would erode my fighting spirit."

"Nonsense. I just wrote down how I cherished our childhood days, the same way you daydreamed in the tunnel."

He looked embarrassed, "He said you didn't show any hatred toward US imperialists, and other soldiers doubted your family background. When I told them your father used to be an accountant, and was neither landlord nor capitalist, that stopped the questions. But I worried my political director might write to your leader about you. So I stopped writing to you."

"Thank you for your concern. Why did you feel free to write me again in the summer of 1959, when I was on the construction site in Fujian?"

He held his mouth open to show me his poorly implanted denture, "In late March, our detachment entered Tibet from the north to suppress the rebels. I fell off a cliff with my horse. Most of my teeth were knocked out, and I was in a coma for a week. In the hospital, nobody checked my mail, and my mom got your address from your parents."

"Ouch, I'm sorry to hear about your injury. So, you no longer blame me for not joining the army? Or do you?"

His smile became uneasy, "You work in Beijing as a technical cadre. I'm an uncouth bumpkin."

I laughed: "You're trusted as the political backbone of your working unit."

"That's what our army commissar said at our farewell

meeting. The financial and commercial systems need us war-toughened soldiers to form their political cores. So we should be happy."

I nodded, "I guess so. In previous years, most demobilized soldiers were sent to factories, mines, or transportation systems as disciplinary forces. Now it's the turn of the financial and commercial systems to recruit people like you."

He snorted: "Who knows? Last spring, I was promoted to Company Commander and assigned to mountain drills for the pending war with India. Then, the security force in Jiangxi discovered that my father had served with the KMT tank troops, and arrested him. My transfer is definitely related to my father's problem. I'm no longer considered reliable enough to hold a gun."

"I know how you feel. No matter what it is, don't take it personally. You've done enough for the country."

"I'll obey the Party without a grudge. But I feel beaten by my father's historical problem."

I lowered my voice, "Just between you and me, your father's service in the KMT troops during World War II was a patriotic deed, though it's now considered counterrevolutionary. That's his misfortune rather than his fault. I don't think he's a sinner, but he must be sentenced to jail to keep public hatred high against Taiwan."

He looked only partially convinced, "You're quite the intellectual now." He put a hand to his heart, "But thanks for saying that."

In a state-owned restaurant, he treated me to supper, and we were seated in a small room away from the main hall. I enjoyed the local specialties, which I hadn't tasted before, especially fresh shrimps fried with green peas and rice-coated, steamed pork ribs. I didn't know how he paid for the meal, or even if he did.

The manager personally acted as our waiter, refilling our dishes amply and presenting a basin of water for us to clean our hands and faces. When he walked to the kitchen, I asked my friend, "Do you know I'm in big trouble?"

He wiped his face with the warm towel the manager offered him, "When my mother told me about it, she cursed, 'That bastard Wang deserves hacking into pieces.' Sorry for your misfortune."

I wrung my towel unconsciously until the water ran into my sleeve, "Wang has abused his power to trap married women. The most hateful is the attitude of the Party leaders of the factory. They're too indulgent with a habitual offender."

He brandished his fists, "Let's punish him to counter the cover-up. The simplest way is to ambush him and beat him up. If you like, we can do it right away. Master Yuan has come back to the town, he is no longer as meek as he was in the past. He could be your first ally and follower."

I paused for a minute, "To attack him in a dark place is not our purpose. We should let the public anger against Wang lead the local power by the nose."

"Let's rack our brains and figure out a plan. Let's go see my mom first, and we can walk around our elementary school and the places we used to hang out."

32

The next day, a Saturday, Hao Ding took the day off, and we hiked to An'yuan, the coalmining town about five kilometers east of the county center, where his mother still lived in a house on a foothill. In her mid-fifties, she looked healthy and had a good complexion.

Upon my calling her 'Auntie Ding', she hurried out to cross the threshold. Holding my hands, she talked to her son, "I'm so glad you two are getting together again. From 1949 to 1952, Dapeng went to high school at the county center, and he came to see me every Sunday, and I would cry after he left."

I pointed at the slope in front of their house, "After you marched away with the army, Auntie often stood there, staring at the clouds and mountains. I knew she was missing you, it was as if you were ambushing the enemy just on the other side of the valley."

Soon after we sat down, she went to the kitchen to cook for us. Following the sizzling sound, the pungent smell of spicy native cooking filled the house.

I was sad for the absence of Grandma Ding, who worked hard to open up patches of wasteland around their house with hand tools, planting wheat and other crops. Sometimes she'd watch us come up the slope after school, holding the long handle of the spade against her shoulder. I missed the fresh sweet potatoes she'd just harvested and boiled in a large cauldron. The condensed juice at the bottom was so tasty and fragrant.

After the early lunch, I suggested we tend to his grandma's grave. We pulled up weeds, filled up the eroded part of the earth mound, and cleaned the ditch around it.

In the afternoon, we walked to the small reservoir, where Hao Ding had taught me to dogpaddle. The weather was cold and the surface covered with duckweed. We sat on the bank wordlessly for a long while. From that elevation, we started climbing Cow Back Mountain, where we used to challenge each other to see who could reach the summit first. Above the forest of tea trees, only wild grasses grew on the slope. I didn't know the name of the tall ones, but felt intimate with their dog-tail shape. They lined our path, yellow in the season, nodding in the breeze as in the past. He pulled one of them, biting its stem and spitting out the dregs.

I asked him, "Do you remember the poem Teacher Meng taught us in the spring of 1948? You were excited by the story."

"I forget the poem, but remember the story. The two young men, Di Zu and Kun Liu, of the Eastern Han Dynasty, aspired to become generals and defend the empire. They got up at midnight, at the first crowing of the roosters, to practice sword fighting, and they eventually became generals."

I clapped, "Good memory. We didn't have swords, but we climbed this mountain every morning before daybreak and kept up the exercise for a year. You've defended our country like the two ancient heroes."

On our way back to the county center, I asked him, "Have you met Wang?"

"Yes. His position in charge of personnel gives him the chance to come around. Every week he comes to bargain with us for rare supplies above and beyond factory worker's ration."

"How does he behave?"

"He keeps grinning cheekily at our young saleswomen. Once he held one of their hands on the countertop for minutes while praising her new wristwatch. After my criticism, the few easygoing girls stopped smiling to him. Seeing my straight face, he pulled in his horns. But it's harder to alter his evil character."

I slapped my thigh, "Only when we know our enemy, can we defeat him."

Hao Ding looked galvanized, "Sounds like you have a plan. Tell me."

"Please tell me your plan first."

He suggested we each write the plan in a few words on one palm then open it to show the other at the same time. His mischievous nature, often on display in our early days, came back to me.

We stopped to write the words on our palms. As it turned out, the idea on my palm, "Lure the enemy in deep," was less explicit than the one on his: "Set up a sex trap."

I laughed, "Great minds think alike." But a problem occurred to me: "Who can play the bait? It's hard to find a pretty woman with guts."

"And a sense of justice." Hao Ding grew apprehensive, "None of the women in our store has such unusual qualities."

"Let me look for a woman to play the key role while knocking together a group of fighters."

33

The next day, Sunday, the mess hall at the main coal mine branch offered salted pork for lunch as a reward to the miners and staff members working on the holiday. My friend Kai Tao got an extra red ticket for the meal from an officemate who wanted to spend the day at home in the county center. Kai Tao invited me to enjoy the pork and we took a commuter train for the 15 kilometers to get there before noon.

Ten minutes after the five service windows had opened, one of the waiting lines became disturbed. Coyote Tian, with his blue, woolen, Mao-style jacket and five-angled hat, was being punched by two men. He fended off their punches and retreated, smiling cheekily, "No, no, don't listen to gossip. A revolutionary soldier should depend on the Party organization to solve any problems." This was the first time I'd seen him since 1946, and in his disgraceful state. Still carrying the features of a ruffian, he looked masculine, with powerful arms and agile steps.

Someone shouted, "Look, our trade union chairman is under attack!"

Others echoed, "The cuckold is fighting desperately. He is ready to risk his life!"

All the rude comments made it clear that Captain Zhou, Minqing's husband, and his brother, an electrician, were punishing Tian in public. They charged forward like red-eyed bulls.

Tian was trained by a famous local boxing master, and his martial-arts skills made him a match for five men at least. When he was putting his bowls aside and taking off his jacket, ready to counterattack, I worried about Zhou. However, Tian seemed weakened by his guilty conscience.

Viewers jeered him and cheered for the Zhou brothers. At first, the two brothers were indeed no match for Tian. Captain Zhou stumbled several times. Once, when he was pushed to the windowsill with no room to retreat, onlookers blocked Tian. When Tian's fist slammed into Zhou's chest, I heard sighs of pity from the crowd.

Zhou's brother was a desperado. He rammed Tian from behind and knocked him down. Tian rolled nimbly and, still lying down, launched a double kick at the brother's belly and crotch. At the same time, Captain Zhou started vomiting. The stink of alcohol and sour food left no doubt that a hangover had handicapped him. The brothers both looked disabled. Tian's few followers shouted to urge him, "Get up, run away quickly!"

Captain Zhou swooped down before Tian could leap to his feet. They rolled over and over, struggling to choke each other. Zhou's brother limped back into the ring, hitting Tian with a stool until he let go of Captain Zhou—who continued to throw up. His stomach's sludge covered Tian's head. When Tian tried to wipe the vomit from his face, Zhou pulled out his commando knife, which he'd kept as a souvenir. His trembling hand found Tian's left ear, and in one vicious swipe, he cut it off in a whole piece.

Tian screamed horribly. The crowd closed in to watch him writhing in blood. And the two brothers also lay in sludge.

That evening, soon after I'd lit our kerosene lamp, my younger brother Youzhi ushered in two cousins of the Xu family, Zhongyuan Xu and Jiujiu Xu, both born in Jiangxi and five years younger than me. I hadn't seen them since 1952, the day they carried my luggage to the railway station when I left home for university.

I was excited, "Both of you are so grown up now. I wouldn't have recognized you. Sit down, please. Normally travelers should take the initiative to visit friends. Now, you've done the reverse, coming to see me. I'm embarrassed by not having treats for you."

A technician working at the county's industrial department, Zhongyuan looked quite distinguished, with his long hair and dark-rimmed glasses, "Don't feel bad. We're wartime friends."

He'd brought a basket of cured meat, preserved eggs, baked yams, and fried peanuts, all wrapped in dried lotus leaves instead of paper, "Jiujiu repaired a truck for a People's Commune on New Year's Day and got a rich dinner in return, and this basket of food. We hope it can express our sympathy for you, our big brother and master."

Jiujiu, a railway mechanic, was tall and muscular. He pushed all the delicacies over to me then pulled a bottle from his overcoat pocket, "Please drink. The liquor comes from Zhongyuan. As an inspector, he can get pure wine without a ration coupon."

Zhongyuan opened the bottle and insisted I take the first sip. Never having had alcohol before, I tasted enough just to wet my lips. Then he held the bottle high to pour the burning wine into his mouth before passing it to Jiujiu, "Let's celebrate Coyote Tian's downfall and wish for Shit Wang's doom!"

My older brother Haitao was in bed already. Hearing the hubbub in the shared dining room, he got up and came out to join us. Jiujiu handed him the bottle and he took a long draft. During the 1955 Campaign of Eliminating Counterrevolutionaries, when Haitao was teaching at the miners' evening school, Tian, then the principal, had thrown him to the masses. His hatred, accumulated from the two-month public disgrace and six-year unemployment, seemed to have found a hole to vent through. He pounded a fist on the table: "An unjust man finds no support."

He took one more drink, making the sound of a babbling brook. With slurred words, he said, "Good will be rewarded with good, and evil with evil. If retribution hasn't come, it means the time is not yet ripe."

Youzhi and I tugged him back into his room while he kept mumbling, "Heaven has eyes, and sees everything clearly." He was soon snoring on his bed.

I returned to the table, "What's the public reaction to this bloody battle?"

"Some people say Captain Zhou went too far," Zhongyuan said, "but many call him a hero, a great man."

"What punishment will the authorities mete out to him?"

"Who knows? Zhou has a perfect family background and personal history."

"No big deal," Youzhi said, "Captain Zhou deserves special consideration. He fought in the War of Liberation and the Korean War. His father died on the Red Army's Long March in 1934. Local government must consider the generations' glory."

Youzhi dumped the lotus leaves and cleaned the table. Then Zhongyuan bent over the table and whispered to us. All four heads converged at the lamp to listen.

"Almost every morning around ten o'clock, I see Shit Wang enter our county hall, pushing a bicycle. He comes to pick up the factory's share of coupons for some irregular goods. Sometimes on my field trips I meet him riding back on the road. The kilometer-long foothill road he has to take is quiet, an ideal place to ambush him."

"What?" I said, "What do you mean?"

Zhongyuan raised a fist, "To be a great man, you have to fight like Captain Zhou."

Jiujiu opened his shoulder bag to show me dozens of steel balls, retrieved from used axle bearings, with diameters of up to half an inch. Then he took out a slingshot, "Three of these primitive weapons would be enough to knock him off his bike and unconscious."

Zhongyuan looked at me, "Do you have the guts to take the final step?"

With his left hand he gripped something imagined, and with his right, slashed the air with his palm, "If I were you, I'd cut off Wang's ear to make him and Tian two of a kind. The right ear is best, to make his criminal stigma symmetrical to Tian's left one."

Before I could answer, Zhongyuan said, "Your honor is our honor. Your humiliation is ours, too."

Jiujiu nodded, "We'll go to jail with you."

I assumed the tone of a venerable elder: "We two families have come to Jiangxi as refugees. As the second generation, our roots are still shallow. No local power or force will stand up for us if we get into trouble."

With tilted head and folded arms, Youzhi scowled, "Dapeng, you're always full of fears. That's why Pig Wang dares go that far. The young workers in Chuju's factory have looked forward to your action. They're disappointed by your inaction."

"I understand all too well how difficult it is to hold back anger. But smart revenge is worth the wait. Your way would draw all of us into deep water. Also, we can't copy Captain Zhou's example and get my wife's confession by torture. After all, Chuju is one of the sisters in our refugee community."

Youzhi slapped the table, "If you can't rise up to avenge yourself, then let us punish Wang to defend the honor of our family and our refugee community. In my presence, angry young men called you a coward, a spineless worm, a cuckold. If that can be tolerated, what can't?"

I jumped to my feet with both fists hitting the center of the table. Jiujiu nimbly pressed the base of the kerosene lamp to keep it from toppling. I pointed at my brother, "Don't you know how vulnerable your own situation is? Father was scared every Eve of National Day for the last three years when the police station warned you and other unreliable elements not to be unruly. How can you forget 'the Iron Fist of the Proletarian Dictatorship' stuff that the police spout?"

The two cousins looked at each other in despair. Youzhi turned his back to me.

A few minutes later, Zhongyuan murmured, "The anger against Wang is stored like fuel. It'll blaze up as long as we can light a fire."

I shook my head, "We have no human testimony or material evidence; so how can we punish Wang as a criminal? It's stupid to act like a tail wagged by the gossiping crowds. A well-conceived plan should work to incite them, guide their rage to burn Wang, and cause no damage to us."

Jiujiu looked up, "You have a well-conceived plan?"

"And a native Jiangxi veteran to join us."

Youzhi turned to face me, smiling through his residual ire, "Who?"

I scanned the three faces, all tight with eagerness, "This must be kept absolutely secret. If it leaks out, our plan will be ruined."

They answered in unison, "We know that."

I briefed them on the scheme. They all nodded with admiration. Zhongyuan said, "Old ginger is spicier than us tender ones."

"Don't rejoice too soon. We haven't found a woman to play the key role. But we should act as soon as possible. Any delay means hitches. Please don't go anywhere in the next few days, be on standby to act anytime."

34

The next morning, Monday, a telegram came from my division leader, asking me to return to Beijing by next Friday morning. My task was to check a whole set of lab equipment before shipping it to Albania, our steadfast European ally against Khrushchev.

Faced with having to abort our plan, a remote possibility

crossed my mind: Huiyin, a woman who'd grown up in our neighborhood. Since her older sister, Huiwen, had married Kai Tao, my high-school classmate, Huiyin had regarded me as her family friend.

During the summer of 1952, at the age of 13, Huiyin walked six hours under the scorching sun to help her friend Qishen sell straw sandals to the coal miners and quarry workers. Since Qishen's father had been sentenced to jail as a small-time officer in the KMT army, her mother had woven straw sandals to make a living. While some of her classmates looked down on Qishen as political trash, Huiyin helped her earn money to continue her studies. I hadn't seen her in nine years. Recalling the tremendous humanity she'd shown in her formative years, I still had faith in her.

I shoved the telegram into my pocket and hurried to Kai Tao's home. He wasn't at home. His wife, Huiyin's sister, told me that Huiyin was an actress at the Jiangxi Opera Troupe and assured me she'd be happy to see me, and that I had been a frequent topic of conversation at their family gatherings over the past ten years. I didn't reveal my plan to her. Instead, I talked with her about something else. Finally, I asked, "Are you a distant relative of Master Yuan? I have an impression that you are. Maybe Kai Tao told me."

"Yuan's wife is my second cousin, but she's very close to us, especially as she took good care of Huiyin, like an older sister, when they were both children."

I sighed, "Master Yuan is a great human being, more than a model worker. He's kept quiet for years since his wife was enticed by Huaizhong Wang."

"He isn't so great. He obeys the Party but doesn't show enough forgiveness to his wife. Since that scandal was exposed, he's been sulkily drinking alcohol, slamming doors and using foul-mouthed curses at home. His wife often cries behind him."

"I heard she had an accident in a workshop, where her two

pigtails were drawn into the belt of a lathe. How serious was that?"

Huiwen shrank her head and shoulders together, "Horrible. All her hair and scalp were pulled off. A lot of blood was shed. After she got out of the hospital, Huiyin helped to get a wig for her. It's expensive and not sold to individuals. You need a special order from a performance unit."

"You sisters should work on Master Yuan. If his wife isn't happy, he can't be happy."

"We did, but to little effect. You know how bad our customs are, and people's habits too. Once a street boy insulted Yuan as 'a man wearing a green hat'—the slang for cuckold; he rushed home and beat up his wife. To vent his hatred, he snatched her wig and ran away from her. Finally, Huiyin asked him to surrender the wig, because it was ordered in the name of her troupe. He didn't resist."

Learning the inside story, I became sure that Huiyin must have her own grudge against Wang for ruining someone so close to her.

I went to the theater around 12:30 pm, when the performers took a break after lunch, scattering themselves among the auditorium seats.

Unlike the bashful girl of nine years before, Huiyin was now a poised, lively, open actress. Her athletic physique, lithe steps, and broad gestures instantly convinced me that she was exactly the woman who could pull off our plan.

She led me to a quiet corner, "What a nice surprise. I never expected a visit from you."

I laughed, "As the proverb says, 'Never go to the temple for nothing.' I wouldn't have come if I didn't have something to ask of you."

"How intriguing. What?"

"We need a cameo performer for a short live drama at the department store's warehouse. We need you to play the part of a store clerk."

She frowned, "That simple? Why do you need me?" Then she brightened: "There's a trick in here, isn't there?"

"Not on you. The simple play will have a big impact. However, without your charm and artful performance, we can't bring the drama alive. We don't yet have a script, it's all in Hao Ding's mind. He can explain it to you clearly in five minutes. Trust me, I'm your family friend."

She laughed, "Don't fool me, big brother. How can you ask me to commit to something when I don't know what it is?"

After she promised to keep our plan secret, no matter whether she would join us or not, I whispered in order to brief her on our ideas.

She turned solemn: "If I did that, the whole city would regard me as a treacherous and frolicsome woman. I'm sorry for disappointing you."

I was ready to leave. Still, I said, "The world has changed, humans too. Since you once hiked six hours under the scorching sun to sell straw sandals for your poor friend, I hoped you would take up cudgels for a just cause. Sorry, I've asked you too much."

As if her self-esteem was hurt, she stretched an arm to stop me, "I'm not a coward. And I hate Huaizhong Wang too. He's damaged my cousin and Yuan's family."

Her indignation gave me new hope. I said, "We share a bitter hatred of the enemy. Don't worry about how people view you. The thornier you are, the farther sexual predators stay away from you. I like seeing you as a female warrior, not a meek fair lady."

She stood, arms akimbo and took a deep breath, then said, "Okay, I'll ask Hao Ding and find out what it's really all about."

35

On February 21, the first Tuesday after the 1961 Spring Festival, Hao Ding kept the employees studying the recent editorials of *The People's Daily* at the front area of the store. A poster on the door announced 'Closed for Inventory'.

At 8:30 am I walked in the back door of the warehouse. Huiyin was already there. Her gaiety and excitement told me that Hao Ding had briefed her on our plot and she was looking forward to her role. She wore a cotton-padded, military overcoat. Underneath it, she had decked herself out in a pink, short-sleeved shirt, a dark, hand-woven vest, and a white silk skirt, all a bit gaudy for the coalmining town.

Around 9:00 am, all our fighters were present. Hao Ding cranked the telephone, which was connected to a battery as large as a wine bottle, to confirm the ten o'clock appointment. The reply from the other end sounded loud and pleasant. It was the first time I heard Wang's voice.

Youzhi introduced me to Master Yuan. He was of middling height and sturdy build. His benevolent smile, like that of an old monk, and his strong muscles, lent his features the look of a diligent and obedient paragon of socialism. His wide shoulders and narrow waist formed a triangle, a sign of masculinity, and gave me a burst of confidence that we might win. Three years before, when the Party leaders asked him to be quiet, he hadn't flared up. Now, whether sitting or standing, he looked on edge. With a tightened fist, as large as a bowl, he kept punching the wooden posts of the storage hall, itching for battle.

Hao Ding gave Huiyin the distribution list of consumer goods for state industrial enterprises in the county and showed her their locations on the ground floor and the loft. Then he reviewed his troops and looked each of us in the eye: "Are you ready? Man your posts!"

With a rope in his hand, Ding climbed the ladder to the loft then slipped through a dormer window onto the roof. I sat on the floor behind two rows of clothes racks, while Youzhi, Master Yuan, and the Xu cousins all took their hiding places.

Soon, Huiyin's melodious voice rang at the door, "Comrade Wang, are you coming to check the special rations items?"

Wang's voice replied, now smooth and charming, "Ah, I didn't expect to see you here. You obviously practice Chairman Mao's teaching, 'Artists have to go down to grassroots' units to observe and learn from real life.' How nice! Your audience will love you more than ever."

I peeked between the hanging overcoats to watch them walk in. He was taller and more muscular than me, had an authoritative bearing, and bore no visible scars.

Huiyin studied her list, "Your factory will get three bicycles, two sewing machines, and—"

"That's not fair. I've given your store a diesel engine and an electric motor, they'll get you a lot of food from People's Communes."

"Shut up! We're fair and impartial." But her voice was coy and sweet.

His right hand was already on her waist and inching to her front. She clutched the papers, elbows together, as if to protect her chest. Then, struggling to free herself, she twisted her body to face him, "You're awfully daring. Do you know who my future father-in-law is? He'll crush you like an ant."

Wang grinned, "I don't know who he is, just like you don't know how much I adore you."

She pushed his chin to make him release her, "Behave yourself. Let's get down to business. Next, leather shoes and woolen knitting yarn." Huiyin climbed the ladder.

Wang followed at her heels and his face touched her calves. She stopped and turned to face him, "Keep your distance."

He paused for a moment. When she'd almost reached the loft, he leapt up and pulled her legs astride his neck. She kicked and wriggled: "Help! Save me!"

I sprinted out of the clothes racks to hit Wang's legs with a hardwood stick. He jerked. Climbing to the loft, Huiyin threw off his grip, her shoes, and her underwear, which Wang had grasped in his teeth.

Zhongyuan Xu dashed out from a cluster of furniture, raised his stick high and aimed for Wang's hips, but instead hit the ladder as it slid and rotated. Wang fell on top of him. The stick snapped and Zhongyuan's glasses flew to the ground. His cousin, Jiujiu, trapped in the narrow space between the fallen ladder and the wall, didn't have room to swing his stick and so threw his body at Wang. Clutching each other's arms, they fought with their elbows and knees. As their bodies twisted together, I tried to jab the beast at bay with my stick, but missed.

With Wang getting the upper hand, Youzhi grabbed a bicycle tire off a shelf to yoke his neck. Wang suddenly rotated to press Jiujiu's head on the ground with his body. During Jiujiu's seconds of unconsciousness, Wang got the tire off his head and tugged Youzhi, who tumbled forward into Wang's neck hold.

Master Yuan jumped out from behind the L-shaped counter, but had difficulty attacking Wang without hurting our own people. Then, he kicked Wang's back. The blow of Yuan's soft, cloth shoe wasn't enough to free Youzhi from Wang's grasp. Yuan took advantage of his standing position to launch a double punch to the side of Wang's skull. Wang looked faint and released Youzhi. But in a surprise move he also propped himself up on one of Yuan's legs and rammed his head into Yuan's groin. While Yuan writhed on the floor and Wang struggled to stand up, Jiujiu came around and found his stick. Wang grabbed the other end of my stick and kicked out at me, trying to make me let go of it.

At that point, a loop of rope tumbled from the loft and accurately fell around Wang's neck. Hao Ding, once a fighter in Tibet, displayed his skill as a cavalryman and lassoed Wang to end the battle.

While we were tying Wang's hands and feet with hemp ropes, Master Yuan gagged him with the red underwear he'd bitten off Huiyin, "Keep the material evidence of your crime."

Zhongyuan put the ladder back firmly in position for Huiyin to descent from the loft. She found her shoes and fetched a pair of shorts from a rack. Before leaving, she slapped both sides of Wang's face with her palm and the back of her hand in quick succession, "Dirty swine!"

As for casualties on our side, I saw a bump on the right side of Jiujiu's head, and Master Yuan was stiffly walking off the pain in his groin. From a shelf, I found a bottle of pain-relief lotion for Yuan and a pack of adhesive bandages for Jiujiu.

The Xu cousins moved up a wooden bench and laid it in front of Wang. He wriggled desperately, but we tied him up squarely in a prone position.

Hao Ding picked up a four-foot bamboo lath, about one-and-a-half-inches wide and a half-inch thick, the kind of material peasants used to build shed walls. He asked, "Now, who's going to whip him?"

Jiujiu raised his hand. But Zhongyuan pushed Master Yuan to the front, "Whoever has a family background of three generations of poor peasants, and he himself is a model worker is the most eligible to punish this bad element."

Yuan took off his warm jacket and rolled up his shirtsleeves. The bamboo lath whistled in the air and cracked on Wang's rump. Wang twitched and groaned.

After Jiujiu counted to 20, Hao Ding gestured to pause, then he yelled at Wang, "Prick up your dog ears! How many women have you enticed and assaulted?"

"None."

Yuan rubbed his groin and picked up a shoulder pole, twice as wide and heavy as the lath. Wang grunted with each of the three strikes, then confessed: "One, only one."

Yuan pulled Wang's pants down to expose his hindquarters. Ten hits directly on the skin rapidly changed its color from pale to crimson, and blood started to ooze. Wang moaned: "Two, only two, that's all!"

Hao Ding roared, "Five, at least five, by our investigation."

Jiujiu opened his electrician's knife and pulled Wang's head up by the hair, "If you continue to defy us, I'll cut off your ears."

"No, don't! Only three! And you may have a joint investigation with our Party committee."

Youzhi slapped his face, "Have you counted Chuju Wu?"

"Yes! Altogether, three. If I lie, kill me."

I gave Youzhi a clipboard and paper, "Let the beast write a statement of repentance."

Youzhi and the Xu cousins retied Wang to free his right arm. Then Hao Ding said, "Write what I say word-for-word."

With a shaking hand, Wang wrote awkwardly in the prone position. Every time he stopped, Master Yuan whipped him until he finished the dictation and signed his name.

> I, Huaizhong Wang, have taken advantage of my power to trap three married women, including Chuju Wu. If later investigation proves that I've concealed any crime, I'll accept double punishment.

Jiujiu found a stamp pad and tried to get Wang's fingerprint with red ink but couldn't pry his thumb open. With a decisive strike, Master Yuan helped Jiujiu finish the task.

I puffed air to dry the ink and folded it carefully. Youzhi reminded me, "Keep it in the inner pocket of your jacket and make photocopies in Beijing."

Our buddies took turns having lunch. When the store employees swarmed the warehouse to see what was happening, I went to Hao Ding's office, where I used red paper and a brush pen to write a long banner, 'Open Trial on Rapist Huaizhong Wang!' With white paper I also wrote a poster denouncing Wang.

New observers kept coming, "Where's the rapist!"

At two o'clock, Hao Ding shut the gate to the warehouse yard and kept the crowds on the street. With a tin megaphone, he announced, "Today, in broad daylight, this sexual offender attempted to rape a woman at our department store. Fortunately, our highly vigilant masses saved the victim in time."

Catcalls shot from the crowd, "Kill him!"

Hao Ding waved his palms downward for quiet, "Chairman Mao has taught us, the strength of our dictatorship lies in the combination of an apparatus of suppression and mass movement. As masses, we've done a great job to catch him in the act. The next step is to parade him through the streets, then turn him in to our government."

Master Yuan set Wang's feet free and tied his hands behind his back. As soon as Yuan, holding the free end of the rope around Wang's neck, led him out to the street, women spat at him, and children threw clumps of dirt. They kept asking Hao Ding, "Where's the woman victim?" He answered, "By our custom, to release her name would be hurting her a second time. We'll let the court know."

Youzhi rushed to cap Wang's head with a wastepaper basket styled like a top hat and emblazoned with the words, 'Rapist Caught in the Act'.

I walked at the tail of the column with the long banner and denouncing poster folded under my arm and a bottle of glue in my pocket. We set out from the warehouse, marched into a back street, skirted a middle school at the west end of the town, and then went along the main street to reach the vegetable market. In the middle of our route, a teenage boy appeared to lead the parade, beating a gong to clear the way, "Down with the bad element Huaizhong Wang!" Echoing the slogan in chorus, the column of two lines had grown into a shapeless human flood.

The vegetable market was roofed but had no walls, it was vacant in the late afternoon. When master Yuan and the Xu cousins were tying Wang to a brick column, I pasted the denouncing poster on a blackboard chalked with the prices of the day's produce. Viewers immediately thronged around me. I squeezed away and listened to them recite my phrases:

> Huaizhong Wang is a bad element who sharpened his wits to penetrate the Party and sought honor through fraud and deception. For many years, he has abused his office's power and authority to entice and harass married women, disgracing their husbands and ruining their families. His criminal deeds have damaged our socialist cause and sullied the glory of the Party. A sham is a sham, and the mask must be stripped off.
>
> This morning, he was caught while attempting to rape a female comrade. All those who have harbored him and covered up his sins must be held responsible.
>
> We solemnly and strongly demand that the County Security Bureau severely punish Huaizhong Wang and his co-conspirators without mercy.
>
> The Alliance of Victimized Husbands and the Supporting Masses.

On the outskirts of the crowd, I found Hao Ding and whispered to him, "We've done enough. Let's retreat before the backlash comes."

"Yes, you have to go back to Beijing right away. The local Party leaders won't be happy with your call to deal with Wang's protectors. Let me deal with the aftermath."

We wedged our way into the crowd to pull Master Yuan, Youzhi, and the two Xu cousins to the outskirts. It was difficult to persuade them. They were eager to beat up Wang in front of the whole town. I said, "We did what we set out to do. Now's the time to walk away before we become targets."

At that moment, the crowd was in a tumult. Chuju showed up with a bucket whose stench opened a right-of-way through the crowd. She poured the whole bucket of human waste over Wang's head and body. The foul smell dispersed the crowd and left Wang alone. Her action slaked my hatred. *She doesn't love Wang?*

I rushed home and grabbed the belongings I'd packed in the early morning. Before I could say any parting words to my parents, Youzhi arrived, "Little Tiger reached the market with a squad of militia from the factory. They're washing Wang and getting ready to take him away."

As I tied my two bags together and loaded them on my shoulder, a hubbub on the street approached our front door. I heard Little Tiger's voice, "Is Liu's family here?"

My two brothers tried to stop him. Father beseeched, "You're Dapeng's good friend, and he's the victim of Wang. Why can't you stand by him?"

"Uncle Liu. You don't know the rules of the new society. You can't shield him from his wrongdoing."

Youzhi took my bags and pulled me out the back door. We ran through a vegetable garden and took the shortcut toward the railway station. When we reached the narrow lane behind the station, Little Tiger, with his wiry body and springy movement, and two members of the militia caught up with us, all with sticks. The Xu cousins also arrived and stood in front of me. Little Tiger dropped his stick to the ground and walked around the cousins to get to me.

Suddenly, Little Tiger gripped my collar and thrust a ball of crumpled paper inside my shirt, its brittle edges chafing my skin, "You're too smart. From your handwriting, I immediately knew you were the ringleader."

He dragged me toward the ticket window. With his fist on high, he shouted, "Get out of town! If I see you around here again, I'll arrest you!"

Youzhi and the Xu cousins freed me from his grasp, "Don't you see we're sending him off?"

Hao Ding must have been hiding around there. As soon as Little Tiger and his men left, he showed up. He'd arranged a seat in the caboose for me, "The caboose is attached to a cargo train, the safest way out of here. The Ministry of Railways has its own police system, independent from the public security forces."

Haitao helped my parents find me in the caboose. With a feeble, discontinuous voice, Father wheezed out, "We've heard the news and rushed here." Mother gripped my hand, "It's stupid to risk your future over a loose woman. A man should worry about gaining honor and official rank, not about lacking a wife."

I urged the crowd go home. Hao Ding waited for two hours until the train was moving. He assured me he'd deal with the aftermath of our joint operation. I said goodbye to everybody and gave special thanks to Hao Ding. As the train sped up, leaving our town behind, I took out the ball of crumpled paper. It was the poster denouncing Wang in my handwriting. I shredded the evidence against me into small pieces. The train accelerated, and I let them fly out the window.

PART THREE

1

Feeling like a bird that had lost his mate in a storm, I returned to Beijing. The place where I'd perched for so many years seemed alien.

As an emergent side assignment, I spent a whole week examining the equipment to aid Albania and checking it against an inventory list. As Chairman Mao had praised that small country as, "A beacon of socialism lighting up Europe," Party Secretary Jiang earnestly pronounced it a task vital for international revolution: "Each specific tool, all accessories, and the rare lab materials must be accurately placed and ready for use. Not a single error is allowed."

Jiang personally rechecked all the wooden boxes. I sealed them with reverence and awe. Only after delivering them to the shipping company could I return to my research work.

Languidly, we congregated in the large, warmer office with its east-facing windows. At eight o'clock every morning, like many people did to the friends they met on the street, we greeted one another by pressing each other's foreheads to check for edema, a symptom of malnutrition and an early stage of a fatal health problem. My skin felt tight all over my face, and the dent on my leg after a thumb press needed several minutes to disappear.

Most people had little work to do but many documents to study. Unlike my idle coworkers, I had to preside over group discussions and take minutes. Besides working on my research paper, I collected data on foreign cases of dam-foundation reinforcement against sliding and leaking.

With my heart still fluttering with anger and frustration from my home visit, it took a tremendous effort to bring my mind back to the work I was doing. Sometimes the odor of human waste that Chuju poured on Wang seemed to linger on, serving as evidence against her that she'd lied to me—her barbaric action implied an emotional entanglement with Wang. Had his sexual assault of Huiyin meant betrayal to Chuju?

On March 4, the monthly payday, I received my 62 yuan. That evening I mailed 20 yuan to Father. After my wedding, I had reduced the monthly remittance to 15 yuan, but his deteriorating health, despite my own difficulties, obliged me to return to the original level.

In a shopping center next to the post office, I looked around for something nutritious to send to him. All I could find was powdered baby food with a label that promised it was, 'Enriched with Multi-Vitamins'. I wasn't sure how much the supposedly enriched baby food could improve Father's edema or jaundice, but at least it would be a spiritual consolation to him.

Returning to the institute, I found my coworkers packed into Old Lou's room to celebrate his leaving for family unification. He'd graduated in 1948 and married the chief ward nurse at a mental hospital in Guangzhou. For a decade, both their leaders had asked them to overcome the personal hardship of separation for the great socialist cause.

Now, so many patients had asked for sick leave and nutritional supplements that the hospital system changed the criteria for diagnosing hepatitis. The year before, doctors had set the transaminase blood level at 60 ppm for it to be considered hepatitis. This year, the threshold was 200 ppm. Regardless, Lou's indicator was above two hundred. Factually disabled, he was allowed to go.

While we said our farewells, Lou was slumped on a pile of comforters and pillows in a corner, trying to open his eyes for the sake of courtesy. As a fellow sufferer of spousal separation, I grieved for the loss of both his health and research. A devoted engineer, he'd recently become a pioneer in directional blasting to build rock-filled dams. As his reputation rose and his expertise was in great demand, the doctors forbade him to work due to the risk of succumbing to a potentially fatal illness.

I vowed not to become crippled like Lou before gaining the right to live with my wife, either Chuju or someone else.

My fate would be determined by the Party branch leaders, and it was difficult to feel them out about my problem. The next morning, on my way to the Beijing Library, I went downtown to see my former boss, Director Gu. As he had hoped and predicted, he now headed the Institute of Construction Technology, a branch of the General Bureau of Waterpower Development. It seemed to me that Chairman Mao still considered those veteran cadres as assets of the Revolution, though it was necessary to humiliate some of them as an education in loyalty.

He greeted me with the air of a hero staging a comeback. As in his heyday, he wore the olive-beige Mao suit. His modulated voice sounded as proud as in the past, before he'd been battered by the 1959 Anti-right-deviation-opportunists Campaign.

I shook his hand with gusto, "Now I can call you Director Gu out loud again."

Sitting in his leather swivel chair, he smoked stylishly, like the early Bolshevik agitators we saw in the movies, "You were the only one with the courage to call me that when I was struck down to dust."

Before I explained what I'd come for, he leaned over his desk and looked at me, "I know your situation, because my wife still works at the Party committee office of your institute."

I knocked on his desk, "How could I expect that a local Party leader would sabotage my marriage, and that no other leaders would care about my suffering or his crimes?"

He looked calm, "Don't be weighed down—it happens. During the guerrilla war, women were rare in the barren, ragged areas under our control. Then too, big shots snatched wives or girlfriends from their subordinates. It was no big deal."

His confidential manner put me at ease, "I didn't know that."

"To seize power, we lost uncountable lives. In the mid-forties

I couldn't imagine we'd win the whole nation so soon. When we were ready to die every day, nobody could argue over women."

"I heard some women comrades took sexual relationships with men as lightly as drinking a cup of water. Was that true?"

"That's what we called it, the cup-of-water philosophy. It was popular among Russian women during the October Revolution and the Civil War. After our victory, we didn't talk about the dark side of the Revolution. Instead, we set new rules. You intellectuals are too tender. Heaven won't collapse."

"But I'm caught in a dilemma. I have no chance to live with Chuju, and divorce would take a long time." I wasn't sure if he'd forgotten his informal promise, made the night of my wedding, ten months before. Staring at his ashtray, I mumbled, "As a newly established research unit, you must have a quota of Beijing residences. I wonder if you can help me."

He exhaled a long trail of smoke, "Hopefully Beijing Municipality will give us a new quota soon. It wouldn't be a problem at all to transfer your wife to our office, if you joined our team. I've already talked to your division leaders. They're very stubborn about keeping you. Our door is open to you— you're welcome anytime. In the meantime, be practical. Reach to the head of your institute for help."

"How?"

"Where there's a will, there's a way. Go to work on Professor Huang, your chief scientist."

"The political cadres see him as a bourgeois expert, reused by the Revolution. They just pretend to respect him."

Gu waved the hand with the cigarette, "The wind is changing. The Party's central committee has worked on a 14-point regulation for scientific research. The new policy will give scientists like Huang the power to make decisions on research work."

"Does that mean the 1958 slogan, 'Put the Party Secretary in Command', would be overridden?"

"Yes, it does. Quietly." He pointed the two fingers holding

the cigarette at my chest, "The regulation also stresses how to bring about achievements by talented people. The new tide will push Professor Huang to the front line. Unfortunately, scientists like him are rare and getting old, and the growth of young talents has been stunted by political campaigns. I would liken him to a brilliant general leading a weak army. Eager to have successors, he'll pay special attention to you."

I shook my head, "He doesn't have the power to help me with a family reunion. Given his nature, I doubt he'll meddle in such headaches."

Walking me out of his office, Gu stopped at the door, and pondered a while, "Let me commit one of the mistakes of liberalism again to leak a little internal news. All the research centers are obligated to select their seed players and cultivate them with special care. I'm sure you'll be one of the seeds handpicked by your division Party branch and presented to Professor Huang. Young man, cheer up and aim high. Once you become a star in your field, our system will take good care of you. Your problem will be gone."

"Before I can reach that stage, Chuju will have flown away."

"If Chuju shows sincere remorse, give her a chance to give up evil and return to good. If she's incorrigible, just let her go. With your new status, you'll be able to find a woman who outshines her."

His final remark sounded similar to what Mother had said about how a man should worry about honor and rank rather than about a wife. I sighed, "Maybe I better divorce Chuju right away."

A cunning smile flitted across his face, "The leaders are anxious to see your achievement as an indicator of their wise leadership, but they won't give a damn about your personal suffering. Hence, your request for divorce will show where your priority lies. It will also measure your weight in the hearts of your division leaders, pushing them to take a clear-cut stand, either bringing Chuju to Beijing or expediting the court's approval of your divorce."

I blinked, "So, asking for divorce would be more effective than begging for reunion? Only an old guard like you could have such a masterful mind."

He tapped my shoulder, "Keep quiet."

A state-owned photo shop required an official introduction letter in order to duplicate Wang's statement of confession, and it was expensive. I asked Dr Peng, the electricity expert, who'd grown up and been educated in Japan, for help. During my stressful honeymoon, his Japanese wife, Noriko, had had difficulty writing her anti-Khrushchev article for her own political harvest, and I helped her as a ghostwriter. Now, returning my favor, the couple used their wide-angle camera and developing equipment to make the enlarged copies for me.

I immediately wrote a letter to the civil court of Pingxiang County asking for a divorce from Chuju, attaching a photocopy of Wang's written confession statement as my evidence.

2

One night in mid-March, when I passed by the front gate, the old man guarding the reception room slid the window open to wave me in. He opened his cabinet and took out a parcel for me. Some men idling nearby came up and began pinching it.

"I bet there's cans of sardines and meat."

"What's in the bottles? Fish oil or vitamins?"

"Open it!"

My heart was pounding. The package was from Hong Kong. I wondered who there had remembered me at this bad time.

It was wrapped in tough fabric, sewed with tight stitches, and weighed about ten pounds. The feminine handwriting, in brushstrokes, told me the sender was Ziwei Cao. Fortunately, she had written her address in English and translated her name using the Wade–Giles system, while the crowd around me knew only the Pinyin style, which our government had adopted. Without the sender's exact name, the gossips would lack steam.

Ziwei had used my old address, which had only been valid until October 1957. That meant the post office had tracked me through two relocations and a large-scale merger. What elaborate, meticulous handling! It was hard to believe, given the attention the authorities paid to mail from abroad, that the parcel had got through.

Stroking her dear handwriting on the wrapping, I sensed the cylindrical shape of a bottle, also the flat surface of a can. I believed the hungry onlookers had guessed right, and I was moved by her solicitude. The guard gave me a pair of scissors, and the covetous eyes focused on the parcel in my hands. Awakening from the bittersweet memories of our university days, I began to worry about the potential troubles her goodwill might provoke. The parcel might indicate a kind of Overseas Relationship, which was a special column that had to be filled out for personnel registration, especially for security clearance.

I put down the scissors, "Sorry. I have to ask my division leader for instructions on how to deal with this."

The ravenous crowd booed and hooted. A draftswoman at our instrument factory jeered at me: "We never knew your political consciousness was so high."

I took to my heels. The purchasing clerk at our warehouse shouted behind me, "No nonsense, miser!"

Back at the dorm I hid the parcel under my bed. In the middle of the night, I rolled to the edge of my bed and reached under to make sure the package was still there. Lying awake, I wondered what kind of high-protein food could be in it, guessing it might be a more effective cure for Father's illness than the powdered baby food I'd bought. As the malnutrition took its toll, many young women weren't menstruating, and men were becoming impotent. With that dreary picture in my mind, I was grateful that the famine had diffused my libido like anesthesia, numbing my sensibility to my broken marriage.

However, my early-stage edema could be worsening, leading to hepatitis and death. Hot Chili and her husband told me that, from the autopsies of people who had died of starvation, they found their livers had become dark, and had shrunk to the size of a walnut. My transaminase blood level reached 90 ppm qualifying me as a hepatitis patient by the previous year's criteria. Now, even though I felt pain, medical doctors denied my request for some food supplements by this year's criteria, two hundred ppm. I couldn't see the size and color of my liver, but it was reasonable to keep a small portion of the food in the parcel for myself.

The problem was the place where the parcel came from. In the past few years, anyone having a visitor from Hong Kong had been annoyed by our security office and suspected by coworkers. Scarier still, my former classmate Huihe Lin, who'd slipped from our farm and attempted to escape to Hong Kong, had recently got a 15-year jail sentence. A few days before I returned to Beijing, he was displayed at a rally in our auditorium, handcuffed and escorted by armed police.

I hadn't heard from Ziwei for four and a half years, and her image had become elusive in my mind. In peaceful times, I imagined her as a fairy, blessing me from the sky; during political storms, I feared her being demonized as a British imperialist. I had no way of knowing if she was studying, working, or married. Nor did I know her father's political status. In 1955, she had been interrogated and abused due to her correspondence with him, yet the next year, the Cantonese provincial government granted her a passport to let them reunite. A kind of mystery surrounding her and her family haunted me.

3

The next morning, the parcel under my bed looked like a bomb to me. I got up early and took it to my office. From my cabinet under the desk, I found my old diary and the few letters I'd kept. Ziwei, in the 3x4-inch picture, stared at me as tenderly as the day we parted, and with the same air of serene dignity that I'd so admired. I couldn't help re-reading the letter, which she wrote on the eve of her leaving for Hong Kong.

Now, deep in crisis, I felt a new hatred piling on top of my old sadness for a broken dream. The parcel from a long-disappeared friend suddenly showed the great strength and compassion I desperately needed.

I took the scissors from an adjacent desk and cut the stitches. What the busybodies in the receptionist's room had speculated about were indeed there: cans of sardines, meat, and multi-vitamins. The package also had bags of glucose powder, bottles of fish oil, and herbal elixir.

I unfolded the enclosed note.

> Dapeng, my schoolmate,
>
> Without knowing your present address, I will tentatively send this small package, hoping it finds its way to you. After your reply arrives, I will send you more. Time goes fast. During the years, you must have made a great leap with your academic work, and your life must have changed dramatically. I'm awaiting your good news.
>
> As for me, living abroad is a constant struggle. I have studied English literature and shall get my BA this coming summer. My time spent learning Russian seems wasted, but it is helpful to my new discipline, and sometimes helps me find temporary jobs. Please write to me at the return address.
>
> Sincerely,

Ziwei

I knew censorship didn't allow me to say much. I tried to take a chance, touching the undeclared limit. Before breakfast, I finished a letter that would let her read something between the lines.

> Dear Ziwei,
> You can't imagine how much I was elated by the arrival of your parcel. Accompanying the nutritious food, it brings me the compassion of a faithful friend after a long period of disappearance. Time and distance have never made my belief waver: your heart remains pure and innocent no matter where you are. How nice it would be if the storm of the summer of 1955 had not occurred! Our old dream as naïve students vanished like a flash, but it comes back to torment me during the nationwide famine and my personal disaster. If you were here, I would have a trustworthy and clear-minded listener to pour out my grief to, which I feel would be shameful and useless to entrust to others. No, that's an utter illusion. I have to struggle silently to get out of this quagmire of bad luck.
> Recalling the enchanting campus of our school and the rough road of the past years, I feel obliged to say thank you. You helped me get rid of my aloofness and arrogance and pushed me to melt into the mainstream. Also, I want to tell you that I've carried the Russian–Chinese dictionary you sent me in 1956 like a soldier with his gun, and now I can read Russian technical articles fluently. On the other hand, I might've let you down with *Fathers and Sons*, though I've kept your bilingual copy in good shape. I've only read the first few pages in four and a half

years.

Are you still single or do you have someone in your life? I believe your professional pursuits and willingness to struggle alongside your man will lay a common ground for building a long-lasting mutual understanding. I'm waiting for your good news. I have much to say, but this piece of paper is too short to contain my words and emotions. I hope you can come back to build up our great motherland.

Dapeng

I hesitated. Could Ziwei understand my situation from the ambiguous words, 'my personal disaster', and 'this quagmire of my bad luck'? If I touched on details, the security inspector might take it as criticism of the Party. With a determined sigh, I sealed the envelope. At lunchtime, I took a bus and trolley to reach Beijing's main post office and send the letter by registered airmail.

Five days later, as I sat by my desk imagining a Hong Kong mailman in a green uniform pushing the doorbell at Ziwei's residence, the office phone rang. The female security clerk on the third floor asked me to go upstairs to meet her boss. *Gosh.* I'd never set my foot in that gruesome place. Her flat tone signaled something ominous.

When I knocked on her door, she came out to lead me to the room across the corridor. The security chief, Comrade Bai, a middle-aged man, who usually looked like a gentle teacher, was sitting on the couch with a raging air. Older Sister Rong, the vice secretary of our division's Party branch was also there, flustered like a mother seeing her son caught stealing. Before I could figure out if it was proper for me to sit down, Bai put a folder on the tea table and pulled out the letter I'd mailed to Ziwei.

He pointed a finger at me and roared, "Where have you seen *famine* in our country? Does socialism allow anyone to starve? Please tell me what kind of grief you have, or why you trust an overseas Chinese person more than our revolutionary comrades?"

Rong beat the drum for him, "We've overestimated your consciousness. How can you be so sure that that woman remains pure and innocent after living in a dirty capitalist society for so many years? Your muddy mind and unhealthy emotions have made you an easy prey for a class enemy. If our mail inspectors hadn't worked diligently enough, your letter would've badly damaged our country's reputation."

I didn't sense any anger or hatred from her dutiful words, which sounded like a monk's recital of scriptures. Obviously, with strong backing from her husband—as the number-two leader of our institute, commanding the lower-rank cadres—she just showed a condescending respect to Bai.

When my fear faded, I reached out for the letter: "I want it back."

Bai swiftly put it in the folder, "Out of the question. We should preserve it with your dossier."

Rong looked bored, "How about letting him write a positive, pleasant letter to bolster our country's image?"

Bai nodded slowly, "If his new letter passes inspection, then we can give him back the old one."

I said, "If you don't give the old one back to me, I won't write a new one. Then the sender of the parcel will think it's been lost."

Rong speared me with a look, "Behave yourself." Then she turned to Bai, "He's generally a good comrade, he works hard and he's loyal to the Party. But he's a young man and so is bound to make mistakes. We need to be more patient in educating him. Please let me handle the case. I won't give him back the old letter until the new one has been proven politically correct."

Without waiting for Bai's reply, she gave me a final lecture, "These days, our enemies gloat over our difficulties and wait for our collapse. Ziwei Cao must've been confused by the international anti-Chinese, anti-communist chorus. If your letter sings a happy song, it will be a blow to enemy slander."

Back at our office, I beckoned Dong Long to come outside with me. In a quiet corner of the backyard, I told him what had happened with the parcel, "Rong is asking me to reject Ziwei's gift with a written statement. But it would violate my conscience and hurt Ziwei badly."

He answered without a second thought, "No big deal. Ziwei will be excited you got the package and understand why your reply is written like an official statement."

"It's wrong to lie to her. I don't want to hurt a good friend."

"Be practical. Rong has given you a way to get out of trouble."

That afternoon, I drafted a short letter with the tone and phrases I'd learned from *The People's Daily*. Before Rong left for the day, I got her review and approval.

> Ziwei, My Schoolmate,
>
> I have not seen you for four and a half years, but I have never relaxed my worry about how you could survive in a hellish capitalist society. Like all your former schoolmates, I have waited for your return to our motherland, where you were nurtured and cultivated into a professional.
>
> I'm moved by your concern for my wellbeing, but your parcel was not necessary. Please don't send anything again, since I have everything I need. Our current problems arise from US imperialists, Soviet revisionists, and three years of natural disasters. Our difficulties are temporary, inevitably part of our unprecedented cause. The road of Revolution is tortuous, but the future is bright. Under the wise leadership of the Party and Chairman Mao, we are

fully confident we will overcome all setbacks and obstacles, and are determined to win worldwide victory for communism.

With compatriotic salutations,

Dapeng

4

The famine brought most capital-intensive construction to a halt. At the same time, our ministry received reports of impending disasters in the upcoming flood season. Hundreds of dams, hastily designed and poorly built nationwide during the Great Leap, would be the sources of massive amounts of death rather than key projects of flood-control and irrigation.

One day, Secretary Jiang called me into his office. With an air of someone delivering a prize, he said, "An emergency delegation plans to inspect the arch dam at Hengshan Reservoir in Shanxi Province. Our ministry has invited about 20 nationally renowned experts to meet in Beijing, and Professor Huang is the delegation's technical head. I think the inspection would be a great learning opportunity for you. I asked Huang if you could go with him. He's accepted you."

I'd heard that Huang had already chosen three aides for the inspection. One was China's former chief engineer on the joint Sino–Soviet water project design in Leningrad. Another was a Moscow-trained structural engineer, and the third, a senior geologist.

"My experience and rank certainly don't equal those of his other aides," I said, "Did he accept me only out of respect for you?"

He laughed, "Don't think the famous experts know everything. They made names for themselves in the past but sometimes have a hard time living up to them. Throw away your blind faith in bourgeois academic tyrants. You've studied dam foundation stability problems more thoroughly than the other delegates." He slapped my shoulder, "Show your guts! We support you."

Obviously, he wanted me to rub shoulders with those expert engineers. Although his trust and high expectations couldn't relieve my personal suffering, Director Gu's pragmatic view helped me look at this assignment in a new way. Huang's important role under the Party's new pro-expert policy might be my best hope. It would be a long-haul struggle but not too remote a possibility.

On the train to Shanxi, I knocked on the door of Huang's compartment and asked, "Do you need me to work on any data preparation or calculations for your speech?"

"Not now. Come on in." In a fatherly manner, he gestured for me to sit down.

He was probably in his early sixties but looked older. His round face was outlined with sparse hair. He had flaccid muscles and wore thick lenses. His reputation had preceded him since his partial lung excision had been the first open-chest operation done in China by a Chinese doctor, trained in the US. Though battered several times in political campaigns, he remained outspoken.

This was the first time I'd met him in a private setting. I felt ashamed at having joined the crowd to criticize such an honest scholar as an imperialist flunky.

I gingerly sat by the window, "I regret my speech against you at the 1958 Open Heart to the Party rally held by our division. It was a blind accusation and insulting."

Reclining on pillows and blankets, he nodded with forgiveness, "I appreciate your discovery of conscience. I don't take such organized torment personally."

"We shouldn't have been so easily whipped up to fight like children."

A spasm distorted his face, "It happened. And it might happen again after the famine is over. But I believe most people will learn from our past mistakes."

"In 1946," I said, "when Russian soldiers raped Chinese women in Northeast China and looted factory equipment left behind by the Japanese, you supported university students in Nanjing demanding that the Soviet Red Army withdraw from China. You did the right thing. In 1958, your patriotic action was blamed for splitting Sino–Soviet unity. Now we're cursing the Soviet Union as harshly as we can."

"It's a long story." He shook his head, "Anyway, the way you practice shows that you have a clear mind. My emphasis that researchers must know foreign languages has drawn attacks from some of your peers. But you've quietly improved your ability to read Russian and English. It takes guts to study English, a devil's language in the eyes of radicals."

"I'm still green, and my theoretical foundation is too weak for me to become a qualified scientist yet."

"It takes time. Your division Party branch is paying special attention to nurturing you as a seed player. I too feel obliged to help you grow. I've gone over your draft of the article, 'Primary Report on the Sliding Stability of Concrete Dams on Rock Foundations'. It'll be printed as the lead article of the first issue of the *Journal of Hydraulic Engineering*, coming out early next year. It's a good start for you."

Since this magazine was jointly sponsored by our ministry and the Chinese Academy of Sciences, my former classmates would consider it a remarkable achievement. Most of them were still doing support work, while I'd emerged as a primary member of our research group. I was elated by the news. We arrived at Datong and stayed at the best hotel in that middle-sized city. With a provincial cadre accompanying us, we not only ate well, but also got to enjoy some sightseeing. Historical sites that were normally closed were open for us. Besides the Palace of Heaven's Emperor, we visited the Yungang Grottoes, built circa 386–534. Astonished by the relief sculptures, continuous and integrated, carved from a massive granite foothill, I sighed, "To chisel away those rocks little by little, some stone carvers must've spent their whole life in the cave."

"You bet," our tour guide said, "Old county annals say some sons carried on their fathers' work carving them."

Professor Huang lowered his voice, "We need such devotion today. The Great Leap has made many scientists boastful, exaggerating their achievements to fool the Party and the public. If someone announces he's written ten research theses in a year, don't believe him, he must be a liar. We should learn from the ancient stone carvers—be dedicated and faithful."

On the third day, a Czechoslovakian tour bus came to our hotel. It was the most powerful and reliable vehicle made in socialist countries, and beautiful too. It took our delegation to the dam site while Professor Huang and the bureau chief rode in a small car. Most of the hundred kilometers of country road was 'paved' with only pebbles and sand, and it took us four hours. On both sides of the highway, elms, poplars, and other trees whose names I didn't know had had their bark stripped to a height of five or six feet. The chilly scene reminded me of what a coworker said after coming back from a survey site in Shanxi: "Peasants are eating the bark off trees."

Local people and cadres in Shanxi Province had built the Hengshan Arch Dam, it was three-hundred-feet tall and double-convex, world-class in terms of complexity and scale. It was completed in just two years with the most meager budget and primitive tools. They relied mainly on university students to design it without adequate geological surveys or hydrological data, then mobilized peasants to erect it. Standing on its crest, I could imagine how much labor they'd all donated and how much personal sacrifice it required.

The inspection delegation soon discovered two major flaws in the dam that threatened its safety. First, the gate at the bottom wasn't large enough to discharge the floodwaters expected during the rainy season. The delegation proposed that a bypass discharge tunnel be retrofitted immediately.

A second problem: a thin, weak, horizontal layer of clay set in the arch dam's left shoulder would probably slide away when the reservoir was full. On this point I had something to say. However, when I raised my hand and stood up, the senior delegates started whispering to each other, scratching their heads, or going to the restroom. The noises distracted the audience from me.

Professor Huang, in the chairman's seat, hit the table several times with his pen, "I need your attention!"

As the crowd turned quiet, I walked to the blackboard, "Leaders, experts, comrades, please listen to me, a rank-and-file soldier on the scientific front. My knowledge is limited, but my sense of duty for the socialist cause urges me to speak before you great masters. A year ago, the Malpasset Dam in France collapsed. The geological conditions leading to the disaster were similar to what we now see at the Hengshan Dam. The French case is a timely lesson. Based on their experience, we can estimate how low the shear strength of the shoulder's clay may be. See for yourself, it's alarming."

When I'd written down my test results from various dam sites and the comparable data collected from foreign journals, half of the senior experts rushed to the blackboard and eagerly copied them into their notebooks.

Huang nodded to me with a smile.

We had one afternoon free during the field conference, and we younger delegates climbed the main peak of Hengshan, one of five celebrated Sacred Mountains of China. When the group of hikers set out, Professor Huang sighed and shook his head, "I can't drag myself up this damn mountain. Dapeng, you go—and don't stop until you reach the top."

I felt restored by the meals the county government had treated us to all week. With renewed energy, I took up the challenge. From the base of the mountain I endured a strenuous five-hour trek to reach the summit, a vertical rise of four thousand feet. At one point, I caught up with one of Huang's aides, a geologist. Though eight years older than me, his profession had trained him to be a better climber, and so he coached me on how to control my pace and conserve energy.

On the final stretch, I looked up at the huge temple on the summit. With eaves upturned to the sky, it looked lofty and magnificent. A Taoist monk, dressed like a peasant, stood at the head of the steps to greet us. He had been caring for the religious complex since the Liberation and had been required to live on his own crops. With no pilgrims visiting anymore, he received no donations.

We dozen hikers gathered around him. After his brief introduction to the temple's history, he put on a long face, "Someone stole the two sacks of oats I hid under the altar. Growing them on the mountain is backbreaking."

Looking at the monk's unhappy face, I could only think that the thief was a hardened bandit, like Huaizhong Wang, and probably an atheist. How else could he have gone so far as to steal food from a monk and his god? None of us intended to donate. Though all capable of climbing to the summit were low-ranking personnel, and, more or less, we all had some money to give, supporting religion was considered a wrongdoing.

The holy atmosphere induced me to contemplate the concepts of emptiness and nothingness, which the Taoist and Buddhist philosophers had spent their entire lives trying to comprehend. But the ideas were too abstruse for me. Huang's image, with both hands holding his walking stick, was fixed in my mind. I felt he was watching me climb to the cloud-capped heights, as he'd watched me climb rugged scientific mountains. He needed people like me to relay with him in his race. I needed him to push our institute's Party leaders to consider my reunion with Chuju. Immediately after I had left home, Wang's factory set him free, and blamed our punishment of him as an anarchist melodrama. As long as Chuju remained under Wang's shadow, I was on tenterhooks day and night.

Professor Huang left the dam site two days before the rest of us. The night before leaving, he summoned me to his room. In pajamas, he looked at ease and said confidently, "Please take care of miscellaneous affairs for the delegation and safeguard the aging experts on the way back to Beijing."

"No problem, I'll do my best."

I was ready to return to my room, but he had more to say: "Your speech at the field meeting was impressive. After a few nervous minutes, you did attract your audience and command the scene. On the spot, an old delegate whispered to me the traditional maxim, 'A youth is to be regarded with respect'."

I blundered forward, "I'm one of the million university graduates trained after the Liberation. Mentally, I'm prepared to wallow for a long time at the bottom of the hierarchy."

He kept quiet, reaching for the thermos and pouring a cup of tea for me. While I regretted my indiscreet remark, he spoke emotionally, "For a society that tells itself we believe in equality and fairness our ranks are rigidly stratified."

His complaint startled me, and I became bolder, "A poorly educated cadre who joined the Party before 1938 can be put in charge of a university, steel mill, museum, hospital, everything. Cadres who joined between 1938 and 1945 would be made section chiefs. Those who dangle from between 1945 and 1949 are qualified only to be office heads."

He raised a palm to curb my speaking in that direction, "That's related to power structures, not to our business. Why should we call professionals from the old society and those trained in the West 'old-fashioned intellectuals'? They're paid well, but subjected to a policy of uniting, using, and remolding, which makes them always feel guilty."

I nodded, "Especially after top scientists and artists have been punished for saying that universities should be run by professors or filmmaking by directors. Opinions like these are condemned as an attempt to abolish the Party's leadership. So, people like me have to keep our mouths shut, like cicadas in winter."

He took out a tiny snuff bottle from his pajama pocket and sniffed noisily. I guess it contained some powder prescribed for his perspiration problem. Then, he continued, "Politically, yes, you're bound to have a slip of the tongue if you talk too much. Academically, do not refuse to shoulder responsibility. Now, while you're studying hard, and most technical cadres have resigned themselves to the political trend, even the senior experts live off their earlier triumphs. Someday, when our leaders decide to make radical changes, only people like you will catch the historical opportunity. The day will come, sooner or later, because our country can't survive without changing its course. Do you understand?"

These words, deeply buried in his heart, he entrusted me to hear. Before I could find a fitting reply, he tightened his pajama belt, sat on the edge of the sofa, and jovially began to talk about the Beijing opera: "The new libretto describes Liang Zhuge, the legendary strategist at the end of Han Dynasty, as a young man."

"Interesting. And daring. Operagoers have gotten used to seeing him as an old man."

"When he walked out of his thatched house as a young man to command the army of the Shu Kingdom, the audience was thrilled. I was moved by his farewell lyrics, 'Phoenixes perch on sky-touching parasol trees, how high do they aim? Ten thousand miles.' You should be inspired like that."

5

By April, spring could be seen in the tender willow twigs. Unlike in normal years, rather than aesthetic, people now found them edible. When I came back from Shanxi, my coworkers had begun to mix the pulp of willow leaves with flour to supplement our food rations. They were bitter, and processing them required a huge effort. After grinding a large pile of the leaves, mixing them with water, and filtering the mash through cloth, they yielded only a small edible portion. When it was my turn to work the stone mill, two hours of pushing and pulling the handle exhausted me, and that day I had to eat more than I usually allowed myself. Soon, by consensus, we abandoned that option.

Because of our leaders' trust, I was assigned to draft a section of the ten-year research plan for our ministry. My former classmates considered my rise a remarkable success.

When Secretary Jiang invited me to attend a discussion on the design of Beijing's first subway again, I refused to go, showing him the ridge of scar on my scalp earned from the confidential pamphlets. He spoke with the force of justice: "Let me tell you something about Marshal Chen, the current minister of foreign affairs. In 1927, after cracking down on the military insurgence, he went to gather the Party's residual forces in Jiangxi, but his former guerrilla soldiers suspected him of being a traitor sent back by the KMT government. They tied him up, hung him from a tree, and hit him with the brass head of a long smoking pipe. At a recent speech, he recalled those peasant fighters with noble respect."

Having no way to argue with his high criteria, I obeyed him.

During a morning break, Jiang happened to be in our office when a nosy female coworker asked me, "What's the latest with you and your wife?"

I scowled and muttered, "Stalemate."

Before she could ask another obnoxious question, Jiang made a gesture to stop me talking, "Dapeng, please go see Older Sister Rong."

When I entered the division leaders' office, Jiang followed on my heels and quietly advised, "Don't say too much from now on. You must consider the difficulties for your wife if she comes here and everybody knows what she's done."

His fishy words sounded premature. Why would he say anything now? When Rong waved me over to sit down, Jiang walked into his inner office.

She took a bunch of letters from a drawer. Sitting opposite her, I caught a glimpse of the red-character letterhead. They came from the court of Pingxiang County and the Party committee of Chuju's factory.

She said calmly, "Now, two months after your home visit, Huaizhong Wang has withdrawn his forced confession, and Chuju Wu denies your accusation of her adultery with Wang." I started to say something, but she held up a palm to stop me, "So, the court is having difficulty making a decision. As usual, the judge aims at helping married couples to reconcile. And Chuju's leaders are asking us to help relocate her to Beijing."

I sat up, surprised, "Are you going to do that?"

"We're pleading with the institute's Party committee to lobby Beijing's Public Security Bureau. As soon as we get a residence permit for Chuju, we'll send the order for her transfer. The factory is willing to let her leave."

This unexpected development verified my former leader Director Gu's judgment. I said thanks and stood up. Rong's face turned tough, "The local Party leaders at your hometown are lenient and forgiving."

"Yes, I know."

"I doubt you really know. They let you go without holding you responsible for your anarchist action, but you don't know what principles you've walked all over. Look at the scenario from their angle: you gathered a mob of backward elements to punish your personal enemy, a Party member. Such a mistake can be downplayed, but also can be criticized from a class-struggle viewpoint. It has definitely revealed your insufficient political consciousness."

I said nothing and waited.

She shifted in her chair to a less stern position, "Have you seen the movie *The Red Detachment of Women*?"

"Yes."

She smiled like an older sister, "What was the main point you learned from it?"

I tried to answer as correctly as possible: "The heroine hates the despotic landlord, who abused her as a slave. During an ambush, she shoots him without an order to do so, which ruins the detachment's whole military operation. After the Party leaders' patient education, she finally understands the principle. Revolution is not for personal vengeance, but for the emancipation of all mankind."

She sighed, "You seem to understand the principle, but only when it doesn't contradict your interests. This time, swayed by personal hatred, you threw the Party's wisdom to the winds. I worry about you." Her tone suggested there would be no more backlash from our vengeance on Wang.

That evening, I felt relaxed. At midnight, while the sighs and moans of lonely men drifted like ghosts through the corridor, I began to look forward to Chuju's arrival. The psychological torture and the year of sex deprivation had ground me down, and I couldn't see the end of my starvation. I believed that in the relatively purified ranks in Beijing, rather than Wang's bandit's lair, Chuju would turn over a new leaf in life. Of course, if things went in the opposite direction, which was possible considering Wang still held his position, my temporary relief would be like drinking poison to quench thirst.

I remembered the gunshots lacerating the quiet air of my hometown during the execution of local KMT officials in 1949. The banners on the rally ground and slogans shouted by the crowds all claimed, "Debts of blood must be paid in blood." No matter what the future developments would be, I had a secret claim. Chuju should pay her debts of sex to me in sex.

The next morning, I wrote a letter.

Dear Chuju,

Can you imagine that our division's Party branch is urging higher-up committees to transfer you to our institute? When the secretary told me this himself, I couldn't believe my ears. It's incredible at such a difficult time, when current policy generally only allows people to leave, rather than enter, Beijing. What favored treatment! It revives me!

Soon, I believe, you can leave our town, a quagmire for you now, and start a new job and a new life. I hope you see the great opportunity our division Party branch can offer us. It hasn't come easily. Let's forget the painful past, heal our wounds, and revive our old dream.

Love,

Dapeng

With a relieved heart, I mailed the letter. It was around our anniversary, May 8. Though nervous about the reunion, I hoped for Chuju's joyful reply and further news about her residence permit.

Dong Long was happy for me. He suggested that I buy a nice pair of dress shoes, which he saw at a store, in anticipation of my happy reunion with Chuju. As he said, the price, 26 yuan, looked high, but was the same as before the inflation. And he gave me his shoe ration coupon for the year. So, I bought them. Alone in my room, waiting for the fantastic moment of Chuju's arrival, I appreciated their streamlined shape and square toes.

6

A few days later, while I was waiting for Chuju's happy

response, a registered letter from my younger brother Youzhi
arrived.

> Since your home visit, Chuju and Wang have
> been shamelessly indulging in adultery, and the
> public is choked with silent fury. As Wang is now
> attending a Party training program at Jiujiang, the
> harbor city on the Yangtze, his absence allows the
> eruption of a volcano of anger. Workers in righteous
> indignation take the opportunity to vent their long-
> accumulated anger toward him. All the walls in
> Chuju's factory have been plastered with posters in
> large characters and cartoons attacking the vile
> couple. They're painful for me to read or look at.
>
> Chuju has been missing for two days! Rumors
> say she's hiding somewhere in Jiujiang, plotting in
> desperation to reunite with Wang. Some say she's
> had an abortion to get rid of a wild seed. Her sinful
> deeds have shamed our family and blemished our
> ancestors. I hate that I can't act like Song Wu, the
> legendary hero of the Song Dynasty, who killed his
> lewd sister-in-law and her paramour to revenge his
> older brother. Nevertheless, I'll fight with you side-
> by-side to punish Wang and defend our family
> honor.
>
> Thanks to the justice-seeking masses, Chuju is
> revealed for what she is and is no longer able to
> hoodwink you. I hope you can be strong enough to
> take the blow and get rid of her, like dumping a
> bucket of dirty water. I've sent a similar letter to the
> leaders of your division's Party branch, hoping they
> can take good care of you.

The next day, during the morning break, an officemate
brought in the mail. I received a letter from Chuju. The

envelope, nearly as thin as an empty one and slovenly addressed, suggested no good news. Though I was eager to read it, my trembling hands delayed. The one page of almost illegible handwriting showed the intensity of her panic, and its blunt message left no doubt she'd already made up her mind.

Dapeng,

Sorry for the pains I've caused you. I'm fleeing the furious mobs in our factory. They're mercilessly humiliating me, happy to see my total destruction. Since our relationship is fatally damaged and the chance for us to live together comes too late, there's no way for me to return to you.

I'd never thought our marriage could be broken up in such an ugly way, and we three sisters all fall into misfortune. My oldest sister's husband has been in jail for 12 years. Minqing has been crippled by her husband and will use a pair of crutches forever, the result of another unhappy marriage. In the light of my current situation, my miserable mother might not live long.

I've admired you since I was a child, and I appreciate your arduous struggle for career advancement and our possible future reunion. However, I can no longer live like a widow with a living husband. Since your home visit, I've often blamed myself for my own weak character, unable to resist seduction in my lonely life. Now, when other roads are blocked to me, I want to liberate myself and get out of practically being a widow.

Please get rid of me, just like kicking a rock out of your path.

Chuju

I let out a roar and tore the letter into pieces. Slumping in my chair, head in my hands, I obsessed over the terrible scenario now facing me.

Several colleagues came over and speechlessly stood near me. Dong Long gathered the paper shreds and pieced them together on the desk, "What a conniver!"

Aiming jostled him to read the letter then pounded my desk, "She's trampled you and defied our socialist system!"

A few days later, Father wrote to inform me that Chuju had been found, brought back to the factory, locked in a room, and forced to write confessions and self-criticism. Father also met Auntie Wu, her mother, to declare the end of our families' ties, begun in 1938 when the Japanese troops pushed us into Jiangxi together.

Then a letter came from Wang's wife, full of grief, "Your wife brought her services into our home while I was away ... We have three children and had a nice life together. Why should our home be broken?"

Paired with Chuju's words, "Please get rid of me, just like kicking a rock out of your path," I now realized without a doubt what they were up to. Wang was trying to divorce his wife and replace her with Chuju. I vowed that plot wouldn't succeed.

With a short note, I answered the woman: "For the sake of your children, you should refuse a divorce. That is the only way to foil their schemes."

Vice Secretary Lanyu Rong, with a soft heart under her Bolshevik crust, privately conferred with me, expressing solicitude from our division Party branch. As a final touch, she said, "Some people have smooth lives, others don't. We want you to be strong."

Normally I preferred to face hardships quietly rather than begging for help or mercy. Now, the game was as good as lost. I had only one possible move. I pleaded, "Could our leaders continue the effort to bring Chuju and me together?"

Rong frowned, "Since her wrongdoing has been caught by the masses, our plan and effort to help your reunion must be suspended. After the factory's Party committee has reached a verdict on her case, we'll discuss what to do."

Like a head-on blow, Rong's words plunged me into darkness. I knew it was no use to repeat my entreaty.

I started a series of letters asking for Huaizhong Wang to be punished. The first two were addressed to the Jiangxi Province Industrial Bureau and the Party's provincial supervisory committee, requesting they do something to salvage the Party's reputation. That's all I was able to do at the moment.

That night, I went to see Director Gu at his new place downtown. Though it was already 11 o'clock, he listened to my grievance patiently. Finally, he offered his clear-cut advice: "You need to change your one-track mind and be realistic. The quickest way to save yourself is divorce. You're young and on the way up. Once you're single, nice girls will become available. Even a former comrade-in-arms, a high-ranking cadre now, is asking me to look for a good man for his daughter."

Most of my coworkers also urged me to divorce to rid myself of the pain and legal burden. Seeing no other way out, I wrote a letter to Pingxiang County Civil Court to inquire about divorce procedures. A quick response from the court told me that I didn't have to appear to apply for a divorce, which could be done via correspondence. The court would investigate and decide whether I had sufficient grounds.

I still had much to say to Chuju. I took out the long letter from under my mattress. I didn't want to read what I'd written, I had just tried to express my feelings fully and strongly. For several months, since the day before I left Pingxiang, I'd kept adding to it when the spirit moved me. No matter what it amounted to—a review, a complaint, a confession, or an accusation—I didn't care. I was as crazy as an ancient scholar burning a letter to a deceased lover, though I was writing to an unfaithful wife. It was 16-pages long already.

7

In late June, students and government employees in Beijing hurried to help the peasants harvest wheat, as in previous years. Our institute needed to dispatch a hundred workers to a village near Tianjin. I voluntarily joined the taskforce.

The first day, I worked hard to keep up with the others in the fields. That night, moisture rising from the dirt floor passed through my thin layer of loose straw, soaking my sheet. In sweat-drenched underwear, I became chilled and began to shiver. I struggled out to work, but by noon I had a high fever. The scorching sun made it difficult for me to breathe. Drinking polluted water from the fly-mottled ditch was taking its toll. The second night, I got up at least ten times, and stepped over my sleeping roommates to run to the stubbly wheat field to relieve myself.

At first, I assumed I had only diarrhea, but the symptoms grew to resemble severe dysentery, which I'd suffered from in 1944, when we refugees crowded into a foothill village. Unlike then, now—under the simultaneous attacks of illness, famine, and my wife's betrayal—I felt I could die.

All day, every day, I lay alone on the ground on a loose layer of mildewed straw. Above the damp straw under my bed sheet I spread a large cloth coated with oil, to prevent moisture from seeping up from the soil. Tung oil extracted from a Chinese variety of paulownia is highly repellant to water and termites. People in my home province believed it to be the best for painting coffins. During our town's evacuation in 1944, my father used that very cloth to protect our belongings from the rain. Then, in October 1949, he gave it to me to wrap my belongings in when I boarded at high school. It had followed me ever since. Though threadbare in places and no longer very waterproof, in my fevered stupor, I took in its strong odor. It wafted from around my pillow and evoked the newly painted coffins of my childhood town.

Trying not to disturb me, my coworkers whispered as they walked past. In my clouded thoughts, they were planning how to wrap the oilskin tarp around my corpse. I was sure Chuju would not attend my funeral.

A healthcare worker gave me a few pills, and over the next several days, I lay in bed, waiting for them to work. Gradually, I ran to the latrine less often, but I was still too weak to remain standing.

On the evening of the sixth day, a truck from the institute arrived laden with cabbages and supplies. Our harvest team commander persuaded the driver to take me back to the institute. I cleared a corner of the truck bed as my nest. Surrounded by freight, I sat on my sleeping roll wrapped in the tarpaulin, leaning against crates and baskets. The country road we took was bumpy, and the smell of cabbage and earthy potatoes was nauseating. As evening came the stars blinked, as if imitating Chuju's aloofness over my suffering. For the first time in my life, I was attacked by both natural and manmade calamities.

8

Alongside the good medical care given by the two nurses at our small clinic, my coworkers at the dorm treated me nicely. Holding teacups and cigarettes, they often spent time with me, creating instant tea parties.

The famine suspended political struggles for the time being. Without the constant inciting of suspicion among our coworkers, human relations within our dorm became warmer and more carefree than before.

As winter approached, I often stayed in the southern room opposite mine. Sunlight slanted through the window, creating slowly shifting warm spots on the beds.

And there was a new attraction, an electric iron that Dong Long bought at a secondhand store and anchored upside down, supporting it with an inverted bamboo stool. We thus had a miniature stovetop on which to reheat mess-hall food. We treated ourselves to boiled spinach with soy sauce, which, without oil, tasted like grass, but gave us something to chew. Sometimes we would make salty, hot soup to share with our dorm mates, warming our bodies and spirits.

The two single men, Junior Mu and Minggui An, frequently came to my room for a casual chat. Since they were also the only two Party members of our research group living in the bachelors' dorm, their show of warmth reflected the concern of the Party branch, which had cleared the friendship between us of ideological barriers.

Mu had a strong sense of duty to enhance morale in our ranks and guard Party interests; however, most of the time, technical experts dominated group meetings, which frustrated him and hurt his self-esteem. Seeing that the timid scholars would keep a respectful social distance, he sought comradeship elsewhere. Given his broad smile and open-mindedness toward me, I assumed he'd heard positive comments about me at the Party's cell meetings. Minggui An, still haunted by his 1959 public humiliation and the rudeness of the other coworkers, was eager for my support and understanding.

One day, I presided over our group study of materialist dialectics through Chairman Mao's work, *On Contradiction*. Everybody recited, "External causes are the conditions for change, and internal causes are the basis. External causes become operative through internal causes." Every speaker then quoted the oft-repeated adage: "The right temperature can change an egg into a chicken, but no temperature can change a stone into a chicken because of their different compositions."

The officemate, whom we'd once criticized at a group meeting for hiding in the dorm to study math during office hours, took the opportunity to make a nasty remark: "I get it.

If a stupid man had a chance to study abroad, he would return as stupid as before." Sitting opposite the desk, An glowered at the offender. He knew, as did all of our group members, the innuendo was aimed at him. For years, jealous coworkers had laughed at him for squandering his opportunity to study in the Soviet Union and learning little of use due to his shaky knowledge of basic physics.

I said, "We should use Chairman Mao's work to enhance our own political consciousness, not to judge others' problems. And we should work to increase group unity, not undermine it."

After the meeting, I dragged the offender by his collar and pressed him to apologize to An. He gave me a cheeky grin, "I'm nobody. A great man gives no thought to my casual words."

Later I told An, "You should forgive him. He suffered from mental problems when he was a teenager." An smiled gratefully. The incident brought us closer, and after that he opened up more about his true feelings.

On New Year's Eve, 1962, our institute's YL held a dance party to display revolutionary optimism. The young female lab workers, recruited from small towns in 1956, were shy but eager to participate. Equipped with basic ballroom skills learned in Russia, Minggui An warmly offered to help them. But one after another they declined his offer. Frustrated, he put his heavy coat on and rushed out. I followed him to his dorm.

He threw his hat and scarf onto his bed, "Those moron girls. They still treat me as politically suspect."

"Don't think that way. They're not as snobbish as you think."

"Yes, they are. They all danced with me on the Tenth National Day in 1959. Now, they refuse me because I'm a political suspect." He started crying, "Dapeng, you can prove my loyalty to the Party and how much I love Chairman Mao.

Can't you?"

"Yes, I can. But you must've said something wrong."

"I privately complained to the typist, Big Sister Cui, about how Party cadres in the countryside have bullied peasants." He gnashed his teeth with hatred, "She looked like a gentle, honest woman. How could I expect her to blab my words during the 1959 campaign? I was put on stage with Director Gu and denounced as a right-wing opportunist."

I pressed his shoulder, urging him to sit down, "I don't want to say anything different from public opinion, but as your friend, I certainly feel you've been punished too harshly just for immaturity. Your study in the Soviet Union allowed you to miss the 1957–58 storms at home. When you returned, you knew nothing of the new tricks. You're not the only one. Many Soviet-trained guys were hit."

He blinked, "Nobody told me that. You're smart."

"I'm not smart. But as an onlooker, I see the game more clearly than you do." I hesitated, "May I say something more about what you've neglected?"

"Yes, please."

Knowing he was an honest man from a peasant family, I assumed the manner of a village elder, "People around us are all poor, but everyone dreams of having something fancy. Your camera, radio, wool coat, and fur hat brought back from Soviet Union have made them jealous. And your mixing Russian into casual chat has added fuel to their envy. In peaceful times, they only gossiped behind your back, harshly measuring your ability and work performance against those rare belongings. Then, the 1959 campaign gave the jealous ones a chance to cheer for your downfall. When a wall is about to fall, everybody wants to give it a push. Don't take it personally."

He smiled through his tears, "I should've known you earlier."

One or two evenings a week, Junior Mu and Minggui An absented themselves from the dorm. I knew they were attending inner-Party briefings and listening to speeches from top Party leaders. Around ten o'clock I'd hear their steps on our staircase. Often, they came to see me before returning to their rooms.

I was usually in bed reading. They'd stand in the middle of the small room, excited to have privileged information. Each liked to start a story with, "They say …" Much of the news—such as how the Soviet Union had exploited China in trade by imposing unfair exchange rates, or how Khrushchev had forced China to pay more than three billion US dollars for the arms supplied by Stalin during the Korean War—confirmed what I'd already heard.

One evening they arrived full of news about Albania and Cuba. Junior Mu, in the manner of a man of combat, shook his fists to stress his points, "They say, because the Albanian Communist Party supported us in our dispute with the Russians, Soviet submarines surfaced in the Adriatic during their withdrawal. Khrushchev, the son of a bitch, did that to signal to the Western imperialists that they can invade that poor country."

Minggui An spoke proudly of China's aid to Cuba, "They say, during the Bay of Pigs Invasion last April, Soviet bombers and missiles were deployed just for blackmail purposes. They didn't work at all, like scarecrows. On the other hand, our arms shipments arrived on time and played an important role in defeating the US troops. Che Guevara personally tested several anti-tank grenades made by us. He was pleased."

After An and Mu left, enchanting scenes of Cuba and Albania, which I'd seen in our documentaries, danced in my mind. A vigilant Albanian soldier stood atop a high peak, facing the Adriatic Sea, an eagle hovering against a blue sky. Happy Cubans danced under palm trees on a Caribbean beach. I was warmed by their concern.

They must've been instructed to stay close to me and nurture me as a potential candidate for Party membership, but they didn't know how to proceed. Instead, they just told me what had excited them. In my solitude, the special treat of having classified information refreshed me like ginseng. I also realized that the closer I grew to the Party, the more informed I would be.

                                    9

In the spring of 1962, Professor Karl Terzaghi—an international giant in our field, and Huang's instructor at Harvard University in the late thirties—published an article emphasizing the significance of natural rock stresses in tunnel design. It caused Huang great exuberance. He asked me to write a paper for our engineering community calling for awareness and going into the technical details. He titled it, 'A Review of the Techniques of Rock Stresses Measurement', and promised to have it published in a later issue of the *Journal of Hydraulic Engineering*. I could tell that, besides the importance of the theme, he wanted to fully bring out the latent potential of his disciples.

As a parallel mission, he told me to organize a group of field experiments and be ready to join a national taskforce at the Yili River Power Station in Yunnan Province. It was originally designed by Czechoslovakian experts, who'd left China following the split in the socialist camp. I was excited that we were to replace the Czechoslovakian experts and clean up the mess left by our Great Leap. Carrying the specific question raised by Karl Terzaghi, I felt challenged to answer it and come up with practical solutions for the Yili River engineering problem.

In three months, I summarized what I'd learned from Western publications and drafted a report on natural rock stresses for Professor Huang's examination. On an August afternoon, he rang and asked me to pick up my manuscript, which he'd reviewed. I went to his office. Sitting in a leather chair, he showed me what he had marked in the margins and asked me to revise accordingly. When I stood to leave, he raised his hand.

After a lengthy pause, he said, "You're in your prime and lucky to be dealing with a world-class problem. I'm glad you're working hard to meet the challenge, even as most people stay idle during the famine. I believe that these times produce their heroes. In the next seven or eight years, our own experts, genuine experts, will come out ahead internationally."

His earnest air conveyed his high expectations for me. Feeling energized, and closer than ever to Professor Huang, I stifled an impulse to appeal for help, "I consider myself the most fortunate one. With your hands-on instruction and the division Party branch's support, I've been compelled to work harder and more efficiently so as not to let you and the other leaders down."

My aggrieved tone, contradicting my decisive words, seemed to have confused him: "Is something wrong?"

I lowered my head, "I married two years ago but have only spent five days with my wife. She's still a thousand miles away, and has been involved in a scandal with her boss. We have no way to be reunited. I know it's utterly improper to bother you with my personal troubles, but I hope you would help me if a chance comes up."

As he cleaned his glasses with a handkerchief, the wrinkles on his face contorted into irregular patterns, "It's a pity that we have a hundred ways to waste people's talent. I'm willing to help you but unable to do so right now." He put his glasses on, "In the next two or three years, after finishing the tasks you've undertaken, you'll be outstanding in your field. Then I can speak aloud to push your case through my higher-ups."

"Is the work in my hands so crucial?"

My question galvanized him, and he rocked forward in his chair, "Karl Terzaghi's article specifically spells out his anxiety about tunnels built through basalt. The cooling process during its formation develops vertical joints and cuts basalt into detached columns, so that the horizontal stress might be zero. It's very bad for a tunnel's stability. We have a high pressure conduit and an underground plant excavated in solid basalt."

"Along with the Himalayas," I said, "the upheaval of the mountains around Yili Station has been continuing for millions of years. In that region, the horizontal stresses must be greater than the vertical ones, dominating them. The large folds of rock formations in the geological maps demonstrate this."

"But you have to prove this by field measurements. If you can find the numerical values of the natural stresses in the basalt, not only will our design of the underground structures be based on a new concept, but a gap in science and technology will have been filled." He tapped the desk with one hand and rocked gently in his swivel chair, "If things go very well, Karl Terzaghi might invite you to visit him in the US."

I smiled, "It sounds like a dream. The US is our number-one enemy. Without Party membership, my going abroad is like climbing into the sky."

With lips tightened, he nodded as if turning his thoughts to things distant, "He has students everywhere, and some of them are well established in Europe. So, going to England is more realistic. I hope you get the chance to learn advanced measuring techniques from the West. Hast, the Swedish professor, has done an excellent job in the deep gold mines of South Africa."

I shook my head in disbelief while he spoke almost to himself. Then he slid his chair sideways, into close range. In a low voice, he said, "Under the pincer attack of the US and the USSR, we have to reach out and expand our ties with Western Europe and Japan. A silent selection is going on for candidates to study abroad."

"I guess this time, fewer will be selected, but they will be of better quality than those sent to the Soviet Union in the fifties."

He patted the edge of his desk, "In that whole decade, our leaders emphasized political performance to the extreme, so we sent a lot of mediocre graduates. The wrong policy has stunted the growth of our culture and science. It probably led the Soviets to believe that all Chinese people have low IQs."

I replied equally quietly: "I heard Lizhi Xu, the talented mathematician and Party member, studied in London after the Liberation. He must've won respect there. He should be a good example for our leaders as to why to pick the best professionals—while keeping Party membership a must, as Xu is, of course."

He stood up and roamed from the desk to the sofa and typewriter table, stretching his arms and twisting his neck, "This time you're in good shape and stand a better chance than other potential nominees."

"I hope I get the chance but don't count on it. In 1956, I flirted with candidacy for graduate study in the Soviet Union. It ended up as a joke."

"Things have changed. Since our country can no longer afford to send mediocre personnel abroad, the final decision can't be made solely by political cadres. I'll be in a position to recommend and defend the person I consider most qualified."

"Thank you for your special teaching and support. But Party membership supersedes all other conditions."

"That's why your division's Party leaders have paid so much attention to you. You must comply with their requirements. Two years from now, if you can achieve what we've planned, I'll be bold and support you to win all the rewards you deserve, including the opportunity to study in Western Europe."

I smiled, "If Heaven bestows such a windfall on me, my other problem will be easily solved."

He sighed, "There's no Heaven. You have to struggle. Until you get a break from your bad luck, show great patience and self-restraint."

10

The summer of 1962 drew to a close as the last August heat-wave subsided. With September came the launch of tourist season in Beijing. The capital-city residents sensed signs of economic recovery earlier than people elsewhere because Beijing enjoyed food-supply priority. With more meat and vegetables available for residents in our mess hall, everyone in our dorm felt awakened, as if from a long hibernation.

Under the Party's new policy, the previously banned piece-rate wage system was restored, and every factory worker received a bonus for above-quota production. Meanwhile, free markets in rural areas, once viewed as hotbeds of capitalism, were allowed to exist, even flourish. Grocery stores had additional goods, such as cookies, candies, and cooking oil, some at fixed prices, others negotiable, showing that the government would allow higher prices. These new measures had a healing effect and helped salvage the nation's economy.

Some moderates on the Party's central committee seemed eager to heal the spiritual wounds the previous campaigns had inflicted on the nation's intellectuals. When their passionate, supportive speeches were read aloud by our institute's Party secretary, it warmed our hearts. For several weeks, our political studies were officially entitled Meeting of Venting Grievances, or Immortals' Meeting, and the secretary pledged there would be neither retaliation nor punishment for anything we said.

I believed his sincerity, but this promise would become void if he or his boss should one day be knocked down. While old hands remained skeptical, three excited young men in our group talked as if they were in a comedic skit, laughing about the Great Leap and People's Communes. I slackened my job of taking minutes, not jotting down their harsh words, especially sensitive requests like, "let's reexamine the 1957 Anti-Rightist Campaign." I hoped, without the words on record, people with average memories would forget what these rough-and-ready guys had said.

Meanwhile, another new Party program, Reexamination and Differentiation, exonerated most Party members who, in 1959, were labeled as right-deviating opportunists. Our ministry held special rallies to apologize for the groundless allegations against such people as Director Gu and Minggui An. Only a few top leaders in our ministry weren't exonerated, due to their close ties to Dehuai Peng, the former defense minister.

On weekends, the music of *Madame Butterfly* flowed from the radio. A few left-wing foreign films playing in urban theaters were meant to remind us of capitalist societies' inequality and injustice, but the landscape and lifestyles we saw on the other side of the globe were like fresh air. All those new things indicated that our cultural inspectors had loosened their censorship, and had a more tolerant view of capitalism.

While a spring-like atmosphere drew those around me to shopping or sightseeing, I tried to make use of my spare time by studying math. Then a judge from my home county sent me a letter.

> Based on the conclusions of the Party committee at Chuju Wu's working unit, I will approve your divorce. Before issuing the certificate, I want to give you a chance to reconsider. She has admitted to having committed adultery, an unforgivable mistake, under the influence of bourgeois ideology, and has repented for squandering your patience. As she has shown remorse in court and said, "If my husband can forgive me, we don't have to divorce," I need to know your final decision.

My feelings were mixed. I was barely moved by Chuju's remorse, as it came so late. After she'd destroyed the bridge between us, nobody could bring her to me. If we could live together, she might turn over a new leaf. If only someone could authorize that, I wouldn't care about the cost.

With the letter in my pocket, I waited outside the division leader's office, reading the posters and bulletins on the walls. Around six o'clock, Lanyu Rong led me in and waved me over to take a seat on the sofa. As usual, our technical director sat in a corner like a wooden statue. His presence didn't bother me, but I couldn't relax once I spotted Secretary Jiang in the inner room eavesdropping.

I quietly gave the letter to Rong. She read it carefully, her finger tracing the lines, then returned it to me, "You should make your own decision."

I pressed my hands against my throbbing temples, "I don't know what to do. If we were now living together, I would swallow my pride, bear the pain, and try to forgive her. If we're kept a thousand miles apart, our marriage is only a burden to us both, a bleeding wound, and divorce the only option."

Rong dropped her official air, poured me a cup of tea, and spoke like a big sister, "We've worked hard to get a residence permit for Chuju and almost succeeded. What a pity she ruined it and dragged you into hot water. Now, we don't have a perfect record with which to compete with other divisions on your behalf. Their candidates for family reunion are also highly qualified, but their wives have fine moral characters. If we insist on giving the golden opportunity to a woman with a bad reputation, we'll be accused of losing our principles. You've failed because of Chuju's behavior, not because we gave up."

Despite her soft manner, her decisive words made it clear the door for Chuju to come to Beijing was permanently shut. I raised my head to face her, "I want to relocate to Changsha, even to my home county, because there are no measures that save both my career and my marriage."

Rong scowled: "No. The Party entrusts you with important tasks and wants to cultivate you as an expert."

"Thanks to the Party organizations and various leaders. But, as an ordinary worker, I'm not indispensable. It's easy to find someone to substitute for me."

She slapped her desk, "We've increasingly put more responsibility on you and happily seen your growth. Please don't belittle the tasks on your shoulders for personal purposes. These are not personal matters. How can you abandon the Revolution for a worthless woman?"

A whimpering noise came from my throat, "Then I'm at a dead end. The only exit is divorce."

She spread out both hands to show her inability to help, "You have to make your own decision."

Secretary Jiang drifted in from the inner room and stood in front of us. His eyes blinked rapidly behind his glasses, and then the words came out, as solemn as his speech on stage: "We see you as an asset to our professional ranks. It would be wrong to let a loose woman hold you back and demoralize you. I hope you can have enough willpower to stand the severe test of personal disaster."

He folded his arms across his chest and focused on a remote object outside the window. In a more sentimental tone, he said, "In the early fifties, when we read the Soviet novel *How the Steel Was Tempered* and then watched the movie, we all vowed to learn from the main character, Pavel Korchagin. We were all touched by Pavel's fortitude in parting from Tonya, his girlfriend since high school, because her cheap individualism had become unbearable to him. Pavel's final statement to Tonya was, 'I would be a poor husband to put you before the Party, for I shall always put the Party first, and you and my other loved ones second.' It has become the strongest voice of the times."

Such popular phrases from the early fifties, which once reverberated over our land, now sounded out of tune. While I felt the air swell in my ears, Rong added, "Since Khrushchev's betrayal of communism, the Soviets have forgotten the tradition of the October Revolution—but we haven't. Instead, we carry it on."

I returned to my dorm, my stomach in spasms from hunger. Having had no dinner, I lay in bed, unable to sleep. After hours of hesitation, I got up and wrote a letter to the judge, "To emancipate myself from the painful relationship, I resolutely confirm my request for divorce."

I stayed awake the rest of the night, lost in thought. Mailing that letter would be like spilling water on the ground. There would be no way to retrieve it. A marriage foreclosed, with conjugal rights virtually unconsummated, would be an incomplete cycle of human life. Mailing that letter now would be my unconditional surrender to brutal mockery.

After another fitful sleep and more hours of contemplation, I stashed the letter to the court under my mattress.

That evening, I took it out and looked at it, feeling I was not ready to mail it. Then, I walked to the nearby post office and mailed the long letter to Chuju, a pamphlet into which I had poured my heart since the tragedy first struck. She probably wouldn't read it. To sting her to do so, I added a big-character note on top of the 40 pages:

> I hope the remorse you have shown to the judge is sincere, and this letter will help you to recognize what a disaster you've brought me. If you can search your soul to reveal your sin, open your heart to repent, and make a truthful pledge to me, I'll seriously negotiate with you. Before our wedding, you vowed to be single forever if I didn't marry you. Then, facing Director Gong as our witness, you promised to make a clean break with Wang. You can't get around such cheating and betrayal without examining them, nor by only lightly touching upon them.

11

October 1, 1962, was National Day, when the whole nation celebrated our recovery from the three-year disaster, I waited for Chuju's response to my long letter. The day before, my high-school friend Hot Chili, the cardiologist, had invited me twice over the phone to have dinner with her family for the holiday. She was happy about her new two-bedroom apartment, a luxury for low-ranking professionals.

The famous Fuwai Hospital stood near the tower of Fucheng Gate, offsetting the shabby roadside stores. Its modern facilities, carefully selected medical crews, and well-manicured gardens served only high-ranking officials and celebrities. Without my acquaintance with Hot Chili as my entrée, I wouldn't have been able to approach it.

In the late afternoon, I signed the guest ledger in the reception hall and made my way to her home near the Inpatient Department. While her husband, Dr Cai, was busy in the kitchen, Hot Chili started the conversation: "My younger sister graduated from Xi'an Teachers University last summer. She's teaching at a high school in Beijing. You remember her?"

"Of course," I sensed where this was going, "She had a fine singing voice too. I can remember her standing on tiptoes when she hit the high notes of *The White-Haired Girl* during the 1950 high tide in the struggle against the landlords."

"She was Chuju's classmate," Hot Chili said, "We talked about Chuju, and frankly, she had good things to say about her—a quiet, shy, and well-disciplined girl. People liked her. Do you know what aspect of her has impressed me the most?"

"You're not easily impressed."

"I was deeply touched by Chuju. In 1955, during the Campaign of Eliminating Counterrevolutionaries, my father was arrested. He was accused of burning all classified documents he'd held as the personnel manager of the Fuxin Coal Mine Bureau in 1948. That happened when the communist army was approaching and the nationalist government's employees were hastily evacuating."

"I read the few lines about your father's case in *The Yangtze Daily*. I was sure he'd just carried out the order from his boss to burn the documents. Why should he be accused of acting in a personal manner? The next year I heard your father was released."

"We were both in Wuhan then. You didn't contact me for a whole year."

"I was very busy with my last year of school; it would have taken a long day to visit your campus."

"That's probably true. But I suspected you were also afraid of meeting me, the daughter of a counterrevolutionary."

"Sorry for not having expressed my sympathies at that time."

"If you had, it would have violated our political code. But it was hard for my younger sister to be shunned while all her friends stayed away from my family for a whole year. Chuju was the only exception. She walked my sister to school every day as though nothing had happened to us."

Before I could respond, she said, "Don't you think this proves Chuju is honest and sincere, rare qualities nowadays?"

I shook my head and leaned against the wall behind my stool, "I don't deny what you said. An ancient poem taught us, 'Spring water remains crystal clear in the mountains, but turns turbid rushing to the plain.' She's no longer the same Chuju."

She stood up, "I believe she got taken advantage of. You should forgive her. If she can escape our hometown, things might work out, you know?"

She paced to the window and pointed to the neighboring wing of the grayish-yellow building: "The cozy life in the suite-like wards of our hospital has made some old jerks reluctant to leave. They keep coming up with new symptoms, anything to stay. If you forgive Chuju and withdraw the case from the court, I'll pressure some high-ranking patients to help you get a

Beijing residence permit for her."

"How can you do that? Please don't sweet talk me like a bratty child."

"If I'd said this two years ago, you'd have blamed me for bragging. But, now, the big-shot patients have gotten to trust me, believing that I just say harsh words to their faces, and won't report their behavior behind their backs. Those pampered lords are mortally afraid of death. They hope I have a bag of tricks to keep them alive a little longer. Now, a sixth-rank cadre is very submissive to me. He used to be the boss of the current minister of public security."

Her husband, Dr Cai, had finished cooking. Their bigger bedroom was also the sitting and dining room. He started setting the table, "Some Chinese experts have recently come back from Canada and Australia, and joined the research divisions at our center, such as plastic surgery and dermatology. We'll help you to gain access to them."

After we finished dinner and he took the dishes to the kitchen, I said to Hot Chili, "He spoils you. You've become bossier."

She laughed, "Maybe. But I'm not pushing you to forgive Chuju, just hoping you have a broad mind and can prepare yourself for a reconciliation."

At around 5:30 pm, the din from the yard and a distant rumble from the street informed me that crowds were flooding toward Tiananmen Square and occupying the high ground of downtown Beijing to see the fireworks for National Day.

Hot Chili put a sweater on and hung a jacket on her arm, "We're escorting some big-shot patients to the hill on the north side of the Palace Museum, the best place to see the fireworks. We have a special pass and reserved seats over there."

"May I go with you?"

"No. You stay here until we come back."

"Why?"

"We need you to help entertain our guest."

"Who's that?"

Someone knocked on the door.

Hot Chili opened the door, and I saw a young woman with a resemblance to Hot Chili's mother, and who was a head taller than her father. She must be Hot Chili's younger sister. Though we hadn't seen each other for ten years, she called me by name at first sight. Then, she turned back to someone lagging behind in the dim hallway, "Come on in. Nobody will eat you up."

The two sisters pulled in nobody else but Chuju. I was shocked by the whole plot. That afternoon, while Hot Chili was persuading me to drop my request for a divorce, her sister had hidden Chuju somewhere else.

Before I could say anything, Hot Chili led her husband and sister outside. Closing the door, she said, "Be nice to her. You're 28 now. Don't you remember the saying, 'A premier's heart is large enough to pole a boat in'? A great man should be big-hearted."

12

Chuju was dressed in the sapphire-blue, cashmere sweater and navy-blue, wool-blend pants I'd bought her for our wedding, and she'd kept them like new. Even her handbag was the one I gave her. She was playing the part of a sinner returning to virtue.

I walked to the window while she stood by the door. From the height of the third floor, I watched the noisy crowd on the ground, "When did you come?"

"Yesterday." Her tone was standoffish.

I turned to assess her expression. She blushed, but her color faded in seconds. Recalling the scene of our last parting and what she'd promised Gong, the director of the women's association of her factory, I was filled with fresh hatred: "It's time for us to get the divorce certificate. Did you ask the court to hold off?"

"I begged the judge to give me a final chance, and Director Gong personally talked to him to prove my sincerity."

"Sincerity? When hundreds of posters in the factory revealed your scandal with Wang, you wrote to ask me to kick you like a rock out of my path. In fact, you'd kicked me out of your way to marry Wang. Is that sincerity?"

She sat down on the bed, "Sorry, Dapeng, the mobs made my name stink. I was afraid you'd toss me out like a pair of worn-out shoes. In desperation, I turned to Wang for a way to escape from my doom, it wasn't by choice."

"And now, since the Party committee foiled Wang's plot to divorce his wife, you're driven to the wall, and you come to pick me up like a scrap of wood you'd thrown into the ditch. How can I forgive you for all the insults and damage? Have you read my long letter?"

"Yes. It awakens me from a nightmare."

"I doubt it."

"I read it all. I'm not an intellectual, but I know I was wrong. When my mind is all mixed up, I can't answer your questions point-by-point."

"What guarantees you'll be a faithful wife?"

She got up from the bed, shuffled across the room, and knelt at my feet. Holding my thighs, she sobbed, "It's all my fault. You can punish me, beat me up, but don't let me go. I'll take good care of you and be a model wife." She jerked spasmodically, "I'm going to serve you like your dog to make up for what I did."

Her voice was piteous. I stroked her hair, "The night before I left our town, 20 months ago, you refused to sleep with me. Soon after I left, you delivered your sexual services to Wang's home when his wife was away."

"I'm guilty, Dapeng. I know how much you've suffered

since our wedding. I owe you a debt of gratitude. I promise to be nice to you forever. I want to repay you with all I have and in every way I can."

She stopped sobbing. Her arms tightened around me, and her head rolled and rubbed against my belly. In the chilly autumn weather, the thin fabric of my pants offered no insulation against the heat and friction from her face, and her feverish movements began to overpower my resolution. As she slid down farther and her nose wriggled into my crotch, the 28-month-old passions, which were so hard to suppress on the wet floor at Beijing Railway Station when I pulled her up from behind, were reignited. They anesthetized me and obliterated all the pain and bitterness she'd caused me.

When I lifted her from the floor, she pressed her wet lips on mine. Her probing tongue released an intoxicating sensation I'd never before experienced, as if casting an anchor into the depths of my heart.

Gradually, we shifted toward the bed.

The minute she spread a blanket to cover the bed and lined the central area with a towel taken from her bag, I saw a hot Chuju for the first time. I was spellbound, unable to resist.

Returning to me stark naked, she lay down, "Poor Dapeng, you squandered the night we had in Changsha. You shouldn't have been so nervous. We should've stayed together that night."

I sighed, "I enjoyed our wedding night. The marriage certificate was our permit, I wasn't afraid and didn't want to hurry. I thought we'd be together from then on, and forever. Who could have expected that your period would end the honeymoon? And then that Wang, the raven, would occupy my nest?"

"Don't say anymore." She muffled my mouth with a breast, then turned and pulled me on top of her. With her arms and legs twining around me like grape vines, she wrapped herself around me with maximum contact. Her tender skin slid over me like silk, and a rich fragrance rose from her neck and shoulders. It was the green perfume, Dew on Flowers, advertised as distilled from honeysuckle flowers and lotus leaves. Slowly, her meticulous caressing released passion from my frustration.

She stopped my frantic movements in the beginning and took the lead in setting my tempo and range. As time spun out, her delicate smell mesmerized me, and I felt like an immortal mounting the clouds. The fireworks projected into the sky above downtown Beijing were crackling, spluttering and whistling. The festival atmosphere and collective gaiety had also dispersed the anger and sadness gnawing at my heart. At that moment, my body and soul were entirely under her control. She guided me with her body's signals and pressure, as if following a premeditated routine, to achieve a satisfaction I'd never imagined, synchronizing her orgasm with mine.

Her wild and experienced action had captured me. At last, I had the sex I'd hoped for. Though not enough to soothe my 28-month ordeal, it was a sizable amount, salvaged from our wrecked marriage. Lying calmly beside her, I felt it would not be as easy to leave her as I'd phrased in the letter to the court, which was still lying under my mattress in the dorm. *How nice if we could have lived like tonight ever since our wedding, or even from now on.* My abandoned desire to get together with her was rekindled, even though another part of me couldn't see any way we could live together.

The first round of fireworks was over; it must have been nine o'clock. During the interlude, the loudspeakers all over the city charged the air with the song 'Ode to the Motherland' to further boost the morale of the millions dancing and watching on the ground. The majestic martial music represented a strong, unified will, warning me no unauthorized plan or choice would prevail. In an hour or so, Hot Chili and her sister would come back and ask me what agreement we'd reached. I had no answer ready, and there would be no more time left for us to remain together. I wanted to salvage more from what was left for me. My desperate greed excited me again.

In the flush of her bewitching charm, she followed my lead. Facing sexual starvation, fully aroused again, she was more unbridled than ever. She turned to sit up and completed a half a somersault to straddle me. Her head bent and back arched, she held my head as if I was a breast-feeding baby until her mad moving had extracted the last drop of my essence.

The fireworks and martial songs had subsided, and the distant jabber of the returning crowds urged me to get dressed. Chuju restored the bed to its original shape. I waited for our hostess's family to come home while Chuju washed the towel in the kitchen, the only place with a sink.

The aftertaste of the night's activity depressed me with a sickening sweetness and extreme exhaustion. I was followed by an insipid sense, as if chewing wax. Feeling no willpower remained within me to resist her, I became hopelessly insecure. Later, when Hot Chili urged me to stay in the small room with Chuju for the night and the next few days, I said, "No, I need time to make a sober estimation of our situation. I'll answer you as soon as possible."

In my dorm, I lay awake until the next morning. Reviewing the scene at Hot Chili's home, I saw Chuju's skillful performance as a playback of her escapades with her boss. I felt nauseated by my shameful acceptance of sexual gratification with an elusive or non-existent love. She might love me temporarily as another man, not her husband, and her love was uncatchable and contaminated. Like a beggar overfed with oily food after a long period of starvation, I wanted to throw up everything I'd taken from her.

I felt sorry for her, too, because now things would go against her wishes. Perhaps I shouldn't have taken up her offer before making up my mind.

The next day I went to the hospital. During a brief interruption in her consultations, I apologized to Hot Chili for not following her passionate plan, and for squandering her goodwill and help. I handed her 30 yuan for Chuju, enough for a hard seat on the train home. That was all I had.

In the main post office of the Western District, I sent the letter to the Pingxiang County Court by registered mail. The moment the clerk stamped the postmark and threw the letter into a collection box, the last bond between Chuju and me was broken.

Two weeks later, in the middle of October, I received the certificate of divorce. It kept the phrases shown in the letter from the judge, which blamed Chuju's mistake of adultery under the influence of bourgeois ideology, and condemned her for squandering my patience and forgiveness during my home visit.

13

As my new routine began, I scrubbed my body with icy tap water in the lavatory. In the dim light, I ran through the woods and vegetable patches to reach a park, where, along with a large group, I practiced Tai chi with a famous master. The weather was cold but bearable. Coming back, I felt fresh and energized. Unlike some passive workers rushing along on bikes or packed into buses every day, I was lucky to have a long-term goal and some freedom to arrange my own schedule.

As long as Professor Huang expected me to become a genuine expert in my field and have a chance to study in Western Europe, I couldn't slacken for a single day. Sometimes I felt it was laughable to emulate Gou Jian, King of Yue, who slept on brushwood and licked pigs' gallbladders for 20 years until his final victory. Most of the time I tried to generate the willpower of ancient heroes to conquer my loneliness.

I stayed in the office for New Year of 1963. Thumbing through recent issues of an international journal, I found some papers written by Western scientists that made predictions with sophisticated math but didn't yet have the experimental data to support their conclusions. I guessed they couldn't afford to use enormous amounts of manpower as we had done. On the opposite side of the coin, our data from field testing were gained with great administrative effort and human cost but lay sleeping as raw materials. If I could process them with modern numerical analyses, the results would be valuable and impressive to a potential foreign adviser. He might guide me to get my paper published at an international conference. As the initial concept made me exuberant, I pounded my chest.

Then my shortage of certain skills cooled me down. I needed to study some specific algorithms and computer technology before I could solve the problems in my mind. The preparation alone might take me two years. Now, as the first step of a long journey, I began to read an introductory book on the binary system of computation and machine language. Since the 104 Machine, the first generation of transistor computers, had recently become available in China, the science and technology elites had been thronging around the few computation stations open to guest users. So far, I'd only had a tour through a hall with a 104 Machine flashing in red and green lights. Right now, I was busy with my mission of Yili Power Station. Later on, I'd punch holes on the black tapes to input my data and get my hands on the machine to print the results.

Around two o'clock, Dong Long came to our office. He grabbed the book I was reading and turned its pages. With a twisted jaw, he said, "Don't follow the fashion so quickly. I worry you'll stretch yourself too thin."

"I'm just curious about the new technology. I don't have time to really go into it, and no access to a computer. No harm to study the ABCs of it."

He suggested going to a restaurant and, on the way, swimming at the preparatory school for returning overseas Chinese people not far from our compound.

I was surprised, "That's a fancy place, and the pool isn't

open to the public."

"Yes, only celebrities and well-connected people can enjoy such a luxury in Beijing. I don't know how, but our administrator arranged a special session for us. What a deal: for 40 fens you'll see an exotic landscape and swim in the winter."

"I don't have swimming shorts."

"You can use my spare pair."

"How long have you been swimming there? You must have connections?"

"I don't go very often, only sometimes. My older brother is the chief commander of a regional garrison in our home province. I have a special card."

The school was located within a noisy district but hidden from the shabby surroundings by high brick walls. The campus looked like a large garden with a European-style architectural complex. Since many students were away for the winter vacation, the serenity accented the setting's aristocratic ambiance. In the twilight, I saw three young ladies, probably in their early twenties, sauntering near our path. Unlike us, bundled in bulky, cotton-padded coats, they wore colorful sweaters, close-fitting jackets, and skirts. Of gentle mien and dignified bearing, they reminded me of Ziwei Cao. During our schooling together, she'd tried hard to get rid of the Western influence from her upbringing and missionary school. Now, after living for eight years in the West, she had probably returned to her original self and become more bourgeois.

Dong Long looked in the same direction, "These fair ladies are treated like state guests, but political cadres probably see them as capitalist puppies or poisonous seeds. They might awaken your memory of Ziwei."

I slapped his back, "You're sharp, but I'm no longer 19. Ten years ago, Ziwei impressed me with her natural beauty. Now, the first thing that strikes me about these women is their innocence and vulnerability. When the next purge arrives, young girls who have grown up abroad will be an easy herd to prey on."

The glass-paneled swimming hall was heated with steam. The few returning overseas Chinese people shouted in mixed Cantonese and English. Their swimming skills, carefree manners, well-developed muscles, and tanned skin contrasted sharply with our scrawny physiques and self-restrained spirits. When I took a rest in a corner, Dong Long swam up to me, puffing, "Do you see a new purge brewing?"

"Sure. In recent months, Chairman Mao stressed we must talk about class struggles every year, every month, and every day. The Party Central has chosen certain rural areas to launch a pilot experiment called the Four Cleanups Movement. I feel the wind gathering clouds on the horizon."

He blinked for a while, "You shouldn't be afraid of that."

"The parcel sent by Ziwei two years ago must have alerted the security system that I have an overseas relationship. That could be used as ammunition against me, or at least act as a stumbling block on my way to Party membership."

"That makes sense, but you can't do anything about it."

"I have to do something about it. As people often say, 'Repair the roof before it rains.'"

14

The next Sunday, on my way back to our dorm from the office, I passed by the low brick wall near the leaders' apartments, where Lanyu Rong was pinning washing to a long rope hung between two trees. I slowed down. When she nodded to me, I said, "How are you, Big Sister Rong?"

"How are you, Dapeng?" She stepped a few yards closer and looked at the scars on my face, "When are you going to have plastic surgery?"

I'd delayed the discussion with Hot Chili about the surgery because I had worried she might hold a grudge against me for not following her advice about Chuju. Still, I said, "Before I go to Yunnan, I hope. But I don't know if it's possible."

We seemed to have nothing else to say, and she went back to hanging clothes. I stuttered, "I have a request to the Party's organization. It might be a wrong idea."

She beckoned to me, "Come in for a cup of tea."

I jumped over the fence and helped her stretch the wet things on the line. I hesitated, feeling embarrassed about disturbing her husband, the number-two leader of our institute, "I don't want to interrupt Director Su's peace. He needs to have a good rest."

"No problem. He's easygoing, he only looks solemn."

Since her husband was the number-two chief of our institute, their family could live in a three-bedroom apartment with a bright sitting room. Seated opposite her, sipping fragrant tea, I didn't know how to raise my request. Instead, I was engrossed by the combination of her innate purity and her upbringing in the violent Revolution.

Rumor had composed a story of her marriage. Sometime in 1947, when the PLA seized the northern city where, at the age of 16, she worked at a post office, Su, 30 years older than her, led a squad of detectives searching for residual KMT forces and found her playing with her friends in a park. Su followed her, and her boss helped him to marry her. The marriage might not have been happy at the beginning. Now they had four children and lived an easy and harmonious life. One thing was for sure, the old man wanted to please her all the time and acted upon whatever she insisted on.

She broke my reverie with a tray of soft candy, "The project in Yunnan isn't easy. Local leaders describe it as shoring up the third line of defense against a possible world war launched by the two superpowers. We trust you. I can see Professor Huang is counting on you and anxious about what results you'll get. Do you have any personal difficulties? What's your request to the Party branch?"

"Two years ago, we dealt with the parcel sent to me from Hong Kong. Ever since then, Comrade Bai, the head of our security office, has watched me with a suspicious air. In the past, whenever he met me on the road he would smile at me like a friend. So I want to ask the Party to find out the political status of my former schoolmate, Ziwei Cao."

She shook her head, "Don't look for trouble with someone overseas. There are so many women in Beijing, why look so far away for what's right under your nose?"

"Please don't misunderstand my intention. What I'm asking for is political clearance. I don't want a problem popping up in the next rectification or blocking my way into the Party. A pressing matter at the moment is my plan to do joint research with my peers in the defense industry. Without excellent political clearance, they'll turn me down flat. Since I have basic trust in Ziwei, I believe the investigation will get the result I'm hoping for."

She grinned in doubt, "Why, after a separation of so many years, do you still trust her?"

I leaned towards her: "Okay, I have a theory. A speculation, really, but it seems logical. During the 1955 Campaign of Eliminating Counterrevolutionaries, the student inquisitors were amateurs. Most likely, they sent an investigating letter to the residents' committee of the street in Guangzhou where her mother lived, and the committee replied with its suspicion of her father. Later, when the provincial public security bureau issued her a passport to visit her father, the highly professional security officers must've based their permission on accurate and positive information. So I choose to trust what the professionals trusted."

She pondered a while, "Plausible. But the process of getting information from abroad is an administrative labyrinth. We don't have a just cause to disturb the huge secret system."

In for a penny, in for a pound. I couldn't retreat: "Ziwei is an ordinary resident in Hong Kong, and I need to know only her political attitude or affiliation. I believe every educated Chinese person living abroad, or every government employee with overseas relatives, must have a special file in our security system. Her name must be in the sorting list of our overseas investigators, so the information must be here already. Can you help me out? I also hope the clearance can expedite my application for Party membership, even though my conditions for acceptance aren't quite mature yet."

She looked at her fingernails, then at me, "That's positive. Let me discuss it with the other leaders. Anything else important to tell me that you've seen or heard?"

I tried for a smile, "Since we left the 304th Geological Survey Brigade in western Hunan, the Wuhan branch of the Chinese Academy of Sciences has continued our work there. Its team leader, Guo, told me a story in a recent letter. In the winter of 1961, a geologist in his mid-thirties asked for a three-month leave to look for a spouse. The brigade leaders accused him of making trouble and rallied the masses to criticize him. He secretly sent a letter to Chairman Mao. Chairman Mao shocked the whole brigade by writing with a brush pen in the margin of the letter, 'If the situation you've presented is true, three months isn't too long, and you may leave until you've found a wife.' What a supreme instruction."

Rong grinned, "Really? I never heard that."

"Who would dare make up a story like that? The provincial Party committee treated it as top priority and dispatched a special envoy to the 304th. All the frustrated bachelors in that survey field said that Chairman Mao's solicitude had warmed their hearts like sunshine."

Seemingly warmed by the same sunshine, she said, "We've been taught by the Party to concern ourselves with the life of the masses. Now that even Chairman Mao, unimaginably busy, has shown such care for geologists, I feel duty-bound to help you. If our investigation tells that Ziwei Cao remains single and patriotic, that would be a double blessing on you."

"If that happens, I'll write to Chairman Mao for permission to write to her."

Her smile emerged. She pointed a finger at me, "Shut up."

15

Telegrams from the local leaders in Yunnan Province, endorsed by our ministry head, came, one after another, to require Structural Engineer Kang and me to arrive at Yili Power Station by the end of February. Due to our low ranks, we were not eligible to take an airplane. Once we reached the railway's southern terminal, we would face many days of hard travel by bus and truck through the mountains. As a special case—an emergency task—we were authorized to fly from Guangxi to Yunnan at the end of our railway trip.

Kang was well known in structural analysis. In his mid-forties, tall with a round face and long hair, he wore a bleached uniform, which his brother-in-law, a demobilized PLA soldier, had given him. It looked like a wide robe folded into creases, with the sleeves covering his fingertips. To keep the cuffs of the sleeves on his wrists, he habitually kept his hands up to his chest, whether talking or walking. His glasses frequently slid down to his nostrils, and so he kept his chin up to face his listener. Such physical features made him resemble Confucius carved in wood, hence he was called Confucian Kang.

In private conversation, he used natural language, avoided political clichés, and told the truth. Traveling with him, especially when he was bemoaning the state of the universe and pitying the fate of mankind, was like returning to the days before 1949, as if Confucian tradition still filled the air we breathed.

He had been geographically separated from his family for ten years. His wife taught at a countryside school and they had three children. Without enough grain distributed from the

People's Commune, they had to spend a large portion of their income to buy rice on the black market. However, he seemed to have forgotten such personal problems.

The construction site looked like a war zone after the Great Leap, the famine, and the sudden departure of the Czechoslovakian experts following the breakup of the Sino–Soviet relationship. Since Czechoslovakia had torn up its treaty with China on this project, the contracted supply of hydraulic turbines and special steel conduits was suspended.

Heavy equipment lay in the warehouse yard almost concealed by weeds. The 36-volt bulbs inside the tunnel had all been stolen by the workers and connected in series of six to match the 220-volt power supply in the living area. Half the wooden ties under the light-gauge railway had been used as fuel during the interruption.

We walked through the section of the high-pressure conduit built four years earlier. Under a flashlight, the concrete appeared loose and porous, and even shoes lost by hastily retreating crews were cast into it, as we saw on other sites. Water and silt from springs bubbled from weld seams, and flakes of rust a millimeter thick, a product of post-installation erosion, peeled from the steel conduit.

The leaders from our ministry and Yunnan Province, along with the invited experts, and guest workers, including Kang and I, held a summit on the site. As a consensus, they decided to demolish the poorly built sections of the project and halt construction until we could conduct thorough field experiments.

Confucian Kang took the position as the director of the steel conduit, full-scale pressure testing group, which was stationed near the bureau's headquarters. I was the vice director of the rock mechanics group.

The water-intake canal and the underground plant had an elevation difference of two thousand one hundred feet. My group was stationed at the middle height between them, where we could reach various sections of the tunnel. The provincial waterpower research center sent us six skillful men from Kunming. Adding local technicians and staffers to the group, we formed a team of 40 men and two women. And as our budget was to be covered as a part of the power plant's investment, we would have more than we needed.

I was exuberant to have such rich human and material resources. However, when I left the hostel for my field station, Kang looked at me over the dropping frame of his glasses, "Don't be too optimistic. We have people from four organizations. Peasants say, 'The fragrance of a newly built latrine will last for only three days.' Now, we're singing the song of large-scale communist cooperation, but soon we might face a situation like the one in the period of the Warring States, when China was divided into seven kingdoms."

I sighed, "That's too bad. Everybody is politically skilled after a 14-year class struggle. And the Sino–Soviet debate has taught us how to quote words and phrases from the Party's documents as weapons."

"Don't worry. If we're honest with the majority, we can survive and make progress."

A Party member from Wuhan, with the surname Lan, was appointed as our group director. His upturning chin, arms of two different lengths, and his unyielding air—of a bearer of principles—gave me a sense of discord and a presentiment of inner struggle. While I was trying to establish friendships with our group members, he checked everyone's family background, political stance, and personal problems, even urged them to render others' information. In less than a week, people called him Commissar Lan, likening him to the Party leaders in the Soviet's Red Army. Ironically, he wasn't irritated, while I saw more satire than compliment in it.

The local workers were mostly simple and warm, but they ignored etiquette while making fun of others. They even used coworkers' physical defects as inspiration for nicknames. However, I was glad to hear 'Commissar' being tossed around.

A Party member called Bing, who came from Wuhan along with Lan used to be a mechanic at an arsenal before going to university and was handy with instruments. Physically small, with dark skin and bristling hair, he often smiled, making wrinkles like fish tails spread toward his temples. Everybody liked him as an amiable man and an ingenious scientist. The native Yunnan coworkers called him Adept Bing. It also sounded well-fitting.

While Commissar Lan, a loner in solitary splendor, busied himself as if he was a secret agent for the police in the movies, I concentrated with my group members on technology and spent most of my time in the tunnel. With my high goal of answering the question raised by Karl Terzaghi, which would pave my way to Western Europe, I avoided confronting him as much as was possible.

Following on my heels, Junior Yu, a 1962 graduate, was sent by our institute to support me. An excellent ping-pong player, he arrived when the ongoing amateur contest had reached its semi-finals. He was likely to be the bureau champion, and he made a lot of friends through the game. Such an off-duty victory facilitated our work, especially when his fans at the machine shop and the logistics warehouse could help us.

Since measuring rock stresses needed new technology, we had to demonstrate what we thought would work. Unwilling to drop his pretentious airs and learn from others, Commissar Lan chose a corner and worked solely with a young man from Wuhan. They followed a book published by the Colorado School of Mines, which gave all the details of the techniques used to measure the rock stresses underneath the foundation of the Hoover Dam. They ground out a small area in the tunnel wall and polished it in order to attach strain gauges, then they used a drill to cut a circular groove around the gauges, deep enough to relieve the natural stresses in the rock. From the readings of the strain gauges and the physical parameters of the rock, we could calculate the original stresses.

The technique looked mature and not difficult to master. But the strain gauges, the glue, and the electronic readout device—all made in China—were not yet reliable. We all doubted his choice but didn't speak out.

I prepared something along the lines of Hast, a Swedish professor, who had invented a magnetic transducer and applied it successfully in the gold mines of South Africa. With help from my peers at Beijing Tectonics Research Center, I made the transducers and found them applicable at Yili River. However, the transducers needed to be installed deep in a hole, and we didn't have a compact geological drill nor a drill bit inlaid with diamonds. To cut the cylindrical slot concentric with the hole to relieve the stresses, we had to use a pneumatic drill to smash the rock. It was time-consuming and dangerous for the drillers. Yu and I decided to stash our devices away for future use.

Adept Bing had worked day and night to copy, from an advertising photo, a transducer made in Western Germany. The materials he used, such as violin strings, headphone magnets, and an oscilloscope, were all available and reliable. We were happy to see the vibrating wire transducer was stable and waterproof. Even the drillers were amused by the green ellipse shown on the fluorescent screen of the cathode ray tube. Still, we hadn't gotten any convincing data.

16

The bureau leaders, used to seeing a dynamic scene with large amounts of troops going full steam ahead, began to lose patience with our slow progress. They tried to find out an ideological cause for the unsatisfactory situation.

Section Chief Yang, assigned to be our political supervisor and administrative supporter, had implicit faith in Lan. It was graphically displayed on his astonished face when Lan told him, "I graduated from the Moscow Power Engineering Institute." That, plus his full CCP membership, must have made him the only red expert among us. As Yang's tough nature, tempered as a guerrilla soldier before 1949, was still overbearing, he could fire at anyone among us with the munitions Lan provided.

During a weekly briefing in the middle of May, Yang blamed someone's unhealthy mentality, criticizing me without naming me: "Someone seems to have been depressed by a broken marriage. A revolutionary man shouldn't behave like that. Compared with the great cause of building up our strategic rear, such personal misfortune is negligible."

My rage was almost uncontrollable. How could Lan go so far as to dig up my private complaints as a trophy to present to District Chief Yang? Nevertheless, when all the group members stared at me, either showing sympathy or waiting for my response, I kept silent as if I wasn't aware that Yang had targeted at me.

That night, I couldn't sleep. Among the four bunks in our bedroom, I chose the narrowest one, which was near the door and separated from the other three with a wooden partition. Commissar Lan, Adept Bing, and Junior Yu arranged their bunks in a U-shape, with a desk at the center. The first night we moved in, I found that the two Party members, Lan and Bing, acted like strangers toward each other. Behind the scenes, they must have fought like Bolsheviks. Now, I was facing an asymmetric war, launched by a tyrant.

I didn't know whether Commissar Lan was asleep or monitoring me in the darkness when the wind bellowed from the middle of the night to the dawn. The deep canyon functioned as a huge chimney, sucking air to the upper stream of the channel. I remembered what Father once told me: "The Chinese character forbearance consists of two parts, a knife blade on top of a heart. Its pictographic shape tells us how difficult it is to tolerate something intolerable."

I didn't need to look far back for a lesson. The skeleton-like image of Old Ye, my coworker and roommate in Beijing, came to warn me. At the end of 1959, when he returned to Beijing from Wuhan, a registered letter had followed him to our division leaders, accusing him of disobeying the local Party branch at the Three Gorges Dam Foundation Research Group. He was sent to labor in Anhui, the province with the highest death toll from starvation. A year later he came back with TB.

Ancient heroes liked to say in their adversity, "A lack of forbearance in small matters upsets great plans." I decided not to make the same mistake as Old Ye had. Professor Huang was expecting me to achieve something big rather than to defeat Lan. I had to endure hardships and humiliation in order to carry out my mission, on which I'd based my future. I needed success to turn the tide of my bad luck. For the purpose of my going abroad, I had to foil his attempt to accuse me of disobeying the local Party's leadership. I believed Lan's evil deeds would probably bring him to ruin.

A week later, District Chief Yang blamed three young men anonymously, "Some comrades seem to have forgotten one of the Eight Points for Attention issued by the PLA, 'Do not take liberties with women.' Their recent jokes certainly showed disrespect for women."

As soon as Yang left, the three young men, who had laughed at the female geologist for her way of eating, demanded an explanation from Lan. One of them, a guy from Kunming, led the attack, "You must be the tattletale because you were the only witness at the scene. We were just amused when she ate fried dough with her heels raised and her hand stretched up in the air holding the end. Sure, we mimicked her, but she wasn't offended, she even laughed too. How can you exaggerate a friendly joke to the level of disrespecting women? Why are you making trouble for us out of nothing?"

Junior Yu was also one of the three, "You're damaging our

reputation to demonstrate your political sharpness. Social climbers trampling on others' heads are in for a fall."

The next morning, Lan accused Yu of peeking into his diary and asked me to criticize him. That gave me an opportunity, "Don't be so sensitive. I can't see any motive for him to read your diary unless it contains a secret innovation or a literary masterpiece."

Yu said, "I just stood behind you for a second to fold my comforter. Reading your diary would pollute my eyes. If you're writing sinister stuff, go somewhere else."

Sooner than I'd expected, Lan had become isolated. And his isolation made him even more suspicious of us. We had a humble office in a corner of the quadrangle around the basketball field. In the evenings, we often met there in threes or fives, chatting for a while. Two men complained that, in the dusk, Lan had snooped over like a thief, tiptoeing under the eaves.

One morning Lan found the experimenters from Kunming rapidly copying field records in their bedroom before their second shift. He shouted, "The original data are government property and secret! Nobody can copy them!"

The guys said, "The four participating units are equal to one another. We need a copy of everything we've created here as our reference for later work. None of the four can monopolize the data."

"I know your research center in Wuhan is affiliated with the central government. But it's not necessarily superior to our provincial one in Kunming."

"If you think anyone of us is politically unreliable, please ask the security force to arrest him."

The dispute continued into the evening's political study. At my turn, I said, "Any possible loss or damage—even a smear on the original sheets—is reason enough for the duplication of the original records. It's helpful to scatter, and preserve, the data in case of a world war. But you have to report the matter to the bureau's security office."

Lan gave me a ferocious stare.

We set up our readout station outside the tunnel and above the entrance to avoid the high degree of humidity. One afternoon, from that position, we saw Lan walking up the slope toward us, obviously to observe the ongoing measurement. The three men from Kunming plus Junior Yu impulsively shut up their folders and put their helmets on, ready to stalk off into the tunnel. When they were about to turn off the power to the devices, I gripped Junior Yu's upper arm and made him sit down, "You can't boycott Lan like that, he's still our leader." The other guys looked at each other and returned to their seats.

July 1, 1963, the 42nd birthday of the CCP, we joined the local technical staff to study the recent articles published by *The People's Daily,* all specifically written to condemn Khrushchev and the Soviet Communist Party. In the evening, Lan was supposed to preside over our group discussion, but he came ten minutes late. When he walked into the office, nobody intended to surrender a place for him to sit.

The man from Kunming, nicknamed Rooster, shouted, "Look at our group leader!" I was nervous about what he was going to say. He was skinny, energetic, and agile. His owlish face and jerky hand gestures suggested he was ready to fight anyone, anytime. Once he'd boasted to me about a brawl with a veteran, who'd joined the 1954 battle to defeat French troops in Vietnam. In the first round of the boxing match in their office, he'd dislocated the veteran's elbow.

"Look at our group leader," Rooster said again. "Round head, fluffy fringe of hair, nasty smile—he looks just like Khrushchev."

His coworkers from Kunming booed and hooted, "Yeah, good eye."

Lan slammed his pad onto a desk. "Your surprise attack on a comrade just proves you're a conspirator like Khrushchev."

Rooster stepped forward toward him. "You look like Khrushchev not only physically, but also spiritually. Let me tell you why. You studied in Moscow from 1953 to 1958, when Khrushchev publicly denied Stalin and restored capitalism to the Soviet Union. At that right time and right place, an arrogant, scheming guy like you must've become a disciple of Khrushchev." Rooster didn't have a good reputation, and he was too wanton that night. If nobody dared curb him, he'd become big trouble for the whole group.

When they began to grab each other's sleeves, I yelled, "Stop! If two monks don't care if they hurt each other, they still have to spare Buddha's feelings. Today is the Party's birthday. I've heard both of you sing 'The Party Is My Mother.' How can you keep fighting on our mother's birthday?"

The laughing crowd brought Rooster back to his seat. Some of them asked me to preside over the night's discussion. I waved the pad. "I'm not eligible to be the chairperson, but I'll volunteer to take minutes. Please say something about how to keep the CCP's glorious traditions and how to learn from model Party members."

17

One evening in late July, Adept Bing remained in the tunnel after the others had left for dinner. Sitting on an inverted bucket, he held his head with both hands, a letter pressed to his head. I peeked and saw the red words 'Party Committee' on the letterhead. I squatted by him, "What's wrong? Has the crossfire here reached Wuhan?"

He raised his head, showing his face stained with rock powder and tears, "The villain sues his victim first. The trouble is, our leaders believe him."

He crumpled the letter and crammed it into a pocket. I asked, "What does it say?"

"My leaders accuse me of colluding with local backward elements to form an opposition faction. They order me to stop any divisive activity, apologize to Lan, and immediately take a sincere attitude of supporting him. Otherwise, the Party will punish me."

I pulled his arm to stand him up and drag him to dinner, "Don't worry. Lan can't shut out the sky with one hand. The majority of our group will prove you're the good guy and he isn't."

He stood up but was reluctant to move, "I'm in a no-win situation. He's a darling of the Party committee. If his plot succeeds, I'll be labeled as an anti-Party sectarian."

"No. He's so isolated here. It's hard for him to get away. The problem is, if we fail to accomplish our mission, none of us can go home. Please take the lead and act like a man. Don't let our boat sink."

"I'm skilled with instruments, not at writing and speaking. You take the lead, you get along with the majority and can unite them."

"I'm not a Party member."

"You'll be one soon. And you represent the most prestigious research center. It's natural for you to take up the leadership as the vice director." I stretched out my hand, "If you, as a Party member, support me, I'll do everything I can to keep our group from falling apart."

He gripped my hand tightly, "Let's fight side-by-side."

In the meantime, the Construction Bureau's Party committee assigned Comrade Shi as the Party branch secretary to supervise our group. Inspired by common sense, it was an emergency measure to overhaul a dysfunctional, collapsing organization. Shi looked 50 years old, but was probably younger. Constant shortness of breath and asthma suggested he suffered from silicosis, a job-related disease for many stonemasons. For weeks, I never saw him smile. His long, narrow face and bronze skin, roughened by densely spaced wrinkles, awed me with its somberness and latent suspicion. He tried to talk to as many of the team as possible, but he was poor with words. They all avoided him after the awkward interviews. Then he sat alone in the office all day. His confused expression betrayed that he was at a loss as to what to do.

The secretary's inaction and Adept Bing's full support encouraged me to take on the overall responsibility like a captain. In the daytime, I collaborated with Bing in the tunnel, and at night, I stayed in the room at the district hostel assigned to us for instrument calibration. Besides routinely checking the records and clarifying problems with other group members, I began to process the data we'd accumulated to get some preliminary results. Seeing the fruit of their hard work boosted morale, and most of our group was excited.

The young fellows showed a hunger for knowledge, and tried to make up for their loss due to the Great Leap and the famine. To satisfy their desire, I worked late into the night for two weeks to translate a French article that had been published three years earlier by the scientist who'd invented one of our ongoing tests. They made enough mimeographed copies for all their coworkers. Likewise, I let them take notes from the final draft of my manuscript, which had been accepted by the *Journal of Hydraulic Engineering*.

Sooner than expected, my active role had given an impetus to production and drawn the group members to rally round Adept Bing and me. I felt I was nearing a result that was internationally sought after and walking on the road that would lead me to study in Europe.

In August and September, we got more results than we had in the previous four months. Using the momentum to further quicken our pace, I began to outline our final report. In the introduction, I acknowledged all the personnel from the four participating organizations as equal comrades. That simple step thrilled the local workers and won their favor. I felt I'd gained enough prestige to prod a few of the sluggards among us.

One very early morning, around two o'clock, a local technician and I were still working to improve the transducer when Secretary Shi came in. He was smiling like a village patriarch and carrying a basket with two bowls of spicy noodles and crumbled eggs. A quilt over the lid kept in the warmth. We took the hot food as an undeclared award. While enjoying the noise we made sucking the noodles, he spoke to the technician, "Dapeng has worked really hard. We should let his leaders in Beijing know how high his socialist consciousness is."

I declined politely: "You've overly praised me. I just do my share of the task."

"Don't be too humble. You deserve a citation. Tell me, do you have any ideas to speed up the work? Thousands of workers are being paid, but they're still waiting for our results. The Party leaders are burning with impatience."

"We want to restart construction as soon as possible. But this is the first time we've tried anything like this in China, and we have to start from scratch. People like Adept Bing have worked desperately hard, and we've made good progress. Now we need to improve our leadership in two ways. One is using our resources rationally, and the other is mobilizing the enthusiasm of the group members."

Shi sat up straighter and leaned toward me, "Great. Do you have a detailed plan?"

"Yes. Since the transducer developed by Bing is stable, and the data measured with it are accurate, we should continue to work along those lines. But when the rock isn't intact, the core with transducers attached to it falls apart. So, under those conditions, I suggest using the method of partial stress relief, as shown by the French paper I've just translated. For that purpose, we need to design a special flat jack to apply hydraulic pressure in order to measure the natural rock stress. We can make the jack right here in the local machine shop rather than waiting for Shanghai or Beijing. Once that's done, we can divide our force into two parallel groups and double our speed."

"Wonderful." Shi paused for a second, "Some people have requested that Lan's experiment is stopped, saying his results aren't reliable. What's your opinion?"

"I suggest leaving him alone. The method he's adopted is well known and standard. We should help him enhance the dependability of the readout device with collective wisdom. If we have a discussion on the problem, I'll offer what I've learned from Japanese and French exhibitions in Beijing. In the meantime, we should criticize the attitude of those gloating over Lan's technical difficulty. It's our collective problem, not his personal problem. If you feel it's proper, you might warn Rooster, the bellicose guy from Kunming, about provoking Lan."

Shi nodded ponderously, "You're gaining a proletarian's broad mind. Now, the second problem: how to raise morale."

I laughed, "Sorry, I've talked like a leader."

"You're a growing leader and carrying heavy burdens for the Revolution."

"Generally, most of us work well. Only two men seem to be in troubled water. They can't work normally. If you can help to unburden them of their problems, our group will become a great fighting unit."

"I know. Electrician Wan is demoralized because his wife abandoned him after she got a higher education. Poor man, he'd cut himself to the bone saving money to finance her studies."

I sighed, "What a loss both in love and finance. He's a native-born Yunnan resident and respects you. I'm sure you could help him brace up."

"I'll do that. The other guy, Gloomy Duan as you've heard, is also depressed by a marriage that's falling apart. He's often absent-minded at work and his mood affects our other comrades from Kunming. I have a hard time convincing him of anything because he's an intellectual and I'm a boorish stone carver. It's better if you work on him."

In the following weeks, Electrician Wan no longer dozed off in a nook during working hours. Besides taking care of the power supply and wire connections, he always found a chance to help others. One day, when he was holding a light above the heads of those who were bent over fixing the transducers on the rock surface, Secretary Shi happened to be there watching. I nudged Shi and whispered, "Your influence on Electrician Wan is like setting up a pole in the sunshine and seeing its shadow."

He pulled me aside, "It's your turn to shake up Duan, the most experienced of the guys from Kunming. If you can get him moving, the other five will tag along."

18

At the end of October, we were measuring rock stresses around the underground plant. The crisscross network of large halls and side caves, not yet lined with concrete, looked like purgatory from a Buddhist picture book. The ragged surfaces of massive rocks loomed like monsters above our heads in the dim light. The tunnel connected to the plant, at an elevation of two thousand one hundred feet, was venting air like a huge chimney; the cold and damp made my knees and shoulders sore. When the air compressor cut out for a while, Electrician Wan and Rooster huddled up for a nap, with their heavy coats bundling their bodies. Gloomy Duan and I picked up some scrap lumber to build a fire. We faced the flame to keep our chests warm while enduring the chilly wind on our backs.

Duan was born in the far north then assigned to Yunnan upon graduation from geology school. He married a woman in

Kunming in 1958 but had been absent from home for fieldwork most of the time since then. A year earlier, he'd learned that his wife had had a secret affair with another man, and he'd become irritable and grouchy.

He recalled, "I respected her like a guest and never yelled at her or complained." He rotated his body clockwise, drawing a fist back to his shoulder as if to accumulate energy, "Enemies are bound to meet on a narrow road. Eight months ago, around Chinese New Year, I encountered the whore and her wild goat in the largest department store in Kunming, right on the landing between the first and second floors. I waited for them to come up and face me."

Electrician Wan woke up and sat straight, "What happened next?"

With fury and full strength, he punched the air, "My wife rolled to the bottom of the steps."

Wan nodded in admiration, "I should've been tough like that. But you have no way to punish the wild goat."

"I'll do it when a chance comes up."

"If we're all stuck here," I said, "how can you get a chance? While you're away from Kunming, your marriage is deadlocked and the evil couple is enjoying a good time."

He was rendered speechless. So, I told him about Chuju while adding wood fragments to the fire. The scene of parading Huaizhong Wang on the street made the two rock with laughter.

Electrician Wan, a mild and taciturn man, never rejoiced like that at hearing another's story. He insisted on giving me a sweet potato, which he'd baked in the hot ashes for an hour, as if rewarding a victorious fighter. I took a third of it, leaving the rest for him to share with Gloomy Duan.

As a final touch, I said, "We're fellow sufferers. Please work hard and finish this job as quickly as possible. Then you can go home to punish your enemies. That's the only way we can help each other."

Rooster sat up shivering and stuffed tobacco into his pipe, "You three should set up a Club of Miserable Husbands."

"Don't listen to him," I said, "A dog's mouth yields no ivory. We're not miserable. We're turning defeat into victory. You're both young, and a great adventure lies ahead. Let's walk out of the shadows and push out our chests."

In the days that followed, a revitalized Gloomy Duan led the other fieldworkers as a foreman to assist Adept Bing at the testing site, while I concentrated on data processing, my preparations for applying the French method, and the conceptual draft of the final report.

Winter came. When the Four Cleanups Movement engulfed the nation's countryside, the rectification, dubbed the Socialist Education Movement, got underway in every industrial sector. On the construction site, all leading Party cadres were required to make a clean breast of their mistakes by public confession and submission to mass criticism. This was known as *taking a bath*. Those who were scrubbed thoroughly by the masses could be allowed to *pass the trial*. The campaign was commanded by a special working team dispatched by a higher-up Party committee, and all the bureau's local Party cadres were scrutinized by the team.

Commissar Lan, as a guest worker, was not required to be treated as one of the campaign targets. Nevertheless, a dozen group members ganged up to demand his taking a bath. When the campaign leaders deferred answering the request, Lan was so scared that he lost sleep for several nights, rapidly pacing to and fro on the balcony like a leopard in a cage.

As members of the masses, we attended the rally to receive our socialist education. Listening to the Party cadres' self-criticism was insipid and boring. Soon after the general screening, and the relatively clean ones had been allowed to pass, those who were once guilty of corruption or misconduct were forced to repeat their confessions until the masses and the working team considered they'd shown enough remorse. However, the public fury over the misappropriation of public property quickly faded, while fascination with sexual scandal lingered.

The case of Dou, vice secretary of the bureau's Party committee, electrified the wearied audience. He'd married a peasant woman with bound feet during the time of the guerrilla war; then, when he was sent to a university for crash courses, he had an affair with a young woman on campus. His wife had forgiven him but constantly held mahjong games at home to interrupt his social life. Now, the masses wouldn't let him pass and, as rumors had circulated, demanded he admit the details of his story.

Perhaps scared by such a public psychological grilling, the head of the design group, Dafu Ge, a beloved role model and Party member, disappeared. A week later, his body was found, shapeless, at the bottom of the flood-discharge well of the reservoir around ten miles upstream on the Yili River. The search team accessed the site through the horizontal tunnel from the riverbed. The well, excavated from hard rock, was two- or three-hundred-feet deep and anchored with radial reinforcement bars along the circumference of the uneven surface for future concrete lining. The steel bars pointed toward the center of the well like countless knifes, and Ge had jumped into the well. To recover the rest of his body, workers had to climb along the bars to collect his dismembered limbs and peel off his innards at various elevations.

The cause of his suicide was kept secret, but Confucian Kang attended the silent burial. On Sunday afternoon, at the bureau's hostel, Kang shook his head, "I never expected a hardworking, selfless man would end up like this. His wife and child were kept in Anhui, and he was allowed to visit them once in two years. Travel expenses made them broke forever. The beautiful nanny at the kindergarten sympathized with him and was very open to him. After years of self-restraint, he'd finally fallen in love with her. The woman found herself pregnant just as the campaign blaze was approaching."

Taking a bath sounded mild, but Dafu Ge's death showed it could turn bloody. The faction angry at Commissar Lan couldn't pass up the chance. Toward the end of the year, when my final report had nearly taken shape and been substantiated with enough convincing data to satisfy the designers, the anti-Lan faction demanded that the local Party committee host a political evaluation.

Adept Bing sought my support for his initiative, "This is the only way to protect me. Without a formal evaluation endorsed by the local Party organization, Lan will fabricate false accusations against me when we go back to Wuhan, and I'll have no way to defend myself."

Since everyone in our group would have to pass a public hearing, the men from Kunming cheered in support of Bing's request, plotting to turn Lan's session into taking a bath. They would rally together to grill him in public like Vice Secretary Dou and send him back to Wuhan with a bad evaluation. The brewing attack would create chaos, interrupt the harvest of our fieldwork and sabotage my personal agenda. I wanted to wrap up the collective business as soon as possible, and return to prepare my paper for certain international conferences or publication. I decided to defuse the pending war.

The Party committee's envoy sent from Wuhan to rescue Lan knew that my vote would be crucial. He asked me to deny the need for a political evaluation.

I wanted to protect Bing without joining the war against Lan. As an alternative, I asked Secretary Shi to get a consensus at a group meeting to issue Bing a certificate of merit as the number-one model worker. Shi thought it was a good idea and did what I suggested. Touching the red stamp of the bureau's Party committee on the honor certificate, I pleaded with Adept Bing, "Look, this is your amulet. Secretary Shi will give it to you at a ceremony in the presence of Lan and your Party committee's envoy."

To talk Rooster and his fellows from Kunming out of their plot, I said point blank, "First, the leaders of the Construction Bureau don't want to make an enemy of any participating unit. Second, Lan isn't a class enemy, and we're bound to work with him again somewhere else. Finally, when Secretary Shi stands by me, your plan won't get popular support."

Rooster fumed, "You pretend to be fair, but you're currying favor with the big organization in Wuhan at the sacrifice of us small fishes."

"Secretary Shi and I will veto your votes."

Rooster stamped his foot, "You're a stupid, softhearted bookworm. You let the poisonous snake go now, he'll come back to bite you once he gets the chance."

I smiled, "Old friends, please don't measure a gentleman's heart with a villain's mind. Adept Bing is protected and honored, Commissar Lan has been in hot water long enough, and you guys haven't lost anything. This ending is better than we expected. Lan's suffering will be a lesson to him, and we can keep the bridge open to future cooperation instead of unexpected retaliation."

The envoy from Wuhan, a university schoolmate, shook my hand, "Thank you for helping us overcome a crisis."

The day we shut down the experimental station, Commissar Lan looked emotional when he apologized to me, "Sorry for my misunderstanding and disrespect. A man of substance doesn't like to show off. Your patience and diplomacy are worthy of emulation."

I was shocked by his humility, "You're overrating me." As parting words, I simply said, "Someday we'll meet again on another project."

Finally, our field experiments had opened the road to restarting construction. The full-scale conduit test, in which Kang had been actively involved, was completed successfully under water pressure, breaking the Swedes' record. The natural stresses measured by our group in the basalt stratum also proved the natural laws of regional structural geology, giving the designers a new concept and answering Karl Terzaghi's question.

The Construction Bureau held a farewell banquet as a treat for us. After a few slugs of hard liquor, Secretary Shi stood up, the wrinkles in his face writhing with emotion, "I'm a poorly educated man. Unlike many other intellectuals, Dapeng respects me and listens to me. During my suffering, he stood by me, and by the Party branch, taking full leadership to prevent the group from collapse. We should cite him highly and send a certificate of merit to the Party committee of his institute."

His words, which carried a certain weight and authority, were printed in the bureau's mimeographed bulletin the same day. Confucian Kang got a copy and folded it into his pocket, "I'll personally show it to Professor Huang and your division leaders."

The next day a jeep was arranged to take us, the five guests from Wuhan and Beijing, to Kunming.

19

Professor Huang received Kang and me the day after we returned to Beijing. We reported our results to him triumphantly.

"Wonderful!" He slapped the leather sofa, "You've made a big step forward, and your performance can be seen as world class. Please prepare two papers, one for the next symposium of the International Conference on Large Dams, the other for the European magazine *Géotechnique*."

Soon after the meeting, I met Lanyu Rong in the hallway. She signaled at me to follow her to the division leaders' office, where she showed me the mimeographed bulletin, which Confucian Kang had brought back from Yunnan. With a confidential air, she said, "A double happiness has descended upon you. Congratulations! While we wait for your certificate of merit to be sent to us from Yunnan, let me tell you the news about Ziwei Cao."

Like thunder cracking through the sky, her happy voice brought my back straight up. But I thought it better not ask anything or show any emotion while she stared at me, watching my response. Then, she said slowly, "Your judgment was correct. Ziwei becoming a 1955 campaign target was based on erroneous information provided by the street residents' committee in Guangzhou. Actually, her father is our own comrade working overseas, resourcefully covering up his clandestine mission with commercial activities, and the provincial security leaders knew his identity. So, she has suffered for the larger interests of the Revolution. Her persecution at university and complaints in Hong Kong afterward have led the KMT intelligence to believe that her father is anti-communist. As a result of her torment, her father gained firmer trust from our enemies."

Such a conclusion called forth in me deep reverence for the father and daughter, "The situation is complicated, and the road of the Revolution is tortuous."

"In some cases," Gan said, "our clandestine workers risk their lives in Taiwan and other Southeast Asian regions, and their wives and children have been treated as counterrevolutionary dependents at home."

"Life is incredibly difficult for them."

She assumed her lecturer look and stance, "We have no reason to complain or be disheartened about the danger and trouble they've endured."

"That's a good way to look at it. Is Ziwei still in Hong Kong?"

"She's studying in London to get her doctoral degree in

English literature. Her father remains in Hong Kong. Both keep low profiles."

A rock had been taken off my heart. Yet I maintained a nonchalant tone, "So, may I write to her?"

"What for?"

"Urging her to come back. She's trained in both Russian and English, a rare professional that our country needs for the international class struggle."

She hemmed and hawed, "Yes or no. Your friendship can help her make the decision to return to the motherland. But only if our government asks you to do so. You know the rules. I don't see that the time is ripe. If you act presumptuously, the negative effect would be hard to estimate, it might ruin the joint effort of the Party branch with Professor Huang for your study abroad."

I shook Gan's hand, "Thank you and the Party organization for finding out about her situation. It must've taken painstaking efforts."

She gave me a wry smile, "Personally, I hope you'll eventually be able to work things out with her. But for now, you need to keep on respecting the line between China and overseas."

"Of course. Under the State Council, there must be an office in charge of receiving overseas Chinese people. I hope you can find a way to have Ziwei's name registered and request that they inform me when she comes back for a visit."

She shrugged, "I'll try, but I don't know if it's feasible."

It was at this time of convalescence for our country and our personal lives that we lost the beloved structural engineer, nicknamed Confucian Kang. Approaching Chinese New Year, February 13, 1964, most men living in the bachelors' dorm on our southern compound had left to visit their wives or parents. Nobody heard him fall and hit his temple on the corner of an iron coal stove. It happened in the wee hours and on his way to the lavatory. Not until daybreak was he found lying across the corridor. His body was already stiff, and the pool of blood blackened. Most likely, his high blood pressure and dizziness had caused his death.

Before sending a telegram to his wife, the division leaders had checked to see what valuables he'd left behind. They'd found only 0.37 yuan change in his pocket and a watch on his wrist. His wife and three children cried all the way from Hunan Province to Beijing for the funeral. His boss, the division Party branch secretary, paid his condolences to the widow. Finally, he said, "We'd already moved his name to number one on the waiting list for family reunion. What a pity."

Near the end of the memorial service, Professor Huang was shivering and repeatedly hitting the cement floor with his stick. I held his arm, urging him to go back to his office before the other mourners started to leave. Once we got there, he slipped into a chair and could no longer hold back his emotion, wailing throatily through a spasmodic cough.

I was worried about his physical condition. A large portion of a lung had been excised during an operation, and he was currently suffering from asthma and heart disease. I poured hot water from the thermos into his teacup and helped relieve the stress by massaging his arms and shoulders.

A long while later, he looked calmer. In a feeble voice, he said, "If he'd had a diploma from the Soviet Union, his engineering rank would've been at least sixth instead of eighth, and his family separation problem would've been resolved years ago."

"A couple of designers told me that his actual ability was higher than some professors of structural analysis."

"Certainly true." He swiveled his chair to face me. As if giving away a secret, he watched me intensely, "Nobody cares for anyone, but our hierarchy system cares for the higher-ups."

"I'm ranked eleventh. My problem will remain as long as I stay on the bottom of the hierarchy, maybe forever."

He rested his head sideways on the back of the sofa, "I feel I've lost one of my arms, but we have to accept the tragedy. Please finish the two papers I asked you and Kang to write, now you have to deal with them alone. I'll toil with my old bones to help you. I hope you have a meteoric rise in the world's eyes to match your real ability. The quickest way is to study in the West and get recognition of your talent from abroad."

"Wishful thinking. I'll do my best but prepare for the worst."

Huang struggled to sit upright, "Don't despair. Believe what an ancient sage said, that things will develop in the opposite direction when they become extreme. Some researchers of your age in the high-tech sector and defense industry have begun to trickle into Western Europe and Japan quietly. Chances are not far away, but the selection of personnel is tough and secret. No matter how skimpy a quota our institute gets, I'm rooting for you."

"Thank you for your care and coaching. I won't slacken my effort, no matter what my fate may be."

When I was ready to leave his office, something seemed to come to his mind: "Oh. You have to learn to speak English. There's a set of records imported from England at our library, sealed by dust for years. You'll find it very helpful."

His solicitude and expectation made me feel better for the moment. Once I was alone, though, all I could think about was how I'd lost a loyal, entertaining, and wise friend and a talented and trusted work colleague. Goodbye, Confucian Kang.

From the library I borrowed the box of elementary English records published by the Linguaphone Institute, Ltd, London, with a book attached to it. Now all I needed was a turntable to play them and a radio set to amplify the sound. The two devices would cost two hundred yuan. More troublesome was the lack of a private place to use them; flagrantly studying English would jangle the nerves of the vigilant and draw fire.

As an alternative, I copied the text of the first five lectures line by line into my pocket notebook, memorizing the sentences until I had the right equipment and a safe place. My ambition to gobble up the whole book occupied my mind and helped fill my empty life. From then on, I went to the mess hall ten or 20 minutes later than the others in order to steal some privacy in my dorm or office. Not knowing the correct pronunciation, I tried to remember the vocabulary just as I did with chemical symbols.

In the vast western suburb of Beijing, there were few bus lines. To visit other research facilities, I would borrow a bicycle from the division office or from a friend. To utilize the hours spent on the road, I would be slowed down by reciting the text; often I got off the bike and pushed it to the roadside to open my notebook and find the words which had just escaped me.

20

My stay on the construction site at the Yili River allowed me to avoid the psychological melee within our institute during the 1963 salary adjustment. After a seven-year freeze, only 40 percent of state employees could get a raise, and public debate on everyone's merits and faults became relentless. The Party branch committee made the final decision while conducting the nominations and comparisons as a mass movement of self-education. Away from Beijing, I could imagine the grueling tension of judging one another's eligibility in the same office. Nevertheless, as a result of the salary adjustment, my monthly pay was increased from 62 to 75 yuan.

In the meantime, the bachelors' dorm teemed with new excitement. The government had decided to grant geographically separated couples 12 paid days a year for conjugal visits. Either spouse could travel, and their roundtrip train or bus fare would be reimbursed. Up until then, they'd had to eat the cheapest food at the mess hall all year long to accumulate the money for a home visit.

Soon after the exuberance died down, I saw the dark side of the unprecedented benefit. It would lessen spousal suffering but by no means end it. Like an analgesic for chronic pain rather than surgery to end its cause, it implied the impossibility of permanent family reunions for the foreseeable future. For me, even that temporary relief came too late. If the new policy had been in effect two years earlier, I'd have gone to see Chuju right at the time of her desperation, and we might've found a way to save our marriage. Even up to the time I received my divorce certificate, Hot Chili still pushed me to remarry Chuju and I was moved by her persuasion. However, harsh local customs made it difficult for Chuju to stay single, and I did not have any vacations or money to visit her at that time. The circumstances propelled me to cut the Gordian knot.

Nevertheless, since single employees could enjoy the same benefit to visit their parents, I took a vacation in March 1964 in order to go home. With my increased salary and the money saved from reimbursed railway fees, I'd accumulated 50 yuan for my older brother's family, with whom my parents were now living. The miscellaneous gifts I brought with me would immensely endear me to Father's few surviving friends. Grand Front Gate cigarettes and biscuits in tins painted with a golden rooster, not seen in local stores, would especially surprise them.

Father looked quite healthy, compared with his state three years previously when he was on the verge of death. The first thing he asked was, "Where did you get those rare food and tonics? They saved my life."

"Ziwei Cao, my university friend, sent them to me from Hong Kong."

"You should find a way to express our gratitude to her."

"I will."

On the first day of my stay, I mostly sat silently with my

parents, wondering how many times I would ever see them again. Under her flaccid, drooping eyelids, Mother's eyes constantly beamed anxiety at me. Sometimes she gazed at Father as if hoping he would have some words to make me happy. Father seemed at ease, relating the fateful stories of our acquaintances to distract me from my pensive state.

On an impulse, after receiving my sizable wad of money, my sister-in-law killed the only old hen she'd raised. As well as stewing the meat, she fried the giblets with hot pepper and celery, a popular local dish.

The fourth evening, my high school friend Kai Tao and his wife, Huiwen, came to see me, and we went to watch a movie. Thanks to the temporarily relaxed censorship, the theater was playing a French film, *The Three Musketeers*, dubbed into Chinese.

Walking toward the theater, Kao Tao briefed me about Chuju's situation, "She married a high-school friend, Yang, a nice young man, but a bit of a sissy. He wasn't allowed to go to college because his father's a soldier in Taiwan. They're both 25 now. Yang is okay to Chuju, but his mother loathes her as a jinx, an unlucky star to bring her family ruin. With her husband in the Taiwanese Army, the old woman can't hold her head up on the street. Every holiday, as a political fine, the neighborhood committee orders her and other class enemies to sweep the streets without pay. At home, as the mother-in-law, she throws her weight around."

"Once," Huiwen said, "when Chuju came home late at night without pre-permission, her mother-in-law refused to open the door and scolded her in a high-pitched voice: 'Don't you know how stinky your name is? Why are you still so wild? If you don't behave yourself, I won't need you as a daughter-in-law. You can stay out overnight wherever you like.' Chuju cried in the cold air until the grandma of another family, who shared the house, let her in."

I felt sorry for Chuju. She shouldn't have come to such bad

circumstances, which now only dampened the funny French movie.

As the movie ended, viewers funneled to the exit. Unexpectedly, at the jammed gate, Chuju appeared abreast of me, and we stood only six inches apart. For a moment, before a stranger wedged himself into the gap between us, we caught each other's eye. I saw her peach-pink face turn pale. Her transient gaze carried intricate and volatile meaning, too mysterious for me to decipher. From the resonance of my heart, I seemed to have sensed the signals of her sorrow, regret, hatred, pleading for forgiveness, and many other mixed feelings.

The pressure of the crowd from behind separated us briefly. As I was shunted aside, I could see her bobbing in the human stream. Having conspicuously gained weight, and with her hair disheveled, Chuju conveyed the image of a hatching hen taking care of her chick. With her blouse unbuttoned, she was breast-feeding a baby, perhaps a half-year old. It was hard to reckon by its size.

The wild scene in Hot Chili's home flashed back to me, and I was flustered by the timing. Could this be my child? I calculated that almost 18 months had elapsed since then.

It was drizzling. When Kai Tao and Huiwen found me on the sidewalk, Chuju stood a few meters away, using the open flap of her blouse to shield the baby, "Chuju," Huiwen called out, "Come over to see our old friend."

Chuju threw out her chest and combed her hair with fingers, then stepped toward me. Unprepared, I shook her hand but asked only about her oldest sister: "Is Minying still in Yunnan?"

"Yes, teaching at a kindergarten. Her husband has five more years to serve in jail as a war criminal."

"Please remember me to her. We were classmates at elementary school for six years. I wish her well and hope she can come back to work in our hometown."

She looked into my eyes, "I will."

I couldn't help but sneak a quick look at the baby, "He's big for three months."

Huiwen stifled a smile and asked, "How old is he now?"

"Almost five months."

The worst possibility had been ruled out. I took a longer look, "He's healthy and handsome."

Chuju smiled, "I hope he becomes a good scholar like Uncle Dapeng."

"He'll surpass us, the older generation. Take good care of yourself."

A woman around 60 hurried up and held an umbrella above her head. Chuju started to run with her. Seeing her hunch over to protect her child from the rain, I imagined she might react that way to avoid our eyes stabbing her back.

I asked Kai, "Is that her mother-in-law? She seems nice enough."

"She's protecting her grandson, not Chuju. Good thing Chuju had a boy. Otherwise, she'd catch hell from the witch."

I watched them walk away. My break with Chuju was clear and complete, leaving only my sorrow for her sisters' tragedy and her own fate.

On the sixth day, I decided to leave, and told my parents I was in a hurry to accomplish many things. I wanted to have my plastic surgery, and the rare peaceful intermission was an opportunity. They were happy about my plan and urged me to go. For 12 years they'd patiently accepted not seeing me around while hoping for a better future for me.

Through intermittent drizzle, we walked like snails to the railway station. Mother tilted her umbrella to hide her tears and repeated one more time, "Father and I are candles in the wind. If you remain single, we can't close our eyes when we die."

Father stifled a sob, "I believe you'll reach your ambition. It all depends on human effort. In case we don't live long enough to see your success, please don't forget to report it to us during the memorial ceremony."

21

I returned to Beijing in late March. When the new academic
year began, it was a season of political study. Though my injury
was job-related, a skin graft of about one and a half inches
wouldn't be covered by our free medical care system. Nor did
our contract hospital have such technology, which was still in
the research stage at some famous facilities. I braced myself to
see Hot Chili, and found her new apartment one night.

Her husband and she both had a salary raise in 1963. Since
they had a baby girl, their living space was larger than the
previous one. Her good mood enabled her to spare my feelings
more than I'd expected, "You haven't come to see us for a year
and a half. I know why: because you rejected my advice to keep
Chuju, you doubted I would help you with your surgery. Am I
such a narrow-minded person?"

Though I'd been accustomed to her tone since high school,
it was hard to take, especially in the presence of her husband,
Dr Cai. I smiled, "Come on, I've never underestimated your
broad mind and kindness, 'A premier's heart is large enough to
pole a boat in.' You used this proverb to persuade me to
forgive Chuju. Now, I present it to you as a compliment."

After I told her my situation, including the year in Yunnan,
she stopped digging at me, "Research into skin grafts has
recently made a lot of progress in Beijing. The risk is much
lower than before."

Through the couple's connections, a surgeon trained in
Canada and now working in Beijing at a famous medical center
accepted me as one of his experimental subjects. I could now
receive treatment not available to ordinary people.

With a patch of skin peeled from my neck, the doctor
replaced the scar on my right cheek; then a piece of skin was

transplanted from my thigh to cover up the cut on my neck. The operation was done in early May. During the follow-up exams he assured me that the operation had been successful. He would monitor my healing process to see if corrective surgery was necessary. With gauze pads stuck to my face and neck, I participated in all activities as usual.

At a big rally, the Party chief of our institute briefed us that the current task of the whole country's economic development was *readjustment, consolidation, filling out, and raising standards.* Following up on the national direction, Professor Huang reported the fruits of our implementation of the Fourteen-point Regulation of Scientific Research. Toward the end, he cited a few young and middle-aged researchers for their outstanding progress. Then he stressed my article and the efforts I'd expended to improve experimental techniques. In front of a thousand employees, he added, "If I'd personally conducted the tests and written the article, I couldn't have done as well as Comrade Dapeng Liu."

Sitting in the next seat, Minggui An nudged me. I looked straight at Huang and the lectern to ignore the converging stare of the audience. Later, outside the auditorium, one of my former classmates came over and shook my hand with too firm a grip. Words oozed between his teeth, "What a great, fair-haired boy you are now."

I could feel a harmonious environment forming around me as a result of my enhanced status, especially when political cadres whom I barely knew tried to help me to look for a suitable spouse among their relatives. One day, in the hallway of our office building, a former campus beauty from our school days even suggested that I take her younger sister's hand, a girl from their respectable family and a senior medical-school student. I politely declined their goodwill because I'd made up my mind to approach Ziwei, and I had a roadmap in mind. I was sure she was still single, otherwise the leaders would've required me to give up the idea of looking for her.

Immediately after the rally, our group leader, Old Ma, volunteered to take one month of physical labor at a farm. On the eve of his departure, he asked me to draft the ten-year plan for rock-mechanics research, in two versions—one for the academic world and the other for the waterpower industry—due to the dual authority our institute answered to. Though he sneaked away at a critical juncture, shirking his responsibility and making me his shield, I forgave him. He'd fully engaged with politics and mentally abandoned study for a decade. Deep down, I saw his withdrawal from the headaches of power as an opportunity for me to boldly come out.

I bit the bullet and struggled through all of April and May for a presentable result. My friend, who'd jeered at me and called me a fair-haired boy, preyed upon me again during the final discussion, presided over by Professor Huang, when I was the only one of my rank who sat among the senior scientists and division directors: "You look like the point of an awl sticking out of a bag, letting your talent show itself."

Since the goal of the plan was to catch up with Western science and technology within our field, I read quite a few pertinent magazines that had been imported in recent years. In the reference room of the Machinery Import Company, I learned what progress Western Europe had made in construction tools and monitoring instruments. The neat photos and precise specifications of the commercial devices fed me with fancies. How much work we could do with them! Seeing me taking notes day after day, an old clerk, knowledgeable and nosy, looked sympathetically at me, "How much foreign currency does your working unit have?"

I pointed to my introduction letter, "As you can see, we don't belong to the defense industry or a high-tech-related sector. Very little foreign currency is given to us. Every year we apply for it, but our research group only got, just once, ten thousand US dollars to buy equipment from Switzerland. That was eight years ago."

He left me alone when some other readers came in. From his professional manner and pure English, I guessed he might've been engaged in foreign trade before 1949. After ushering the newcomers to the right shelves, he came back to sit by me, "Your handwriting is elegant."

I made a face, "Thank you, but sorry, I can't speak English."

"You're young and just need a chance to practice." He tapped my introduction letter, "Unlike your institute, which is administered by a civil industrial ministry, military research centers have a lot of foreign currency. They've bought almost all they want, even some items embargoed by the Western imperialists. I doubt they know how to use all of those fancy, expensive gadgets."

The old man's information inspired me to visit a research center affiliated with the PLA Navy. It was located in a quiet valley in a mountainous region west of Beijing. The receiving officer opened only a non-sensitive area, the material testing lab, to me. I was dazed by the array of new machines imported from Western countries, including recent US products. The automatic-control devices and measuring instruments made me especially envious. However, the large hall looked like an exhibition setting, neat and bright, without a trace of ongoing, advanced research.

I asked the scientist about the feasibility of borrowing or renting their equipment. He answered positively. Returning to my office, I felt my vision was too narrow. To go beyond that idea, I wrote a proposal for joint research on problems common to both civil and military projects. It was the right time, when the nation was mobilizing its resources to shore up the third line of defense, and hundreds of large factories were moving from the coast to settle in the ragged southwestern areas. Placing important factories in deep mountains and core plants underground was the number-one principle for selecting sites for new or relocated projects.

While dozens of tunnels were under construction for

railway networks, factories, and grain depots, our system started to build underground power stations with coal burners that vented smoke from the hilltops. Their mania felt like the approach of a world war, and, more practically, I found myself predicting how many casualties and disasters would occur before the war broke out.

To substantiate my proposal, I joined the fieldwork on the upper Yellow River to monitor the arched roof of an underground power plant. The excavated hall, with a 130-foot span, looked magnificent, but its design wasn't based on scientific theory. Also, the monitoring devices were copied from coal-mine safety controls and not suitable for our purpose. Then I went to China's largest coal mine, in Shanxi Province, where engineers and construction workers were rebuilding the section destroyed by a 1959 disaster that had broken the world record for deaths in a gas explosion.

I had no access to look at the ambitious military fortresses. Still, I visited tunnel sites along the railway triangle connecting the three provinces of Southwest China, where the PLA Railway Corps was doing something people normally couldn't imagine. With simple tools and equipment, it overcame the difficulties through human endurance and the spirit of sacrifice. At a staff office in a valley of Sichuan, an army engineer wearing a captain's epaulets received me. In the tunnel under excavation, he answered all my questions frankly. However, when I asked about casualties, he declined to answer, using a quotation from Mao: "Wherever there is struggle there is sacrifice, and death is a common occurrence."

Returning with him to his office, I followed quietly and gazed around. In a corner shed, staff members were peeling residual paper off used wreaths and pasting on new stripes with words of mourning for the coming memorial service. The twigs woven around the frames had lost their luster and were even withered and sallow. It was sad to guess how many times they must have reused the wreaths. The sky was misty, and the steep rock walls darkened the bottom of the narrow glen. I couldn't see a victorious prospect ahead. The whole setting looked like a section of Purgatory. I wondered if I was progressing toward my dream of having a family at all by being there. If I had to do so, I'd like to suffer and to risk my life alone, and avoid having a beloved one to be buried with me.

During my general survey, I was annoyed and angered by the lords in Beijing—far removed from the working people and reality—and the news media holding back unpleasant information. Being deeply aggrieved, I wrote a proposal for a joint military–civil study on the design and construction of underground structures, aiming at minimizing the death rate before an international war took place, and accelerating our preparedness. As a fanciful hope, I suggested that the authorities concerned might organize a professional study tour in Western Europe.

While the Gulf of Tonkin incident alarmed us about the possibility of the Vietnam War expanding to China, we kept on working. To speed up our readiness for the war, the designers of several large-span underground plants abandoned the traditional concrete linings in order to shorten construction time. The new lining system, with steel mesh, anchors, and gunite would provide the excavated caves with quicker and safer protection. However, it was a new technology even in the West. Our hastily manufactured pneumatic equipment didn't work well, and the additives to accelerate the adhesion of sprayed concrete were not fast enough. In contrast with the slogan 'Run a Race with the US Imperialists', posted everywhere on the site, large portions of concrete had fallen to the floor, and the man controlling the nozzle failed to realize thick layers, especially when spraying overhead. As an urgent measure of war preparation, I urged that this should be the most pressing subject of our study tour.

In the meantime, I rewrote the report, 'Catching up with Western Tunneling Technology', which I'd drafted in Fujian in the winter of 1959, and attached it as an appendix to the proposal.

Professor Huang promised to present my proposal to the planner of the Science Commission under the State Council. Meanwhile, he would approach the leaders of the Defense Science Commission to look for an opportunity to use their facilities, and to form a group with them to visit Sweden, Japan, or South Africa in order to study rapid underground construction.

22

I casually browsed *The People's Daily* on a Friday afternoon in late November, and saw a photo of the Great Yangtze River Bridge at Wuhan, with the caption, 'Compatriots from Hong Kong and Macao Highly Praise their Motherland for her Reconstruction Achievement'. I felt it insipid. However, viewing it again made me fidgety, because the woman facing the camera resembled Ziwei, though she was much older than her image in my memory. We hadn't seen each other for eight years, and the black-and-white photo printed on rough paper must look older than the real person.

I waited for the ending of the day, then went to the Committee of Overseas Chinese Affairs, downtown east, and asked if my boss had registered the name of my possible visitor, Ziwei Cao, with its service center. The receptionist, a young man sitting behind the counter with his head tilted and one eye shut, asked to see my ID. He answered, "We don't deal with individuals like you. Please let your leaders approach us through the administration system."

On Saturday evening, I went to the two fancy hotels, famous for housing overseas Chinese tourists. The front desks at both places asked if I had an official introduction letter to authorize my inquiry. I gave up my search, blaming myself,

"You're out of your mind. There're so many people who look like each other. Don't make trouble out of nothing."

The next Monday, when I was calibrating an instrument, Lanyu Rong, vice secretary of the division's Party branch, came to see me in the quiet lab instead of using the phone to summon an ordinary worker to her office as she usually did. I left the machine to greet her.

Her smile, plain and solemn, often led me to see, inside her beautiful skin, a woman with a soul and mind well cultivated by the Party since she joined the Revolution at the age of 16. However, in 1961, when a rank-and-file Party member had complained to her about his wife remaining in Qinghai, next to Tibet, she did mobilize her old husband to use his connections in the security system and helped the woman move to Beijing. At the time, I was envious of that lucky man, but now I saw Comrade Rong's caring for him flicker with human spirit.

With a confidential air, she said, "Your university friend, Miss Ziwei Cao, is arriving in Beijing next week as a member of the Hong Kong Patriotic Touring Group. Since we registered her name, the Office of Overseas Chinese Affairs under the State Council has informed our ministry. She's requested to meet you privately, or at least see you at the scheduled gala celebration. Since she's a pro-China activist and left-winger, our higher-up leaders have granted you the privilege of visiting her at the hotel. Do your best to impress her with our country's prosperity and your personal progress."

"I'll take it on as an important political mission." I showed an impassionate face, and felt my soul ascending to the sky.

"The United Front Line is our party's magic weapon for victory in the Revolution. Winning overseas support is as important as building up the third line of defense. You know what to say and how to say it during the meeting. Just dress neatly and speak with national pride."

I followed her to the door and stopped in front of her, "Could you go with me?"

"Why?"

"I need a supervisor and witness."

"You're overly cautious." She blinked for a few seconds, "Let me ask the foreign affairs office of our ministry for instructions."

I was worried about my appearance. The bandages had come off five months ago, but my right cheek still looked thickened, red, and irregular. When I smiled, my expression was unnatural, even distorted. That night, I sat at the desk in my dorm in a trance, staring into Old Ye's pocket mirror. Dong Long came in and took a seat on my bed. I told him about the good news and my anxiety. As always, the peasant's son had a practical suggestion.

"Ask the doctor to put a soothing pad on it. It'll fade the color. Then you can lift the pad and show her what a fresh skin graft looks like. She'll assume it's still getting better."

After a few days of wearing the new pad, my request for Rong to escort me got a positive answer. She managed to have our institute's only sedan, a Polish-made Warsaw, take us to the hotel, New Overseas Home, where Ziwei was staying. The beetle-shaped car, painted in yellowish green, was the humblest one assigned to cadres with ranks equal or lower to bureau chief in Beijing.

It was a Tuesday afternoon. For the first time, I put on my new leather shoes, which I had bought in anticipation of a happy reunion with Chuju, and which had lain on my bookshelf until now. Also I wore a dark-blue, serge jacket of the Dr Sun Yat-sen style, actually a Western coat with the collar buttoned up, which my father had bought before 1949 but never wore. To match the jacket, I spent 44 yuan on a tailor-made pair of olive-gray, woolen pants, and 15 yuan for a white polyester shirt imported from Japan, to make a white border around the collar like the Catholic priests do, a style kept up by our famous Beijing opera actors.

Such an outfit, copied from off-stage entertainers, might have looked sharp within our own community but made me feel like a clodhopper as soon as we walked into the Westernized hotel. Rong wore a dark-gray, woolen coat over a traditional blouse with an oil-green, satin sheen. The foreign guests playing billiards were polite and pretended not to notice us passing through the lobby. On the other hand, some Chinese clerks, all in suitable attire, cast haughty sideway glances at us hayseeds. I wanted to back out and run away, except Ziwei was waiting for me, which made my getup even more mortifying.

Rong looked at ease. Her mien as a pretty, rural, northern woman and her confidence as a Party cadre seemed unaffected by the foreign setting.

We sat by the window of the second-floor parlor waiting for Ziwei. The bleak streets under the gray sky, full of motor vehicles moving with the flux of bicyclists, reminded me of where I belonged. From what I'd gathered about the Party's ambitions and strategy, the luxurious environment was designed to please foreigners, serving China's long-term goal. Despising the extravagance of the external bourgeois world, I was anxious to make sure Ziwei was still single and interested in me. My only confidence came from the fact that my leaders had not told me otherwise. Also I wondered how, under Rong's sharp nose, I could convey to Ziwei my craving for a revival of our old romance. She came to supervise rather than help me.

For long, boring minutes, Gan reclined on the sofa with her neck against the headrest, gazing up at the crystal chandeliers. Suddenly, she straightened her back and stood up. With quizzical eyebrows, she greeted someone approaching us from behind me, "Miss Cao?"

"Just call me Ziwei." The melodic voice, once familiar, seemed to come from outer space. Like a robot triggered by a signal, I jumped to my feet and turned my body to face the two women shaking each other's hand. It took a moment for my blurred eyes to relay a clear vision of Ziwei. While her student image had been frozen in my mind for eight years, I found her mutated into a bourgeois lady. Still athletic and carrying traces of her younger days, she now posed with the grace of a Western public figure in a documentary movie. She spoke sonorously and laughed heartily, in sharp contrast with the withdrawn, bashful women of Mainland China.

I admired her but sensed the immense distance between us. Her stylish, white jacket and golden necklace over a light blue gown made her overly glamorous, cutting her off from the austere society outside the hotel, and from my life.

She held my upper arms with both hands in an easy, unaffected manner. Still, her tight grip and blush perhaps hinted at well-smothered emotion. Then, she tilted back and looked me up and down as if not seeing the gauze pad on my face, "You're quite the scholar now. The glasses add an even more intelligent look."

I touched her elbows for a second, and then my hands hung awkwardly.

She turned to a man unexpectedly standing behind her, "George, this is Dapeng, whom I've frequently talked about. Can't you see the wisdom glowing from his eyes?"

As my heart sank, George stepped forward to shake hands. With ostentatious warmth and an unnatural tone, he said, "Yes, indeed. Seeing is believing."

His colorful outfit, the ring on his finger, and the English name attached to his Cantonese face and physique—all in real life rather than on stage—should have amused me. But their obviously close relationship delayed my response, "You overseas Chinese people are courteous and generous with compliments. We've gotten used to criticism and self-criticism."

"That's why people like you are mentally stronger than the intellectuals abroad," Ziwei said, "They're pampered by a cozy life and are too self-centered."

I tilted my head toward Rong, "Compared with veterans, I'm still weak, but more practical and less tender than before."

Facing Rong and me, Ziwei explained her situation, "I stayed in Hong Kong for five years and got my bachelor's degree in English. Since then I've been studying comparative literature at the University of Cambridge, England."

I forced a smile, "That's great. Your skills in Russian and English are badly needed for the international revolution. Is George also from London?"

George said, "I'm in New York, getting my PhD in economics at Columbia University."

"Your expertise will be very helpful to our economic development."

Ziwei said, "He worries that what he's learned about a market economy can't be applied to China's centrally-planned economy."

George frowned for a moment, "I still need a few more years to finish my studies. Right now, our battles with Chinese anti-communist scholars and KMT thugs require me to stay in New York."

Gazing at Rong, Ziwei held my hand, "We constantly fight against the pro-Taiwan students and scholars in Hong Kong, London, and New York. We need comrades like Dapeng. With his eloquence and ability to write quickly, he could be a core fighter among us."

"What I'm doing here now is also backing your overseas struggle," I said, "The stronger our motherland becomes, the prouder and more confident you'll feel abroad." I opened my palms to Ziwei and George, "You prove that everybody can be noble, even while living in the capitalist world."

Rong gave the final touch, "All patriotic Chinese people can make a contribution to China, no matter where they are."

Ziwei held her palms together and turned to face me, "We have to admit that the West has advanced in science, so I hope you get the chance to study in the UK or the US. My father has connections and would like to help you financially."

"My current work gives me great opportunity to grow. As for my future, I'll comply with whatever the Party needs me to do."

Ziwei waved for us to sit down, then leaned over the armrest next to mine, "Are you still single?"

I gazed at the woolen carpet, "Yes."

"Why? No woman is perfect. You shouldn't nitpick."

I looked up at Rong, who sat opposite Ziwei across the coffee table, calm and expressionless. I said, "I'm working in the frontier of my field, and my leaders have put increasingly heavier responsibility on me. In our tradition, by the time a man is 30, he should be well established. I hope I can reach that point before having a family."

Rong nodded, "You've almost attained it."

While she switched to chat with Ziwei, George bent forward and smiled to me. At this moment, I peeped at the ring on the middle finger of Ziwei's right hand. Repelling its distraction, I asked George about his life in the US, specifically what kind of mathematics was required to understand modern economics. The common topic helped dilute the uneasiness between us, "What's the major difference between Americans and Asians studying on your campus?" I asked.

"Many students from Taiwan and Hong Kong choose majors they're not really interested in and instead keep their eyes on the job market. Most of them want to immigrate. The Western students study what they love. Generally, we have better grades but the Westerners are more creative."

"I hope you can write some articles about your observations and experiences. They could be valuable to our educational leaders. I worry the Western scientists don't have a clear mind about which class they're serving with their creativity."

"So far, we've orally offered some suggestions and proposals when your leaders have solicited our opinions at forums. Your leaders were warm and modest. You're right, they also stressed the importance of a class stance for scientists."

As it turned dark, Rong tapped her watch, "Dapeng, it's time for us to leave. These travelers have a very tight schedule."

Ziwei said, "No, you've come a long way from the western suburbs to meet us. We have much to say. The traffic is heavy now, and it's dinner time. We can't let you leave starving. Who knows when we can meet again?"

She walked around the table and put an arm around Rong's shoulders, "You, Big Sister, take the lead to stay, and Dapeng must follow you."

I heard a voice like a deep bell tolling behind us, "How can you go without talking to me?" A man in his late fifties in a gray woolen sport coat strode up to join us, "Sorry, a phone call from your foreign-trade leader detained me. I apologize for coming late."

His fit physique and handsome face presented an aged version of Ziwei. Unlike the rustic, rich businessmen I saw in my hometown before 1949, this Westernized man looked quite stylish and diplomatic. Perhaps his wealth let him speak louder than us, the poor majority, just as high-ranking cadres did, with their political superiority.

Ziwei introduced him to Rong, "Papa, this is Dapeng's boss, a leader of his research division."

Then he shook my hand, "You must be Dapeng. I saw your photo and read your letter to Ziwei, which she's meticulously preserved. Ah, I've waited for years to meet such a brilliant and handsome young man."

Ziwei was jittery, squirming like a spoiled child, "Papa, you talk too much. I never knew you had such a big mouth."

I felt uneasy about the edge in Mr Cao's words, which might hurt George, but gave me hope. George lagged behind and looked around, as if distracted by interesting people.

I said, "Uncle Cao, you're the first red capitalist I've met. What an honor for me."

Tilting his head toward me, indeed like an uncle, he said, "In Hong Kong and London, I'm a capitalist: returning home, I'm your comrade."

He spread his arms around Rong's shoulders and mine, pushing us to leave, "Everyone must be hungry now. I'm inviting you have dinner with us to celebrate our historical meeting at the great victorious time of our country."

Already made uneasy by the luxurious setting and imagining how expensive the meal would be, I said, "I appreciate your profound sentiment of friendship but must decline the offer. We can't get a reward without deserving it."

Rong nodded to approve my expression.

Uncle Cao insisted on leading us to the dining hall, "Just make yourself at home. Don't regard us as outsiders. Besides myself, I'm inviting you also on behalf of Ziwei's mother. I hope you don't hurt all of us."

Rong finally said to me, "It would be ungracious not to accept Mr Cao's kindness."

My first Western meal consisted of a piece of salmon, slices of beets, a seaweed soup, and caviar spread on bread. I'd never tasted any of them before.

The round table was spacious enough for five guests. Mr Cao chose to chat with Comrade Rong, as if to shield his daughter. George graciously sat between Rong and me, leaving me free to talk to Ziwei.

First things were first: "The food and remedies you sent kept my early-stage edema from getting worse. They also saved my father's life. We're deeply grateful to you. I'm so, so sorry about replying to you with such an ugly note."

She pretended to watch something at the far end of the hall. Her Adam's apple bobbed up and down, and her breathing became heavy for a few moments. Then she turned to me with a cold smile, "I understand. You followed a formula. Still, it hurt."

"You understand why I wrote the propaganda piece. But you don't understand what I was eager to say but couldn't."

"You can say it now."

I twisted my mouth to point at Rong, who was absorbed in Uncle Cao's narrative, "I'll do that today, before leaving."

Ziwei nodded, then stared at my bandage. I tore off the adhesive tape, "I recently had surgery to replace the burned skin. It's as big as a silver dollar. The doctor predicts the color of the patch will become natural and the boundary gradually fuzzy."

She paled, "What happened? When?"

"A fire in a tunnel, 1959."

She lowered her head and put her right hand on my left arm, "Poor Dapeng. I wasn't by your side."

Though nervous, I put my hand on hers and let it stay there as long as Rong was raptly listening to Uncle Cao.

Ziwei bent forward and whispered, "Are you really happy? Tell me the truth."

I stared at the food on my plate, "Yes."

"You don't look like it."

"I'm just tired." I raised my head and sat upright, "Can you …" The words wouldn't come.

Ziwei stopped eating, and her hand remained on my arm. I couldn't help but stare at the back of her hand.

She rotated her palm and grinned, "I know you hate the ring. It's incompatible with the Revolution. But we have to follow the customs abroad."

I tried to laugh, "No. I don't care what kind of ring you wear. I was recalling the ballroom dance party on the Chinese New Year of 1956. Your hands were swollen with chilblains, and some patches of skin had turned purple."

She signed, "Almost nine years have passed."

I couldn't hide my obsession with her pink, creamy hand on my arm. A poem by Lu of the Song Dynasty popped into my mind. Years after Lu's mother had forced him to divorce his beloved wife, he encountered her and her new husband in a park. She graciously presented him with a cup of wine, which provoked his deep sorrow and eternal regret. The poem crystalized indelible passion and a celebrated gift, and it affected readers almost eight centuries after his death. I asked Ziwei, "Do you remember the first line of Lu's poem?"

"'With your pink, creamy hands, you offered me a cup of yellow wine.'"

Our time was running out. I pushed ahead, "Your pink, creamy hands are so dear to me. I want to hold them and keep you by my side from now on."

Her eyes became teary, "It's possible. No matter what happened during those years, I'm still single."

I was carried away by her single status, but tried to keep my voice unperturbed, "Does the ring mean you're engaged?"

She stared into my eyes with an assurance, "Miserable man, don't you see it's on the middle finger of my right hand. According to overseas custom, an engagement ring should be on the third finger of a woman's left hand."

I abruptly stood and raised my glass, "Thanks to our host, Uncle Cao, and to our two young overseas friends. I propose a toast, to everybody's health and to the prosperity of our great motherland."

George had been drinking a long draft beer and showed his empty glass to us. As he left the seat to refill it, his muscular back and energetic stride showed he was a healthy, happy man. I whispered to Ziwei, "Your boyfriend?"

"No, fellow left-wing student." Rong was craning her ears towards us, and Ziwei started to speak in a normal voice, "We meet here to coordinate our activities in Europe and North America. There're too many Taiwanese spies in Hong Kong."

"The fight must be tough, with the KMT getting support from Western reactionaries."

"Yes, but we're not isolated."

Calmed down from the initial impact of her being single, I said, "It's incredible. A lady like you can't lack suitors, but you're not ready to settle down."

"I've met some eligible men, mostly Chinese. I gave up because they all lack the kind of charisma I've craved. But I don't know what exactly it is."

"I know." Uncle Cao turned to approach her ear, "Many old novels used the same two lines of verse to describe the unshakable love of the heroine: 'No rivers can impress me since I've seen the great sea; and no other clouds are as celestial as those above Wushan Mountain.' The repetition had made them into a cliché until 1949 when writers stopped quoting them."

Ziwei pushed her father's head away, "They're too genteel. I don't understand."

"Ah, my child, you understand. Don't miss today's chance."

Rong pricked up her ears, "What are they so caught up in talking about?"

Uncle Cao laughed, "A Song Dynasty poem."

Rong smiled, "Unlike us cadres from worker or peasant families, the intellectuals always have something foreign or ancient to babble on about."

As George returned, Ziwei left for a while and came back with a gorgeous plastic bag, which she pushed into my hands, "Dapeng, here are two small gifts for you. The warm jacket is from me, and my father gives you this slide rule."

I looked at Rong, while pushing the bag back to Ziwei, "No. They're expensive. I can't accept them."

Ziwei said, "Please accept them. We all know the saying, 'The gift itself may be as light as a goose feather, but brought from afar, it conveys deep feeling.' Don't make us feel bad." She turned to Rong, "Big Sister, please help us persuade him."

Rong said, "Slide rules aren't consumer goods and this one can improve your work. The jacket is durable, protective gear for your fieldwork, especially in cold weather. Both are practical. You can take them."

I put the bag on a nearby chair and presented Ziwei with a brown envelope containing two issues of the *Journal of Hydraulic Engineering*. She thumbed through the pages to find the two articles I wrote, "Wow. This magazine is a big deal, it's available to foreign countries, and every article has an English synopsis."

"But that's not really a gift," I said, "just my bragging." I reached into my bag and pulled out a tin cylinder wrapped in pink paper: "I'm afraid it's very cheap, but I know you've been craving it." I handed it to Ziwei.

She shook the package, sniffed it, gave me a puzzled smile, and then unwrapped it, "Oh my gosh, Xiaogan sesame candy!" She laughed with delight, "You're right, I have been craving it since our Wuhan days." She rotated the tin, looked at the photo on the side—a still from the movie *The Heavenly Maid and the Mortal Man*—and flashed me a quick, intimate smile.

Rong frowned, "Sesame is a controlled crop. How did you get that?"

"I assisted Professor Huang on an errand at the Friendship Hotel. He bought it for me there with his special card as a People's Congress member."

Rong sighed and looked at Mr Cao, "Dapeng has never been accused of coming to a meeting unprepared." She nudged me, "How about the two pamphlets? They're your prize."

I sheepishly handed Ziwei the two propaganda books, *Long Live Leninism* and *Selected Theses on Socialism*. She turned to the first page of each book. One carried the words, 'Awarded to Comrade Dapeng Liu, a 1958 model socialist worker'. The other was dated 1962 and addressed me as a creative socialist laborer.

Ziwei clicked her tongue, "You're really going to be a red expert." She scanned a few paragraphs of the two books, "Wow, I didn't know Khrushchev was so bad. There's so much new jargon and so many new concepts I don't understand."

Rong said, "You can ask Dapeng. He's written a good ideological summary for criticizing Soviet revisionists."

I gave Ziwei a sly smile the others couldn't see, "Do you have any questions?"

She looked at the others and said, "Don't let me bore you with my ignorance."

They all finished eating, but were still seated at the table. She pulled me over to a couple of chairs farther away, sat down next to me, and skimmed a finger under a line in the pamphlet as if asking a question about it, "Can you apply for government sponsorship to study in Western Europe?"

I was nervous but tilted my head like an easygoing tutor, "That would draw a suspicion of disloyalty for admiring Western culture. Usually, an individual's request from bottom to top gets no answer. It's like throwing a stone into the sea."

"Then what can we do?"

I glanced at Rong. She was telling Uncle Cao and George about her 1949 role as a telegraph operator in a security unit at Guangzhou, the last stronghold of the routed KMT. I pointed at the book, "If your father requests that my leaders let him sponsor my study abroad, they'd take it seriously from the angle of the United Front Line. It might be handled from top to bottom as a special case."

"Would the offer of financial aid help?"

"I don't know. The idea of private aid makes our leaders nervous, but Uncle Cao's offer might prod them into action."

She nodded at me with a perceptive stare, then sat next to her father until Rong had finished her story of the horrible evening, October 14, 1949, when the retreating KMT army demolished the major bridge to cut Guangzhou into two parts.

She pulled her father aside. They stood up and whispered briefly in Cantonese and English, which neither Rong nor I could understand. Rong stood up and put on her overcoat, "Our meeting is mutually encouraging and unforgettable."

Uncle Cao urged her to sit down and urged the waitress to serve the dessert quickly.

While we ate ice cream and pineapple cake, Uncle Cao lost no time in working on Rong, "I would like to support Dapeng to study in England. I have the money and connections over there, but the political qualifications here are the most difficult part. I formally propose my idea to you here and now. Could you take the trouble to go through the administrative process?"

Rong seemed perplexed, "It's a big issue, too big for me to be of much help. The only thing I can promise is to report your suggestion to my superiors. If they are not opposed to it, I'll do my best."

Uncle Cao burst into hearty laugher, "With your big heart wanting to help Dapeng, all the hurdles in our system will step aside to let him pass. I'll lobby the big shots I know. Let's work both lines."

Remaining in high spirits, Uncle Cao turned to face me, "I know many middle-class people in the wider London area, left wingers, and local Marxists. In the early fifties, I helped a guy, Mr Hu, get elected as Chairman of the Chinese Student Association at the University of London, defeating the pro-Taiwan candidate. Now, Professor Hu is teaching international law in Shanghai. If you have the chance to go to London, please ask Hu for the details."

Ziwei suggested a final drink, "Cheers, to a rich and strong motherland."

The bubbling champagne tasted sweet and mild, even to me, a non-drinker. However, two rounds of drinks served by her pink, creamy hand made me tipsy. Both the wine and the new hope were intoxicating. Compared with Poet Lu, how lucky I was.

The next moment, I began to worry. If things didn't go well, I might never see Ziwei again. My palate sensed a bitter and salty taste; my backward-flowing tears polluted the beautiful wine and spoiled its delicacy.

We said goodbye and shook hands with one another. Ziwei and I gripped each other's palm with crashing force as if to acknowledge the night's smothered passion and bind our tacit understanding for our future union.

On the way back to our institute, I sat in the back seat. Insufficient voltage for the street lamps made the light yellowish orange, like the color of champagne. I suddenly saw the windshield of the Warsaw as a giant wineglass and, through the transparent wine, Ziwei's long, tender, shapely fingers. They were even more attractive than they had been eight years earlier.

Rong said, "It's funny. Mr Cao obviously prefers you to George as a son-in-law."

The remark put me on high alert, "I don't know how serious Mr Cao is. Maybe he said so much just for fun. Did I say anything wrong today?"

She looked at me carefully, "No, you did very well. Both your speech and manner were proper."

23

In the winter of 1964, a nationwide evaluation of cadres was unfolding to settle every state employee's political and professional accounts for the past eight years. While mutual criticism was rigorous, self-analysis couldn't pass without collective consensus. The day when each of my officemates received a slip of paper stating the final assessment presented as the Party branch's conclusive comments, I saw few smile. In two extreme cases, a young woman cried to Lanyu Rong, and a middle-aged man argued with Secretary Jiang with trembling hands. They knew the negative conclusions of the Party branch would darken their future.

In Rong's office, she issued my slip of paper to me. I skimmed it, "You've actively responded to the Party's call during every campaign, strenuously completed tasks without fear of hardship and danger, consistently improved your professional skills, and made remarkable contributions. You've shown great teamwork spirit, uniting people of various habits and personalities."

Much better than I'd expected.

As for my shortcomings, the Party branch repeated what I said with my self-analysis: "I've found myself to have a tendency to slacken in terms of ideological remolding."

In a benevolent tone, Rong said, "We five committee members didn't have conflicting opinions about you. That's unusual. Soon, the conditions to qualify you as a Party member will be mature."

"Thank you for your help and encouragement." When I said that, my real concern was with Mr Cao's proposition. I guessed such an offer had passed over Comrade Rong like water off a duck's back. I wanted to know the feasibility of his idea, especially if Rong would drive her old man to push it through the bureaucratic maze.

Not knowing how to broach the question, I called her by name, "Big Sister Rong …"

"What? Get it off your chest."

"Is there a way to combine government authorization with private financial support for my studying abroad?"

"You mean what Ziwei's father suggested? Since you're not his immediate relative, I see no reason to accept his offer. You should count on our own system. No matter how scanty the quota or funds, Professor Huang considers you first in line to go. He's in a position to help you, and we're supportive."

As the escalation of the Vietnam War stimulated the boom in our underground construction, the Chinese Society of Civil Engineering, Beijing Chapter, held a Sunday meeting to let four research centers report their experiences with large-scale tunneling. During my 45-minute speech, a man in the middle row, around 40 years old and wearing glasses, kept grinning at me as if he needed my special attention. It was distracting, but I couldn't remember who he was.

When I was returning to my seat, he greeted me in the aisle and led me to the yard, "Don't you recognize me? Liangzuo Qi, I taught you wood structures."

Though most of my classmates treated that course lightly, considering our major was in heavy construction, as course representative I'd met him frequently. He'd impressed me with his broad smile, ruddy complexion, and energetic tennis playing. In 1957, I'd heard he was labeled a rightist and sent to a labor camp in Hubei. Now he was no longer an athletic young man. His vitality had faded, his skin had become dry and ashen, and his body looked too small for his overcoat. I tried to identify this withered man with my former happy teacher, "How have you been all these years?"

"I spent three years on farmland in Hubei. Then, at the end of 1960, my mother died in Hong Kong, and I was allowed to attend her funeral. Unexpectedly, I fell ill and had my gallbladder removed. During my recovery, I found a job and began to work as a structural engineer in Hong Kong."

His status as an overseas Chinese person alarmed me. I asked, "What kind of wind has blown you here?"

"Wuhan University has decided to remove my rightist label, officially called 'taking off the hat', due to my good performance at the farm and patriotic behavior overseas. I came for the ceremony of rehabilitation. Before going back, I'm taking a tour of Beijing."

"That's wonderful for you. Few of the 1957 targets have been rehabilitated so early. I wish you good luck from now on."

"I'm lucky. My boss paid for me to take a PhD program in structural mechanics at the University of Wales in Swansea, England. I competed with the younger generation and got all the required units in three semesters. After this tour, I'll go

back to work out my research topic with my adviser. Then I'll
finish my thesis while taking charge of designing the largest
gym in Hong Kong."

My heart was itching with envy, "You're learning the new
concepts and new theories. Westerners are trying to use
computers in structural analysis. That's a revolution in itself.
We still use the forties' procedures and hand-cranked
calculating machines that make designers' offices sound like
textile mills."

"My boss also promises to let me inspect and learn from
famous gyms around the world. I plan to visit 30 big cities."

"Your experiences will be valuable to China. Are you
married?"

"Yes, and I have a son, he's one year old."

After the meeting, he insisted on inviting me for dinner at a
fancy restaurant, which only foreigners and Beijing dignitaries
patronized. I felt apprehensive that accepting his invitation
without pre-authorization might be a liability for me. The
waiters and waitresses serving foreigners there were probably
very watchful: "Thank you for your hospitality, but I'm not
supposed to go to that extravagant place."

On the other hand, his going to London would be a
Heaven-sent chance to get a message to Ziwei. I suggested a
tavern favored by ordinary people.

Sitting among the Beijing natives, I enjoyed the peripheral
sound of Mandarin and the local slang. In contrast with the icy
weather outside, the dining hall was as warm as spring, with
steam rising from the chafing dishes. This was my first taste of
thin slices of mutton scalded in boiling water. My teacher,
seven years older than me, behaved like a long-separated
brother. While following Chinese etiquette and dropping well-
done slices into my bowl of sauce, he told me about his plan to
emigrate to Canada and keep his job in Hong Kong. His wife
would take the exam to get a Canadian license as a certified
public accountant. Then they would settle down in the suburbs

of Toronto.

Full and tipsy, he sighed complacently, "Later on, I'll get a MSc in geotechnical engineering, probably from the University of Toronto. Only when you understand the behaviors of foundations can you become an excellent structural engineer. After I retire, my children will get a good education in North America."

"You can do all this because you're a citizen of Hong Kong now?"

"Yes, it's easy to move around within the British Commonwealth of Nations."

The glowing charcoal under the copper chafing dish cast red rays on the glasses of wine and the tiny bubbles sent up by the famous bamboo-leaf wine. The good time and his sincerity made me feel that the political line between us was dim and remote. So I decided to fully trust him, and I briefed him on my sad story with Chuju and possible future with Ziwei.

With a page torn from my notebook, I wrote down from memory the full short text of our divorce certificate, actually a denouncement of Chuju. I folded the piece of paper and gave it to my teacher, "Please find Ziwei Cao and give this to her along with the story of my last eight years."

He slid it into his wallet, "Not many overseas Chinese people are studying English literature nowadays. I won't have any problem finding her at Cambridge. I'll tell her how much your former teachers are fond of you, and what big progress you've made in your field. Today's speech proves you're a real expert in underground structures."

24

In October 1964, during an international conference in Madrid, Professor Huang met the famous European geotechnical engineering experts. They mourned for Karl Terzaghi, who'd passed away a year before. As an unanswered question raised by the founding father, his disciples and admirers were all interested in rock stresses measured in basalt areas. Since the information about Yili Power Station was still classified, and the draft of my article hadn't gone through a security check, Huang had to get permission from the head of the PRC delegation to present, in general terms, our data and geological descriptions. Still, some of them expressed the intention to invite me as a visiting scholar. King's College London even offered a stipend for a year.

When he returned home, Huang asked me to become better prepared while waiting for political authorization to go abroad. The Swedish method invented by Professor Hast had been successfully used in deep gold mines. I should continue the work I'd started in 1963.

After that, he told me, "For an adult to learn speak a foreign language is very slow and frustrating. You have to practice it right away and make every minute and second count. We've proposed two candidates as visiting scholars in Europe for two years, and you're one of them. The other will be sent to Holland to study irrigation. We don't know how long it takes to pass scrutiny, maybe one or two years. That's a long time to wait for approval, but a short time to learn to speak English."

To free myself from the awkwardness of studying English like a mute, I talked to the electronics technician who'd helped me with my instrumentation. He jostled among children and electronics amateurs to search for components at bargain stores. In a week, he had made a tiny amplifier for driving a headphone, and I spent only 15 yuan for the materials. I tested it with Minggui An's turntable, which he'd brought back from the Soviet Union, and the system worked well. I was excited not only to have solved the problems with space and privacy, but also for the small step I'd made toward studying in England near Ziwei. She must speak British English fluently and would act like a relative, orienting me in the outlandish locale.

Gradually, the ESL book enhanced my appetite for more of the basics of Western society. In the winter of 1964, I read an abridged English copy of *David Copperfield* and a translated version of *Pride and Prejudice*. I also watched several British movies dubbed into Chinese, such as *The Pickwick Papers* and *Hamlet*. They touched me with something new and fresh but I didn't know exactly what it was.

One evening, free from collective activity, I strolled in the farmland on the north side of our compound, reading my pocket notebook until the sunset glow faded. As night's dome dropped, resting its edge on the horizon of the wheat field, darkness seemed to shorten the distance from where I stood to the English-speaking world, which I imagined flashing ahead on the other side of the western mountains of Beijing. On my way to the dorm, as I walked carefully on the uneven earth, a scarecrow shaking in the chilly wind startled me. I bowed to it, and the sentence I'd memorized from the ESL book popped out: "Sir, I'm sorry to trouble you, but would you be kind enough to tell me where the nearest post office is?" Were Westerners really so polite?

All the good news promised that 1965 would be a victorious year for China. Our formal relationship with France was established in 1964, following the success of our first nuclear bomb experiment, and the Games of the New Emerging Forces held in Jakarta had shown that the solidarity between China and Indonesia would be a decisive factor in Asia. Under Chairman Mao's new strategy, we stopped cursing the developed capitalist countries as US appendages. Instead, they were an intermediate zone between the two superpowers on one side and the force of national independence movements on the other. We should do our best to unite with Western European countries and Japan, and win them over from the US and the

USSR. Miraculously, my dream of going to England suddenly appeared to fit the historical trend.

A few days after the Chinese New Year, February 2, 1965, my former teacher Qi came to Beijing as a guest of Qinghua University. His lectures in numerical analysis and computer programming languages, newly developed in the West, were fresh to China and were warmly welcomed by the teachers and engineers in Beijing.

Most exciting and thrilling to me, his trip brought me a letter from Ziwei. As he was regarded as a patriotic personage, his name was listed at our customs inspection post for exemption from the security search. Ziwei's letter wasn't opened.

> Your former teacher, Liangzuo Qi, relayed your sad story and gave me the piece of paper as evidence of your innocence. I cried for being robbed of the love I'd thought belonged to me. For all those years, I'd never considered any other suitors for my future spouse because they lacked certain qualities you possess. Dapeng, I hated you. Why should you have allowed yourself to be degraded by marrying such a shady woman? I wanted to beat you up over and over again.

> When I cried again, I blamed myself for leaving you in a lovelorn state, especially during that difficult time. I hate my wrong decision in 1956 to go abroad; otherwise, you wouldn't have been exposed to that horrid woman. Now, while I write this letter, my mind is as confused as a tangled ball of yarn.

> While I no longer feel you're as pure and innocent as I used to think, you seem more indispensable to me than ever. Please tell me what's going on with your application for studying in England. If you need our help, my father can make a special trip to China. In case you're not able to go abroad, just tell

me the truth, I'll quit my PhD program and come back to you.

During my homecoming visit last year, a leader at the Committee of Overseas Chinese Affairs, State Council, promised to place me in a suitable position whenever I return to our motherland. Even now my English is good enough to take a teaching job in Beijing.

Along with the letter, she sent me a photo taken in Paris at the Eiffel Tower. She was wearing colorful sports attire. With one hand touching the visor of her hat, she was intensely focused on a formation of birds flying in echelon, which were captured in the upper-left corner of the picture. On the back of the photo, she'd written, 'Autumn, 1964'. Above the date, she quoted two lines from a Tang Dynasty poem:

> Climbing the height to heed you,
> My heart follows vanishing wild geese.

My world brightened as I looked at Ziwei's letter and photo, manifesting her forgiveness, her passionate devotion. A heavy load had been lifted off my heart. I regretted marrying a depraved woman. How I'd damaged Ziwei's true love. I prayed that Ziwei would stay with me forever and punish me for my wrongs.

Acknowledgements

Many thanks to Clifton Hawkins, the first American to encourage me to write about how millions of Chinese lived their lives during modern times. I'd like to express my gratitude to Carlos Smith for his dedicated proofreading, to Megan Timberlake, Jeffrey Michels, Gilbert Couts, and Steve Boga, who reviewed my early drafts, and to Sylvie Carberry, who checked my later revisions. Their selfless support opened my eyes to the moral merits of critical Western intellectuals, with whom I share great affinities.

Andrew Hilleman taught me some basic principles of writing a novel. Peter Gelfan's coaching helped me form the final shape of this book.

My heartfelt thanks to Harvard Square Editions for discovering my work and guiding me along the path and for their expertise and passionate help.

More books from
Harvard Square Editions:

People and Peppers, Kelvin Christopher James
Gates of Eden, Charles Degelman
Love's Affliction, Fidelis Mkparu
Transoceanic Lights, S. Li
Close, Erika Raskin
Anomie, Jeff Lockwood
Living Treasures, Yang Huang
Nature's Confession, J.L. Morin
Love and Famine, Han-ping Chin
Dark Lady of Hollywood, Diane Haithman
How Fast Can You Run, Harriet Levin Millan
Appointment with ISIL, Joe Giordano
Never Summer, Tim Blaine
Parallel, Sharon Erby